SANT' ILARIO

◆ CLUNY CLASSICS ◆

Visit WWW.CLUNYMEDIA.COM *for other titles*
from the Catholic literary tradition, including:

RICCARDO BACCHELLI
The Mill on the Po

ROBERT HUGH BENSON
Come Rack, Come Rope
Dawn of All
Lord of the World

GEORGES BERNANOS
Joy
Under the Sun of Satan

G. K. CHESTERTON
Wanderings over the World

MYLES CONNOLLY
Dan England and the Noonday Devil
Mr. Blue

F. MARIAN CRAWFORD
Saracinesca
Sant' Ilario
Don Orsino
Corleone

ALICE CURTAYNE
House of Cards

GERTRUD VON LE FORT
The Veil of Veronica

MARIELLA GABLE, O.S.B. (EDITOR)
Many-Colored Fleece: Short Stories

JOSÉ MARÍA GIRONELLA
The Cypresses Believe in God
One Million Dead
Peace After War

RUMER GODDEN
A Breath of Air
Five for Sorrow, Ten for Joy
In This House of Brede

CAROLINE GORDON
The Malefactors

CARYLL HOUSELANDER
The Dry Wood

ELISABETH LANGGÄSSER
The Quest

BRUCE MARSHALL
Father Malachy's Miracle
A Thread of Scarlet

FRANÇOIS MAURIAC
The Desert of Love
Thérèse: A Portrait in Four Parts
Vipers' Tangle

DOROTHY L. SAYERS
Whose Body?

IGNAZIO SILONE
Fontamara
Bread and Wine
The Seed Beneath the Snow

SIGRID UNDSET
The Burning Bush
The Wild Orchid
The Longest Years

HELEN C. WHITE
A Watch in the Night

SANT' ILARIO

A Novel

F. Marion Crawford

With an Introduction by Stephen Schmalhofer

CLUNY
Providence, Rhode Island

CLUNY MEDIA EDITION, 2023

This Cluny edition is an unabridged republication of the
1905 Macmillan edition of *Sant' Ilario*.

For information regarding this title
or any other Cluny Media publication,
please write to info@clunymedia.com, or to
Cluny Media, P.O. Box 1664, Providence, RI 02901

✢ VISIT US ONLINE AT WWW.CLUNYMEDIA.COM ✢

ISBN (paperback) | 978-1685951979
ISBN (hardcover) | 978-1685952037

Cover design by Clarke & Clarke
Cover image: George Inness, *View of Rome
from Tivoli* (detail), 1872, oil on canvas
Courtesy of Wikimedia Commmons

CONTENTS

TO *My Wife*
THIS SECOND PART OF *Saracinesca*
IS LOVINGLY DEDICATED

In memoriam
GERALD RUSSELLO (1971-2021)

Cluny is pleased to republish Francis Marion Crawford's SARACINESCA tetralogy in remembrance of the life in faith and letters of Gerald Russello. He was a great friend and advisor to Cluny, especially in his role as Editor of *The University Bookman*, a publication of The Russell Kirk Center.

Gerald's Sicilian faith is all anyone needs. Go to confession. Say the rosary. Hear Mass as often as you can. The saints are God's friends, so ask them for help.

Gerald could have kept his editing and writing in the moonlight. Despite the extra scrutiny he risked as a practicing lawyer in Manhattan, he brought his extracurricular work into the light of day. He was a lighthouse for young professionals. Gerald knew firsthand that financial and legal work can be both intensely stressful and numbingly boring. The temptation is to escape to the republic of letters. While he fought that temptation, Gerald's writing was enriched by his experience of serious, sustained professional excellence.

Gerald helped to keep alive the legacy of Russell Kirk, Orestes Brownson, and Christopher Dawson. Gerry Russello from Brooklyn coulda, shoulda, woulda lived as an intellectual in their mold. But he had a touch more Walter Bagehot in him than he liked to admit. He worked at the center of things and lived in the service of the permanent things.

Gerald Russello is irreplaceable but he joins the saints. *Requiescat in pace.*

✳ INTRODUCTION ✳

As Garibaldi menaced the Eternal City with his revolutionary army, foreigners in Rome put out their national flags in a bid for immunity, which gave the city a festive appearance incongruous with the anxious popular mood. A large banner over the Santa Maria Sopra Minerva appealed to the highest sovereign for protection: "The ancient war against the Church is renewed. We, O Romans, will oppose it with our arms—prayer!"

On their path to Rome, the Piedmontese were met by armed resistance from the *Papalini*, the Zouaves serving Pope Pius IX. Their ranks were filled by Catholic gentlemen, many forgoing pay, from "the oldest and noblest families in Europe, who marched cheerfully in the ranks shoulder to shoulder with devout peasants and working men from Tyrol, Bavaria, Ireland, and other Catholic countries," writes Mary Fraser, sister of novelist Francis Marion Crawford. A great Romantic, Crawford found the last days of the Papal States irresistible as the raw material for his Roman tetralogy following the Saracinesca family.

Another great Romantic, Russell Kirk, never visited Rome without Crawford's two-volume history of the city. In *Ave Roma Immortalis*, Crawford gives the historical context for the opening scenes of his novel *Sant' Ilario*:

> On by the Borgo Santo Spirito, opposite the old church of the Penitentiaries, stands the Palazzo Serristori, memorable in the revolutionary movement of 1867. It was then the barracks of the Papal Zouaves—the brave foreign legion enlisted under Pius the Ninth, in which men of all nations were enrolled under officers of the best blood in Europe, hated more especially by the revolutionaries because they were foreigners, and because their existence, therefore, showed a foreign sympathy with the temporal power, which was a denial of the revolutionary theory which asserted the Papacy to be without friends in Europe. Wholesale murder by explosives was in its infancy then as a fine art; but the spirit was

willing, and a plot was formed to blow up the castle of Sant' Angelo and the barracks of the Zouaves. The castle escaped because one of the conspirators lost heart and revealed the treachery; but the Palazzo Serristori was partially destroyed. The explosion shattered one corner of the building. It was said that the fuse burned faster than had been intended, so that the catastrophe came too soon. At all events, when it happened, about dark, only the musicians of the band were destroyed, and few of the regiment were in the building at all, so that about thirty lives were sacrificed, where the intention had been to destroy many hundreds. In the more sane condition of Europe today, it seems to us amazing that Pius the Ninth should have been generally blamed for signing the death warrant of the two atrocious villains who did the deed, and for allowing them to be executed.

The explosion at the Serristori barracks creates a collision between members of the Saracinesca and Montevarchi families with collateral damage across several characters in Roman society.

Anastase Gouache is Rome's favorite society artist. At the end of *Saracinesca*, the boyish Gouache puts down his paints and picks up his musket as a newly enlisted Zouave. "When Gouache put on the gray jacket, the red sash and the yellow gaiters, he became a man." He is content within the martial routine and *esprit de corps* of the Zouaves until his peace is shattered by every Frenchman's weakness: a beautiful young woman.

The delicate Donna Faustina Montevarchi is eighteen years old and a recent graduate of the convent school of the Sacro Cuore atop the Spanish Steps. There she acquired "the French language, a slight knowledge of music, a very limited acquaintance with the history of her own country, a ready memory for prayers and litanies—and her manners. Manners among the Italians are called education."

Here is the challenge for any Roman novelist: every landmark has layers of true history threatening to outshine your fiction. These were the golden days of the Society of the Sacred Heart when St. Madeleine Sophie Barat's mission and example drew over three thousand young women into religious life. In the convent next to the Sacro Cuore at the time of Crawford's novel, Pauline Perdrau, a young postulant of the Society, sought permission to paint the Blessed

Virgin Mary in a chapel niche. Perdrau finished her fresco in 1844 to polite nods from her sisters and perhaps some snickering. Their rudeness would have been confessable if the fresco had been better. Painted wet, it was too brightly colored, even ugly. When Pius IX visited the chapel, against the wishes of the Mother Superior, he asked to see the painting concealed behind a curtain. The passage of time had dried the wet fresco and (perhaps through the intercession of a higher artist) softened the colors. The pontiff was delighted. "Truly she is Mater Admirabilis!" It is the custom to place a replica of the painting in all the Sacred Heart schools around the world. In Perdrau's painting as in heaven, Our Lady patiently bears all things, even schools that have forgotten her Son.

The Montevarchi are a rich noble family living in the old patriarchal style in Rome. Their married adult children live in perfect obedience in different wings of the palazzo. "Don Lotario's request that his wife might have a sitting-room of her own was looked upon as an attempt at a domestic revolution, and the privilege was only obtained at last through the formidable intervention of the Duke of Agincourt, the Duchessa's own father." All meals were served on silver plates "from motives of economy, for the simple reason that metal did not break."

Prince Montevarchi's thrift masks his avarice. In a perversion of generosity, he is greedy for his daughters and desires to marry them off to rich suitors. For Faustina, he hopes for a match with a young man from an old family. Only a Frangipani or Colonna will do. For the boisterous Flavia, he despairs until the unexpected appearance of another Saracinesca in Rome. Formerly a rural innkeeper, the physically formidable Marchese di San Giacinto explains his relationship to the elderly Prince Saracinesca:

> My great-grandfather was two years older than yours. You know he never meant to marry, and resigned the title to his younger brother, who had children already. He took a wife in his old age, and my grandfather was the son born to him. That is why you are so much older than I, though we are of the same generation in the order of descent.

In other words, if his great-grandfather had not resigned his title in perpetuity, the humble, rough-cut San Giacinto would sit as Prince Saracinesca in Rome. With a little legal pruning and grafting, the entire family tree of the Saracinesca would have been altered. St. Ignatius of Loyola cautions that Satan "begins by suggesting thoughts that are suited to a devout soul and ends by suggesting his own." As Montevarchi ponders the meaning of justice, he receives an evil suggestion from the Tempter.

The Montevarchi maintain a private library filled with antiquarian treasures and family archives. The private libraries of Roman nobles have long been priceless resources for historians and researchers. The anti-papal German historian Ferdinand Gregorovius wrote his multi-volume history of Rome (destined for the *Index Librorum Prohibitorum*) in the private libraries of the Colonna, Gaetani, Orsini, and Chigi families. One can measure the distance between the Rome of the nineteenth and twenty-first centuries in Gregorovius' diary entry: "The Jesuits have made their first attack; I must be prepared for the consequences." From behind the dusty shelves of the Montevarchi library creeps one of Crawford's great antagonists, Arnold Meschini. "He studied law and had practised for some time, when he had suddenly abandoned his profession in order to accept the ill-paid post of librarian." Common courtesy assumes that he simply had a fanatic's love of medieval lore, genealogy, and calligraphy. These are all means to an end for Meschini. He loves money and has acquired an unusual talent for forgery.

Aquinas teaches that suspicion denotes evil thinking based on slight indications while St. Madeleine Sophie Barat warns of the small infidelities that lead away from beatitude:

> In speaking of infidelities, I do not mean faults that the weakness of our nature causes…but those that close our hearts and keep our Lord at a distance; those little voluntary infidelities to which we easily give in: a light that we do not wish to follow, an inspiration that we resist…

While Anastase and Faustina meet secretly at Sunday Mass, and San Giacinto pursues Faustina with the directness of a man accustomed to achieving his goals, Prince Sant' Ilario and his wife Corona are led by a series of small confusions and miscommunications into dangerous suspicion. They have wealth, honor, and beauty but a rupture in their love for each other threatens body and soul. Only an act of heroic sacrifice can repair the wound.

"Every wedding is a society wedding; it is on the well-being of the family that society depends," writes Monsignor Ronald Knox in *Bridegroom and Bride*

(1957). In *Sant' Ilario*, Francis Marion Crawford shows the many ways to fight for God, for Country, and for Family.

Stephen Schmalhofer
Feast of St. Thomas Aquinas, A.D. 2023
Mount Alvernia

✳ SANT' ILARIO ✳

CHAPTER I

TWO years of service in the Zouaves had wrought a change in Anastase Gouache, the painter. He was still a light man, nervously built, with small hands and
feet, and a delicate face; but constant exposure to the weather had browned his
skin, and a life of unceasing activity had strengthened his sinews and hardened
his compact frame. The clustering black curls were closely cropped, too, while
the delicate dark moustache had slightly thickened. He had grown to be a very
soldierly young fellow, straight and alert, quick of hand and eye, inured to that
perpetual readiness which is the first characteristic of the good soldier, whether
in peace or war. The dreamy look that was so often in his face in the days when
he sat upon a high stool painting the portrait of Donna Tullia Mayer, had given
place to an expression of wide-awake curiosity in the world's doings.

Anastase was an artist by nature and no amount of military service could
crush the chief aspirations of his intelligence. He had not abandoned work since
he had joined the Zouaves, for his hours of leisure from duty were passed in his
studio. But the change in his outward appearance was connected with a similar
development in his character. He himself sometimes wondered how he could
have ever taken any interest in the half-hearted political fumbling which Donna
Tullia, Ugo Del Ferice, and others of their set used to dignify by the name of
conspiracy. It seemed to him that his ideas must at that time have been deplorably confused and lamentably unsettled. He sometimes took out the old sketch of
Madame Mayer's portrait, and setting it upon his easel, tried to realise and bring
back those times when she had sat for him. He could recall Del Ferice's mock
heroics, Donna Tullia's ill-expressed invectives, and his own half-sarcastic sympathy in the liberal movement; but the young fellow in an old velveteen jacket
who used to talk glibly about the guillotine, about stringing-up the clericals to

street-lamps and turning the churches into popular theatres, was surely not the energetic, sunburnt Zouave who had been hunting down brigands in the Samnite hills last summer, who spent three-fourths of his time among soldiers like himself, and who had pledged his honour to follow the gallant Charette and defend the Pope as long as he could carry a musket.

There is a sharp dividing line between youth and manhood. Sometimes we cross it early, and sometimes late, but we do not know that we are passing from one life to another as we step across the boundary. The world seems to us the same for a while, as we knew it yesterday and shall know it tomorrow. Suddenly, we look back and start with astonishment when we see the past, which we thought so near, already vanishing in the distance, shapeless, confused, and estranged from our present selves. Then, we know that we are men, and acknowledge, with something like a sigh, that we have put away childish things.

When Gouache put on the gray jacket, the red sash and the yellow gaiters, he became a man and speedily forgot Donna Tullia and her errors, and for some time afterwards he did not care to recall them. When he tried to remember the scenes at the studio in the Via San Basilio, they seemed very far away. One thing alone constantly reminded him disagreeably of the past, and that was his unfortunate failure to catch Del Ferice when the latter had escaped from Rome in the disguise of a mendicant friar. Anastase had never been able to understand how he had missed the fugitive. It had soon become known that Del Ferice had escaped by the very pass which Gouache was patrolling, and the young Zouave had felt the bitterest mortification in losing so valuable and so easy a prey. He often thought of it and promised himself that he would visit his anger on Del Ferice if he ever got a chance; but Del Ferice was out of reach of his vengeance, and Donna Tullia Mayer had not returned to Rome since the previous year. It had been rumoured of late that she had at last fulfilled the engagement contracted some time earlier, and had consented to be called the Contessa Del Ferice; this piece of news, however, was not yet fully confirmed. Gouache had heard the gossip, and had immediately made a lively sketch on the back of a half-finished picture, representing Donna Tullia, in her bridal dress, leaning upon the arm of Del Ferice, who was arrayed in a capuchin's cowl, and underneath, with his brush, he scrawled a legend, "Finis coronat opus."

It was nearly six o'clock in the afternoon of the 23rd of September. The day had been rainy, but the sky had cleared an hour before sunset, and there was a sweet damp freshness in the air, very grateful after the long weeks of late summer. Anastase Gouache had been on duty at the Serristori barracks in the Borgo Santo Spirito and walked briskly up to the bridge of Sant' Angelo. There was not much movement in the streets, and the carriages were few. A couple of officers were lounging at the gate of the castle and returned Gouache's salute as he passed. In the middle of the bridge he stopped and looked westward, down the short reach of the river which caught a lurid reflection of the sunset on its eddying yellow surface. He mused a moment, thinking more of the details of his duty at the barracks than of the scene before him. Then he thought of the first time he had crossed the bridge in his Zouave uniform, and a faint smile flickered on his brown features. It happened almost every day that he stopped at the same place, and as particular spots often become associated with ideas that seem to belong to them, the same thought almost always recurred to his mind as he stood there. Then followed the same daily wondering as to how all these things were to end; whether he should for years to come wear the red sash and the yellow gaiters, a corporal of Zouaves, and whether for years he should ask himself every day the same question. Presently, as the light faded from the houses of the Borgo, he turned away with an imperceptible shrug of the shoulders and continued his walk upon the narrow pavement at the side of the bridge. As he descended the step at the end, to the level of the square, a small bright object in a crevice of the stones attracted his attention. He stooped and picked it up.

It was a little gold pin, some two inches long, the head beaten out and twisted into the shape of the letter C. Gouache examined it attentively, and saw that it must have been long used, for it was slightly bent in more than one place as though it had often been thrust through some thick material. It told no other tale of its possessor, however, and the young man slipped it into his pocket and went on his way, idly wondering to whom the thing belonged. He reflected that if he had been bent on any important matter he would probably have considered the finding of a bit of gold as a favourable omen; but he was merely returning to his lodging as usual, and had no engagement for the evening. Indeed, he expected no event in his life at that time, and following the train of his meditation he smiled a little when he thought that he was not even in love. For a Frenchman, nearly thirty years of age, the position was an unusual one enough. In Gouache's case it was especially remarkable. Women liked him, he liked them, and he was constantly in the society of some of the most beautiful in the world.

Nevertheless, he turned from one to another and found a like pleasure in the conversation of them all. What delighted him in the one was not what charmed him most in the next, but the equilibrium of satisfaction was well maintained between the dark and the fair, the silent beauty and the pretty woman of intelligence. There was indeed one whom he thought more noble in heart and grander in symmetry of form and feature, and stronger in mind than the rest; but she was immeasurably removed from the sphere of his possible devotion by her devoted love of her husband, and he admired her from a distance, even while speaking with her.

As he passed the Apollo theatre and ascended the Via di Tordinona the lights were beginning to twinkle in the low doorways, and the gas-lamps, then a very recent innovation in Rome, shone out one by one in the distance. The street is narrow, and was full of traffic, even in the evening. Pedestrians elbowed their way along in the dusk, every now and then flattening themselves against the dingy walls to let a cab or a carriage rush past them, not without real risk of accident. Before the deep, arched gateway of the Orso, one of the most ancient inns in the world, the empty wine-carts were getting ready for the return journey by night across the Campagna, the great bunches of little bells jingling loudly in the dark as the carters buckled the harness on their horses' backs.

Just as Gouache reached this place, the darkest and most crowded through which he had to pass, a tremendous clatter and rattle from the Via dell' Orso made the hurrying people draw back to the shelter of the doorsteps and arches. It was clear that a runaway horse was not far off. One of the carters, the back of whose waggon was half-way across the opening of the street, made desperate efforts to make his beast advance and clear the way; but the frightened animal only backed farther up. A moment later the runaway charged down past the tail of the lumbering vehicle. The horse himself just cleared the projecting timbers of the cart, but the cab he was furiously dragging caught upon them while going at full speed and was shivered to pieces, throwing the horse heavily upon the stones, so that he slid along several feet on his head and knees with the fragments of the broken shafts and the wreck of the harness about him. The first man to spring from the crowd and seize the beast's head was Anastase. He did not see that the same instant a large private carriage, drawn by a pair of powerful horses, emerged quickly from the Vicolo dei Soldati, the third of the streets which meet the Via di Tordinona at the Orso. The driver, who owing to the darkness had not seen the disaster which had just taken place, did his best to stop in time; but before the heavy equipage could be brought to a stand Anastase had been thrown to the ground, between the hoofs of the struggling cab-horse and the feet of the startled pair of bays. The crowd closed in as near as was safe, while the confusion and the shouts of the people and the carters increased every minute.

The coachman of the private carriage threw the reins to the footman and sprang down to go to the horses' heads.

"You have run over a Zouave!" some one shouted from the crowd.

"Meno male! Thank goodness it was not one of us!" exclaimed another voice.

"Where is he? Get him out, some of you!" cried the coachman as he seized the reins close to the bit.

By this time a couple of stout gendarmes and two or three soldiers of the Antibes legion had made their way to the front and were dragging away the fallen cab-horse. A tall, thin, elderly gentleman, of a somewhat sour countenance, descended from the carriage and stooped over the injured soldier.

"It is only a Zouave, Excellency," said the coachman, with a sort of sigh of relief.

The tall gentleman lifted Gouache's head a little so that the light from the carriage-lamp fell upon his face. He was quite insensible, and there was blood upon his pale forehead and white cheeks. One of the gendarmes came forward.

"We will take care of him, Signore," he said, touching his three-cornered hat. "But I must beg to know your revered name," he added, in the stock Italian phrase. "Capira—I am very sorry—but they say your horses—"

"Put him into my carriage," answered the elderly gentleman shortly. "I am the Principe Montevarchi."

"But, Excellency—the Signorina—" protested the coachman. The prince paid no attention to the objection and helped the gendarme to deposit Anastase in the interior of the vehicle. Then he gave the man a silver scudo.

"Send some one to the Serristori barracks to say that a Zouave has been hurt and is at my house," he said. Therewith he entered the carriage and ordered the coachman to drive home.

"In heaven's name, what has happened, papa?" asked a young voice in the darkness, tremulous with excitement.

"My dear child, there has been an accident in the street, and this young man has been wounded, or killed—"

"Killed! A dead man in the carriage!" cried the young girl in some terror, and shrinking away into the corner.

"You should really control your nerves, Faustina," replied her father in austere tones. "If the young man is dead, it is the will of Heaven. If he is alive we shall soon find it out. Meanwhile I must beg you to be calm—to be calm, do you understand?"

Donna Faustina Montevarchi made no answer to this parental injunction, but withdrew as far as she could into the corner of the back seat, while her father supported the inanimate body of the Zouave as the carriage swung over the uneven pavement. In a few minutes they rolled beneath a deep arch and stopped at the foot of a broad marble staircase.

"Bring him upstairs carefully, and send for a surgeon," said the prince to the men who came forward. Then he offered his arm to his daughter to ascend the steps, as though nothing had happened, and without bestowing another look on the injured soldier.

Donna Faustina was just eighteen years old, and had only quitted the convent of the Sacro Cuore a month earlier. It might have been said that she was too young to be beautiful, for she evidently belonged to that class of women who do not attain their full development until a later period. Her figure was almost too slender, her face almost too delicate and ethereal. There was about her a girlish look, an atmosphere of half-saintly maidenhood, which was not so much the expression of her real nature as the effect produced by her being at once very thin and very fresh. There was indeed nothing particularly angelic about her warm brown eyes, shaded by unusually long black lashes; and little wayward locks of chestnut hair, curling from beneath the small round hat of the period, just before the small pink ears, softened as with a breath of worldliness the grave outlines of the serious face. A keen student of women might have seen that the dim religious halo of convent life which still clung to the young girl would soon fade and give way to the brilliancy of the woman of the world. She was not tall, though of fully average height, and although the dress of that time was ill-adapted to show to advantage either the figure or the movements, it was evident, as she stepped lightly from the carriage, that she had a full share of ease and grace. She possessed that unconscious certainty in motion which proceeds naturally from the perfect proportion of all the parts, and which exercises a far greater influence over men than a faultless profile or a dazzling skin.

Instead of taking her father's arm, Donna Faustina turned and looked at the face of the wounded Zouave, whom three men had carefully taken from the carriage and were preparing to carry upstairs. Poor Gouache was hardly recognisable for the smart soldier who had crossed the bridge of Sant' Angelo half an hour earlier. His uniform was all stained with mud, there was blood upon his pale face, and his limbs hung down, powerless and limp. But as the young girl looked at him, consciousness returned, and with it came the sense of acute suffering. He opened his eyes suddenly, as men often do when they revive after being stunned, and a short groan escaped from his lips. Then, as he realised that he was in the presence of a lady, he made an effort as though to release himself from the hands of those who carried him, and to stand upon his feet.

"Pardon me, Madame," he began to say, but Faustina checked him by a gesture.

Meanwhile old Montevarchi had carefully scrutinised the young man's face, and had recognised him, for they had often met in society.

"Monsieur Gouache!" he exclaimed in surprise. At the same time he made the men move on with their burden.

"You know him, papa?" whispered Donna Faustina as they followed together. "He is a gentleman? I was right?"

"Of course, of course," answered her father. "But really, Faustina, had you nothing better to do than to go and look into his face? Imagine, if he had known you! Dear me! If you begin like this, as soon as you are out of the convent—"

Montevarchi left the rest of the sentence to his daughter's imagination, merely turning up his eyes a little as though deprecating the just vengeance of heaven upon his daughter's misconduct.

"Really, papa—" protested Faustina.

"Yes—really, my daughter—I am much surprised," returned her incensed parent, still speaking in an undertone lest the injured man should overhear what was said.

They reached the head of the stairs and the men carried Gouache rapidly away; not so quickly, however, as to prevent Faustina from getting another glimpse of his face. His eyes were open and met hers with an expression of mingled interest and gratitude which she did not forget. Then he was carried away and she did not see him again.

The Montevarchi household was conducted upon the patriarchal principle, once general in Rome, and not quite abandoned even now, twenty years later than the date of Gouache's accident. The palace was a huge square building facing upon two streets, in front and behind, and opening inwards upon two courtyards. Upon the lower floor were stables, coach-houses, kitchens, and offices innumerable. Above these there was built a half story, called a mezzanino—in French, *entresol*, containing the quarters of the unmarried sons of the house, of the household chaplain, and of two or three tutors employed in the education of the Montevarchi grandchildren. Next above, came the "piano nobile," or state apartments, comprising the rooms of the prince and princess, the dining-room, and a vast suite of reception-rooms, each of which opened into the next in such a manner that only the last was not necessarily a passage. In the huge hall was the dais and canopy with the family arms embroidered in colours once gaudy but now agreeably faded to a softer tone. Above this floor was another, occupied by the married sons, their wives and children; and high over all, above the cornice of the palace, were the endless servants' quarters and the roomy garrets. At a rough estimate the establishment comprised over a hundred persons, all living under the absolute and despotic authority of the head of the house, Don Lotario Montevarchi, Principe Montevarchi, and sole possessor of forty or fifty other titles. From his will and upon his pleasure depended every act of every member of his household, from his eldest son and heir, the Duca di Bellegra, to that of Pietro Paolo, the under-cook's scullion's boy. There were three sons and four daughters. Two of the sons were married, to wit, Don Ascanio, to whom his father had given his second title, and Don Onorato, who was allowed to call himself Principe di Cantalupo, but who would have no legal claim to that distinction after his father's death. Last of the three came Don Carlo, a young fellow of twenty years, but not yet emancipated from the supervision of his tutor. Of the daughters, the two eldest, Bianca and Laura, were married and no longer lived in Rome, the one having been matched with a Neapolitan and the other with a Florentine. There remained still at home, therefore, the third, Donna Flavia, and the youngest of all the family, Donna Faustina. Though Flavia was not yet two and twenty years of age, her father and mother were already beginning to despair of marrying her, and dropped frequent hints about the advisability of making her enter religion, as they called it; that is to say, they thought she had better take the veil and retire from the world.

The old princess Montevarchi was English by birth and education, but thirty-three years of life in Rome had almost obliterated all traces of her nationality.

That all-pervading influence, which so soon makes Romans of foreigners who marry into Roman families, had done its work effectually. The Roman nobility, by intermarriage with the principal families of the rest of Europe, has lost many Italian characteristics; but its members are more essentially Romans than the full-blooded Italians of the other classes who dwell side by side with the aristocracy in Rome.

When Lady Gwendoline Fontenoy married Don Lotario Montevarchi in the year 1834, she, no doubt, believed that her children would grow up as English as she herself, and that her husband's house would not differ materially from an establishment of the same kind in England. She laughed merrily at the provisions of the marriage contract, which even went so far as to stipulate that she was to have at least two dishes of meat at dinner, and an equivalent on fast-days, a drive every day—the traditional trottata—two new gowns every year, and a woman to wait upon her. After these and similar provisions had been agreed upon, her dowry, which was a large one for those days, was handed over to the keeping of her father-in-law and she was duly married to Don Lotario, who at once assumed the title of Duca di Bellegra. The wedding journey consisted of a fortnight's retirement in the Villa Montevarchi at Frascati, and at the end of that time the young couple were installed under the paternal roof in Rome. Before she had been in her new abode a month the young Duchessa realised the utter hopelessness of attempting to change the existing system of patriarchal government under which she found herself living. She discovered, in the first place, that she would never have five scudi of her own in her pocket, and that if she needed a handkerchief or a pair of stockings it was necessary to obtain from the head of the house not only the permission to buy such necessaries, but the money with which to pay for them. She discovered, furthermore, that if she wanted a cup of coffee or some bread and butter out of hours, those things were charged to her daily account in the steward's office, as though she had been in an inn, and were paid for at the end of the year out of the income arising from her dowry. Her husband's younger brother, who had no money of his own, could not even get a lemonade in his father's house without his father's consent.

Moreover, the family life was of such a nature as almost to preclude all privacy. The young Duchessa and her husband had their bedroom in the upper story, but Don Lotario's request that his wife might have a sitting-room of her own was looked upon as an attempt at a domestic revolution, and the privilege was only obtained at last through the formidable intervention of the Duke of Agincourt, the Duchessa's own father. All the family meals, too, were eaten together in the solemn old dining-hall, hung with tapestries and dingy with the dust of ages. The order of precedence was always strictly observed, and though the cooking was of a strange kind, no plate or dish was ever used which was not of solid silver, battered indeed, and scratched, and cleaned only after Italian ideas, but heavy and massive withal. The Duchessa soon learned that the old Roman houses all used silver plates from motives of economy, for the simple reason that metal did not break. But the sensible English woman saw also that although the most rigid economy was practised in many things, there was lavish expenditure in many departments of the establishment. There were magnificent horses in the stables, gorgeously gilt carriages in the coach-houses, scores of domestics in bright liveries at every door. The pay of the servants did not, indeed, exceed the average earnings of a shoe-black in London, but the coats they wore were exceeding glorious with gold lace.

It was clear from the first that nothing was expected of Don Lotario's wife but to live peaceably under the patriarchal rule, making no observations and offering no suggestions. Her husband told her that he was powerless to introduce any changes, and added, that since his father and all his ancestors had always lived in the same way, that way was quite good enough for him. Indeed, he rather looked forward to the time when he should be master of the house, having children under him whom he might rule as absolutely and despotically as he was ruled himself.

In the course of years the Duchessa absorbed the traditions of her new home, so that they became part of her, and as everything went on unchanged from year to year she acquired unchanging habits which corresponded with her surroundings. Then, when at last the old prince and princess were laid side by side in the vault of the family chapel and she was princess in her turn, she changed nothing, but let everything go on in the same groove, educating her children and managing them, as her husband had been educated and as she herself had been managed by the old couple. Her husband grew more and more like his father, punctilious, rigid; a strict observant in religious matters, a pedant in little things, prejudiced against all change; too satisfied to desire improvement, too scrupulously conscientious to permit any retrogression from established rule, a model of the immutability of an ancient aristocracy, a living paradigm of what always had been and a stubborn barrier against all that might be.

Such was the home to which Donna Faustina Montevarchi returned to live after spending eight years in the convent of the Sacro Cuore. During that time she had acquired the French language, a slight knowledge of music, a very limited acquaintance with the history of her own country, a ready memory for prayers and litanies—and her manners. Manners among the Italians are called education. What we mean by the latter word, namely the learning acquired, is called, more precisely, instruction. An educated person means a person who has acquired the art of politeness. An instructed person means some one who has learnt rather more than the average of what is generally learnt by the class of people to whom he belongs. Donna Faustina was extremely well educated, according to Roman ideas, but her instruction was not, and was not intended to be, any better than that imparted to the young girls with whom she was to associate in the world.

As far as her character was concerned, she herself knew very little of it, and would probably have found herself very much embarrassed if called upon to explain what character meant. She was new and the world was very old. The nuns had told her that she must never care for the world, which was a very sinful place, full of thorns, ditches, pitfalls and sinners, besides the devil and his angels. Her sister Flavia, on the contrary, assured her that the world was very agreeable, when mamma happened to go to sleep in a corner during a ball; that all men were deceivers, but that when a man danced well it made no difference whether he were a deceiver or not, since he danced with his legs and not with his con-science; that there was no happiness equal to a good cotillon, and that there were a number of these in every season; and, finally, that provided one did not spoil one's complexion one might do anything, so long as mamma was not looking.

To Donna Faustina, these views, held by the nuns on the one hand and by Flavia on the other, seemed very conflicting. She would not, indeed, have hesi-tated in choosing, even if she had been permitted any choice; for it was clear that, since she had seen the convent side of the question, it would be very interesting to see the other. But, having been told so much about sinners, she was on the look-out for them, and looked forward to making the acquaintance of one of them with a pardonable excitement. Doubtless she would hate a sinner if she saw one, as the nuns had taught her, although the sinner of her imagination was not a very repulsive personage. Flavia probably knew a great many, and Flavia said that society was very amusing. Faustina wished that the autumn months would pass a little more quickly, so that the carnival season might begin.

Prince Montevarchi, for his part, intended his youngest daughter to be a model of prim propriety. He attributed to Flavia's frivolity of behaviour the difficulty he experienced in finding her a husband, and he had no intention of exposing himself to a second failure in the case of Faustina. She should marry in her first season, and if she chose to be gay after that, the responsibility thereof might fall upon her husband, or her father-in-law, or upon whomsoever it should most concern; he himself would have fulfilled his duty so soon as the nuptial benediction was pronounced. He knew the fortune and reputation of every marriageable young man in society, and was therefore eminently fitted for the task he undertook. To tell the truth, Faustina herself expected to be married before Easter, for it was eminently fitting that a young girl should lose no time in such matters. But she meant to choose a man after her own heart, if she found one; at all events, she would not submit too readily to the paternal choice nor appear satisfied with the first tolerable suitor who should be presented to her.

Under these circumstances it seemed probable that Donna Faustina's first season, which had begun with the unexpected adventure at the corner of the old Orso, would not come to a close without some passage of arms between herself and her father, even though the ultimate conclusion should lead to the steps of the altar.

The men carried the wounded Zouave away to a distant room, and Faustina entered the main apartments by the side of the old prince. She sighed a little as she went.

"I hope the poor man will get well!" she exclaimed.

"Do not disturb your mind about the young man," answered her father. "He will be attended by the proper persons, and the doctor will bleed him and the will of Heaven will be done. It is not the duty of a well-conducted young woman to be thinking of such things, and you may dismiss the subject at once."

"Yes, papa," said Faustina submissively. But in spite of the dutiful tone of voice in which she spoke, the dim light of the tall lamps in the antechambers showed a strange expression of mingled amusement and contrariety in the girl's ethereal face.

CHAPTER II

"You know Gouache?" asked old Prince Saracinesca, in a tone which implied that he had news to tell. He looked from his daughter-in-law to his son as he put the question, and then went on with his breakfast.

"Very well," answered Giovanni. "What about him?"

"He was knocked down by a carriage last night. The carriage belonged to Montevarchi, and Gouache is at his house, in danger of his life."

"Poor fellow!" exclaimed Corona in ready sympathy. "I am so sorry! I am very fond of Gouache."

Giovanni Saracinesca, known to the world since his marriage as Prince of Sant' Ilario, glanced quickly at his wife, so quickly that neither she nor the old gentleman noticed the fact.

The three persons sat at their midday breakfast in the dining-room of the Palazzo Saracinesca. After much planning and many discussions the young couple had determined to take up their abode with Giovanni's father. There were several reasons which had led them to this decision, but the two chief ones were that they were both devotedly attached to the old man; and secondly, that such a proceeding was strictly fitting and in accordance with the customs of Romans. It was true that Corona, while her old husband, the Duca d'Astrardente, was alive, had grown used to having an establishment exclusively her own, and both the Saracinesca had at first feared that she would be unwilling to live in her father-in-law's house. Then, too, there was the Astrardente palace, which, could not lie shut up and allowed to go to ruin; but this matter was compromised advantageously by Corona's letting it to an American millionaire who wished to spend the winter in Rome. The rent paid was large, and Corona never could have too much money for her improvements out at Astrardente. Old Saracinesca wished that the tenant might have been at least a diplomatist, and cursed the American by his gods, but Giovanni said that his wife had shown good sense in getting as much as she could for the palace.

"We shall not need it till Orsino grows up—unless you marry again," said Sant' Ilario to his father, with a laugh.

Now, Orsino was Giovanni's son and heir, aged, at the time of this tale, six months and a few days. In spite of his extreme youth, however, Orsino played a great and important part in the doings of the Saracinesca household. In the first place, he was the heir, and the old prince had been found sitting by his cradle with an expression never seen in his face since Giovanni had been a baby. Secondly, Orsino was a very fine child, swarthy of skin, and hard as a tiger cub, yet having already his mother's eyes, large, coal-black and bright, but deep and soft withal. Thirdly, Orsino had a will of his own, admirably seconded by an enormous lung power. Not that he cried, when he wanted anything. His baby eyes had not yet been seen to shed tears. He merely shouted, loud and long, and thumped the sides of his cradle with his little clenched fists, or struck out straight at anybody who chanced to be within reach. Corona rejoiced in the child, and used to say that he was like his grandfather, his father and his mother all put together. The old prince thought that if this were true the boy would do very well; Corona was the most beautiful dark woman of her time; he himself was a sturdy, tough old man, though his hair and beard were white as snow, and Giovanni was his father's ideal of what a man of his race should be. The arrival of the baby Orsino had been an additional argument in favour of living together, for the child's grandfather could not have been separated from him even by the quarter of a mile which lay between the two palaces.

And so it came to pass that they all dwelt under the same roof, and were sitting together at breakfast on the morning of the 24th of September, when the old prince told them of the accident which had happened to Gouache.

"How did you hear the news?" asked Giovanni.

"Montevarchi told me this morning. He was very much disturbed at the idea of having an interesting young man in his house, with Flavia and Faustina at home." Old Saracinesca smiled grimly.

"Why should that trouble him?" inquired Corona.

"He has the ancient ideas," replied her father-in-law.

"After all—Flavia—"

"Yes Flavia, after all—"

"I shall be curious to see how the other one turns out," remarked Giovanni. "There seems to be a certain unanimity in our opinion of Flavia. However, I daresay it is mere gossip, and Casa Montevarchi is not a gay place for a girl of her age."

"Not gay? How do you know?" asked the old prince. "Does the girl want Carnival to last till All Souls'? Did you ever dine there, Giovannino?"

"No—nor any one else who is not a member of the most Excellent Casa Montevarchi."

"Then how do you know whether it is gay or not?"

"You should hear Ascanio Bellegra describe their life," retorted Giovanni.

"And I suppose you describe your life to him, in exchange?" Prince Saracinesca was beginning to lose his temper, as he invariably did whenever he could induce his son to argue any question with him. "I suppose you deplore each other's miserable condition. I tell you what I think, Giovanni. You had better go and live in Corona's house if you are not happy here."

"It is let," replied Giovanni with imperturbable calm, but his wife bit her lip to control her rising laughter.

"You might travel," growled the old gentleman.

"But I am very happy here."

"Then what do you mean by talking like that about Casa Montevarchi?"

"I fail to see the connection between the two ideas," observed Giovanni.

"You live in precisely the same circumstances as Ascanio Bellegra. I think the connection is clear enough. If his life is sad, so is yours."

"For downright good logic commend me to my beloved father!" cried Giovanni, breaking into a laugh at last.

"A laughing-stock for my children! I have come to this!" exclaimed his father gruffly. But his features relaxed into a good-humoured smile, that was pleasant to see upon his strong dark face.

"But, really, I am very sorry to hear this of poor Gouache," said Corona at last, returning to the original subject of their conversation. "I hope it is nothing really dangerous."

"It is always dangerous to be run over by a carriage," answered Giovanni. "I will go and see him, if they will let me in."

At this juncture Orsino was brought in by his nurse, a splendid creature from Saracinesca, with bright blue eyes and hair as fair as any Goth's, a contrast to the swarthy child she carried in her arms. Immediately the daily ovation began, and each of the three persons began to worship the baby in an especial way. There was no more conversation, after that, for some time. The youngest of the Saracinesca absorbed the attention of the family. Whether he clenched his little fists, or opened his small fat fingers, whether he laughed and crowed at his grandfather's attempts to amuse him, or struck his nurse's rosy cheeks with his chubby hands, the result was always applause and merriment from those who looked on. The scene recalled Joseph's dream, in which the sheaves of his brethren bowed down to his sheaf.

After a while, however, Orsino grew sleepy and had to be taken away. Then the little party broke up and separated. The old prince went to his rooms to read and doze for an hour. Corona was called away to see one of the numberless dressmakers whose shadows darken the beginning of a season in town, and Giovanni took his hat and went out.

In those days young men of society had very little to do. The other day a German diplomatist was heard to say that Italian gentlemen seemed to do nothing but smoke, spit, and criticise. Twenty years ago their manners might have been described less coarsely, but there was even more truth in the gist of the saying. Not only they did nothing. There was nothing for them to do. They floated about in a peaceful millpool, whose placid surface reflected nothing but their own idle selves, little guessing that the dam whereby their mimic sea was confined, would shortly break with a thundering crash and empty them all into the stream of real life that flowed below. For the few who disliked idleness there was no occupation but literature, and literature, to the Roman mind of 1867, and in the Roman meaning of the word, was scholarship. The introduction to a literary career was supposed to be obtained only by a profound study of the classics, with a view to avoiding everything classical, both in language and ideas, except Cicero, the apostle of the ancient Roman Philistines; and the tendency to clothe stale truisms and feeble sentiments in high-sounding language is still found in Italian prose and is indirectly traceable to the same source. As for the literature of the country since the Latins, it consisted, and still consists, in the works of the four poets, Dante, Tasso, Ariosto, and Petrarch. Leopardi is more read now than then, but is too unhealthily melancholy to be read long by any one. There used to be Roman princes who spent years in committing to memory the verses of those four poets, just as the young Brahman of today learns to recite the Rig Veda. That was called the pursuit of literature.

The Saracinesca were thought very original and different from other men, because they gave some attention to their estates. It seemed very like business to try and improve the possessions one had inherited or acquired by marriage, and business was degradation. Nevertheless, the Saracinesca were strong enough to laugh at other people's scruples, and did what seemed best in their own eyes without troubling themselves to ask what the world thought. But the care of such matters was not enough to occupy Giovanni all day. He had much time on his hands, for he was an active man, who slept little and rarely needed rest. Formerly he had been used to disappear from Rome periodically, making long journeys, generally ending in shooting expeditions in some half-explored country. That was in the days before his marriage, and his wanderings had assuredly done him no harm. He had seen much of the world not usually seen by men of his class and prejudices, and the acquaintance he had thus got with things and people was a source of great satisfaction to him. But the time had come to give up all this. He was now not only married and settled in his own home, but moreover he loved his wife with his whole heart, and these facts were serious obstacles against roughing it in Norway, Canada, or Transylvania. To travel with Corona and little Orsino seemed a very different matter from travelling with Corona alone. Then there was his father's growing affection for the child, which had to be taken into account in all things. The four had become inseparable, old Saracinesca, Giovanni, Corona, and the baby.

Now Giovanni did not regret his old liberty. He knew that he was far happier than he had ever been in his life before. But there were days when the time hung heavily on his hands and his restless nature craved some kind of action which should bring with it a generous excitement. This was precisely what he could not find during the months spent in Rome, and so it fell out that he did very much what most young men of his birth found quite sufficient as an employment; he spent a deal of time in strolling where others strolled, in lounging at the club, and in making visits which filled the hours between sunset and dinner. To him this life was new, and not altogether tasteful; but his friends did not fail to say that Giovanni had been civilised by his marriage with the Astrardente, and was much less reserved than he had formerly been.

When Corona went to see the dressmaker, Giovanni very naturally took his hat and went out of the house. The September day was warm and bright, and in such weather it was a satisfaction merely to pace the old Roman streets in the autumn sun. It was too early to meet any of his acquaintance, and too soon in the season for any regular visiting. He did not know what to do, but allowed himself to enjoy the sunshine and the sweet air. Presently, the sight of a couple of Zouaves, talking together at the corner of a street, recalled to his mind the accident which had happened to Gouache. It would be kind to go and see the poor fellow, or, at least, to ask after him. He had known him for some time and had gradually learned to like him, as most people did who met the gifted artist day after day throughout the gaiety of the winter.

At the Palazzo Montevarchi Giovanni learned that the princess had just finished breakfast. He could hardly ask for Gouache without making a short visit in the drawing-room, and he accordingly submitted, regretting after all that he had come. The old princess bored him, he did not know Faustina, who was just out of the convent, and Flavia, who amused many people, did not amuse him in the least. He inwardly rejoiced that he was married, and that his visit could not be interpreted as a preliminary step towards asking for Flavia's hand.

The princess looked up with an expression of inquiry in her prominent blue eyes, as Sant' Ilario entered. She was stout, florid, and not well dressed. Her yellow hair, already half gray, for she was more than fifty years old, was of the unruly kind, and had never looked neat even in her best days. Her bright, clear complexion saved her, however, as it saves hundreds of middle-aged Englishwomen, from that look of peculiar untidiness which belongs to dark-skinned persons who take no trouble about their appearance or personal adornment. In spite of thirty-three years of residence in Rome, she spoke Italian with a foreign accent, though otherwise correctly enough. But she was nevertheless a great lady, and no one would have thought of doubting the fact. Fat, awkwardly dressed, of no imposing stature, with unmanageable hair and prominent teeth, she was not a person to be laughed at. She had what many a beautiful woman lacks and envies—natural dignity of character and manner, combined with a self-possession which is not always found in exalted personages. That repose of manner which is commonly believed to be the heirloom of noble birth is seen quite as often in the low-born adventurer, who regards it as part of his stock-in-trade; and there are many women, and men too, whose position might be expected to place them beyond the reach of what we call shyness, but who nevertheless suffer daily agonies of social timidity and would rather face alone a charge of cavalry than make a new acquaintance. The Princess Montevarchi was made of braver stuff, however, and if her daughters had not inherited all her unaffected dignity they had at least received their fair share of self-possession. When Sant' Ilario entered, these two young ladies, Donna Flavia and Donna Faustina, were seated one on each side of their mother. The princess extended her hand, the two daughters held theirs demurely crossed upon their knees. Faustina looked at the carpet, as she had been taught to do in the convent. Flavia looked up boldly at Giovanni, knowing by experience that her mother could not see her while greeting the visitor. Sant' Ilario muttered some sort of civil inquiry, bowed to the two young ladies and sat down.

"How is Monsieur Gouache?" he asked, going straight to the point. He had seen the look of surprise on the princess's face as he entered, and thought it best to explain himself at once.

"Ah, you have heard? Poor man! He is badly hurt, I fear. Would you like to see him?"

"Presently, if I may," answered Giovanni. "We are all fond of Gouache. How did the accident happen?"

"Faustina ran over him," said Flavia, fixing her dark eyes on Giovanni and allowing her pretty face to assume an expression of sympathy—for the sufferer. "Faustina and papa," she added.

"Flavia! How can you say such things!" exclaimed the princess, who spent a great part of her life in repressing her daughter's manner of speech.

"Well, mamma—it was the carriage of course. But papa and Faustina were in it. It is the same thing."

Giovanni looked at Faustina, but her thin fresh face expressed nothing, nor did she show any intention of commenting on her sister's explanation. It was the first time he had seen her near enough to notice her, and his attention was arrested by something in her looks which surprised and interested him. It was something almost impossible to describe, and yet so really present that it struck Sant' Ilario at once, and found a place in his memory. In the superstitions of the far north, as in the half material spiritualism of Polynesia, that look has a meaning and an interpretation. With us, the interpretation is lost, but the instinctive persuasion that the thing itself is not wholly meaningless remains ineradicable. We say, with a smile at our own credulity, "That man looks as though he had a story," or, "That woman looks as though something odd might happen to her." It is an expression in the eyes, a delicate shade in the features, which speak of many things which we do not understand; things which, if they exist at all, we feel must be inevitable, fatal, and beyond human control. Giovanni looked and was surprised, but Faustina said nothing.

"It was very good of the prince to bring him here," remarked Sant' Ilario.

"It was very unlike papa," exclaimed Flavia, before her mother could answer. "But very kind, of course, as you say," she added, with a little smile. Flavia had a habit of making rather startling remarks, and of then adding something in explanation or comment, before her hearers had recovered breath. The addition did not always mend matters very much.

"Do not interrupt me, Flavia," said her mother, severely.

"I beg your pardon, were you speaking, mamma?" asked the young girl, innocently.

Giovanni was not amused by Flavia's manners, and waited calmly for the princess to speak.

"Indeed," said she, "there was nothing else to be done. As we had run over the poor man—"

"The carriage—" suggested Flavia. But her mother took no notice of her.

"The least we could do, of course, was to bring him here. My husband would not have allowed him to be taken to the hospital."

Flavia again fixed her eyes on Giovanni with a look of sympathy, which, however, did not convey any very profound belief in her father's charitable intentions.

"I quite understand," said Giovanni. "And how has he been since you brought him here? Is he in any danger?"

"You shall see him at once," answered the princess, who rose and rang the bell, and then, as the servant's footsteps were heard outside, crossed the room to meet him at the door.

"Mamma likes to run about," said Flavia, sweetly, in explanation. Giovanni had risen and made as though he would have been of some assistance.

The action was characteristic of the Princess Montevarchi. An Italian woman would neither have rung the bell herself, nor have committed such an imprudence as to turn her back upon her two daughters when there was a man in the room. But she was English, and a whole lifetime spent among Italians could not extinguish her activity; so she went to the door herself. Faustina's deep eyes followed her mother as though she were interested to know the news of Gouache.

"I hope he is better," she said, quietly.

"Of course," echoed Flavia, "So do I. But mamma amuses me so much! She is always in a hurry."

Faustina made no answer, but she looked at Sant' Ilario, as though she wondered what he thought of her sister. He returned her gaze, trying to explain to himself the strange attraction of her expression, watching her critically as he would have watched any new person or sight. She did not blush nor avoid his bold eyes, as he would have expected had he realised that he was staring at her.

A few minutes later Giovanni found himself in a narrow, high room, lighted by one window, which showed the enormous thickness of the walls in the deep embrasure. The vaulted ceiling was painted in fresco with a representation of Apollo in the act of drawing his bow, arrayed for the time being in his quiver, while his other garments, of yellow and blue, floated everywhere save over his body. The floor of the room was of red bricks, which had once been waxed, and the furniture was scanty, massive and very old. Anastase Gouache lay in one corner in a queer-looking bed covered with a yellow damask quilt the worse for a century or two of wear, upon which faded embroideries showed the Montevarchi arms surmounted by a cardinal's hat. Upon a chair beside the patient lay the little heap of small belongings he had carried in his pocket when hurt, his watch and purse, his cigarettes, his handkerchief and a few other trifles, among which, half concealed by the rest, was the gold pin he had picked up by the bridge on the previous evening. There was a mingled smell of dampness and of stale tobacco in the comfortless room, for the windows were closely shut, in spite of the bright sunshine that flooded the opposite side of the street.

Gouache lay on his back, his head tied up in a bandage and supported by a white pillow, which somehow conveyed the impression of one of those marble cushions upon which in old-fashioned monuments the effigies of the dead are made to lean in eternal prayer, if not in eternal ease. He moved impatiently as the door opened, and then recognising Giovanni, he hailed him in a voice much more lively and sonorous than might have been expected.

"You, prince!" he cried, in evident delight. "What saint has brought you?"

"I heard of your accident, and so I came to see if I could do anything for you. How are you?"

"As you see," replied Gouache. "In a hospitable tomb, with my head tied up like an imperfectly-resurrected Lazarus. For the rest there is nothing the matter with me, except that they have taken away my clothes, which is something of an obstacle to my leaving the house at once. I feel as if I had been in a revolution and had found myself on the wrong side of the barricade—nothing worse than that."

"You are in good spirits, at all events. But are you not seriously hurt?"

"Oh, nothing—a broken collar-bone somewhere, I believe, and some part of my head gone—I am not quite sure which, and a bad headache, and nothing to eat, and a general sensation as though somebody had made an ineffectual effort to turn me into a sausage."

"What does the doctor say?"

"Nothing. He is a man of action. He bled me because I had not the strength to strangle him, and poured decoctions of boiled grass down my throat because I could not speak. He has fantastic ideas about the human body."

"But you will have to stay here several days," said Giovanni, considerably amused by Gouache's view of his own case.

"Several days! Not even several hours, if I can help it."

"Things do not go so quickly in Rome. You must be patient."

"In order to starve, when there is food as near as the Corso?" inquired the artist. "To be butchered by a Roman phlebotomist, and drenched with infusions of hay by the Principessa Montevarchi, when I might be devising means of being presented to her daughter? What do you take me for? I suppose the young lady with the divine eyes is her daughter, is she not?"

"You mean Donna Faustina, I suppose. Yes. She is the youngest, just out of the Sacro Cuore. She was in the drawing-room when I called just now. How did you see her?"

"Last night, as they brought me upstairs, I was lucky enough to wake up just as she was looking at me. What eyes! I can think of nothing else. Seriously, can you not help me to get out of here?"

"So that you may fall in love with Donna Faustina as soon as possible, I suppose," answered Giovanni with a laugh. "It seems to me that there is but one thing to do, if you are really strong enough. Send for your clothes, get up, go into the drawing-room and thank the princess for her hospitality."

"That is easily said. Nothing is done in this house without the written permission of the old prince, unless I am much mistaken. Besides, there is no bell. I might as well be under arrest in the guard-room of the barracks. Presently the doctor will come and bleed me again and the princess will send me some more boiled grass. I am not very fat, as it is, but another day of this diet will make me diaphanous—I shall cast no shadow. A nice thing, to be caught without a shadow on parade!"

"I will see what I can do," said Giovanni, rising. "Probably, the best thing would be to send your military surgeon. He will not be so tender as the other leech, but he will get you away at once. My wife wished me to say that she sympathised, and hoped you might soon be well."

"My homage and best thanks to the princess," answered Gouache, with a slight change of tone, presumably to be referred to his sense of courtesy in speaking of the absent lady.

So Giovanni went away, promising to send the surgeon at once. The latter soon arrived, saw Gouache, and was easily persuaded to order him home without further delay. The artist-soldier would not leave the house without thanking his hostess. His uniform had been cleansed from the stains it had got in the accident, and his left arm was in a sling. The wound on his head was more of a bruise than a cut, and was concealed by his thick black hair. Considering the circumstances he presented a very good appearance. The princess received him in the drawing-room, and Flavia and Faustina were with her, but all three were now dressed to go out, so that the interview was necessarily a short one.

Gouache made a little speech of thanks and tried to forget the decoction of mallows he had swallowed, fearing lest the recollection should impart a tone of insincerity to his expression of gratitude. He succeeded very well, and afterwards attributed the fact to Donna Faustina's brown eyes, which were not cast down as they had been when Sant' Ilario had called, but appeared on the contrary to contemplate the new visitor with singular interest.

"I am sure my husband will not approve of your going so soon," said the princess in somewhat anxious tones. It was almost the first time she had ever known any step of importance to be taken in her house without her husband's express authority.

"Madame," answered Gouache, glancing from Donna Faustina to his hostess, "I am in despair at having thus unwillingly trespassed upon your hospitality, although I need not tell you that I would gladly prolong so charming an experience, provided I were not confined to solitude in a distant chamber. However, since our regimental surgeon pronounces me fit to go home, I have no choice but to obey orders. Believe me, Madame, I am deeply grateful to yourself as well as to the Principe Montevarchi for your manifold kindnesses, and shall cherish a remembrance of your goodness so long as I live."

With these words Gouache bowed as though he would be gone and stood waiting for the princess's last word. But before her mother could speak, Faustina's voice was heard.

"I cannot tell you how dreadfully we feel—papa and I—at having been the cause of such a horrible accident! Is there nothing we can do to make you forget it?"

The princess stared at her daughter in the utmost astonishment at her forwardness. She would not have been surprised if Flavia had been guilty of such imprudence, but that Faustina should thus boldly address a young man who had not spoken to her, was such a shock to her belief in the girl's manners that she did not recover for several seconds. Anastase appreciated the situation, for as he answered, he looked steadily at the mother, although his words were plainly addressed to the brown-eyed beauty.

"Mademoiselle is too kind. She exaggerates. And yet, since she has put the question, I will say that I should forget my broken bones very soon if I might be permitted to paint Mademoiselle's portrait. I am a painter," he added, in modest explanation.

"Yes," said the princess, "I know. But, really—this is a matter which would require great consideration—and my husband's consent—and, for the present—"

She paused significantly, intending to convey a polite refusal, but Gouache completed the sentence.

"For the present, until my bones are mended, we will not speak of it. When I am well again I will do myself the honour of asking the prince's consent myself."

Flavia leaned towards her mother and whispered into her ear. The words were quite audible, and the girl's dark eyes turned to Gouache with a wicked laugh in them while she was speaking.

"Oh, mamma, if you tell papa it is for nothing he will be quite delighted!"

Gouache's lip trembled as he suppressed a smile, and the elderly princess's florid cheeks flushed with annoyance.

"For the present," she said, holding out her hand rather coldly, "we will not speak of it. Pray let us know of your speedy recovery, Monsieur Gouache."

As the artist took his leave he glanced once more at Donna Faustina. Her face was pale and her eyes flashed angrily. She, too, had heard Flavia's stage whisper and was even more annoyed than her mother. Gouache went his way toward his lodging in the company of the surgeon, pondering on the inscrutable mysteries of the Roman household of which he had been vouchsafed a glimpse. He was in pain from his head and shoulder, but insisted that the walk would do him good and refused the cab which his companion had brought. A broken collar-bone is not a dangerous matter, but it can be very troublesome for a while, and the artist was glad to get back to his lodgings and to find himself comfortably installed in an easy chair with something to eat before him, of a more substantial nature than the Principessa Montevarchi's infusions of camomile and mallows.

CHAPTER III

WHILE Giovanni was at the Palazzo Montevarchi, and while Corona was
busy with her dressmakers, Prince Saracinesca was dozing over the *Osservatore
Romano* in his study. To tell the truth the paper was less dull than usual, for
there was war and rumour of war in its columns. Garibaldi had raised a force
of volunteers and was in the neighbourhood of Arezzo, beginning to skirmish
with the outlying posts of the pontifical army along the frontier. The old gentleman did not know, of course, that on that very day the Italian Government was
issuing its proclamation against the great agitator, and possibly if he had been
aware of the incident it would not have produced any very strong impression
upon his convictions. Garibaldi was a fact, and Saracinesca did not believe that
any proclamations would interfere with his march unless backed by some more
tangible force. Even had he known that the guerilla general had been arrested at
Sinalunga and put in confinement as soon as the proclamation had appeared, the
prince would have foreseen clearly enough that the prisoner's escape would be
only a question of a few days, since there were manifold evidences that an understanding existed between Ratazzi and Garibaldi of much the same nature as that
which in 1860 had been maintained between Garibaldi and Cavour during the
advance upon Naples. The Italian Government kept men under arms to be ready
to take advantage of any successes obtained by the Garibaldian volunteers, and at
the same time to suppress the republican tendencies of the latter, which broke out
afresh with every new advance, and disappeared, as by magic, under the depress-
ing influence of a forced retreat.

The prince knew all these things, and had reflected upon them so often that
they no longer afforded enough interest to keep him awake. The warm September
sun streamed into the study and fell upon the paper as it slowly slipped over the
old gentleman's knees, while his head sank lower and lower on his breast. The
old enamelled clock upon the chimney-piece ticked more loudly, as clocks seem
to do when people are asleep and they are left to their own devices, and a few
belated flies chased each other in the sunbeams.

The silence was broken by the entrance of a servant, who would have withdrawn again when he saw that his master was napping, had not the latter stirred
and raised his head before the man had time to get away. Then the fellow came

forward with an apology and presented a visiting-card. The prince stared at the bit of pasteboard, rubbed his eyes, stared again, and then laid it upon the table beside him, his eyes still resting on the name, which seemed so much to surprise him. Then he told the footman to introduce the visitor, and a few moments later a very tall man entered the room, hat in hand, and advanced slowly towards him with the air of a person who has a perfect right to present himself but wishes to give his host time to recognise him.

The prince remembered the newcomer very well. The closely-buttoned frock-coat showed the man's imposing figure to greater advantage than the dress in which Saracinesca had last seen him, but there was no mistaking the personality. There was the same lean but massive face, broadened by the high cheekbones and the prominent square jaw; there were the same piercing black eyes, set near together under eyebrows that met in the midst of the forehead, the same thin and cruel lips, and the same strongly-marked nose, set broadly on at the nostrils, though pointed and keen. Had the prince had any doubts as to his visitor's identity they would have been dispelled by the man's great height and immense breadth of shoulder, which would have made it hard indeed for him to disguise himself had he wished to do so. But though very much surprised, Saracinesca had no doubts whatever. The only points that were new to him in the figure before him were the outward manner and appearance, and the dress of a gentleman.

"I trust I am not disturbing you, prince?" The words were spoken in a deep, clear voice, and with a notable southern accent.

"Not at all. I confess I am astonished at seeing you in Rome. Is there anything I can do for you? I shall always be grateful to you for having been alive to testify to the falsehood of that accusation made against my son. Pray sit down. How is your Signora? And the children? All well, I hope?"

"My wife is dead," returned the other, and the grave tones of his bass voice lent solemnity to the simple statement.

"I am sincerely sorry—" began the prince, but his visitor interrupted him.

"The children are well. They are in Aquila for the present. I have come to establish myself in Rome, and my first visit is naturally to yourself, since I have the advantage of being your cousin."

"Naturally," ejaculated Saracinesca, though his face expressed considerable surprise.

"Do not imagine that I am going to impose myself upon you as a poor relation," continued the other with a faint smile. "Fortune has been kind to me since we met, perhaps as a compensation for the loss I suffered in the death of my poor wife. I have a sufficient independence and can hold my own."

"I never supposed—"

"You might naturally have supposed that I had come to solicit your favour, though it is not the case. When we parted I was an innkeeper in Aquila. I have no cause to be ashamed of my past profession. I only wish to let you know that it is altogether past, and that I intend to resume the position which my great-grandfather foolishly forfeited. As you are the present head of the family I judged that it was my duty to inform you of the fact immediately."

"By all means. I imagined this must be the case from your card. You are entirely in your rights, and I shall take great pleasure in informing every one of the fact. You are the Marchese di San Giacinto, and the inn at Aquila no longer exists."

"As these things must be done, once and for always, I have brought my papers to Rome," answered the Marchese. "They are at your disposal, for you certainly have a right to see them, if you like. I will recall to your memory the facts of our history, in case you have forgotten them."

"I know the story well enough," said Saracinesca. "Our great-grandfathers were brothers. Yours went to live in Naples. His son grew up and joined the French against the King. His lands were forfeited, he married and died in obscurity, leaving your father, his only son. Your father died young and you again are his only son. You married the Signora Felice—"

"Baldi," said the Marchese, nodding in confirmation of the various statements.

"The Signora Felice Baldi, by whom you have two children—"

"Boys."

"Two boys. And the Signora Marchesa, I grieve to hear, is dead. Is that accurate?"

"Perfectly. There is one circumstance, connected with our great-grandfathers, which you have not mentioned, but which I am sure you remember."

"What is that?" asked the prince, fixing his keen eyes on his companion's face.

"It is only this," replied San Giacinto, calmly. "My great-grandfather was two years older than yours. You know he never meant to marry, and resigned the title to his younger brother, who had children already. He took a wife in his old age, and my grandfather was the son born to him. That is why you are so much older than I, though we are of the same generation in the order of descent."

"Yes," assented the prince. "That accounts for it. Will you smoke?"

Giovanni Saracinesca, Marchese di San Giacinto, looked curiously at his cousin as he took the proffered cigar. There was something abrupt in the answer which attracted his attention and roused his quick suspicions. He wondered whether that former exchange of titles, and consequent exchange of positions were an unpleasant subject of conversation to the prince. But the latter, as though anticipating such a doubt in his companion's mind, at once returned to the question with the boldness which was natural to him.

"There was a friendly agreement," he said, striking a match and offering it to the Marchese. "I have all the documents, and have studied them with interest. It might amuse you to see them, some day."

"I should like to see them, indeed," answered San Giacinto. "They must be very curious. As I was saying, I am going to establish myself in Rome. It seems strange to me to be playing the gentleman—it must seem even more odd to you."

"It would be truer to say that you have been playing the innkeeper," observed the prince, courteously. "No one would suspect it," he added, glancing at his companion's correct attire.

"I have an adaptable nature," said the Marchese, calmly. "Besides, I have always looked forward to again taking my place in the world. I have acquired a little instruction—not much, you will say, but it is sufficient as the times go; and as for education, it is the same for every one, innkeeper or prince. One takes off one's hat, one speaks quietly, one says what is agreeable to hear—is it not enough?"

"Quite enough," replied the prince. He was tempted to smile at his cousin's definition of manners, though he could see that the man was quite able to maintain his position. "Quite enough, indeed, and as for instruction, I am afraid most of us have forgotten our Latin. You need have no anxiety on that score. But, tell me, how comes it that, having been bred in the south, you prefer to establish yourself in Rome rather than in Naples? They say that you Neapolitans do not like us."

"I am a Roman by descent, and I wish to become one in fact," returned the Marchese. "Besides," he added, in a peculiarly grave tone of voice, "I do not like the new order of things. Indeed, I have but one favour to ask of you, and that is a great one."

"Anything in my power—"

"To present me to the Holy Father as one who desires to become his faithful subject. Could you do so, do you think, without any great inconvenience?"

"Eh! I shall be delighted! Magari!" answered the prince, heartily. "To tell the truth, I was afraid you meant to keep your Italian convictions, and that, in Rome, would be against you, especially in these stormy days. But if you will join us heart and soul you will be received with open arms. I shall take great pleasure in seeing you make the acquaintance of my son and his wife. Come and dine this evening."

"Thank you," said the Marchese. "I will not fail."

After a few more words San Giacinto took his leave, and the prince could not but admire the way in which this man, who had been brought up among peasants, or at best among the small farmers of an outlying district, assumed at once an air of perfect equality while allowing just so much of respect to appear in his manner as might properly be shown by a younger member to the head of a great house. When he was gone Saracinesca rang the bell.

"Pasquale," he said, addressing the old butler who answered the summons, "that gentleman who is just gone is my cousin, Don Giovanni Saracinesca, who is called Marchese di San Giacinto. He will dine here this evening. You will call him Eccellenza, and treat him as a member of the family. Go and ask the princess if she will receive me."

Pasquale opened his mental eyes very wide as he bowed and left the room. He had never heard of this other Saracinesca, and the appearance of a new member of the family upon the scene, who must, from his appearance, have been in existence between thirty and forty years, struck him as astonishing in the extreme; for the old servant had been bred up in the house from a boy and imagined himself master of all the secrets connected with the Saracinesca household.

He was, indeed, scarcely less surprised than his master who, although he had been aware for some time past that Giovanni Saracinesca existed and was his cousin, had never anticipated the event of his coming to Rome, and had expected still less that the innkeeper would ever assume the title to which he had a right and play the part of a gentleman, as he himself had expressed it. There was a strange mixture of boldness and foresight in the way the old prince had received his new relation. He knew the strength of his own position in society, and that the introduction of a humble cousin could not possibly do him harm. At the worst, people might laugh a little among themselves and remark that the Marchese must be a nuisance to the Saracinesca. On the other hand, the prince was struck from the first with the air of self-possession which he discerned in San Giacinto, and foresaw that the man would very probably play a part in Roman life. He was a man who might be disliked, but who could not be despised; and since his claims to consideration were undeniably genuine, it seemed wiser to accept him from the first as a member of the family and unhesitatingly to treat him as such. After all, he demanded nothing to which he had not a clear right from the moment he announced his intention of taking his place in the world, and it was certainly far wiser to receive him cordially at once, than to draw back from acknowledging the relationship because he had been brought up in another sphere.

This was the substance of what Prince Saracinesca communicated to his daughter-in-law a few minutes later. She listened patiently to all he had to say, only asking a question now and then in order to understand more clearly what had happened. She was curious to see the man whose name had once been so strangely confounded with her husband's by the machinations of the Conte Del Ferice and Donna Tullia Mayer, and she frankly confessed her curiosity and her satisfaction at the prospect of meeting San Giacinto that evening. While she was talking with the prince, Giovanni unexpectedly returned from his walk. He had turned homewards as soon as he had sent the military surgeon to Gouache. "Well, Giovannino," cried the old gentleman, "the prodigal innkeeper has returned to the bosom of the family."

"What innkeeper?"

"Your worthy namesake, and cousin, Giovanni Saracinesca, formerly of Aquila."

"Does Madame Mayer want to prove that it is he who has married Corona?" inquired Sant' Ilario with a laugh.

"No, though I suppose he is a candidate for marriage. I never was more surprised in my life. His wife is dead. He is rich, or says he is. He has his card printed in full, 'Giovanni Saracinesca, Marchese di San Giacinto,' in the most correct manner. He wears an excellent coat, and announces his intention of being presented to the Pope and introduced to Roman society."

Sant' Ilario stared incredulously at his father, and then looked inquiringly at his wife as though to ask if it were not all a jest. When he was assured that the facts were true he looked grave and slowly stroked his pointed black beard, a gesture which was very unusual with him, and always accompanied the deepest meditation.

"There is nothing to be done but to receive him into the family," he said at last. "But I do not wholly believe in his good intentions. We shall see. I shall be glad to make his acquaintance."

"He is coming to dinner."

The conversation continued for some time and the arrival of San Giacinto was discussed in all its bearings. Corona took a very practical view of the question, and said that it was certainly best to treat him well, thereby relieving her father-in-law of a considerable anxiety. He had indeed feared lest she should resent the introduction of a man who might reasonably be supposed to have retained a certain coarseness of manner from his early surroundings, and he knew that her consent was all-important in such a case, since she was virtually the mistress of the house. But Corona regarded the matter in much the same light as the old gentleman himself, feeling that nothing of such a nature could possibly injure the imposing position of her husband's family, and taking it for granted that no one who had good blood in his veins could ever behave outrageously. Of all the three, Sant' Ilario was the most silent and thoughtful, for he feared certain consequences from the arrival of this new relation which did not present themselves to the minds of the others, and was resolved to be cautious accordingly, even while appearing to receive San Giacinto with all due cordiality. Later in the day he was alone with his father for a few minutes.

"Do you like this fellow?" he asked, abruptly.

"No," answered the prince.

"Neither do I, though I have not seen him."

"We shall see," was the old gentleman's answer.

The evening came, and at the appointed hour San Giacinto was announced. Both Corona and her husband were surprised at his imposing appearance, as well as at the dignity and self-possession he displayed. His southern accent was not more noticeable than that of many Neapolitan gentlemen, and his conversation, if neither very brilliant nor very fluent, was not devoid of interest. He talked of the agricultural condition of the new Italy, and old Saracinesca and his son were both interested in the subject. They noticed, too, that during dinner no word escaped him which could give any clue to his former occupation or position, though afterwards, when the servants were not present, he alluded more than once with a frank smile to his experiences as an innkeeper. On the whole, he seemed modest and reserved, yet perfectly self-possessed and conscious of his right to be where he was.

Such conduct on the part of such a man did not appear so surprising to the Saracinesca household, as it would have seemed to foreigners. San Giacinto had said that he had an adaptable character, and that adaptability is one of the most noticeable features of the Italian race. It is not necessary to discuss the causes of this peculiarity. They would be incomprehensible to the foreigner at large, who never has any real understanding of Italians. I do not hesitate to say that, without a single exception, every foreigner, poet or prose-writer, who has treated of these people has more or less grossly misunderstood them. That is a sweeping statement, when it is considered that few men of the highest genius in our century have not at one time or another set down upon paper their several estimates of the Italian race. The requisite for accurately describing people, however, is not genius, but knowledge of the subject. The poet commonly sees himself in others, and the modern writer upon Italy is apt to believe that he can see others in himself. The reflection of an Italian upon the mental retina of the foreigner is as deceptive as his own outward image is when seen upon the polished surface of a concave mirror; and indeed the character studies of many great men, when the subject is taken from a race not their own, remind one very forcibly of what may be seen by contemplating oneself in the bowl of a bright silver spoon. To understand Italians a man must have been born and bred among them; and even then the harder, fiercer instinct, which dwells in northern blood, may deceive the student and lead him far astray. The Italian is an exceedingly simple creature, and is apt to share the opinion of the ostrich, who ducks his head and believes his whole body is hidden. Foreigners use strong language concerning the Italian lie; but this only proves how extremely transparent the deception is. It is indeed a singular fact, but one which may often be observed, that two Italians who lie systematically will frequently believe each other, to their own ruin, with a childlike faith rarely found north of the Alps. This seems to me to prove that their dishonesty has outgrown their indolent intelligence; and indeed they deceive themselves nearly as often as they succeed in deceiving their neighbours. In a country where a lie easily finds credence, lying is not likely to be elevated to the rank of a fine art. I have often wondered how such men as Cesare Borgia succeeded in entrapping their enemies by snares which a modern northerner would detect from the first and laugh to scorn as mere child's play.

There is an extraordinary readiness in Italians to fit themselves and their lives to circumstances whenever they can save themselves trouble by doing so. Their constitutions are convenient to this end, for they are temperate in most things and do not easily fall into habits which they cannot change at will. The desire to avoid trouble makes them the most courteous among nations; and they are singularly obliging to strangers when, by conferring an obligation, they are able to make an acquaintance who will help them to pass an idle hour in agreeable conversation. They are equally surprised, whether a stranger suspects them of making advances for the sake of extracting money from him, or expresses resentment at having been fraudulently induced to part with any cash. The beggar in the street howls like a madman if you refuse an alms, and calls you an idiot to his fellow-mendicant if you give him five centimes. The servant says in his heart that his foreign employer is a fool, and sheds tears of rage and mortification when his shallow devices for petty cheating are discovered. And yet the servant, the beggar, the shopkeeper, and the gentleman, are obliging sometimes almost to philanthropy, and are ever ready to make themselves agreeable.

The Marchese di San Giacinto differed from his relations, the Saracinesca princes, in that he was a full-blooded Italian, and not the result of a cosmopolitan race-fusion, like so many of the Roman nobles. He had not the Roman traditions, but, on the other hand, he had his full share of the national characteristics, together with something individual which lifted him above the common herd in point of intelligence and in strength. He was a noticeable man; all the more so because, with many pleasant qualities, his countrymen rarely possess that physical and mental combination of size, energy, and reserve, which inspires the sort of respect enjoyed by imposing personages.

As he sat talking with the family after dinner on the evening of his first introduction to the household what passed in his mind and in the minds of his hosts can be easily stated.

Sant' Ilario, whose ideas were more clear upon most subjects than those of his father or his wife, said to himself that he did not like the man; that he suspected him, and believed he had some hidden intention in coming to Rome; that it would be wise to watch him perpetually and to question everything he did; but that he was undeniably a relation, possessing every right to consideration, and entitled to be treated with a certain familiarity; that, finally and on the whole, he was a nuisance, to be borne with a good grace and a sufficient show of cordiality.

San Giacinto, for his part, was deeply engaged in maintaining the exact standard of manners which he knew to be necessary for the occasion, and his thoughts concerning his relatives were not yet altogether defined. It was his intention to take his place among them, and he was doing his best to accomplish this object as speedily and quietly as possible. He had not supposed that princes and princesses were in any way different from other human beings except by the accidents of wealth and social position. Master of these two requisites there was no reason why he should not feel as much at home with the Saracinesca as he had felt in the society of the mayor and municipal council of Aquila, who possessed those qualifications also, though in a less degree. The Saracinesca probably thought about most questions very much as he himself did, or if there were any difference in their mode of thinking it was due to Roman prejudice and tradition rather than to any peculiarity inherent in the organisation of the members of the higher aristocracy. If he should find himself in any dilemma owing to his ignorance of social details he would not hesitate to apply to the prince for information, since it was by no means his fault if he had been brought up an innkeeper and was now to be a nobleman. His immediate object was to place himself among his equals, and his next purpose was to marry again, in his new rank, a woman of good position and fortune. Of this matter he intended to speak to the prince in due time, when he should have secured the first requisite to his marriage by establishing himself firmly in society. He meant to apply to the prince, ostensibly as to the head of the family, thereby showing a deference to that dignity, which he supposed would be pleasing to the old gentleman; but he had not forgotten in his calculations the pride which old Saracinesca must naturally feel in his race, and which would probably induce him to take very great pains in finding a suitable wife for San Giacinto rather than permit the latter to contract a discreditable alliance.

San Giacinto left the house at half-past nine o'clock, under the pretext of another engagement, for he did not mean to weary his relations with too much of his company in the first instance. When he was gone the three looked at each other in silence for some moments.

"He has surprisingly good manners, for an innkeeper," said Corona at last. "No one will ever suspect his former life. But I do not like him."

"Nor I," said the prince.

"He wants something," said Sant' Ilario. "And he will probably get it," he added, after a short pause. "He has a determined face."

CHAPTER IV

ANASTASE Gouache recovered rapidly from his injuries, but not so quickly as he wished. There was trouble in the air, and many of his comrades were already gone to the frontier where the skirmishing with the irregular volunteers of Garibaldi's guerilla force had now begun in earnest. To be confined to the city at such a time was inexpressibly irksome to the gallant young Frenchman, who had a genuine love of fighting in him, and longed for the first sensation of danger and the first shower of whistling bullets. But his inactivity was inevitable, and he was obliged to submit with the best grace he could, hoping only that all might not be over before he was well enough to tramp out and see some service with his companions-in-arms.

The situation was indeed urgent. The first article of the famous convention between France and Italy, ratified in September 1864, read as follows:

> Italy engages not to attack the actual territory of the Holy Father, and to prevent, even by force, all attack coming from outside against such territory.

Relying upon the observance of this chief clause, France had conscientiously executed the condition imposed by the second article, which provided that all French troops should be withdrawn from the States of the Church. The promise of Italy to prevent invasion by force applied to Garibaldi and his volunteers. Accordingly, on the 24th of September, 1867, the Italian Government issued a proclamation against the band and its proceedings, and arrested Garibaldi at Sinalunga, in the neighbourhood of Arezzo. This was the only force employed, and it may be believed that the Italian Government firmly expected that the volunteers would disperse as soon as they found themselves without a leader; and had proper measures been taken for keeping the general in custody this would in all probability have followed very shortly, as his sons, who were left at large, did not possess any of their father's qualifications for leadership. Garibaldi, however, escaped eighteen days later, and again joined his band, which had meanwhile been defeated by the Pope's troops in a few small engagements, and had gained one or two equally insignificant advantages over the latter. As soon as it was known that Garibaldi was again at large, a simultaneous movement began, the numerous Garibaldian emissaries who had arrived in Rome stirring up an attempt at insurrection within the city, while Garibaldi himself made a bold dash and seized Monte Rotondo, another force at the same time striking at Subiaco, which, by a strange ignorance of the mountains, Garibaldi appears to have believed to be the southern key to the Campagna. In consequence of the protestations of the French minister to the court of Italy, and perhaps, too, in consequence of the approach of a large body of French troops by sea, the Italian Government again issued a proclamation against Garibaldi, who, however, remained in his strong position at Monte Rotondo. Finally, on the 30th of October, the day on which the French troops re-entered Rome, the Italians made a show of interfering in the Pope's favour, General Menatiea authorising the Italian forces to enter the Papal States in order to maintain order. They did not, however, do more than make a short advance, and no active measures were taken, but Garibaldi was routed on the 3rd and 4th of November by the Papal forces, and his band being dispersed the incident was at an end. But for the armed intervention of France the result would have been that which actually came about in 1870, when, the same Convention being still valid, the French were prevented by their own disasters from sending a force to the assistance of the Pope.

It is not yet time to discuss the question of the annexation of the States of the Church to the kingdom of Italy. It is sufficient to have shown that the movement of 1867 took place without any actual violation of the letter of the Convention. The spirit in which the Italian Government acted might be criticised at length. It is sufficient however to notice that the Italian Government was, as it still is, a parliamentary one; and to add that parliamentary government, in general, exhibits its weakest side in the emergency of war, as its greatest advantages are best appreciated in times of peace. In the Italian Parliament of that day, as in that of the present time, there was a preponderance of representatives who considered Rome to be the natural capital of the country, and who were as ready to trample upon treaties for the accomplishment of what they believed a righteous end, as most parliaments have everywhere shown themselves in similar circumstances. That majority differed widely, indeed, in opinion from Garibaldi and Mazzini, but they conceived that they had a right to take full advantage of any revolution the latter chanced to bring about, and that it was their duty to their country to direct the stream of disorder into channel which should lead to the aggrandisement of Italy, by making use of Italy's standing army. The defenders of the Papal States found themselves face to face, not with any organised and disciplined force, but with a horde of brutal ruffians and half-grown lads, desperate in that delight of unbridled license which has such attractions for the mob in all countries; and all alike, Zouaves, native troops and Frenchmen, were incensed to the highest degree by the conduct of their enemies. It would be absurd to make the Italian Government responsible for the atrocious defiling of churches, the pillage and the shocking crimes of all sorts, which marked the advance or retreat of the Garibaldians; but it is equally absurd to deny that a majority of the Italians regarded these doings as a means to a very desirable end, and, if they had not been hindered by the French, would have marched a couple of army corps in excellent order to the gates of Rome through the channel opened by a mob of lawless insurgents.

Anastase Gouache was disgusted with his state of forced inaction as he paced the crowded pavement of the Corso every afternoon for three weeks after his accident, smoking endless cigarettes, and cursing the fate which kept him an invalid at home when his fellow-soldiers were enjoying themselves amidst the smell of gunpowder and the adventures of frontier skirmishing. It was indeed bad luck, he thought, to have worn the uniform during nearly two years of perfect health and then to be disabled just when the fighting began. He had one consolation, however, in the midst of his annoyance, and he made the most of it. He had been fascinated by Donna Faustina Montevarchi's brown eyes, and for lack of any other interest upon which to expend his energy he had so well employed his time that he was now very seriously in love with that young lady. Among her numerous attractions was one which had a powerful influence on the young artist, namely, the fact that she was, according to all human calculations, absolutely beyond his reach. Nothing had more charm for Gouache, as for many gifted and energetic young men, than that which it must require a desperate effort to get, if it could be got at all. Frenchmen, as well as Italians, consider marriage so much in the light of a mere contract which must be settled between notaries and ratified by parental assent, that to love a young girl seems to them like an episode out of a fairy tale, enchantingly novel and altogether delightful. To us, who consider love as a usual if not an absolutely necessary preliminary to marriage, this point of view is hardly conceivable; but it is enough to tell a Frenchman that you have married your wife because you loved her, and not because your parents or your circumstances arranged the match for you, to hear him utter the loudest exclamations of genuine surprise and admiration, declaring that his ideal of happiness, which he considers of course as quite unattainable, would be to marry the woman of his affections. The immediate result of a state in which that sort of bliss is considered to be generally beyond the grasp of humanity has been to produce the moral peculiarities of the French novel, of the French play, and of the French household, as it is usually exhibited in books and on the stage.

The artist-Zouave was made of determined stuff. It was not for nothing that he had won the great prize which brought him to the Academy in Rome, nor was it out of mere romantic idleness that he had thrown over the feeble conspiracies of Madame Mayer and her set in order to wear a uniform. He had profound convictions, though he was not troubled with any great number of them. Each new one which took hold of him marked an epoch in his young life, and generally proved tenacious in proportion as he had formerly regarded it as absurd; and it was a proof of the sound balance of his mind that the three or four real convictions which he had accumulated during his short life were in no way contradictory to each other. On the contrary, each one seemed closely bound up with the rest, and appeared to bring a fresh energy to that direct action which, with Anastase, was the only possible result of any belief whatsoever.

There was therefore a goodly store of logic in his madness, and though, like Childe Harold, he had sighed to many, and at present loved but one, yet he was determined, if it were possible, that this loved one should be his; seeing that to sigh for anything, and not to take it if it could be taken, was the part of a boy and not of a strong man. Moreover, although the social difficulties which lay in his way were an obstacle which would have seemed insurmountable to many, there were two considerations which gave Anastase some hope of ultimate success. In the first place Donna Faustina herself was not indifferent; and, secondly, Anastase was no longer the humble student who had come to Rome some years earlier with nothing but his pension in his pocket and his talent in his fingers. He was certainly not of ancient lineage, but since he had attained that position which enabled him to be received as an equal in the great world, and had by his skill accumulated a portion of that filthy lucre which is the platform whereon society moves and has its exclusive being, he had the advantage of talking to Donna Faustina, wherever he met her, in spite of her father's sixty-four quarterings. Nor did those meetings take place only under the auspices of so much heraldry and blazon, as will presently appear.

At that period of the year, and especially during such a time of disturbance, there was no such thing as gaiety possible in Rome. People met quietly in little knots at each other's houses and talked over the state of the country, or walked and drove as usual in the villas and on the Pincio. When society cannot be gay it is very much inclined to grow confidential, to pull a long face, and to say things which, if uttered above a whisper, would be considered extremely shocking, but which, being communicated, augmented, criticised, and passed about quickly without much noise, are considered exceedingly interesting. When every one is supposed to be talking of politics it is very easy for every one to talk scandal, and to construct neighbourly biography of an imaginary character which shall presently become a part of contemporary history. On the whole, society would almost as gladly do this as dance. In those days of which I am speaking, therefore, there were many places where two or three, and sometimes as many as ten, were gathered together in council, ostensibly for the purpose of devising means whereby the Holy Father might overcome his enemies, though they were very often engaged in criticising the indecent haste exhibited by their best friends in yielding to the wiles of Satan.

There were several of these rallying points, among which may be chiefly noticed the Palazzo Valdarno, the Palazzo Saracinesca, and the Palazzo Montevarchi. In the first of these three it may be observed in passing that there was a division of opinion, the old people being the most rigid of conservatives, while the children declared as loudly as they dared that they were for Victor Emmanuel and United Italy. The Saracinesca, on the other hand, were firmly united and determined to stand by the existing order of things. Lastly, the Montevarchi all took their opinions from the head of the house, and knew very well that they would submit like sheep to be led whichever way was most agreeable to the old prince. The friends who frequented those various gatherings were of course careful to say whatever was most sure to please their hosts, and after the set speeches were made most of them fell to their usual occupation of talking about each other.

Gouache was an old friend of the Saracinesca, and came whenever he pleased; since his accident, too, he had become better acquainted with the Montevarchi, and was always a welcome guest, as he generally brought the latest news of the fighting, as well as the last accounts from France, which he easily got through his friendship with the young attachés of his embassy. It is not surprising therefore that he should have found so many opportunities of meeting Donna Faustina, especially as Corona di Sant' Ilario had taken a great fancy to the young girl and invited her constantly to the house.

On the very first occasion when Gouache called upon the Princess Monte-varchi in order to express again his thanks for the kindness he had received, he found the room half full of people. Faustina was sitting alone, turning over the pages of a book, and no one seemed to pay any attention to her. After the usual speeches to the hostess Gouache sat down beside her. She raised her brown eyes, recognised him, and smiled faintly.

"What a wonderful contrast you are enjoying, Donna Faustina," said the Zouave.

"How so? I confess it seems monotonous enough."

"I mean that it is a great change for you, from the choir of the Sacro Cuore, from the peace of a convent, to this atmosphere of war."

"Yes; I wish I were back again."

"You do not like what you have seen of the world, Mademoiselle? It is very natural. If the world were always like this its attraction would not be dangerous. It is the pomps and vanities that are delightful."

"I wish they would begin then," answered Donna Faustina with more natural frankness than is generally found in young girls of her education.

"But were you not taught by the good sisters that those things are of the devil?" asked Gouache with a smile.

"Of course. But Flavia says they are very nice."

Gouache imagined that Flavia ought to know, but he thought fit to conceal his conviction.

"You mean Donna Flavia, your sister, Mademoiselle?"

"Yes."

"I suppose you are very fond of her, are you not? It must be very pleasant to have a sister so nearly of one's own age in the world."

"She is much older than I, but I think we shall be very good friends."

"Your family must be almost as much strangers to you as the rest of the world," observed Gouache. "Of course you have only seen them occasionally for a long time past. You are fond of reading, I see."

He made this remark to change the subject, and glanced at the book the young girl still held in her hand.

"It is a new book," she said, opening the volume at the title-page. "It is Manon Lescaut. Flavia has read it—it is by the Abbé Prevost. Do you know him?"

Gouache did not know whether to laugh or to look grave.

"Did your mother give it to you?" he asked.

"No, but she says that as it is by an abbé, she supposes it must be very moral. It is true that it has not the imprimatur, but being by a priest it cannot possibly be on the Index."

"I do not know," replied Gouache, "Prevost was certainly in holy orders, but I do not know him, as he died rather more than a hundred years ago. You see the book is not new."

"Oh!" exclaimed Donna Faustina, "I thought it was. Why do you laugh? Am I very ignorant not to know all about it?"

"No, indeed. Only, you will pardon me, Mademoiselle, if I offer a suggestion. You see I am French and know a little about these matters. You will permit me?"

Faustina opened her brown eyes very wide, and nodded gravely.

"If I were you, I would not read that book yet. You are too young."

"You seem to forget that I am eighteen years old, Monsieur Gouache."

"No, not at all. But five and twenty is a better age to read such books. Believe me," he added seriously, "that story is not meant for you."

Faustina looked at him for a few seconds and then laid the volume on the table, pushing it away from her with a puzzled air. Gouache was inwardly much amused at the idea of finding himself the moral preceptor of a young girl he scarcely knew, in the house of her parents, who passed for the most strait-laced of their kind. A feeling of deep resentment against Flavia, however, began to rise beneath his first sensation of surprise.

"What are books for?" asked Donna Faustina, with a little sigh. "The good ones are dreadfully dull, and it is wrong to read the amusing ones—until one is married. I wonder why?"

Gouache did not find any immediate answer and might have been seriously embarrassed had not Giovanni Sant' Ilario come up just then. Gouache rose to relinquish his seat to the newcomer, and as he passed before the table deftly turned over the book with his finger so that the title should not be visible. It jarred disagreeably on his sensibilities to think that Giovanni might see a copy of Manon Lescaut lying by the elbow of Donna Faustina Montevarchi. Sant' Ilario did not see the action and probably would not have noticed it if he had.

Anastase pondered all that afternoon and part of the next morning over his short conversation, and the only conclusion at which he arrived was that Faustina was the most fascinating girl he had ever met. When he compared the result produced in his mind with his accurate recollection of what had passed between them, he laughed at his haste and called himself a fool for yielding to such nonsensical ideas. The conversation of a young girl, he argued, could only be amusing for a short time. He wondered what he should say at their next meeting, since all such talk, according to his notions, must inevitably consist of commonplaces. And yet at the end of a quarter of an hour of such meditation he found that he was constructing an interview which was anything but dull, at least in his own anticipatory opinion.

Meanwhile the first ten days of October passed in comparative quiet. The news of Garibaldi's arrest produced temporary lull in the excitement felt in Rome, although the real struggle was yet to come. People observed to each other that strange faces were to be seen in the streets, but as no one could enter without a proper passport, very little anxiety gained the public mind.

Gouache saw Faustina very often during the month that followed his accident. Such good fortune would have been impossible under any other circumstances, but, as has been explained, there were numerous little social confabulations on foot, for people were drawn together by a vague sense of common danger, and the frequent meetings of the handsome Zouave with the youngest of the Montevarchi passed unnoticed in the general stir. The old princess indeed often saw the two together, but partly owing to her English breeding, and partly because Gouache was not in the least eligible or possible as a husband for her daughter, she attached no importance to the acquaintance. The news that Garibaldi was again at large caused great excitement, and every day brought fresh news of small engagements along the frontier. Gouache was not yet quite recovered, though he felt as strong as ever, and applied every day for leave to go to the front. At last, on the 22nd of October, the surgeon pronounced him to be completely recovered, and Anastase was ordered to leave the city on the following morning at daybreak.

As he mounted the sombre staircase of the Palazzo Saracinesca on the afternoon previous to his departure, the predominant feeling in his breast was great satisfaction and joy at being on the eve of seeing active service, and he himself was surprised at the sharp pang he suffered in the anticipation of bidding farewell to his friends. He knew what friend it was whom he dreaded to leave, and how bitter that parting would be, for which three weeks earlier he could have summoned a neat speech expressing just so much of feeling as should be calculated to raise an interest in the hearer, and prompted by just so much delicate regret as should impart a savour of romance to his march on the next day. It was different now.

Donna Faustina was in the room, as he had reason to expect, but it was several minutes before Anastase could summon the determination necessary to go to her side. She was standing near the piano, which faced outwards towards the body of the room, but was screened by a semicircular arrangement of plants, a novel idea lately introduced by Corona, who was weary of the stiff old-fashioned way of setting all the furniture against the wall. Faustina was standing at this point therefore, when Gouache made towards her, having done homage to Corona and to the other ladies in the room. His attention was arrested for a moment by the sight of San Giacinto's gigantic figure. The cousin of the house was standing before Flavia Montevarchi, bending slightly towards her and talking in low tones. His magnificent proportions made him by far the most noticeable person in the room, and it is no wonder that Gouache paused and looked at him, mentally observing that the two would make a fine couple.

As he stood still he became aware that Corona herself was at his side. He glanced at her with something of inquiry in his eyes, and was about to speak when she made him a sign to follow her. They sat down together in a deserted corner at the opposite end of the room.

"I have something to say to you, Monsieur Gouache," she said, in a low voice, as she settled herself against the cushions. "I do not know that I have any right to speak, except that of a good friend—and of a woman."

"I am at your orders, princess."

"No, I have no orders to give you. I have only a suggestion to make. I have watched you often during the last month. My advice begins with a question. Do you love her?"

Gouache's first instinct was to express the annoyance he felt at this interrogation. He moved quickly and glanced sharply at Corona's velvet eyes. Before the words that were on his lips could be spoken he remembered all the secret reverence and respect he had felt for this woman since he had first known her, he remembered how he had always regarded her as a sort of goddess, a superior being, at once woman and angel, placed far beyond the reach of mortals like himself. His irritation vanished as quickly as it had arisen. But Corona had seen it.

"Are you angry?" she asked.

"If you knew how I worship you, you would know that I am not," answered Gouache with a strange simplicity.

For an instant the princess's deep eyes flashed and a dark blush mounted through her olive skin. She drew back, rather proudly. A delicate, gentle smile played round the soldier's mouth.

"Perhaps it is your turn to be angry, Madame," he said, quietly. "But you need not be. I would say it to your husband, as I would say it to you in his presence. I worship you. You are the most beautiful woman in the world, the most nobly good. Everybody knows it, why should I not say it? I wish I were a little child, and that you were my mother. Are you angry still?"

Corona was silent, and her eyes grew soft again as she looked kindly at the man beside her. She did not understand him, but she knew that he meant to express something which was not bad. Gouache waited for her to speak.

"It was not for that I asked you to come with me," she said at last.

"I am glad I said it," replied Gouache. "I am going away tomorrow, and it might never have been said. You asked me if I loved her. I trust you. I say, yes, I do. I am going to say good-bye this afternoon."

"I am sorry you love her. Is it serious?"

"Absolutely, on my part. Why are you sorry? Is there anything unnatural in it?"

"No, on the contrary, it is too natural. Our lives are unnatural. You cannot marry her. It seems brutal to tell you so, but you must know it already."

"There was once a little boy in Paris, Madame, who did not have enough to eat every day, nor enough clothes when the north wind blew. But he had a good heart. His name was Anastase Gouache."

"My dear friend," said Corona, kindly, "the atmosphere of Casa Montevarchi is colder than the north wind. A man may overcome almost anything more easily than the old-fashioned prejudices of a Roman prince."

"You do not forbid me to try?"

"Would the prohibition make any difference?"

"I am not sure." Gouache paused and looked long at the princess. "No," he said at last, "I am afraid not."

"In that case I can only say one thing. You are a man of honour. Do your best not to make her uselessly unhappy. Win her if you can, by any fair means. But she has a heart, and I am very fond of the child. If any harm comes to her I shall hold you responsible. If you love her, think what it would be should she love you and be married to another man."

A shade of sadness darkened Corona's brow, as she remembered those terrible months of her own life. Gouache knew what she meant and was silent for a few moments.

"I trust you," said she, at last. "And since you are going tomorrow, God bless you. You are going in a good cause."

She held out her hand as she rose to leave him, and he bent over it and touched it with his lips, as he would have kissed the hand of his mother. Then, skirting the little assembly of people, Anastase went back towards the piano, in search of Donna Faustina. He found her alone, as young girls are generally to be found in Roman drawing-rooms, unless there are two of them present to sit together.

"What have you been talking about with the princess?" asked Donna Faustina when Gouache was seated beside her.

"Could you see from here?" asked Gouache instead of answering. "I thought the plants would have hindered you."

"I saw you kiss her hand when you got up, and so I supposed that the conversation had been serious."

"Less serious than ours must be," replied Anastase, sadly. "I was saying good-bye to her, and now—"

"Good-bye? Why—?" Faustina checked herself and looked away to hide her pallor. She felt cold, and a slight shiver passed over her slender figure.

"I am going to the front tomorrow morning."

There was a long silence, during which the two looked at each other from time to time, neither finding courage to speak. Since Gouache had been in the room it had grown dark, and as yet but one lamp had been brought. The young man's eyes sought those he loved in the dusk, and as his hand stole out it met another, a tender, nervous hand, trembling with emotion. They did not heed what was passing near them.

As though their silence were contagious, the conversation died away, and there was a general lull, such as sometimes falls upon an assemblage of people who have been talking for some time. Then, through the deep windows there came up a sound of distant uproar, mingled with occasional sharp detonations, few indeed, but the more noticeable for their rarity. Suddenly the door of the drawing-room burst open, and a servant's voice was heard speaking in a loud key, the coarse accents and terrified tone contrasting strangely with the sounds generally heard in such a place.

"Excellency! Excellency! The revolution! Garibaldi is at the gates! The Italians are coming! Madonna! Madonna! The revolution, Eccellenza mia!"

The man was mad with fear. Every one spoke at once. Some laughed, thinking the man crazy. Others, who had heard the distant noise from the streets, drew back and looked nervously towards the door. Then Sant' Ilario's clear, strong voice, rang like a clarion through the room.

"Bar the gates. Shut the blinds all over the house—it is of no use to let them break good windows. Don't stand there shivering like a fool. It is only a mob."

Before he had finished speaking, San Giacinto was calmly bolting the blinds of the drawing-room windows, fastening each one as steadily and securely as he had been wont to put up the shutters of his inn at Aquila in the old days.

In the dusky corner by the piano Gouache and Faustina were overlooked in the general confusion. There was no time for reflection, for at the first words of the servant Anastase knew that he must go instantly to his post. Faustina's little hand was still clasped in his, as they both sprang to their feet. Then with a sudden movement he clasped her in his arms and kissed her passionately.

"Good-bye—my beloved!"

The girl's arms were twined closely about him, and her eyes looked up to his with a wild entreaty.

"You are safe here, my darling—good-bye!"

"Where are you going?"

"To the Serristori barracks. God keep you safe till I come back—good-bye!"

"I will go with you," said Faustina, with a strange look of determination in her angelic face.

Gouache smiled, even then, at the mad thought which presented itself to the girl's mind. Once more he kissed her, and then, she knew not how, he was gone. Other persons had come near them, shutting the windows rapidly, one after the other, in anticipation of danger from without. With instinctive modesty Faustina withdrew her arms from the young man's neck and shrank back. In that moment he disappeared in the crowd.

Faustina stared wildly about her for a few seconds, confused and stunned by the suddenness of what had passed, above all by the thought that the man she loved was gone from her side to meet his death. Then without hesitation she left the room. No one hindered her, for the Saracinesca men were gone to see to the defences of the house, and Corona was already by the cradle of her child. No one noticed the slight figure as it slipped through the door and was gone in the darkness of the unlighted halls. All was confusion and noise and flashing of passing lights as the servants hurried about, trying to obey orders in spite of their terror. Faustina glided like a shadow down the vast staircase, slipped through one of the gates just as the bewildered porter was about to close it, and in a moment was out in the midst of the multitude that thronged the dim streets—a mere child and alone, facing a revolution in the dark.

CHAPTER V

GOUACHE made his way as fast as he could to the bridge of Sant' Angelo, but his progress was constantly impeded by moving crowds—bodies of men, women, and children rushing frantically together at the corners of the streets and then surging onward in the direction of the resultant produced by their combined forces in the shock. There was loud and incoherent screaming of women and shouting of men, out of which occasionally a few words could be distinguished, more often "Viva Pio Nono!" or "Viva la Repubblica!" than anything else. The scene of confusion baffled description. A company of infantry was filing out of the castle of Sant' Angelo on to the bridge, where it was met by a dense multitude of people coming from the opposite direction. A squadron of mounted gendarmes came up from the Borgo Nuovo at the same moment, and half a dozen cabs were jammed in between the opposing masses of the soldiers and the people. The officer at the head of the column of foot-soldiers loudly urged the crowd to make way, and the latter, consisting chiefly of peaceable but terrified citizens, attempted to draw back, while the weight of those behind pushed them on. Gouache, who was in the front of the throng, was allowed to enter the file of infantry, in virtue of his uniform, and attempted to get through and make his way to the opposite bank. But with the best efforts he soon found himself unable to move, the soldiers being wedged together as tightly as the people. Presently the crowd in the piazza seemed to give way and the column began to advance again, bearing Gouache backwards in the direction he had come. He managed to get to the parapet, however, by edging sideways through the packed ranks.

"Give me your shoulder, comrade!" he shouted to the man next to him. The fellow braced himself, and in an instant the agile Zouave was on the narrow parapet, running along as nimbly as a cat, and winding himself past the huge statues at every half-dozen steps. He jumped down at the other end and ran for the Borgo Santo Spirito at the top of his speed. The broad space was almost deserted and in three minutes he was before the gates of the barracks, which were situated on the right-hand side of the street, just beyond the College of the Penitentiaries and opposite the church of San Spirito in Sassia.

Meanwhile Donna Faustina Montevarchi was alone in the streets. In desperate emergencies young and nervously-organised people most commonly act in accordance with the dictates of the predominant passion by which they are influenced. Very generally that passion is terror, but when it is not, it is almost impossible to calculate the consequences which may follow. When the whole being is dominated by love and by the greatest anxiety for the safety of the person loved, the weakest woman will do deeds which might make a brave man blush for his courage. This was precisely Faustina's case.

If any man says that he understands women he is convicted of folly by his own speech, seeing that they are altogether incomprehensible. Of men, it may be sufficient for general purposes to say with David that they are all liars, even though we allow that they may be all curable of the vice of falsehood. Of women, however, there is no general statement which is true. The one is brave to heroism, the next cowardly in a degree fantastically comic. The one is honest, the other faithless; the one contemptible in her narrowness of soul, the next supremely noble in broad truth as the angels in heaven; the one trustful, the other suspicious; this one gentle as a dove, that one grasping and venomous as a strong serpent. The hearts of women are as the streets of a great town—some broad and straight and clean; some dim and narrow and winding; or as the edifices and buildings of that same city, wherein there are holy temples, at which men worship in calm and peace, and dens where men gamble away the souls given them by God against the living death they call pleasure, which is doled out to them by the devil; in which there are quiet dwellings, and noisy places of public gathering, fair palaces and loathsome charnel-houses, where the dead are heaped together, even as our dead sins lie ghastly and unburied in that dark chamber of the soul, whose gates open of their own selves and shall not be sealed while there is life in us to suffer. Dost thou boast that thou knowest the heart of woman? Go to, thou more than fool! The heart of woman containeth all things, good and evil; and knowest thou then all that is?

Donna Faustina was no angel. She had not that lofty calmness which we attribute to the angelic character. She was very young, utterly inexperienced and ignorant of the world. The idea which over-towers all other ideas was the first which had taken hold upon her, and under its strength she was like a flower before the wind. She was not naturally of the heroic type either, as Corona d'Astrardente had been, and perhaps was still, capable of sacrifice for the ideal of duty, able to suffer torment rather than debase herself by yielding, strong to stem the torrent of a great passion until she had the right to abandon herself to its mighty flood. Faustina was a younger and a gentler woman, not knowing what she did from the moment her heart began to dictate her actions, willing, above all, to take the suggestion of her soul as a command, and, because she knew no evil, rejoicing in an abandonment which might well have terrified one who knew the world.

She already loved Anastase intensely. Under the circumstances of his farewell, the startling effect of the announcement of a revolution, the necessity under which, as a soldier, he found himself of leaving her instantly in order to face a real danger, with his first kiss warm upon her lips, and with the frightful conviction that if he left her it might be the last—under all the emotions brought about by these things, half mad with love and anxiety, it was not altogether wonderful that she acted as she did. She could not have explained it, for the impulse was so instinctive that she did not comprehend it, and the deed followed so quickly upon the thought that there was no time for reflection. She fled from the room and from the palace, out into the street, wholly unconscious of danger, like a creature in a dream.

The crowd which had impeded Gouache's progress was already thinning when Faustina reached the pavement. She was born and bred in Rome, and as a child, before the convent days, had been taken to walk many a time in the neighbourhood of Saint Peter's. She knew well enough where the Serristori barracks were situated, and turned at once towards Sant' Angelo. There were still many people about, most of them either hurrying in the direction whence the departing uproar still proceeded, or running homewards to get out of danger. Few noticed her, and for some time no one hindered her progress, though it was a strange sight to see a fair young girl, dressed in the fashion of the time which so completely distinguished her from Roman women of lower station, running at breathless speed through the dusky streets.

Suddenly she lost her way. Coming down the Via de' Coronari she turned too soon to the right and found herself in the confusing byways which form a small labyrinth around the church of San Salvatore in Lauro. She had entered a blind alley on the left when she ran against two men, who unexpectedly emerged from one of those underground wine-shops which are numerous in that neighbourhood. They were talking in low and earnest tones, and one of them staggered backward as the young girl rushed upon him in the dark. Instinctively the man grasped her and held her tightly by the arms.

"Where are you running to, my beauty?" he asked, as she struggled to get away.

"Oh, let me go! Let me go!" she cried in agonised tones, twisting her slender wrists in his firm grip. The other man stood by, watching the scene.

"Better let her go, Peppino," he said. "Don't you see she is a lady?"

"A lady, eh?" echoed the other. "Where are you going to, with that angel's face?"

"To the Serristori barrack," answered Faustina, still struggling with all her might.

At this announcement both men laughed loudly and glanced quickly at each other. They seemed to think the answer a very good joke.

"If that is all, you may go, and the devil accompany you. What say you, Gaetano?" Then they laughed again.

"Take that chain and brooch as a ricordo—just for a souvenir," said Gaetano, who then himself tore off the ornaments while the other held Faustina's hands.

"You are a pretty girl indeed!" he cried, looking at her pale face in the light of the filthy little red lamp that hung over the low door of the wine-shop. "I never kissed a lady in my life."

With that he grasped her delicate chin in his foul hand and bent down, bringing his grimy face close to hers. But this was too much. Though Faustina had hitherto fought with all her natural strength against the ruffians, there was a reserved force, almost superhuman, in her slight frame, which was suddenly roused by the threatened outrage. With a piercing shriek she sprang backwards and dashed herself free, sending the two blackguards reeling into the darkness. Then, like a flash she was gone. By chance she took the right turning and in a moment more found herself in the Via di Tordinona, just opposite the entrance of the Apollo theatre. The torn white handbills on the wall, and the projecting shed over the doors told her where she was.

By this time the soldiers who had intercepted Gouache's passage across the bridge, as well as the dense crowd, had disappeared, and Faustina ran like the wind along the pavement it had taken the soldier so long to traverse. Like a flitting bird she sped over the broad space beyond and up the Borgo Nuovo, past the long low hospital, wherein the sick and dying lay in their silence, tended by the patient Sisters of Mercy, while all was in excitement without. The young girl ran past the corner. A Zouave was running before her towards the gate of the barrack where a sentinel stood motionless under the lamp, his gray hood drawn over his head and his rifle erect by his shoulder.

At that instant a terrific explosion rent the air, followed a moment later by the dull crash of falling fragments of masonry, and then by a long thundering, rumbling sound, dreadful to hear, which lasted several minutes, as the ruins continued to fall in, heaps upon heaps, sending immense clouds of thick dust up into the night air. Then all was still.

The little piazza before San Spirito in Sassia was half filled with masses of stone and brickwork and crumbling mortar. A young girl lay motionless upon her face at the corner of the hospital, her white hands stretched out towards the man who lay dead but a few feet before her, crushed under a great irregular mound of stones and rubbish. Beneath the central heap where the barracks had stood lay the bodies of the poor Zouaves, deep buried in wreck of the main building, the greater part of which had fallen across the side street that passes between the Penitenzieri and the Serristori. All was still for many minutes, while the soft light streamed from the high windows of the hospital and faintly illuminated some portion of the hideous scene.

Very slowly a few stragglers came in sight, then more, and then by degrees a great dark crowd of awestruck people were collected together and stood afar off, fearing to come near, lest the ruins should still continue falling. Presently the door of the hospital opened and a party of men in gray blouses, headed by three or four gentlemen in black coats—one indeed was in his shirt sleeves—emerged into the silent street and went straight towards the scene of the disaster. They carried lanterns and a couple of stretchers such as are used for bearing the wounded. It chanced that the straight line they followed from the door did not lead them to where the girl was lying, and it was not until after a long and nearly fruitless search that they turned back. Two soldiers only, and both dead, could they find to bring back. The rest were buried far beneath, and it would be the work of many hours to extricate the bodies, even with a large force of men.

As the little procession turned sadly back, they found that the crowd had advanced cautiously forward and now filled the street. In the foremost rank a little circle stood about a dark object that lay on the ground, curious, but too timid to touch it.

"Signor Professore," said one man in a low voice, "there is a dead woman."

The physicians came forward and bent over the body. One of them shook his head, as the bright light of the lantern fell on her face while he raised the girl from the ground.

"She is a lady," said one of the others in a low voice.

The men brought a stretcher and lifted the girl's body gently from the ground, scarcely daring to touch her, and gazing anxiously but yet in wonder at the white face.

When she was laid upon the coarse canvas there was a moment's pause. The crowd pressed closely about the hospital men, and the yellow light of the lanterns was reflected on many strange faces, all bent eagerly forward and down to get a last sight of the dead girl's features.

"Andiamo," said one of the physicians in a quiet sad voice. The bearers took up the dead Zouaves again, the procession of death entered the gates of the hospital, and the heavy doors closed behind like the portals of a tomb.

The crowd closed again and pressed forward to the ruins. A few gendarmes had come up, and very soon a party of labourers was at work clearing away the lighter rubbish under the lurid glare of pitch torches stuck into the crevices and cracks of the rent walls. The devilish deed was done, but by a providential accident its consequences had been less awful than might have been anticipated. Only one-third of the mine had actually exploded, and only thirty Zouaves were at the time within the building.

"Did you see her face, Gaetano?" asked a rough fellow of his companion. They stood together in a dark corner a little aloof from the throng of people.

"No, but it must have been she. I am glad I have not that sin on my soul."

"You are a fool, Gaetano. What is a girl to a couple of hundred soldiers? Besides, if you had held her tight she would not have got here in time to be killed."

"Eh—but a girl! The other vagabonds at least, we have despatched in a good cause. Viva la liberta!"

"Hush! There are the gendarmes! This way!"

So they disappeared into the darkness whence they had come.

It was not only in the Borgo Nuovo that there was confusion and consternation. The first signal for the outbreak had been given in the Piazza Colonna, where bombs had been exploded. Attacks were made upon the prisons by bands of those sinister-looking, unknown men, who for several days had been noticed in various parts of the city. A compact mob invaded the capitol, armed with better weapons than mobs generally find ready to their hands. At the Porta San Paolo, which was rightly judged to be one of the weakest points of the city, a furious attack was made from without by a band of Garibaldians who had crept up near the walls in various disguises during the last two days. More than one of the barracks within the city were assaulted simultaneously, and for a short time companies of men paraded the streets, shouting their cries of "Viva Garibaldi! Viva la liberta!" A few cried "Viva Vittorio!" and "Viva l'Italia!" But a calm observer—and there were many such in Rome that night—could easily see that the demonstration was rather in favour of an anarchic republic than of the Italian monarchy. On the whole, the population showed no sympathy with the insurrection. It is enough to say that this tiny revolution broke out at dusk and was entirely quelled before nine o'clock of the same evening. The attempts made were bold and desperate in many cases, but were supported by a small body of men only, the populace taking no active part in what was done. Had a real sympathy existed between the lower classes of Romans and the Garibaldians the result could not have been doubtful, for the vigour and energy displayed by the rioters would inevitably have attracted any similarly disposed crowd to join in a fray, when the weight of a few hundreds more would have turned the scale at any point. There was not a French soldier in the city at the time, and of the Zouaves and native troops a very large part were employed upon the frontier. Rome was saved and restored to order by a handful of soldiers, who were obliged to act at many points simultaneously, and the insignificance of the original movement may be determined from this fact.

It is true that of the two infernal schemes, plotted at once to destroy the troops in a body and to strike terror into the inhabitants, one failed in part and the other altogether. If the whole of the gunpowder which Giuseppe Monti and Gaetano Tognetti had placed in the mine under the Serristori barracks had exploded, instead of only one-third of the quantity, a considerable part of the Borgo Nuovo would have been destroyed; and even the disaster which actually occurred would have killed many hundreds of Zouaves if these had chanced to be indoors at the time. But it is impossible to calculate the damage and loss of life which would have been recorded had the castle of Sant' Angelo and the adjacent fortifications been blown into the air. A huge mine had been laid and arranged for firing in the vaults of one of the bastions, but the plot was betrayed at the very last moment by one of the conspirators. I may add that these men, who were tried, and condemned only to penal servitude, were liberated in 1870, three years later, by the Italian Government, on the ground that they were merely political prisoners. The attempt in which they had been engaged would, however, even in time of declared war, have been regarded as a crime against the law of nations.

Rome was immediately declared under a state of siege, and patrols of troops began to parade the streets, sending all stragglers whom they met to their homes, on the admirable principle that it is the duty of every man who finds himself in a riotous crowd to leave it instantly unless he can do something towards restoring order. Persons who found themselves in other people's houses, however, had some difficulty in at once returning to their own, and as it has been seen that the disturbance began precisely at the time selected by society for holding its confabulations, there were many who found themselves in that awkward situation.

As the sounds in the street subsided, the excitement in the drawing-room at the Palazzo Saracinesca diminished likewise. Several of those present announced their intention of departing at once, but to this the old prince made serious objections. The city was not safe, he said. Carriages might be stopped at any moment, and even if that did not occur, all sorts of accidents might arise from the horses shying at the noises, or running over people in the crowds. He had his own views, and as he was in his own house it was not easy to dispute them.

"The gates are shut," he said, with a cheerful laugh, "and none of you can get out at present. As it is nearly dinner-time you must all dine with me. It will not be a banquet, but I can give you something to eat. I hope nobody is gone already."

Every one, at these words, looked at everybody else, as though to see whether any one were missing.

"I saw Monsieur Gouache go out," said Flavia Montevarchi.

"Poor fellow!" exclaimed the princess, her mother. "I hope nothing will happen to him!" She paused a moment and looked anxiously round the room. "Good Heavens!" she cried suddenly, "where is Faustina?"

"She must have gone out of the room with my wife," said Sant' Ilario, quietly. "I will go and see."

The princess thought this explanation perfectly natural and waited till he should return. He did not come back, however, so soon as might have been expected. He found his wife just leaving the nursery. Her first impulse had been to go to the child, and having satisfied herself that he had not been carried off by a band of Garibaldians but was sound asleep in his cradle, she was about to rejoin her guests.

"Where is Faustina Montevarchi?" asked Giovanni, as though it were the most natural question in the world.

"Faustina?" repeated Corona. "In the drawing-room, to be sure. I have not seen her."

"She is not there," said Sant' Ilario, in a more anxious tone. "I thought she had come here with you."

"She must be with the rest. You have overlooked her in the crowd. Come back with me and see your son—he does not seem to mind revolution in the least!"

Giovanni, who had no real doubt but that Faustina was in the house, entered the nursery with his wife, and they stood together by the child's cradle.

"Is he not beautiful?" exclaimed Corona, passing her arm affectionately through her husband's, and leaning her cheek on his shoulder.

"He is a fine baby," replied Giovanni, his voice expressing more satisfaction than his words. "He will look like my father when he grows up."

"I would rather he should look like you," said Corona.

"If he could look like you, dear, there would be some use in wishing."

Then they both gazed for some seconds at the swarthy little boy, who lay on his pillows, his arms thrown back above his head and his two little fists tightly clenched. The rich blood softly coloured the child's dark cheeks, and the black lashes, already long, like his mother's, gave a singularly expressive look to the small face.

Giovanni tenderly kissed his wife and then they softly left the room. As soon as they were outside Sant' Ilario's thoughts returned to Faustina.

"She was certainly not in the drawing-room," he said, "I am quite sure. It was her mother who asked for her and everybody heard the question. I dare not go back without her."

They stopped together in the corridor, looking at each other with grave faces.

"This is very serious," said Corona. "We must search the house. Send the men. I will tell the women. We will meet at the head of the stairs."

Five minutes later, Giovanni returned in pursuit of his wife.

"She has left the house," he said, breathlessly. "The porter saw her go out."

"Good Heavens! Why did he not stop her?" cried Corona.

"Because he is a fool!" answered Sant' Ilario, very pale in his anxiety. "She must have lost her head and gone home. I will tell her mother."

When it was known in the drawing-room that Donna Faustina Montevarchi had left the palace alone and on foot every one was horrorstruck. The princess turned as white as death, though she was usually very red in the face. She was a brave woman, however, and did not waste words.

"I must go home at once," said she. "Please order my carriage and have the gates opened."

Giovanni obeyed silently, and a few minutes later the princess was descending the stairs, accompanied by Flavia, who was silent, a phenomenon seldom to be recorded in connection with that vivacious young lady. Giovanni went also, and his cousin, San Giacinto.

"If you will permit me, princess, I will go with you," said the latter as they all reached the carriage. "I may be of some use."

Just as they rolled out of the deep archway, the explosion of the barracks rent the air, the tremendous crash thundering and echoing through the city. The panes of the carriage-windows rattled as though they would break, and all Rome was silent while one might count a score. Then the horses plunged wildly in the traces and the vehicle struck heavily against one of the stone pillars which stood before the entrance of the palace. The four persons inside could hear the coachman shouting.

"Drive on!" cried San Giacinto, thrusting his head out of the window.

"Eccellenza—" began the man in a tone of expostulation.

"Drive on!" shouted San Giacinto, in a voice that made the fellow obey in spite of his terror. He had never heard such a voice before, so deep, so strong and so savage.

They reached the Palazzo Montevarchi without encountering any serious obstacle. In a few minutes they were convinced that Donna Faustina had not been heard of there, and a council was held upon the stairs. Whilst they were deliberating, Prince Montevarchi came out, and with him his eldest son, Bellegra, a handsome man about thirty years old, with blue eyes and a perfectly smooth fair beard. He was more calm than his father, who spoke excitedly, with many gesticulations.

"You have lost Faustina!" cried the old man in wild tones. "You have lost Faustina! And in such times as these! Why do you stand there? Oh, my daughter! My daughter! I have so often told you to be careful, Guendalina—move, in the name of God—the child is lost, lost, I tell you! Have you no heart? No feeling? Are you a mother? Signori miei, I am desperate!"

And indeed he seemed to be, as he stood wringing his hands, stamping his feet, and vociferating incoherently, while the tears began to flow down his cheeks.

"We are going in search of your daughter," said Sant' Ilario. "Pray calm yourself. She will certainly be found."

"Perhaps I had better go too," suggested Ascanio Bellegra, rather timidly. But his father threw his arms round him and held him tightly.

"Do you think I will lose another child?" he cried. "No, no, no—figlio mio—you shall never go out into the midst of a revolution."

Sant' Ilario looked on gravely, though he inwardly despised the poor old man for his weakness. San Giacinto stood against the wall, waiting, with, a grim smile of amusement on his face. He was measuring Ascanio Bellegra with his eye and thought he would not care for his assistance. The princess looked scornfully at her husband and son.

"We are losing time," said Sant' Ilario at last to his cousin. "I promise you to bring you your daughter," he added gravely, turning to the princess. Then the two went away together, leaving Prince Montevarchi still lamenting himself to his wife and son. Flavia had taken no part in the conversation, having entered the hall and gone to her room at once.

The cousins left the palace together and walked a little way down the street, before either spoke. Then Sant' Ilario stopped short.

"Does it strike you that we have undertaken rather a difficult mission?" he asked.

"A very difficult one," answered San Giacinto.

"Rome is not the largest city in the world, but I have not the slightest idea where to look for that child. She certainly left our house. She certainly has not returned to her own. Between the two, practically, there lies the whole of Rome. I think the best thing to do, will be to go to the police, if any of them can be found."

"Or to the Zouaves," said San Giacinto.

"Why to the Zouaves? I do not understand you."

"You are all so accustomed to being princes that you do not watch each other. I have done nothing but watch, you all the time. That young lady is in love with Monsieur Gouache."

"Really!" exclaimed Sant' Ilario, to whom the idea was as novel and incredible as it could have been to old Montevarchi himself, "really, you must be mistaken. The thing is impossible."

"Not at all. That young man took Donna Faustina's hand and held it for some time there by the piano while I was shutting the windows in your drawing-room." San Giacinto did not tell all he had seen.

"What?" cried Sant' Ilario. "You are mad—it is impossible!"

"On the contrary, I saw it. A moment later Gouache left the room. Donna Faustina must have gone just after him. It is my opinion that she followed him."

Before Sant' Ilario could answer, a small patrol of foot-gendarmes came up, and peremptorily ordered the two gentlemen to go home. Sant' Ilario addressed the corporal in charge. He stated his name and that of his cousin.

"A lady has been lost," he then said. "She is Donna Faustina Montevarchi—a young lady, very fair and beautiful. She left the Palazzo Saracinesca alone and on foot half an hour ago and has not been heard of. Be good enough to inform the police you meet of this fact and to say that a large reward will be paid to any one who brings her to her father's house—to this palace here."

After a few more words the patrol passed on, leaving the two cousins to their own devices. Sant' Ilario was utterly annoyed at the view just presented to him, and could not believe the thing true, though he had no other explanation to offer.

"It is of no use to stand here doing nothing," said San Giacinto rather impatiently. "There is another crowd coming, too, and we shall be delayed again. I think we had better separate. I will go one way, and you take the other."

"Where will you go?" asked Sant' Ilario. "You do not know your way about—"

"As she may be anywhere, we may find her anywhere, so that it is of no importance whether I know the names of the streets or not. You had best think of all the houses to which she might have gone, among her friends. You know them better than I do. I will beat up all the streets between here and your house. When I am tired I will go to your palace."

"I am afraid you will not find her," replied Sant' Ilario. "But we must try for the sake of her poor mother."

"It is a question of luck," said the other, and they separated at once.

San Giacinto turned in the direction of the crowd which was pouring into the street at some distance farther on. As he approached, he heard the name "Serristori" spoken frequently in the hum of voices.

"What about the Serristori?" he asked of the first he met.

"Have you not heard?" cried the fellow. "It is blown up with gunpowder! There are at least a thousand dead. Half the Borgo Nuovo is destroyed, and they say that the Vatican will go next—"

The man would have run on for any length of time, but San Giacinto had heard enough and dived into the first byway he found, intending to escape the throng and make straight for the barracks. He had to ask his way several times, and it was fully a quarter of an hour before he reached the bridge. Thence he easily found the scene of the disaster, and came up to the hospital of Santo Spirito just after the gates had closed behind the bearers of the dead. He mixed with the crowd and asked questions, learning very soon that the first search, made by the people from the hospital, had only brought to light the bodies of two Zouaves and one woman.

"And I did not see her," said the man who was speaking, "but they say she was a lady and beautiful as an angel."

"Rubbish!" exclaimed another. "She was a little sewing woman who lived in the Borgo Vecchio. And I know it is true because her innamorato was one of the dead Zouaves they picked up."

"I don't believe there was any woman at all," said a third. "What should a woman be doing at the barracks?"

"She was killed outside," observed the first speaker, a timid old man. "At least, I was told so, but I did not see her."

"It was a woman bringing a baby to put into the Rota,"[†] cried a shrill-voiced washerwoman. "She got the child in and was running away, when the place blew up, and the devil carried her off. And serve her right, for throwing away her baby, poor little thing!"

In the light of these various opinions, most of which supported the story that some woman had been carried into the hospital, San Giacinto determined to find out the truth, and boldly rang the bell. A panel was opened in the door, and the porter looked out at the surging crowd.

"What do you want?" he inquired roughly, on seeing that admittance had not been asked for a sick or wounded person.

"I want to speak with the surgeon in charge," replied San Giacinto.

"He is busy," said the man rather doubtfully. "Who are you?"

"A friend of one of the persons just killed."

"They are dead. You had better wait till morning and come again," suggested the porter.

"But I want to be sure that it is my friend who is dead."

"Then why do you not give your name? Perhaps you are a Garibaldian. Why should I open?"

"I will tell the surgeon my name, if you will call him. There is something for yourself. Tell him I am a Roman prince and must see him for a moment."

"I will see if he will come," said the man, shutting the panel in San Giacinto's face. His footsteps echoed along the pavement of the wide hall within. It was long before he came back, and San Giacinto had leisure to reflect upon the situation.

He had very little doubt but that the dead woman was no other than Donna Faustina. By a rare chance, or rather in obedience to an irresistible instinct, he had found the object of his search in half an hour, while his cousin was fruitlessly inquiring for the missing girl in the opposite direction. He had been led to the conclusion that she had followed Gouache by what he had seen in the Saracinesca's drawing-room, and by a process of reasoning too simple to suggest itself to an ordinary member of Roman society. What disturbed him most was the thought

---

† The Rota was a revolving box in which foundlings were formerly placed. The box turned round and the infant was taken inside and cared for. It stands at the gate of the Santo Spirito Hospital, and is still visible, though no longer in use.

of the consequences of his discovery, and he resolved to conceal the girl's name and his own if possible. If she were indeed dead, it would be wiser to convey her body to her father's house privately; if she were still alive, secrecy was doubly necessary. In either case it would be utterly impossible to account to the world for the fact that Faustina Montevarchi had been alone in the Borgo Nuovo at such an hour; and San Giacinto had a lively interest in preserving the good reputation of Casa Montevarchi, since he had been meditating for some time past a union with Donna Flavia.

At last the panel opened again, and when the porter had satisfied himself that the gentleman was still without, a little door in the heavy gate was cautiously unfastened and San Giacinto went in, bending nearly double to pass under the low entrance. In the great vestibule he was immediately confronted by the surgeon in charge, who was in his shirt sleeves, but had thrown his coat over his shoulders and held it together at the neck to protect himself from the night air. San Giacinto begged him to retire out of hearing of the porter, and the two walked away together.

"There was a lady killed just now by the explosion, was there not?" inquired San Giacinto.

"She is not dead," replied the surgeon. "Do you know her?"

"I think so. Had she anything about her to prove her identity?"

"The letter M embroidered on her handkerchief. That is all I know. She has not been here a quarter of an hour. I thought she was dead myself, when we took her up."

"She was not under the ruins?"

"No. She was struck by some small stone, I fancy. The two Zouaves were half buried, and are quite dead."

"May I see them? I know many in the corps. They might be acquaintances."

"Certainly. They are close by in the mortuary chamber, unless they have been put in the chapel."

The two men entered the grim place, which was dimly lighted by a lantern hanging overhead. It is unnecessary to dwell upon the ghastly details. San Giacinto bent down curiously and looked at the dead men's faces. He knew neither of them, and told the surgeon so.

"Will you allow me to see the lady?" he asked.

"Pardon me, if I ask a question," said the surgeon, who was a man of middle age, with a red beard and keen grey eyes. "To whom have I the advantage of speaking?"

"Signor Professore," replied San Giacinto, "I must tell you that if this is the lady I suppose your patient to be, the honour of one of the greatest families in Rome is concerned, and it is important that strict secrecy should be preserved."

"The porter told me that you were a Roman prince," returned the surgeon rather bluntly. "But you speak like a southerner."

"I was brought up in Naples. As I was saying, secrecy is very important, and I can assure you that you will earn the gratitude of many by assisting me."

"Do you wish to take this lady away at once?"

"Heaven forbid! Her mother and sister shall come for her in half an hour."

The surgeon thrust his hands into his pockets, and stood staring for a moment or two at the bodies of the Zouaves.

"I cannot do it," he said, suddenly looking up at San. Giacinto. "I am master here, and I am responsible. The secret is professional, of course. If I knew you, even by sight, I should not hesitate. As it is, I must ask your name."

San Giacinto did not hesitate long, as the surgeon was evidently master of the situation. He took a card from his case and silently handed it to the doctor. The latter took it and read the name, "Don Giovanni Saracinesca, Marchese di San Giacinto." His face betrayed no emotion, but the belief flashed through his mind that there was no such person in existence. He was one of the leading men in his profession, and knew Prince Saracinesca and Sant' Ilario, but he had never heard of this other Don Giovanni. He knew also that the city was in a state of revolution and that many suspicious persons were likely to gain access to public buildings on false pretences.

"Very well," he said quietly. "You are not afraid of dead men, I see. Be good enough to wait a moment here—no one will see you, and you will not be recognised. I will go and see that there is nobody in the way, and you shall have a sight of the young lady."

His companion nodded in assent and the surgeon went out through the narrow door. San Giacinto was surprised to hear the heavy key turned in the lock and withdrawn, but immediately accounted for the fact on the theory that the surgeon wished to prevent any one from finding his visitor lest the secret should be divulged. He was not a nervous man, and had no especial horror of being left alone in a mortuary chamber for a few minutes. He looked about him, and saw that the room was high and vaulted. One window alone gave air, and this was ten feet from the floor and heavily ironed. He reflected with a smile that if it pleased the surgeon to leave him there he could not possibly get out. Neither his size nor his phenomenal strength could assist him in the least. There was no furniture in the place. Half a dozen slabs of slate for the bodies were built against the wall, solid and immovable, and the door was of the heaviest oak, thickly studded with huge iron nails. If the dead men had been living prisoners their place of confinement could not have been more strongly contrived.

San Giacinto waited a quarter of an hour, and at last, as the surgeon did not return, he sat down upon one of the marble slabs and, being very hungry, consoled himself by lighting a cigar, while he meditated upon the surest means of conveying Donna Faustina to her father's house. At last he began to wonder how long he was to wait.

"I should not wonder," he said to himself, "if that long-eared professor had taken me for a revolutionist."

He was not far wrong, indeed. The surgeon had despatched a messenger for a couple of gendarmes and had gone about his business in the hospital, knowing very well that it would take some time to find the police while the riot lasted, and congratulating himself upon having caught a prisoner who, if not a revolutionist, was at all events an impostor, since he had a card printed with a false name.

CHAPTER VI

THE improvised banquet at the Palazzo Saracinesca was not a merry one, but the probable dangers to the city and the disappearance of Faustina Montevarchi furnished matter for plenty of conversation. The majority inclined to the belief that the girl had lost her head and had run home, but as neither Sant' Ilario nor his cousin returned, there was much speculation. The prince said he believed that they had found Faustina at her father's house and had stayed to dinner, whereupon some malicious person remarked that it needed a revolution in Rome to produce hospitality in such a quarter.

Dinner was nearly ended when Pasquale, the butler, whispered to the prince that a gendarme wanted to speak with him on very important business.

"Bring him here," answered old Saracinesca, aloud. "There is a gendarme outside," he added, addressing his guests, "he will tell us all the news. Shall we have him here?"

Every one assented enthusiastically to the proposition, for most of those present were anxious about their houses, not knowing what had taken place during the last two hours. The man was ushered in, and stood at a distance holding his three-cornered hat in his hand, and looking rather sheepish and uncomfortable.

"Well?" asked the prince. "What is the matter? We all wish to hear the news."

"Excellency," began the soldier, "I must ask many pardons for appearing thus—" Indeed his uniform was more or less disarranged and he looked pale and fatigued.

"Never mind your appearance. Speak up," answered old Saracinesca in encouraging tones.

"Excellency," said the man, "I must apologise, but there is a gentleman who calls himself Don Giovanni, of your revered name—"

"I know there is. He is my son. What about him?"

"He is not the Senior Principe di Sant' Ilario, Excellency—he calls himself by another name—Marchese di—di—here is his card, Excellency."

"My cousin, San Giacinto, then. What about him, I say?"

"Your Excellency has a cousin—" stammered the gendarme.

"Well? Is it against the law to have cousins?" cried the prince. "What is the matter with my cousin?"

"Dio mio!" exclaimed the soldier in great agitation. "What a combination! Your Excellency's cousin is in the mortuary chamber at Santo Spirito!"

"Is he dead?" asked Saracinesca in a lower voice, but starting from his chair.

"No," cried the man, "questo e il male! That is the trouble! He is alive and very well!"

"Then what the devil is he doing in the mortuary chamber?" roared the prince.

"Excellency, I beseech your pardon, I had nothing to do with locking up the Signor Marchese. It was the surgeon, Excellency, who took him for a Garibaldian. He shall be liberated at once—"

"I should think so!" answered Saracinesca, savagely. "And what business have your asses of surgeons with gentlemen? My hat, Pasquale. And how on earth came my cousin to be in Santo Spirito?"

"Excellency, I know nothing, but I had to do my duty."

"And if you know nothing how the devil do you expect to do your duty! I will have you and the surgeon and the whole of Santo Spirito and all the patients, in the Carceri Nuove, safe in prison before morning! My hat, Pasquale, I say!"

Some confusion followed, during which the gendarme, who was anxious to escape all responsibility in the matter of San Giacinto's confinement, left the room and descended the grand staircase three steps at a time. Mounting his horse he galloped back through the now deserted streets to the hospital.

Within two minutes after his arrival San Giacinto heard the bolt of the heavy lock run back in the socket and the surgeon entered the mortuary chamber. San Giacinto had nearly finished his cigar and was growing impatient, but the doctor made many apologies for his long absence.

"An unexpected relapse in a dangerous case, Signor Marchese," he said in explanation. "What would you have? We doctors are at the mercy of nature! Pray forgive my neglect, but I could send no one, as you did not wish to be seen. I locked the door, so that nobody might find you here. Pray come with me, and you shall see the young lady at once."

"By all means," replied San Giacinto. "Dead men are poor company, and I am in a hurry."

The surgeon led the way to the accident ward and introduced his companion to a small clean room in which a shaded lamp was burning. A Sister of Mercy stood by the white bed, upon which lay a young girl, stretched out at her full length.

"You are too late," said the nun very quietly. "She is dead, poor child."

San Giacinto uttered a deep exclamation of horror and was at the bedside even before the surgeon. He lifted the fair young creature in his arms and stared at the cold face, holding it to the light. Then with a loud cry of astonishment he laid down his burden.

"It is not she, Signor Professore," he said. "I must apologise for the trouble I have given you. Pray accept my best thanks. There is a resemblance, but it is not she."

The doctor was somewhat relieved to find himself freed from the responsibility which, as San Giacinto had told him, involved the honour of one of the greatest families in Rome. Before speaking, he satisfied himself that the young woman was really dead.

"Death often makes faces look alike which have no resemblance to each other in life," he remarked as he turned away. Then they both left the room, followed at a little distance by the sister who was going to summon the bearers to carry away her late charge.

As the two men descended the steps, the sound of loud voices in altercation reached their ears, and as they emerged into the vestibule, they saw old Prince Saracinesca flourishing his stick in dangerous proximity to the head of the porter. The latter had retreated until he stood with his back against the wall.

"I will have none of this lying," shouted the irate nobleman. "The Marchese is here—the gendarme told me he was in the mortuary chamber—if he is not produced at once I will break your rascally neck—" The man was protesting as fast and as loud as his assailant threatened him.

"Eh! My good cousin!" cried San Giacinto, whose unmistakable voice at once made the prince desist from his attack and turn round. "Do not kill the fellow! I am alive and well, as you see."

A short explanation ensued, during which the surgeon was obliged to admit that as San Giacinto had no means of proving any identity he, the doctor in charge, had thought it best to send for the police, in view of the unquiet state of the city.

"But what brought you here?" asked old Saracinesca, who was puzzled to account for his cousin's presence in the hospital.

San Giacinto had satisfied his curiosity and did not care a pin for the annoyance to which he had been subjected. He was anxious, too, to get away, and having half guessed the surgeon's suspicions was not at all surprised by the revelation concerning the gendarme.

"Allow me to thank you again," he said politely, turning to the doctor. "I have no doubt you acted quite rightly. Let us go," he added, addressing the prince.

The porter received a coin as consolation money for the abuse he had sustained, and the two cousins found themselves in the street. Saracinesca again asked for an explanation.

"Very simple," replied San Giacinto. "Donna Faustina was not at her father's house, so your son and I separated to continue our search. Chancing to find myself here—for I do not know my way about the city—I learnt the news of the explosion, and was told that two Zouaves had been found dead and had been taken into the hospital. Fearing lest one of them might have been Gouache, I succeeded in getting in, when I was locked up with the dead bodies, as you have heard. Gouache, by the bye, was not one of them."

"It is outrageous—" began Saracinesca, but his companion did not allow him to proceed.

"It is no matter," he said, quickly. "The important thing is to find Donna Faustina. I suppose you have no news of her."

"None. Giovanni had not come home when the gendarme appeared."

"Then we must continue the search as best we can," said San Giacinto. Thereupon they both got into the prince's cab and drove away.

It was nearly midnight when a small detachment of Zouaves crossed the bridge of Sant' Angelo. There had been some sharp fighting at the Porta San Paolo, at the other extremity of Rome, and the men were weary. But rest was not to be expected that night, and the tired soldiers were led back to do sentry duty in the neighbourhood of their quarters. The officer halted the little body in the broad space beyond.

"Monsieur Gouache," said the lieutenant, "you will take a corporal's guard and maintain order in the neighbourhood of the barracks—if there is anything left of them," he added with a mournful laugh.

Gouache stepped forward and half a dozen men formed themselves behind him. The officer was a good friend of his.

"I suppose you have not dined any more than I, Monsieur Gouache?"

"Not I, mon lieutenant. It is no matter."

"Pick up something to eat if you can, at such an hour. I will see that you are relieved before morning. Shoulder arms! March!"

So Anastase Gouache trudged away down the Borgo Nuovo with his men at his heels. Among the number there was the son of a French duke, an English gentleman whose forefathers had marched with the Conqueror as their descendant now marched behind the Parisian artist, a young Swiss doctor of law, a couple of red-headed Irish peasants, and two or three others. When they reached the scene of the late catastrophe the place was deserted. The men who had been set to work at clearing away the rubbish had soon found what a hopeless task they had undertaken; and the news having soon spread that only the regimental musicians were in the barracks at the time, and that these few had been in all probability in the lower story of the building, where the band-room was situated, all attempts at finding the bodies were abandoned until the next day.

Gouache and many others had escaped death almost miraculously, for five minutes had not elapsed after they had started at the double-quick for the Porta San Paolo, when the building was blown up. The news had of course been brought to them while they were repulsing the attack upon the gate, but it was not until many hours afterwards that a small detachment could safely be spared to return to their devastated quarters. Gouache himself had been just in time to join his comrades, and with them had seen most of the fighting. He now placed his men at proper distances along the street, and found leisure to reflect upon what had occurred. He was hungry and thirsty, and grimy with gunpowder, but there was evidently no prospect of getting any refreshment. The night, too, was growing cold, and he found it necessary to walk briskly about to keep himself warm. At first he tramped backwards and forwards, some fifty paces each way, but growing weary of the monotonous exercise, he began to scramble about among the heaps of ruins. His quick imagination called up the scene as it must have looked at the moment of the explosion, and then reverted with a sharp pang to the thought of his poor comrades-in-arms who lay crushed to death many feet below the stones on which he trod.

Suddenly, as he leaned against a huge block, absorbed in his thoughts, the low wailing of a woman's voice reached his ears. The sound proceeded apparently from no great distance, but the tone was very soft and low. Gradually, as he listened, he thought he distinguished words, but such words as he had not expected to hear, though they expressed his own feeling well enough.

"*Requiem eternam dona eis!*"

It was quite distinct, and the accents sounded strangely familiar. He held his breath and strained every faculty to catch the sounds.

"*Requiem sempiternam—sempiternam—sempiternam!*" The despairing tones trembled at the third repetition, and then the voice broke into passionate sobbing.

Anastase did not wait for more. At first he had half believed that what he heard was due to his imagination, but the sudden weeping left no doubt that it was real. Cautiously he made his way amongst the ruins, until he stopped short in amazement not unmingled with horror.

In an angle where a part of the walls was still standing, a woman was on her knees, her hands stretched wildly out before her, her darkly-clad figure faintly revealed by the beams of the waning moon. The covering had fallen back from her head upon her shoulders, and the struggling rays fell upon her beautiful features, marking their angelic outline with delicate light. Still Anastase remained motionless, scarcely believing his eyes, and yet knowing that lovely face too well not to believe. It was Donna Faustina Montevarchi who knelt there at midnight, alone, repeating the solemn words from the mass for the dead; it was for him that she wept, and he knew it.

Standing there upon the common grave of his comrades, a wild joy filled the young man's heart, a joy such as must be felt to be known, for it passes the power of earthly words to tell it. In that dim and ghastly place the sun seemed suddenly to shine as at noonday in a fair country; the crumbling masonry and blocks of broken stone grew more lovely than the loveliest flowers, and from the dark figure of that lonely heart-broken woman the man who loved her saw a radiance proceeding which overflowed and made bright at once his eyes and his heart. In the intensity of his emotion, the hand which lay upon the fallen stone contracted suddenly and broke off a fragment of the loosened mortar.

At the slight noise, Faustina turned her head. Her eyes were wide and wild, and as she started to her feet she uttered a short, sharp cry, and staggered backward against the wall. In a moment Anastase was at her side, supporting her and looking into her face.

"Faustina!"

During a few seconds she gazed horrorstruck and silent upon him, stiffening herself and holding her face away from his. It was as though his ghost had risen out of the earth and embraced her. Then the wild look shivered like a mask and vanished, her features softened and the colour rose to her cheeks for an instant. Very slowly she drew him towards her, her eyes fixed on his; their lips met in a long, sweet kiss—then her strength forsook her and she swooned away in his arms.

Gouache supported her tenderly until she sat leaning against the wall, and then knelt down by her side. He did not know what to do, and had he known, it would have availed him little. His instinct told him that she would presently recover consciousness and his emotions had so wholly overcome him that he could only look at her lovely face as her head rested upon his arm. But while he waited a great fear began to steal into his heart. He asked himself how Faustina had come to such a place, and how her coming was to be accounted for. It was long past midnight, now, and he guessed what trouble and anxiety there would be in her father's house until she was found. He represented to himself in quick succession the scenes which would follow his appearance at the Palazzo Montevarchi with the youngest daughter of the family in his arms—or in a cab, and he confessed to himself that never lover had been in such straits.

Faustina opened her eyes and sighed, nestled her head softly on his breast, sighing again, in the happy consciousness that he was safe, and then at last she sat up and looked him in the face.

"I was so sure you were killed," said she, in her soft voice.

"My darling!" he exclaimed, pressing her to his side.

"Are you not glad to be alive?" she asked. "For my sake, at least! You do not know what I have suffered."

Again he held her close to him, in silence, forgetting all the unheard-of difficulties of his situation in the happiness of holding her in his arms. His silence, indeed, was more eloquent than any words could have been. "My beloved!" he said at last, "how could you run such risks for me? Do you think I am worthy of so much love? And yet, if loving you can make me worthy of you, I am the most deserving man that ever lived—and I live only for you. But for you I might as well be buried under our feet here with my poor comrades. But tell me, Faustina, were you not afraid to come? How long have you been here? It is very late—it is almost morning."

"Is it? What does it matter, since you are safe? You ask how I came? Did I not tell you I would follow you? Why did you run on without me? I ran here very quickly, and just as I saw the gates of the barracks there was a terrible noise and I was thrown down, I cannot tell how. Soon I got to my feet and crept under a doorway. I suppose I must have fainted, for I thought you were killed. I saw a soldier before me, just when it happened, and he must have been struck. I took him for you. When I came to myself there were so many people in the street that I could not move from where I was. Then they went away, and I came here while the workmen tried to move the stones, and I watched them and begged them to go on, but they would not, and I had nothing to give them, so they went away too, and I knew that I should have to wait until tomorrow to find you—for I would have waited—no one should have dragged me away—ah, my darling!— my beloved! What does anything matter now that you are safe!"

For fully half an hour they sat talking in this wise, both knowing that the situation could not last, but neither willing to speak the word which must end it. Gouache, indeed, was in a twofold difficulty. Not only was he wholly at a loss for a means of introducing Faustina into her father's house unobserved at such an hour; he was in command of the men stationed in the neighbourhood, and to leave his post under any circumstances whatever would be a very grave breach of duty. He could neither allow Faustina to return alone, nor could he accompany her. He could not send one of his men for a friend to help him, since to take any one into his confidence was to ruin the girl's reputation in the eyes of all Rome. To find a cab at that time of night was almost out of the question. The position seemed desperate. Faustina, too, was a mere child, and it was impossible to explain to her the social consequences of her being discovered with him.

"I think, perhaps," said she after a happy silence, and in rather a timid voice—"I think, perhaps, you had better take me home now. They will be anxious, you know," she added, as though fearing that he should suspect her of wishing to leave him.

"Yes, I must take you home," answered Gouache, somewhat absently. To her his tone sounded cold.

"Are you angry, because I want to go?" asked the young girl, looking lovingly into his face.

"Angry? No indeed, darling! I ought to have taken you home at once—but I was too happy to think of it. Of course your people must be terribly anxious, and the question is how to manage your entrance. Can you get into the house unseen? Is there any way? Any small door that is open?"

"We can wake the porter," said Faustina, simply. "He will let us in."

"It would not do. How can I go to your father and tell him that I found you here? Besides, the porter knows me."

"Well, if he does, what does it matter?"

"He would talk about it to other servants, and all Rome would know it tomorrow. You must go home with a woman, and to do that we must find some one you know. It would be a terrible injury to you to have such a story repeated abroad."

"Why?"

To this innocent question Gouache did not find a ready answer. He smiled quietly and pressed her to his side more closely.

"The world is a very bad place, dearest. I am a man and know it. You must trust me to do what is best. Will you?"

"How can you ask? I will always trust you."

"Then I will tell you what we will do. You must go home with the Princess Sant' Ilario."

"With Corona? But—"

"She knows that I love you, and she is the only woman in Rome whom I would trust. Do not be surprised. She asked me if it was true, and I said it was. I am on duty here, and you must wait for me while I make the rounds of my sentries—it will not take five minutes. Then I will take you to the Palazzo Saracinesca. I shall not be missed here for an hour."

"I will do whatever you wish," said Faustina. "Perhaps that is best. But I am afraid everybody will be asleep. Is it not very late?"

"I will wake them up if they are sleeping."

He left her to make his round and soon assured himself that his men were not napping. Then before he returned he stopped at the corner of a street and by the feeble moonlight scratched a few words on a leaf from his notebook.

"Madame," he wrote, "I have found Donna Faustina Montevarchi, who had lost her way. It is absolutely necessary that you should accompany her to her father's house. You are the only person whom I can trust. I am at your gate. Bring something in the way of a cloak to disguise her with."

He signed his initials and folded the paper, slipping it into his pocket where he could readily find it. Then he went back to the place where Faustina was waiting. He helped her out of the ruins, and passing through a side street so as to avoid the sentinels, they made their way rapidly to the bridge. The sentry challenged Gouache who gave the word at once and was allowed to pass on with his charge. In less than a quarter of an hour they were at the Palazzo Saracinesca. Gouache made Faustina stand in the shadow of a doorway on the opposite side of the street and advanced to the great doors. A ray of light which passed through the crack of a shutter behind the heavy iron grating on one side of the arch showed that the porter was up. Anastase drew his bayonet from his side and tapped with its point against the high window.

"Who is there?" asked the porter, thrusting his head out.

"Is the Principe di Sant' Ilario still awake?" asked Gouache.

"He is not at home. Heaven knows where he is. What do you want? The princess is sitting up to wait for the prince."

"That will do as well," replied Anastase. "I am sent with this note from the

Vatican. It needs an immediate answer. Be good enough to say that I was ordered to wait."

The explanation satisfied the porter, to whom the sight of a Zouave was just then more agreeable than usual. He put his arm out through the grating and took the paper.

"It does not look as though it came from the Vatican," he remarked doubtfully, as he turned the scrap to the light of his lamp.

"The cardinal is waiting—make haste!" said Gouache. It struck him that even if the man could read a little, which was not improbable, the initials A. G., being those of Cardinal Antonelli in reversed order would be enough to frighten the fellow and make him move quickly. This, indeed was precisely what occurred.

In five minutes the small door in the gate was opened and Gouache saw Corona's tall figure step out into the street. She hesitated a moment when she saw the Zouave alone, and then closed the door with a snap behind her. Gouache bowed quickly and gave her his arm.

"Let us be quick," he said, "or the porter will see us. Donna Faustina is under that doorway. You know how grateful I am—there is no time to say it."

Corona said nothing but hastened to Faustina's side. The latter put her arms about her friend's neck and kissed her. The princess threw a wide cloak over the young girl's shoulders and drew the hood over her head.

"Let us be quick," said Corona, repeating Gouache's words. They walked quickly away in silence, and no one spoke until they leached the Palazzo Montevarchi. Explanations were impossible, and every one was too much absorbed by the danger of the situation to speak of anything else. When they were a few steps from the gate Corona stopped.

"You may leave us here," she said coldly, addressing Gouache.

"But, princess, I will see you home," protested the latter, somewhat surprised by her tone.

"No—I will take a servant back with me. Will you be good enough to leave us?" she asked almost haughtily, as Gouache still lingered.

He had no choice but to obey her commands, though for some time he could not explain to himself the cause of the princess's behaviour.

"Good night, Madame. Good night, Mademoiselle," he said, quietly. Then with a low bow he turned away and disappeared in the darkness. In five minutes he had reached the bridge, running at the top of his speed, and he regained his post without his absence having been observed.

When the two women were alone, Corona laid her hand upon Faustina's shoulder and looked down into the girl's face.

"Faustina, my child," she said, "how could you be led into such a wild scrape?"

"Why did you treat him so unkindly?" asked the young girl with flashing eyes. "It was cruel and unkind—"

"Because he deserved it," answered Corona, with rising anger. "How could he dare—from my house—a mere child like you—"

"I do not know what you imagine," said Faustina in a tone of deep resentment. "I followed him to the Serristori barracks, and I fainted when they were blown up. He found me and brought me to you, because he said I could not go back to my father's house with him. If I love him what is that to you?"

"It is a great deal to me that he should have got you into this trouble."

"He did not. If it is trouble, I got myself into it. Do you love him yourself that you are so angry?"

"I!" cried Corona in amazement at the girl's audacity. "Poor Gouache!" she added with a half-scornful, half-pitying laugh. "Come, child! Let us go in. We cannot stand here all night talking. I will tell your mother that you lost your way in our house and were found asleep in a distant room. The lock was jammed, and you could not get out."

"I think I will simply tell the truth," answered Faustina.

"You will do nothing of the kind," said Corona, sternly. "Do you know what would happen? You would be shut up in a convent by your father for several years, and the world would say that I had favoured your meetings with Monsieur Gouache. This is no trifling matter. You need say nothing. I will give the whole explanation myself, and take the responsibility of the falsehood upon my own shoulders."

"I promised him to do as he bid me," replied Faustina. "I suppose he would have me follow your advice, and so I will. Are you still angry, Corona?"

"I will try not to be, if you will be sensible."

They knocked at the gate and were soon admitted. The whole household was on foot, though it was past one o'clock. It is unnecessary to describe the emotions of Faustina's relations, nor their gratitude to Corona, whose explanation they accepted at once, with a delight which may easily be imagined.

"But your porter said he had seen her leave your house," said the Princess

Montevarchi, recollecting the detail and anxious to have it explained.

"He was mistaken, in his fright," returned Corona, calmly. "It was only my maid, who ran out to see what was the matter and returned soon afterwards."

There was nothing more to be said. The old prince and Ascanio Bellegra walked home with Corona, who refused to wait until a carriage could be got ready, on the ground that her husband might have returned from the search and might be anxious at her absence. She left her escort at her door and mounted the steps alone. As she was going up the porter came running after her.

"Excellency," he said in low tones, "the Signor Principe came back while you were gone, and I told him that you had received a note from the Vatican and had gone away with the Zouave who brought it. I hope I did right—"

"Of course you did," replied Corona. She was a calm woman and not easily thrown off her guard, but as she made her answer she was conscious of an unpleasant sensation wholly new to her. She had never done anything concerning which she had reason to ask herself what Giovanni would think of it. For the first time since her marriage with him she knew that she had something to conceal. How, indeed, was it possible to tell him the story of Faustina's wild doings? Giovanni was a man who knew the world, and had no great belief in its virtues. To tell him what had occurred would be to do Faustina an irreparable injury in his eyes. He would believe his wife, no doubt, but he would tell her that Faustina had deceived her. She cared little what he might think of Gouache, for she herself was incensed against him, believing that he must certainly have used some persuasion to induce Faustina to follow him, mad as the idea seemed.

Corona had little time for reflection, however. She could not stand upon the stairs, and as soon as she entered the house she must meet her husband. She made up her mind hurriedly to do what in most cases is extremely dangerous. Giovanni was in her boudoir, pale and anxious. He had forgotten that he had not dined that evening and was smoking a cigarette with short sharp puffs.

"Thank God!" he cried, as his wife entered the room. "Where have you been, my darling?"

"Giovanni," said Corona, gravely, laying her two hands on his shoulders, "you know you can trust me—do you not?"

"As I trust Heaven," he answered, tenderly.

"You must trust me now, then," said she. "I cannot tell you where I have been. I will tell you some day, you have my solemn promise. Faustina Montevarchi is with her mother. I took her back, and told them she had followed me from the room, had lost her way in the house, and had accidentally fastened a door which she could not open. You must support the story. You need only say that I told you so, because you were out at the time. I will not lie to you, so I tell you that I invented the story."

Sant' Ilario was silent for a few minutes, during which he looked steadily into his wife's eyes, which met his without flinching.

"You shall do as you please, Corona," he said at last, returning the cigarette to his lips and still looking at her. "Will you answer me one question?"

"If I can without explaining."

"That Zouave who brought the message from the Vatican—was he Gouache?"

Corona turned her eyes away, annoyed at the demand. To refuse to answer was tantamount to admitting the truth, and she would not lie to her husband.

"It was Gouache," she said, after a moment's hesitation.

"I thought so," answered Sant' Ilario in a low voice. He moved away, throwing his cigarette into the fireplace. "Very well," he continued, "I will remember to tell the story as you told it to me, and I am sure you will tell me the truth some day."

"Of course," said Corona. "And I thank you, Giovanni, with my whole heart! There is no one like you, dear."

She sat down in a chair beside him as he stood, and taking his hand she pressed it to her lips. She knew well enough what a strange thing she had asked, and she was indeed grateful to him. He stooped down and kissed her forehead.

"I will always trust you," he said, softly. "Tell me, dear one, has this matter given you pain? Is it a secret that will trouble you?"

"Not now," she answered, frankly.

Giovanni was in earnest when he promised to trust his wife. He knew, better than any living man, how well worthy she was of his utmost confidence, and he meant what he said. It must be confessed that the situation was a trying one to a man of his temper, and the depth of his love for Corona can be judged from the readiness with which he consented to her concealing anything from him. Every circumstance connected with what had happened that evening was strange, and the conclusion, instead of elucidating the mystery, only made it more mysterious still. His cousin's point-blank declaration that Faustina and Gouache were in love was startling to all his ideas and prejudices. He had seen Gouache kiss Corona's hand in a corner of the drawing-room, a proceeding which he did not wholly approve, though it was common enough. Then Gouache and Faustina had disappeared. Then Faustina had been found, and to facilitate the finding it had been necessary that Corona and Gouache should leave the palace together at one o'clock in the morning. Finally, Corona had appealed to his confidence in her and had taken advantage of it to refuse any present explanation whatever of her proceedings. Corona was a very noble and true woman, and he had promised to trust her. How far he kept his word will appear hereafter.

CHAPTER VII

WHEN San Giacinto heard Corona's explanation of Faustina's disappearance, he said nothing. He did not believe the story in the least, but if every one was satisfied there was no reason why he should not be satisfied also. Though he saw well enough that the tale was a pure invention, and that there was something behind it which was not to be known, the result was, on the whole, exactly what he desired. He received the thanks of the Montevarchi household for his fruitless exertions with a smile of gratification, and congratulated the princess upon the happy issue of the adventure. He made no present attempt to ascertain the real truth by asking questions which would have been hard to answer, for he was delighted that the incident should be explained away and forgotten at once. Donna Faustina's disappearance was of course freely discussed and variously commented, but the general verdict of the world was contrary to San Giacinto's private conclusions. People said that the account given by the family must be true, since it was absurd to suppose that a child just out of the convent could be either so foolish or so courageous as to go out alone at such a moment. No other hypothesis was in the least tenable, and the demonstration offered must be accepted as giving the only solution of the problem. San Giacinto told no one that he thought differently.

It was before all things his intention to establish himself firmly in Roman society, and his natural tact told him that the best way to accomplish this was to offend no one, and to endorse without question the opinion of the majority. Moreover, as a part of his plan for assuring his position consisted in marrying Faustina's sister, his interest lay manifestly in protecting the good name of her family by every means in his power. He knew that old Montevarchi passed for being one of the most rigid amongst the stiff company of the strait-laced, and that the prince was as careful of the conduct of his children, as his father had formerly been in regard to his own doings. Ascanio Bellegra was the result of this home education, and already bid fair to follow in his parent's footsteps. Christian virtues are certainly not incompatible with manliness, but the practice of them as maintained by Prince Montevarchi had made his son Ascanio a colourless creature, rather non-bad than good, clothed in a garment of righteousness that fitted him only because his harmless soul had no salient bosses of goodness, any more than it was disfigured by any reprehensible depressions capable of harbouring evil.

There is a class of men in certain states of society who are manly, but not masculine. There is nothing paradoxical in the statement, nor is it a mere play upon the meanings of words. There are men of all ages, young, middle-aged, and old, who possess many estimable virtues, who show physical courage wherever it is necessary, who are honourable, strong, industrious, and tenacious of purpose, but who undeniably lack something which belongs to the ideal man, and which, for want of a better word, we call the masculine element. When we shall have microscopes so large and powerful that a human being shall be as transparent under the concentrated light of the lenses as the tiniest insect when placed in one of our modern instruments, then, perhaps, the scientist of the future may discover the causes of this difference. I believe, however, that it does not depend upon the fact of one man having a few ounces more of blood in his veins than another. The fact lies deeper hidden than that, and may puzzle the psychologist as well as the professor of anthropology. For us it exists, and we cannot explain it, but must content ourselves with comparing the phenomena which proceed from these differences of organisation. At the present day the society of the English-speaking races seems to favour the growth of the creature who is only manly but not masculine, whereas outside the pale of that strange little family which calls itself "society" the masculinity of man is more striking than among other races. Not long ago a French journalist said that many of the peculiarities of the English-speaking peoples proceeded from the omnipresence of the young girl, who reads every novel that appears, goes to every theatre, and regulates the tone of conversation and literature by her never-absent innocence. Cynics, if there are still representatives of a school which has grown ridiculous, may believe this if they please; the fact remains that it is precisely the most masculine class of men who show the strongest predilection for the society of the most refined women, and who on the whole show the greatest respect for all women in general. The masculine man prefers the company of the other sex by natural attraction, and would perhaps rather fight with other men, or at least strive to outdo them in the struggle for notoriety, power, or fame, than spend his time in friendly conversation with them, no matter how interesting the topic selected. This point of view may be regarded as uncivilised, but it may be pointed out that it is only in the most civilised countries that the society of women is accessible to all men of their own social position. No one familiar with Eastern countries will pretend that Orientals shut up their women because they enjoy their company so much as to be unwilling to share the privilege with their friends.

San Giacinto was pre-eminently a masculine man, as indeed were all the Saracinesca, in a greater or less degree. He understood women instinctively, and, with a very limited experience of the world, knew well enough the strength of their influence. It was characteristic of him that he had determined to marry almost as soon as he had got a footing in Roman society. He saw clearly that if he could unite himself with a powerful family he could exercise a directing power over the women which must ultimately give him all that he needed. Through his cousins he had very soon made the acquaintance of the Montevarchi household, and seeing that there were two marriageable daughters, he profited by the introduction. He would have preferred Faustina, perhaps, but he foresaw that he should find fewer difficulties in obtaining her sister for his wife. The old prince and princess were in despair at seeing her still unmarried, and it was clear that they were not likely to find a better match for her than the Marchese di San Giacinto. He, on his part, knew that his past occupation was a disadvantage to him in the eyes of the world, although he was the undoubted and acknowledged cousin of the Saracinesca, and the only man of the family besides old Leone and his son Sant' Ilario. His two boys, also, were a drawback, since his second wife's children could not inherit the whole of the property he expected to leave. But his position was good, and Flavia was not generally considered to be likely to marry, so that he had good hopes of winning her.

It was clear to him from the first that there must be some reason why she had not married, and the somewhat disparaging remarks concerning her which he heard from time to time excited his curiosity. As he had always intended to consult the head of his family upon the matter he now determined to do so at once. He was not willing, indeed, to let matters go any further until he had ascertained the truth concerning her, and he was sure that Prince Saracinesca would tell him everything at the first mention of a proposal to marry her. The old gentleman had too much pride to allow his cousin to make an unfitting match. Accordingly, on the day following the events last narrated San Giacinto called after breakfast and found the prince, as usual, alone in his study. He was not dozing, however, for the accounts of the last night's doings in the *Osservatore Romano* were very interesting.

"I suppose you have heard all about Montevarchi's daughter?" asked Saracinesca, laying his paper aside and giving his hand to San Giacinto.

"Yes, and I am delighted at the conclusion of the adventure, especially as I have something to ask you about another member of the family."

"I hope Flavia has not disappeared now," remarked the prince.

"I trust not," answered San Giacinto with a laugh. "I was going to ask you whether I should have your approval if I proposed to marry her."

"This is a very sudden announcement," said Saracinesca with some surprise. "I must think about it. I appreciate your friendly disposition vastly, my dear cousin, in asking my opinion, and I will give the matter my best consideration."

"I shall be very grateful," replied the younger man, gravely. "In my position I feel bound to consult you. I should do so in any case for the mere benefit of your advice, which is very needful to one who, like myself, is but a novice in the ways of Rome."

Saracinesca looked keenly at his cousin, as though expecting to discover some touch of irony in his tone or expression. He remembered the fierce altercations he had engaged in with Giovanni when he had wished the latter to marry Tullia Mayer, and was astonished to find San Giacinto, over whom he had no real authority at all, so docile and anxious for his counsel.

"I suppose you would like to know something about her fortune," he said at last. "Montevarchi is rich, but miserly. He could give her anything he liked."

"Of course it is important to know what he would like to give," replied San Giacinto with a smile.

"Of course. Very well. There are two daughters already married. They each had a hundred thousand scudi. It is not so bad, after all, when you think what a large family he has—but he could have given more. As for Flavia, he might do something generous for the sake of—"

The old gentleman was going to say, for the sake of getting rid of her, and perhaps his cousin thought as much. The prince checked himself, however, and ended his sentence rather awkwardly.

"For the sake of getting such a fine fellow for a husband," he said.

"Why is she not already married?" inquired San Giacinto with a very slight inclination of his head, as an acknowledgment of the flattering speech whereby the prince had helped himself out of his difficulty.

"Who knows!" ejaculated the latter enigmatically.

"Is there any story about her? Was she ever engaged to be married? It is rather strange when one thinks of it, for she is a handsome girl. Pray be quite frank—I have taken no steps in the matter."

"The fact is that I do not know. She is not like other girls, and as she gives her father and mother some trouble in society, I suppose that young men's fathers have been afraid to ask for her. No. I can assure you that there is no story connected with her. She has a way of stating disagreeable truths that terrifies Montevarchi. She was delicate as a child and was brought up at home, so of course she has no manners."

"I should have thought she should have better manners for that," remarked San Giacinto. The prince stared at him in surprise.

"We do not think so here," he answered after a moment's pause. "On the whole, I should say that for a hundred and twenty thousand you might marry her, if you are so inclined—and if you can manage her. But that is a matter for you to judge."

"The Montevarchi are, I believe, what you call a great family?"

"They are not the Savelli, nor the Frangipani—nor the Saracinesca either. But they are a good family—good blood, good fortune, and what Montevarchi calls good principles."

"You think I could not do better than marry Donna Flavia, then?"

"It would be a good marriage, decidedly. You ought to have married Tullia Mayer. If she had not made a fool of herself and an enemy of me, and if you had turned up two years ago—well, there were a good many objections to her, and stories about her, too. But she was rich—eh, that was a fortune to be snapped up by that scoundrel Del Ferice!"

"Del Ferice?" repeated San Giacinto. "The same who tried to prove that your son was married by copying my marriage register?"

"The same. I will tell you the rest of the story some day. Then at that time there was Bianca Valdarno—but she married a Neapolitan last year; and the Rocca girl, but Onorato Cantalupo got her and her dowry—Montevarchi's second son—and—well, I see nobody now, except Flavia's sister Faustina. Why not marry her? It is true that her father means to catch young Frangipani, but he will have no such luck, I can tell him, unless he will part with half a million."

"Donna Faustina is too young," said San Giacinto, calmly. "Besides, as they are sisters and there is so little choice, I may say that I prefer Donna Flavia, she is more gay, more lively."

"Vastly more, I have no doubt, and you will have to look after her, unless you can make her fall in love with you." Saracinesca laughed at the idea.

"With me!" exclaimed San Giacinto, joining in his cousin's merriment. "With me, indeed! A sober widower, between thirty and forty! A likely thing! Fortunately there is no question of love in this matter. I think I can answer for her conduct, however."

"I would not be the man to raise your jealousy!" remarked Saracinesca, laughing again as he looked admiringly at his cousin's gigantic figure and lean stern face. "You are certainly able to take care of your wife. Besides, I have no doubt that Flavia will change when she is married. She is not a bad girl—only a little too fond of making fun of her father and mother, and after all, as far as the old man is concerned, I do not wonder. There is one point upon which you must satisfy him, though—I am not curious, and do not ask you questions, but I warn you that glad as he will be to marry his daughter, he will want to drive a bargain with you and will inquire about your fortune."

San Giacinto was silent for a few moments and seemed to be making a calculation in his head.

"Would a fortune equal to what he gives her be sufficient?" he asked at length.

"Yes. I fancy so," replied the prince looking rather curiously at his cousin. "You see," he continued, "as you have children by your first marriage, Montevarchi would wish to see Flavia's son provided for, if she has one. That is your affair. I do not want to make suggestions."

"I think," said San Giacinto after another short interval of silence, "that I could agree to settle something upon any children which may be born. Do you think some such arrangement would satisfy Prince Montevarchi?"

"Certainly, if you can agree about the terms. Such things are often done in these cases."

"I am very grateful for your advice. May I count upon your good word with the prince, if he asks your opinion?"

"Of course," answered Saracinesca, readily, if not very cordially.

He had not at first liked his cousin, and although he had overcome his instinctive aversion to the man, the feeling was momentarily revived with more than its former force by the prospect of being perhaps called upon to guarantee, in a measure, San Giacinto's character as a suitable husband for Flavia. He had gone too far already however, for since he had given his approval to the scheme it would not become him to withhold his cooperation, should his assistance be in any way necessary in order to bring about the marriage. The slight change of tone as he uttered the last words had not escaped San Giacinto, however. His perceptions were naturally quick and were sharpened by the peculiarities of his present position, so that he understood Saracinesca's unwillingness to have a hand in the matter almost better than the prince understood it himself.

"I trust that I shall not be obliged to ask your help," remarked San Giacinto. "I was, indeed, more anxious for your goodwill than for any more material aid."

"You have it, with all my heart," said Saracinesca warmly, for he was a little ashamed of his coldness.

San Giacinto took his leave and went away well satisfied with what he had accomplished, as indeed he had good cause to be. Montevarchi's consent to the marriage was not doubtful, now that San Giacinto was assured that he was able to fulfil the conditions which would be asked, and the knowledge that he was able to do even more than was likely to be required of him gave him additional confidence in the result. To tell the truth, he was strongly attracted by Flavia; and though he would assuredly have fought with his inclination had it appeared to be misplaced, he was pleased with the prospect of marrying a woman who would not only strengthen his position in society, but for whom he knew that he was capable of a sincere attachment. Marriage, according to his light, was before all things a contract entered into for mutual advantage; but he saw no reason why the fulfilment of such a contract should not be made as agreeable as possible.

The principal point was yet to be gained, however, and as San Giacinto mounted the steps of the Palazzo Montevarchi he stopped more than once, considering for the last time whether he were doing wisely or not. On the whole he determined to proceed, and made up his mind that he would go straight to the point.

Flavia's father was sitting in his study when San Giacinto arrived, and the latter was struck by the contrast between the personalities and the modes of life of his cousin whom he had just left and of the man to whom he was about to propose himself as a son-in-law. The Saracinesca were by no means very luxurious men, but they understood the comforts of existence better than most Romans of that day. If there was massive old-fashioned furniture against the walls and in the corners of the huge rooms, there were on the other hand soft carpets for the feet and cushioned easy-chairs to sit in. There were fires on the hearths when the weather was cold, and modern lamps for the long winter evenings. There were new books on the tables, engravings, photographs, a few objects of value and beauty not jealously locked up in closets, but looking as though they were used, if useful, or at least as if some one derived pleasure from looking at them. The palace itself was a stern old fortress in the midst of the older part of the city, but within there was a genial atmosphere of generous living, and, since Sant' Ilario's marriage with Corona, an air of refinement and good taste such as only a woman can impart to the house in which she dwells.

The residence of the Montevarchi was very different. Narrow strips of carpet were stretched in straight lines across cold marble floors, from one door to another. Instead of open fires in the huge chimney-places, pans of lighted charcoal were set in the dim, empty rooms. Half a dozen halls were furnished alike. Each had three marble tables and twelve straight-backed chairs ranged against the walls, the only variety being that some were covered with red damask and some with green. Vast old-fashioned mirrors, set in magnificent frames built into the wall, reflected vistas of emptiness and acres of cold solitude. Nor were the rooms where the family met much better. There were more tables and more straight-backed chairs there than in the outer halls, but that was all. The drawing-room had a carpet, which for many years had been an object of the greatest concern to the prince, who never left Rome for the months of August and September until he had assured himself that this valuable object had been beaten, dusted, peppered, and sewn up in a linen case as old as itself, that is to say, dating from a quarter of a century back. That carpet was an extravagance to which his father had been driven by his English daughter-in-law; it was the only one of which he had ever been guilty, and the present head of the family meant that it should last his lifetime, and longer too, if care could preserve it. The princess herself had been made to remember for five and twenty years that since she had obtained a carpet she must expect nothing else in the way of modern improvements. It was the monument of a stupendous energy which she had expended entirely in that one struggle, and the sight of it reminded her of her youth. Long ago she had submitted once and for ever to the old Roman ways, and though she knew that a very little saved from the expense of maintaining a score of useless servants and a magnificent show equipage would suffice to make at least one room in the house comfortable for her use, she no longer sighed at the reflection, but consoled herself with making her children put up with the inconveniences she herself had borne so long and so patiently.

Prince Montevarchi's private room was as comfortless as the rest of the house. Narrow, high, dim, carpetless, insufficiently warmed in winter by a brazier of coals, and at present not warmed at all, though the weather was chilly; furnished shabbily with dusty shelves, a writing-table, and a few chairs with leather seats, musty with an ancient mustiness which seemed to be emitted by the rows of old books and the moth-eaten baize cover of the table—the whole place looked more like the office of a decayed notary than the study of a wealthy nobleman of ancient lineage. The old gentleman himself entered the room a few seconds after San Giacinto had been ushered in, having slipped out to change his coat when his visitor was announced. It was a fixed principle of his life to dress as well as his neighbours when they could see him, but to wear threadbare garments whenever he could do so unobserved. He greeted San Giacinto with a grave dignity which contrasted strangely with the weakness and excitement he had shown on the previous night.

"I wish to speak to you upon a delicate subject," began the younger man, after seating himself upon one of the high-backed chairs which cracked ominously under his weight.

"I am at your service," replied the old gentleman, inclining his head politely.

"I feel," continued San Giacinto, "that although my personal acquaintance with you has unfortunately been of short duration, the familiarity which exists between your family and mine will entitle what I have to say to a share of your consideration. The proposal which I have to make has perhaps been made by others before me and has been rejected. I have the honour to ask of you the hand of your daughter."

"Faustina, I suppose?" asked the old prince in an indifferent tone, but looking sharply at his companion out of his small keen eyes.

"Pardon me, I refer to Donna Flavia Montevarchi."

"Flavia?" repeated the prince, in a tone of unmistakable surprise, which however was instantly moderated to the indifferent key again as he proceeded. "You see, we have been thinking so much about my daughter Faustina since last night that her name came to my lips quite naturally."

"Most natural, I am sure," answered San Giacinto; who, however, had understood at once that his suit was to have a hearing. He then remained silent.

"You wish to marry Flavia, I understand," remarked the prince after a pause. "I believe you are a widower, Marchese. I have heard that you have children."

"Two boys."

"Two boys, eh? I congratulate you. Boys, if brought up in Christian principles, are much less troublesome than girls. But, my dear Marchese, these same boys are an obstacle—a very serious obstacle."

"Less serious than you may imagine, perhaps. My fortune does not come under the law of primogeniture. There is no *fidei commissum*. I can dispose of it as I please."

"Eh, eh! But there must be a provision," said Montevarchi, growing interested in the subject.

"That shall be mutual," replied San Giacinto, gravely.

"I suppose you mean to refer to my daughter's portion," returned the other with more indifference. "It is not much, you know—scarcely worth mentioning. I am bound to tell you that, in honour."

"We must certainly discuss the matter, if you are inclined to consider my proposal."

"Well, you know what young women's dowries are in these days, my dear Marchese. We are none of us very rich."

"I will make a proposal," said San Giacinto. "You shall give your daughter a portion. Whatever be the amount, up to a reasonable limit, which you choose to give, I will settle a like sum in such a manner that at my death it shall revert to her, and to her children by me, if she have any."

"That amounts merely to settling upon herself the dowry I give her," replied Montevarchi, sharply. "I give you a scudo for your use. You settle my scudo upon your wife, that is all."

"Not at all," returned San Giacinto. "I do not wish to have control of her dowry—"

"The devil! Oh—I see—how stupid of me—I am indeed so old that I cannot count any more! How could I make such a mistake? Of course, it would be exactly as you say. Of course it would."

"It would not be so as a general rule," said San Giacinto, calmly, "because most men would not consent to such an arrangement. That, however, is my proposal."

"Oh! For the sake of Flavia, a man would do much, I am sure," answered the prince, who began to think that his visitor was in love with the girl, incredible as such a thing appeared to him. The younger man made no answer to this remark, however, and waited for Montevarchi to state his terms.

"How much shall we say?" asked the latter at length.

"That shall be for you to decide. Whatever you give I will give, if I am able."

"Ah, yes! But how am I to know what you are able to give, dear Marchese?" The prince suspected that San Giacinto's offer, if he could be induced to make one, would not be very large.

"Am I to understand," inquired San Giacinto, "that if I name the amount to be settled so that at my death it goes to my wife and her children by me for ever, you will agree to settle a like sum upon Donna Flavia in her own right? If so, I will propose what I think fair."

Montevarchi looked keenly at his visitor for some moments, then looked away and hesitated. He was very anxious to marry Flavia at once, and he had many reasons for supposing that San Giacinto was not very rich.

"How about the title?" he asked suddenly.

"My title, of course, goes to my eldest son by my first marriage. But if you are anxious on that score I think my cousin would willingly confer one of his upon the eldest son of your daughter. It would cost him nothing, and would be a sort of compensation to me for my great-grandfather's folly."

"How?" asked Montevarchi. "I do not understand."

"I supposed you knew the story. I am the direct descendant of the elder branch. There was an agreement between two brothers of the family, by which the elder resigned the primogeniture in favour of the younger who was then married. The elder, who took the San Giacinto title, married late in life and I am his great-grandson. If he had not acted so foolishly I should be in my cousin's shoes. You see it would be natural for him to let me have some disused title for one of my children in consideration of this fact. He has about a hundred, I believe. You could ask him, if you please."

San Giacinto's grave manner assured Montevarchi of the truth of the story. He hesitated a moment longer, and then made up his mind.

"I agree to your proposal, my dear Marchese," he said, with unusual blandness of manner.

"I will settle one hundred and fifty thousand scudi in the way I stated," said San Giacinto, simply. The prince started from his chair.

"One—hundred—and—fifty—thousand!" he repeated slowly. "Why, it is a fortune in itself! Dear me! I had no idea you would name anything so large—"

"Seven thousand five hundred scudi a year, at five per cent," remarked the younger man in a businesslike tone. "You give the same. That will insure our children an income of fifteen thousand scudi. It is not colossal, but it should suffice. Besides, I have not said that I would not leave them more, if I chanced to have more to leave."

The prince had sunk back into his chair, and sat drumming on the table with his long thin fingers. His face wore an air of mingled surprise and bewilderment. To tell the truth, he had expected that San Giacinto would name about fifty thousand as the sum requisite. He did not know whether to be delighted at the prospect of marrying his daughter so well or angry at the idea of having committed himself to part with so much money.

"That is much more than I gave my other daughters," he said at last, in a tone of hesitation.

"Did you give the money to them or to their husbands?" inquired San Giacinto.

"To their husbands, of course."

"Then allow me to point out that you will now be merely settling money in your own family, and that the case is very different. Not only that, but I am settling the same sum upon your family, instead of taking your money for my own use. You are manifestly the gainer by the transaction."

"It would be the same, then, if I left Flavia the money at my death, since it remains in the family," suggested the prince, who sought an escape from his bargain.

"Not exactly," argued San Giacinto. "First there is the yearly interest until your death, which I trust is yet very distant. And then there is the uncertainty of human affairs. It will be necessary that you invest the money in trust, as I shall do, at the time of signing the contract. Otherwise there would be no fairness in the arrangement."

"So you say that you are descended from the elder branch of the Saracinesca. How strange are the ways of Providence, my dear Marchese!"

"It was a piece of great folly on the part of my great-grandfather," replied the other, shrugging his shoulders. "You should never say that a man will not marry until he is dead."

"Ah, no! The ways of heaven are inscrutable! It is not for us poor mortals to attempt to change them. I suppose that agreement of which you speak was made in proper form and quite regular."

"I presume so, since no effort was ever made to change the dispositions established by it."

"I suppose so—I suppose so, dear Marchese. It would be very interesting to see those papers."

"My cousin has them," said San Giacinto. "I daresay he will not object. But, pardon me if I return to a subject which is very near my heart. Do I understand that you consent to the proposal I have made? If so, we might make arrangements for a meeting to take place between our notaries."

"One hundred and fifty thousand," said Montevarchi, slowly rubbing his pointed chin with his bony lingers. "Five per cent—seven thousand five hundred—a mint of money, Signor Marchese, a mint of money! And these are hard times. What a rich man you must be, to talk so lightly about such immense sums! Well, well—you are very eloquent, I must consent, and by strict economy I may perhaps succeed in recovering the loss."

"You must be aware that it is not really a loss," argued San Giacinto, "since it is to remain with your daughter and her children, and consequently with your family."

"Yes, I know. But money is money, my friend," exclaimed the prince, laying his right hand on the old green tablecover and slowly drawing his crooked nails over the cloth, as though he would like to squeeze gold out of the dusty wool. There was something almost fierce in his tone, too, as he uttered the words, and his small eyes glittered unpleasantly. He knew well enough that he was making a good bargain and that San Giacinto was a better match than he had ever hoped to get for Flavia. So anxious was he, indeed, to secure the prize that he entirely abstained from asking any questions concerning San Giacinto's past life, whereby some obstacle might have been raised to the intended marriage. He promised himself that the wedding should take place at once.

"It is understood," he continued, after a pause, "that we or our notaries shall appear with the money in cash, and that it shall be immediately invested as we shall jointly decide, the settlements being made at the same time and on the spot."

"Precisely so," replied San Giacinto. "No money, no contract."

"In that case I will inform my daughter of my decision."

"I shall be glad to avail myself of an early opportunity to pay my respects to Donna Flavia."

"The wedding might take place on the 30th of November, my dear Marchese. The 1st of December is Advent Sunday, and no marriages are permitted during Advent without a special licence."

"An expensive affair, doubtless," remarked San Giacinto, gravely, in spite of his desire to laugh.

"Yes. Five scudi at least," answered Montevarchi, impressively.

"Let us by all means be economical."

"The Holy Church is very strict about these matters, and you may as well keep the money."

"I will," replied San Giacinto, rising to go. "Do not let me detain you any longer. Pray accept my warmest thanks, and allow me to say that I shall consider it a very great honour to become your son-in-law."

"Ah, indeed, you are very good, my dear Marchese. As for me I need consolation. Consider a father's feelings, when he consigns his beloved daughter—Flavia is an angel upon earth, my friend—when, I say, a father gives his dear child, whom he loves as the apple of his eye, to be carried off by a man—a man even of your worth! When your children are grown up, you will understand what I suffer."

"I quite understand," said San Giacinto in serious tones. "It shall be the endeavour of my life to make you forget your loss. May I have the honour of calling tomorrow at this time?"

"Yes, my dear Marchese, yes, my dear son—forgive a father's tenderness. Tomorrow at this time, and—" he hesitated. "And then—some time before the ceremony, perhaps—you will give us the pleasure of your company at breakfast,

I am sure, will you not? We are very simple people, but we are hospitable in our quiet way. Hospitality is a virtue," he sighed a little. "A necessary virtue," he added with some emphasis upon the adjective.

"It will give me great pleasure," replied San Giacinto.

Therewith he left the room and a few moments later was walking slowly homewards, revolving in his mind the probable results of his union with the Montevarchi family.

When Montevarchi was alone, he smiled pleasantly to himself, and took out of a secret drawer a large book of accounts, in the study of which he spent nearly half an hour, with evident satisfaction. Having carefully locked up the volume, and returned the sliding panel to its place, he sent for his wife, who presently appeared.

"Sit down, Guendalina," he said. "I will change my coat, and then I have something important to say to you."

He had quite forgotten the inevitable change in his satisfaction over the interview with San Giacinto, but the sight of the princess recalled the necessity for economy. It had been a part of the business of his life to set her a good example in this respect. When he came back he seated himself before her.

"My dear, I have got a husband for Flavia," were his first words.

"At last!" exclaimed the princess. "I hope he is presentable," she added. She knew that she could trust her husband in the matter of fortune.

"The new Saracinesca—the Marchese di San Giacinto."

Princess Montevarchi's ruddy face expressed the greatest astonishment, and her jaw dropped as she stared at the old gentleman.

"A pauper!" she exclaimed when she had recovered herself enough to speak.

"Perhaps, Guendalina mia—but he settles a hundred and fifty thousand scudi on Flavia and her heirs for ever, the money to be paid on the signing of the contract. That does not look like pauperism. Of course, under the circumstances I agreed to do the same. It is settled on Flavia, do you understand? He does not want a penny of it, not a penny! Trust your husband for a serious man of business, Guendalina."

"Have you spoken to Flavia? It certainly looks like a good match. There is no doubt about his being of the Saracinesca, of course. How could there be? They have taken him to their hearts. But how will Flavia behave?"

"What a foolish question, my dear!" exclaimed Montevarchi. "How easily one sees that you are English! She will be delighted, I presume. And if not, what difference does it make?"

"I would not have married you against my will, Lotario," observed the princess.

"For my part, I had no choice. My dear father said simply, 'My son, you will pay your respects to that young lady, who is to be your wife. If you wish to marry anyone else, I will lock you up.' And so I did. Have I not been a faithful husband to you, Guendalina, through more than thirty years?"

The argument was unanswerable, and Montevarchi had employed it each time one of his children was married. In respect of faithfulness, at least, he had been a model husband.

"It is sufficient," he added, willing to make a concession to his wife's foreign notions, "that there should be love on the one side, and Christian principles on the other. I can assure you that San Giacinto is full of love, and as for Flavia, my dear, has she not been educated by you?"

"As for Flavia's Christian principles, my dear Lotario, I only hope they may suffice for her married life. She is a terrible child to have at home. But San Giacinto looks like a determined man. I shall never forget his kindness in searching for Faustina last night. He was devotion itself, and I should not have been surprised had he wished to marry her instead."

"That exquisite creature is reserved for a young friend of ours, Guendalina. Do me the favour never to speak of her marrying anyone else."

The princess was silent for a moment, and then began to make a series of inquiries concerning the proposed bridegroom, which it is unnecessary to recount.

"And now we will send for Flavia," said Montevarchi, at last.

"Would it not be best that I should tell her?" asked his wife.

"My dear," he replied sternly, "when matters of grave importance have been decided it is the duty of the head of the house to communicate the decision to the persons concerned."

So Flavia was sent for, and appeared shortly, her pretty face and wicked black eyes expressing both surprise and anticipation. She was almost as dark as San Giacinto himself, though of a very different type. Her small nose had an upward turn which disturbed her mother's ideas of the fitness of things, and her thick black hair waved naturally over her forehead. Her figure was graceful and her movements quick and spontaneous. The redness of her lips showed a strong vitality, which was further confirmed by the singular brightness of her eyes. She was no beauty, especially in a land where the dark complexion predominates, but she was very pretty and possessed something of that mysterious quality which charms without exciting direct admiration.

"Flavia," said her father, addressing her in solemn tones, "you are to be married, my dear child. I have sent for you at once, because there was no time to be lost, seeing that the wedding must take place before the beginning of Advent. The news will probably give you pleasure, but I trust you will reflect upon the solemnity of such engagements and lay aside—"

"Would you mind telling me the name of my husband?" inquired Flavia, interrupting the paternal lecture.

"The man I have selected for my son-in-law is one whom all women would justly envy you, were it not that envy is an atrocious sin, and one which I trust you will henceforth endeavour—"

"To drown, crush out and stamp upon in the pursuit of true Christian principles," said Flavia with a laugh. "I know all about envy. It is one of the seven deadlies. I can tell you them all, if you like."

"Flavia, I am amazed!" cried the princess, severely.

"I had not expected this conduct of my daughter," said Montevarchi. "And though I am at present obliged to overlook it, I can certainly not consider it pardonable. You will listen with becoming modesty and respect to what I have to say."

"I am all modesty, respect and attention—but I would like to know his name, papa—please consider that pardonable!"

"I do not know why I should not tell you that, and I shall certainly give you all such information concerning him as it is proper that you should receive. The fact that he is a widower need not surprise you, for in the inscrutable ways of Providence some men are deprived of their wives sooner than others. Nor should his age appear to you in the light of an obstacle—indeed there are no obstacles—"

"A widower—old—probably bald—I can see him already. Is he fat, papa?"

"He approaches the gigantic; but as I have often told you, Flavia, the qualities a wise father should seek in choosing a husband for his child are not dependent upon outward—"

"For heaven's sake, mamma," cried Flavia, "tell me the creature's name!"

"The Marchese di San Giacinto. Let your father speak. Do not interrupt him."

"While you both insist on interrupting me," said Montevarchi, "it is impossible for me to express myself."

"I wish it were!" observed Flavia, under her breath. "You are speaking of the Saracinesca cousin, San Giacinto? Not so bad after all."

"It is very unbecoming in a young girl to speak of men by their last names—"

"Giovanni, then. Shall I call him Giovanni?"

"Flavia!" exclaimed the princess. "How can you be so undutiful! You should speak of him as the Marchese di San Giacinto."

"Silence!" cried the prince. "I will not be interrupted! The Marchese di San Giacinto will call tomorrow, after breakfast, and will pay his respects to you. You will receive him in a proper spirit."

"Yes, papa," replied Flavia, suddenly growing meek, and folding her hands submissively.

"He has behaved with unexampled liberality," continued Montevarchi, "and I need hardly say that as the honour of our house was concerned I have not allowed myself to be outdone. Since you refuse to listen to the words of fatherly instruction which it is natural I should speak on this occasion, you will at least remember that your future husband is entirely such a man as I would have chosen, that he is a Saracinesca, as well as a rich man, and that he has been accustomed in the women of his family to a greater refinement of manner than you generally think fit to exhibit in the presence of your father."

"Yes, papa. May I go, now?"

"If your conscience will permit you to retire without a word of gratitude to your parents, who in spite of the extreme singularities of your behaviour have at last provided you with a suitable husband; if, I say, you are capable of such ingratitude, then, Flavia, you may certainly go."

"I was going to say, papa, that I thank you very much for my husband, and mamma, too."

Thereupon she kissed her father's and her mother's hands with great reverence and turned to leave the room. Her gravity forsook her, however, before she reached the door.

"Evviva! Hurrah!" she cried, suddenly skipping across the intervening space and snapping her small fingers like a pair of castanets. "Evviva! Married at last! Hurrah!" And with this parting salute she disappeared.

When she was gone, her father and mother looked at each other, as they had looked many times before in the course of Flavia's life. They had found little difficulty in bringing up their other children, but Flavia was a mystery to them both. The princess would have understood well enough a thorough English girl, full of life and animal spirits, though shy and timid in the world, as the elderly lady had herself been in her youth. But Flavia's character was incomprehensible to her northern soul. Montevarchi understood the girl better, but loved her even less. What seemed odd in her to his wife, to him seemed vulgar and ill-bred, for he would have had her like the rest, silent and respectful in his presence, and in awe of him as the head of the house, if not in fact, at least in manner. But Flavia's behaviour was in the eyes of Romans a very serious objection to her as a wife for any of their sons, for in their view moral worth was necessarily accompanied by outward gravity and decorum, and a light manner could only be the visible sign of a giddy heart.

"If only he does not find out what she is like!" exclaimed the princess at last.

"I devoutly trust that heaven in its mercy may avert such a catastrophe from our house," replied Montevarchi, who, however, seemed to be occupied in adding together certain sums upon his fingers.

San Giacinto understood Flavia better than either of her parents; and although his marriage with her was before all things a part of his plan for furthering his worldly interests, it must be confessed that he had a stronger liking for the girl than her father would have considered indispensable in such affairs. The matter was decided at once, and in a few days the preliminaries were settled between the lawyers, while Flavia exerted the utmost pressure possible upon the parental purse in the question of the trousseau.

It may seem strange that at the time when all Rome was convulsed by an internal revolution, and when the temporal power appeared to be in very great danger, Montevarchi and San Giacinto should have been able to discuss so coolly the conditions of the marriage, and even to fix the wedding day. The only possible explanation of this fact is that neither of them believed in the revolution at all. It is a noticeable characteristic of people who are fond of money that they do not readily believe in any great changes. They are indeed the most conservative of men, and will count their profits at moments of peril with a coolness which would do honour to veteran soldiers. Those who possess money put their faith in money and give no credence to rumours of revolution which are not backed by cash. Once or twice in history they have been wrong, but it must be confessed that they have very generally been right.

As for San Giacinto, his own interests were infinitely more absorbing to his attention than those of the world at large, and being a man of uncommonly steady nerves, it seems probable that he would have calmly pursued his course in the midst of much greater disturbances than those which affected Rome at that time.

CHAPTER VIII

WHEN Anastase Gouache was at last relieved from duty and went home in the gray dawn of the twenty-third, he lay down to rest expecting to reflect upon the events of the night. The last twelve hours had been the most eventful of his life; indeed less than that time had elapsed since he had bid farewell to Faustina in the drawing-room of the Palazzo Saracinesca, and yet the events which had occurred in that short space had done much towards making him another man. The change had begun two years earlier, and had progressed slowly until it was completed all at once by a chain of unforeseen circumstances. He realised the fact, and as this change was not disagreeable to him he set himself to think about it. Instead of reviewing what had happened, however, he did what was much more natural in his case, he turned upon his pillow and fell fast asleep. He was younger than his years, though he counted less than thirty, and his happy nature had not yet formed that horrible habit of wakefulness which will not yield even to bodily fatigue. He lay down and slept like a boy, disturbed by no dreams and troubled by no shadowy revival of dangers or emotions past.

He had placed a gulf between himself and his former life. What had passed between him and Faustina might under other circumstances have become but a romantic episode in the past, to be thought of with a certain tender regret, half fatuous, half genuine, whenever the moonlight chanced to cast the right shadow and the artist's mind was in the contemplative mood. The peculiar smell of broken masonry, when it is a little damp, would recall the impression, perhaps; an old wall knocked to pieces by builders would, through his nostrils, bring vividly before him that midnight meeting amid the ruins of the barracks, just as the savour of a certain truffle might bring back the memory of a supper at Voisin's, or as, twenty years hence, the pasty grittiness of rough maize bread would make him remember the days when he was chasing brigands in the Samnite hills. But this was not to be the case this time. There was more matter for reminiscence than a ray of moonlight on a fair face, or the smell of crumbling mortar.

There was a deep and sincere devotion on both sides, in two persons both singularly capable of sincerity, and both foresaw that the result of this love could never be indifference. The end could only be exceeding happiness, or mortal sorrow. Anastase and Faustina were not only themselves in earnest; each knew instinctively that the other would be faithful, a condition extremely rare in ordinary cases. Each recognised that the obstacles were enormous, but neither doubted for a moment that means would be found to overcome them.

In some countries the marriage of these two would have been a simple matter enough. A man of the world, honourable, successful, beginning to be famous, possessed of some fortune, might aspire to marry any one he pleased in lands where it is not a disgrace to have acquired the means of subsistence by one's own talent and industry. Artists and poets have sometimes made what are called great marriages. But in Rome, twenty years ago, things were very different. It is enough to consider the way in which Montevarchi arranged to dispose of his daughter Flavia to understand the light in which he would have regarded Faustina's marriage with Anastase Gouache. The very name of Gouache would have raised a laugh in the Montevarchi household had any one suggested that a woman of that traditionally correct race could ever make it her own. There were persons in Rome, indeed, who might have considered the matter more leniently. Corona Sant' Ilario was one of these; but her husband and father-in-law would have opened their eyes as wide as old Lotario Montevarchi himself, had the match been discussed before them. Their patriarchally exclusive souls would have been shocked and the dear fabric of their inborn prejudices shaken to its deepest foundations. It was bad enough, from the point of view of potential matrimony, to earn money, even if one had the right to prefix "Don" to one's baptismal name. But to be no Don and to receive coin for one's labour was a far more insurmountable barrier against intermarriage with the patriarchs than hereditary madness, toothless old age, leprosy, or lack of money.

Gouache had acquired enough knowledge of Roman life to understand this, and nothing short of physical exhaustion would have prevented his spending his leisure in considering the means of overcoming such stupendous difficulties. When he awoke his situation presented itself clearly enough to his mind, however, and occupied his thoughts throughout the remainder of the day. Owing to the insurrection his departure was delayed for twenty-four hours, and his duty was likely to keep him busily engaged during the short time that remained to him. The city was in a state of siege and there would be a perpetual service of patrols, sentries and general maintenance of order. The performance of labours almost mechanical left him plenty of time for reflection, though he found it hard to spare a moment in which to see any of his friends.

He was very anxious to meet the Princess Sant' Ilario, whose conduct on the previous night had seriously alarmed him. It was to her that he looked for assistance in his troubles and the consciousness that she was angry with him was a chief source of distress. In the course of the few words he had exchanged with her, she had made it sufficiently clear to him that although she disapproved in principle of his attachment to Faustina, she would do nothing to hinder his marriage if he should be able to overcome the obstinacy of the girl's parents. He was at first at a loss to explain her severity to him when she had left her house to take Faustina home. Being wholly innocent of any share in the latter's mad course, it did not at first enter his mind that Corona could attribute to him any blame in the matter. On the contrary, he knew that if the girl's visit to the ruined barracks remained a secret, this would be owing quite as much to his own discretion and presence of mind as to the princess's willingness to help him. Not a little, too, was due to good luck, since the least difference in the course of events must have led to immediate discovery.

A little thought led him to a conclusion which wounded his pride while it explained Corona's behaviour. It was evident that she had believed in a clandestine meeting, prearranged between the lovers at the instigation of Gouache himself, and she had probably supposed this meeting to be only the preliminary to a runaway match. How, indeed, could Faustina have expected to escape observation, even had there been no revolution in Rome, that night? Corona clearly thought that the girl had never intended to come back, that Gouache had devised means for their departure, and that Faustina had believed the elopement possible in the face of the insurrection. Anastase, on finding himself in the small hours of the morning with Faustina on his hands and knowing that discovery must follow soon after day-break, had boldly brought her to the Palazzo Saracinesca and had demanded Corona's assistance.

As the artist thought the matter over, he became more and more convinced that he had understood the princess's conduct, and the reflection made him redden with shame and anger. He determined to seize the first moment that presented itself for an explanation with the woman who had wronged him. He unexpectedly found himself at liberty towards five o'clock in the afternoon and made haste at once to reach the Palazzo Saracinesca. Knowing that no one would be allowed to be in the streets after dark, he felt sure of finding Corona without visitors, and expected the most favourable opportunity for talking over the subject which distressed him.

After waiting several minutes in one of the outer halls he was ushered in, and to his extreme annoyance found himself in the midst of a family party. He had not counted upon the presence of the men of the household, and the fact that the baby was also present did not facilitate matters. Old Saracinesca greeted him warmly; Sant' Ilario looked grave; Corona herself looked up from her game with little Orsino, nodded and uttered a word of recognition, and then returned to her occupation.

Conversation under these circumstances was manifestly impossible, and Gouache wished he had not had the unlucky idea of calling. There was nothing to be done, however, but to put on a brave face and make the best of it.

"Well, Monsieur Gouache," inquired the old prince, "and how did you spend the night?"

He could scarcely have asked a question better calculated to disturb the composure of everyone present except the baby. Anastase could not help looking at Corona, who looked instinctively at her husband, while the latter gazed at Gouache, wondering what he would say. All three turned a shade paler, and during a very few seconds there was an awkward silence.

"I spent the night very uncomfortably," replied Anastase, after hesitating a little. "We were driven from pillar to post, repelling attacks, doing sentry duty, clearing the streets, marching and countermarching. It was daylight when I was relieved."

"Indeed!" exclaimed Sant' Ilario. "I had supposed that you had remained all night at the Porta San Paolo. But there are many contradictory accounts. I was in some anxiety until I was assured that you had not been blown up in that infernal plot."

Gouache was on the point of asking who had told Giovanni that he had escaped, but fortunately checked himself, and endeavoured to turn the conversation to the disaster at the barracks. Thereupon old Saracinesca, whose blood was roused by the atrocity, delivered a terrible anathema against the murderous wretches who had ruined the building, and expressed himself in favour of burning them alive, a fate, indeed, far too good for them. Anastase profited by the old gentleman's eloquence to make advances to the baby. Little Orsino, however, struck him a vigorous blow in the face with his tiny fist and yelled lustily.

"He does not like strangers," remarked Corona, coldly. She rose with the child in her arms and moved towards the door, Gouache following her with the intention of opening it for her to go out. The prince was still thundering out curses against the conspirators, and Anastase attempted to say a word unobserved as Corona passed him.

"Will you not give me a hearing?" he asked in a low tone, accompanying his words with an imploring look.

Corona raised her eyebrows slightly as though surprised, but his expression of genuine contrition softened her heart a little and rendered her answer perhaps a trifle less unkind than she had meant it to be.

"You should be satisfied—since I keep your secret," she said, and passed quickly out.

When Gouache turned after closing the door he was aware that Sant' Ilario had been watching him, by the fixed way in which he was now looking in another direction. The Zouave wished more and more fervently that he had not come to the house, but resolved to prolong his visit in the hope that Corona might return. Sant' Ilario was unaccountably silent, but his father kept up a lively conversation, needing only an occasional remark from Gouache to give a fillip to his eloquence.

This situation continued during nearly half an hour, at the end of which time Anastase gave up all hope of seeing Corona again. The two men evidently did not expect her to return, for they had made themselves comfortable and had lighted their cigarettes.

"Good-bye, Monsieur Gouache," said the old prince, cordially shaking him by the hand. "I hope we shall see you back again alive and well in a few days."

While he was speaking Giovanni had rung the bell for the servant to show the visitor out, an insignificant action destined to produce a rather singular result. Sant' Ilario himself, feeling that after all he might never see Gouache alive again, repented a little of his coldness, and while the latter stood ready to go, detained him with a question as to his destination on leaving the city. This resulted in a lively discussion of Garibaldi's probable movements, which lasted several minutes.

Corona in the meantime had taken Orsino back to his nurse, and had bidden her maid let her know when the visitor in the drawing-room was gone. The woman went to the hall, and when Giovanni rang the bell, returned to inform her mistress of the fact, supposing that Gouache would go at once. Corona waited a few minutes, and then went back to the sitting-room, which was at the end of the long suite of apartments. The result was that she met Anastase in one of the rooms on his way out, preceded by the footman, who went on towards the hall after his mistress had passed. Corona and Gouache were left face to face and quite alone in the huge dim drawing-room. Gouache had found his opportunity and did not hesitate.

"Madame," he said, "I beg your pardon for trespassing on your time, but I have a serious word to say. I am going to the frontier and am as likely to be killed as any one else. On the faith of a man who may be dead tomorrow, I am wholly innocent of what happened last night. If I come back I will prove it to you some day. If not, will you believe me, and not think of me unkindly?"

Corona hesitated and stood leaning against the heavy curtain of a window for a moment. Though the room was very dim, she could see the honest look in the young man's eyes and she hesitated before she answered. She had heard that day that two of her acquaintances had fallen fighting against the Garibaldians and she knew that Anastase was speaking of a very near possibility when he talked of being killed. There were many chances that he was telling the truth, and she felt how deeply she should regret her unbelief if he should indeed meet his fate before they met again.

"You tell me a strange thing," she said at last. "You ask me to believe that this poor girl, of her own free will and out of love for you, followed you out of this room last night into the midst of a revolution. It is a hard thing to believe—"

"And yet I implore you to believe it, princess. A man who should love her less than I, would be the basest of men to speak thus of her love. God knows, if things had been otherwise, I would not have let you know. But was there any other way of taking her home? Did I not do the only thing that was at all possible to keep last night's doings a secret? I love her to such a point that I glory in her love for me. If I could have shielded her last night by giving up my life, you know that I would have ended my existence that very moment. It would have done no good. I had to confide in some one, and you, who knew half my secret, since I had told you I loved her, were the only person who could be allowed to guess the remainder. If it could profit her that you should think me a villain, you might think me so—even you, whom I reverence beyond all women save her. But to let you think so would be to degrade her, and that you shall not do. You shall not think that she has been so foolish as to pin her faith on a man who would lead her to destruction—ah, if I loved her less I could tell you better what I mean!"

Corona was moved by his sincerity, if not by his arguments. She saw all the strangeness of the situation; how he had been forced to confide in some one, and how it seemed better in his eyes that she should know how Faustina had really behaved, than think that the young girl had agreed to a premeditated meeting. She was touched and her heart relented.

"I believe you," she said. "Forgive me if I have wronged you."

"Thank you, thank you, dear princess!" cried Gouache, taking her hand and touching it with his lips. "I can never thank you as I would. And now, good-bye—I am going. Will you give me your blessing, as my mother would?" He smiled, as he recalled the conversation of the previous evening.

"Good-bye," answered Corona. "May all blessings go with you." He turned away and she stood a moment looking after him as he disappeared in the gloom.

She was sorry for him in her heart and repented a little of having treated him so harshly. And yet, as soon as he was gone she began to doubt again, wondering vaguely whether she had not been deceived. There was an odd fascination about the soldier-artist which somehow influenced her in his favour when he was present, and of which she was not conscious until he was out of her sight. Now that she was alone, she found herself considering how this peculiar charm which he possessed would be likely to affect a young girl like Faustina, and she was obliged to acknowledge that it would account well enough for the latter's foolish doings. She could not look into Gouache's eyes and doubt what he said, but she found it hard afterwards to explain the faith she put in him.

She was roused from her short reflection by her husband who, without being observed by her, had come to her side. Seeing that she did not return to the sitting-room when Gouache was gone he had come in search of her, and by the merest chance had overheard the last words which had passed between her and Anastase, and had seen how the latter fervently kissed her hand. The phrase in which she had wished him good luck rang unpleasantly in his ears and startled the inmost sensibilities of his nature. He remembered how she had blessed him once, in her calm, gentle way, on that memorable night of the Frangipani ball nearly three years before, and there was a similarity between the words she had used then and the simple expression which had now fallen from her lips.

Giovanni stood beside her now and laid his hand upon her arm. It was not his nature to break out suddenly as his father did, when anything occurred to disturb his peace of mind. The Spanish blood he had inherited from his mother had imparted a profound reserve to his character, which gave it depth rather than coldness. It was hard for him to speak out violently when under the influence of emotion, but this very difficulty of finding words and his aversion to using them made him more sincere, more enduring and less forgiving than other men. He could wait long before he gave vent to his feelings, but they neither grew cool nor dull for the waiting. He detested concealment and secrecy more than most people, but his disinclination to speak of any matter until he was sure of it had given him the reputation of being both reticent and calculating. Giovanni now no longer concealed from himself the fact that he was annoyed by what was passing, but he denied, even in his heart, that he was jealous. To doubt Corona would be to upset the whole fabric of his existence, which he had founded upon her love and which had been built up to such great proportions during the past three years. His first impulse was to ask an explanation, and it carried him just far enough to lay his hand on his wife's arm, when it was checked by a multitude of reflections and unconscious arguments which altogether changed his determination.

"I thought he was gone," he said, quietly enough.

"So did I," replied Corona, in a cooler tone than she generally used in speaking to her husband.

She, too, was annoyed, for she suspected that Giovanni had been watching her; and since, on the previous evening he had promised to trust her altogether in this affair, she looked upon his coming almost in the light of an infringement upon the treaty, and resented it accordingly. She did not reflect that it was unlikely that Giovanni should expect her to try to meet Gouache on his way out, and would therefore not think of lying in wait for her. His accidental coming seemed premeditated. He, on his side, had noticed her marked coldness to

Anastase in the sitting-room and thought it contrasted very strangely with the over-friendly parting of which he had chanced to be a witness. Corona, too, knew very well that the last words spoken were capable of misinterpretation, and as she had no intention of telling her husband Faustina's story at present she saw no way of clearing up the situation, and therefore prepared to ignore it altogether.

They turned together and walked slowly back in the direction of the sitting-room, neither speaking a word until they had almost reached the door. Then Giovanni stopped and looked at his wife.

"Is it part of last night's secret?" he asked, almost indifferently.

"Yes," answered Corona. "What could you suppose it was? I met him by accident and we exchanged a few words."

"I know. I heard you say good-bye. I confess I was surprised. I thought you meant to be rude to him when we were all together, but I was mistaken. I hope your blessing will profit him, my dear!" He spoke quite naturally and without effort.

"I hope so too," returned Corona. "You might have added yours, since you were present."

"To tell the truth," said Giovanni, with a short laugh, "I fancy it might not have been so acceptable."

"You talk very strangely, Giovanni!"

"Do I? It seems to me quite natural. Shall we go into the sitting-room?"

"Giovanni—you promised to trust me last night, and I promised to explain everything to you some day. You must keep your promise wholly or not at all."

"Certainly," answered Sant' Ilario, opening the door for his wife and thus forcing the conversation to end suddenly, since old Saracinesca must now hear whatever was said.

He would not allow the situation to last, for fear lest he should say something of which he might repent, for in spite of his words he did not wish to seem suspicious. Unfortunately, Corona's evident annoyance at having been overheard did more to strengthen the feeling of resentment which was growing in him than what he had heard and seen a few moments earlier. The way in which she had reproached him with not adding his blessing to hers showed plainly enough, he thought, that she was angry at what had occurred. They both entered the room, but before they had been long together Giovanni left his wife and father and retired to his own room under pretext of writing letters until dinner-time.

When he was alone, the situation presented itself to his mind in a very dis-agreeable light. Corona's assurance that the mystery was a harmless one seemed wholly inadequate to account for her meeting with Gouache and for her kind treatment of him, especially after she had shown herself so evidently cold to him in the presence of the others. Either Giovanni was a very silly fellow, or he was being deceived as no man was ever deceived before. Either conclusion was exasperating. He asked himself whether he were such a fool as to invent a mis-construction upon occurrences which to any one else would have seemed void of any importance whatsoever; and his heart answered that if he were indeed so senseless he must have lost his intelligence very recently. On the other hand to suspect Corona of actually entertaining a secret passion for Gouache was an hypothesis which seemed too monstrous to be discussed. He sat down to think about it, and was suddenly startled by the host of little circumstances which all at once detached themselves from the hazy past and stood out in condemnation of his wife. Gouache, as he himself had acknowledged, had long worshipped the princess in a respectful, almost reverential way. He had taken every occasion of talking with her, and had expressed even by his outward manner a degree of devotion he never manifested to other women. Giovanni was now aware that for some time past, even as far back as the previous winter, he had almost uncon-sciously watched Corona and Anastase when they were together. Nothing in her conduct had excited his suspicions in the least, but he had certainly suspected that Gouache was a little inclined to idolise her, and had laughed to himself more than once at the idea of the French artist's hopeless passion, with some-thing of that careless satisfaction a man feels who sees a less favoured mortal in dangerous proximity to a flame which burns only for himself. It was rather a contemptible amusement, and Giovanni had never indulged in it very long. He liked Gouache, and, if anything, pitied him for his hopeless passion. Corona treated the Zouave in her grand, quiet way, which had an air of protection with it, and Giovanni would have scoffed at the thought that she cared for the man. Nevertheless, now that matters had taken such a strange turn, he recollected with surprise that Gouache was undeniably the one of all their acquaintance who most consistently followed Corona wherever they met. The young man was a favourite in society. His great talent, his modesty, and above all what people were pleased to describe as his harmlessness, made everybody like him. He went everywhere, and his opportunities of meeting the princess were almost numberless. Giovanni had certainly watched him very often, though he was hardly conscious of having bestowed so much attention on the French artist-soldier, that he never failed to glance at his wife when Anastase was mentioned.

Now, and all at once, a hundred details rushed to his recollection, and he was staggered by the vista of incidents that rose before his mind. Within the last twenty-four hours, especially, the evidence had assumed terrible proportions. In the first place there had been that scene in the drawing-room, enacted quietly enough and in a corner, while there were twenty persons present, but with the coolness of two people of the world who know what surprising things may be done unobserved in a room full of people. If Anastase had kissed Corona's hand a little differently, and with the evident intention of being seen, the action would have been natural. But there was a look in Gouache's face which Giovanni remembered, and an expression of kindness in Corona's eyes that he had not forgotten; above all they had both seemed as though they were sure that no one was watching them. Indeed, Sant' Ilario now asked himself how he had chanced to see what passed, and the only answer was that he generally watched them when they were together. This was a revelation to himself, and told much. Then there was her midnight expedition with Gouache, a far more serious matter. After all, he had only Corona's own assurance that Faustina Montevarchi had been in any way concerned in that extraordinary piece of rashness. He must indeed have had faith in his wife to pass over such conduct without a word of explanation. Next came the events of that very afternoon. Corona had been rude to Gouache, had then suddenly left the room, and in passing out had exchanged a few words with him in a low tone. She had met him again by accident, if it had been an accident, and fancying herself unseen had behaved very differently to the young man. There had been a parting which savoured unpleasantly of the affectionate, and which was certainly something more than merely friendly. Lastly, Corona had evidently been annoyed at Giovanni's appearance, a fact which seemed to conclude the whole argument with a terrible certainty.

Finding himself face to face with a conclusion which threatened to destroy his happiness altogether, Giovanni started up from his chair and began to walk backwards and forwards in the room, pausing a moment each time he turned, as though to gather strength, or to shake off an evil thought. In the light of his present reflections an explanation seemed inevitable, but when he thought of that he saw too clearly that any explanation must begin by his accusing his wife, and he knew that if he accused her justly, it would only end in a denial from her. What woman, however guilty, would not deny her guilt when charged with it. What man either, where love was concerned? Giovanni laughed bitterly, then turned pale and sat down again. To accuse Corona of loving Gouache! It was too monstrous to be believed. And yet—what did all those doings mean? There must be a reason for them. If he called her and told her what he felt, and if she were innocent, she would tell him all, everything would be explained, and he would doubtless see that all this damning evidence was no more than the natural outward appearance of perfectly harmless circumstances of which he knew nothing. Ay, but if they were harmless, why should she implore him to ask no questions? Because the honour of some one else was concerned, of course. But was he, Giovanni Saracinesca, not to be trusted with the keeping of that other person's honour as well as Corona herself? Had they ever had secrets from each other? Would it not have been simpler for her to trust him with the story, if she was innocent, than to be silent and ask him to trust her motives? Far simpler, of course. And then, if only a third person's feelings were at stake, what necessity had there been for such a sentimental parting? She had given Gouache a blessing very like the one she had given Giovanni. Worst of all, were not the circumstances the same, the very same?

Giovanni remembered the Frangipani ball. At that time Corona was married to Astrardente, who had died a few days afterwards. Giovanni had that night told Corona that he loved her, in very passionate terms. She had silenced him, and he had behaved like a gentleman, for he had asked her pardon for what he had done. She had forgiven him, and to show that she bore no malice had spoken a kind of benediction—a prayer that all might be well with him. He knew now that she had loved him even then when she repelled him.

And now that she was married to Giovanni, another had come, and had talked with her, and exchanged words in a low tone even as he himself had once done. And she had treated this man roughly before her husband, and presently afterwards had allowed him to kiss her hand and had sent him away saying that she forgave him—just as she had formerly forgiven Giovanni—and praying that all blessings might go with him. Why was it not possible that she loved this man, too? Because she was so grandly beautiful, and dark and calm, and had such a noble fearlessness in her eyes? Other women had been beautiful and had deceived wiser men than Giovanni, and had fallen. Beauty was no argument for the defence, nor brave eyes, nor the magnificent dignity of movement and speech—nor words either, for that matter.

Suspense was agony, and yet a twofold horror seemed the only issue, the one inevitable, the other possible. First, to accuse this woman whom he loved so dearly, and then, perhaps, to hear her deny the charge boldly and yet refuse all explanation. Once more Giovanni rose from his deep chair and paced his room with regular strides, though he scarcely saw the carpet under his feet, nor realised any longer where he was. At last he stopped and laughed. The sound was strange and false, as when a man tries to be merry who feels no mirth.

He was making a desperate effort to shake off this nightmare that beset him, to say to himself that he was but a fool, and that there was no cause for all this suffering which he was inflicting on his heart, nor for all these questions he had been asking of his intelligence. It was surely not true! He would laugh now, would laugh heartily within the next half hour with Corona herself, at the mere thought of supposing that she could love Gouache, Gouache, a painter! Gouache, a Zouave! Gouache, a contemptibly good-natured, harmless little foreigner!— and Corona del Carmine, Duchessa d'Astrardente, Principessa di Sant' Ilario, mother of all the Saracinesca yet to come! It was better to laugh, truly, at such an absurd juxtaposition of ideas, of personalities, of high and low. And Giovanni laughed, but the sound, was very harsh and died away without rousing one honest echo in the vaulted room.

Had Corona seen his face at that moment, or had she guessed what was passing in his mind, she would have sacrificed Faustina's secret ten times over rather than let Giovanni suffer a moment longer as he was suffering now. But Corona had no idea that he could put such a construction upon her doings. He had shown her nothing of what he felt, except perhaps a slight annoyance at not being put in possession of the secret. It was natural, she thought, that he should be a little out of temper, but as she saw no way of remedying the trouble except by exposing to him the innocent girl whom she had undertaken to protect, she held her peace and trusted that her husband's displeasure would soon be past. Had there been more time for reflection on the previous evening, in the interval between her learning from the porter that Giovanni knew of her absence, and her being confronted with Giovanni himself, she might have resolved to act differently; but having once made up her mind that he ought not to know the truth for the present, opposition only strengthened her determination. There was nothing wrong in the course she was pursuing, or her conscience would have spoken and bidden her speak out. Her nature was too like Giovanni's own, proud, reserved, and outwardly cold, to yield any point easily. It was her instinct, like his, to be silent rather than to speak, and to weigh considerations before acting upon them. This very similarity of temper in the two rendered it certain that if they were ever opposed to each other the struggle would be a serious one. They were both too strong to lead a life of petty quarrelling; if they ceased to live in perfect harmony they were only too sure to come to open hostility. There is nothing which will wound pride and raise anger so inevitably as finding unexpected but determined opposition in those who very closely resemble ourselves. In such a case a man cannot fall back upon the comfortable alternative of despising his enemy, since he has an intimate conviction that it would be paramount to despising himself; and if he is led into a pitched battle he will find his foe possessed of weapons which are exactly like his own.

Giovanni and Corona were very evenly matched, as nearly resembling each other as is possible for a man and a woman. Corona was outwardly a little the colder, Giovanni a little the more resentful of the two. Corona had learned during the years of her marriage with Astrardente to wear a mask of serene indifference, and the assumed habit had at last become in some degree a part of her nature. Giovanni, whose first impulses had originally been quicker than they now were, had learned the power of waiting by constant intercourse with his father, whose fiery temper seemed to snatch at trifles for the mere pleasure of tearing them to pieces, and did injustice to the generous heart he concealed under his rough exterior.

Under these circumstances it was not probable that Sant' Ilario would make any exhibition of his jealousy for some time to come. As he paced the floor of his room, the bitterness of his situation slowly sank from the surface, leaving his face calm and almost serene. He forced himself to look at the facts again and again, trying bravely to be impartial and to survey them as though he were the judge and not the plaintiff. He admitted at last that there was undoubtedly abundant matter for jealousy, but Corona still stood protected as it were by the love he bore her, a love which even her guilt would be unable to destroy. His love indeed, must outlast everything, all evil, all disgrace, and he knew it. He thought of that Latin poet who, writing to his mistress, said in the bitterness of his heart that though she were to become the best woman in the world he could never again respect her, but that he could not cease to love her, were she guilty of all crimes. He knew that if the worst turned out true that must be his case, and perhaps for the first time in his life he understood all the humanity of Catullus, and saw how a man might love even what he despised.

Happily matters had not yet come to that. He knew that he might be deceived, and that circumstantial evidence was not always to be trusted. Even while his heart grew cold with the strongest and most deadly passion of which man is capable, with jealousy which is cruel as the grave, the nobility of his nature rose up and made him see that his duty was to believe Corona innocent until she were proved unfaithful. The effort to quench the flame was great, though fruitless, but the determination to cover it and hide it from every one, even from Corona herself, appealed to all that was brave and manly in his strong character. When at last he once more sat down, his face betrayed no emotion, his eyes were quiet, his hands did not tremble. He took up a book and forced his attention upon the pages for nearly an hour without interruption. Then he dressed himself, and went and sat at table with his father and his wife as though nothing had occurred to disturb his equanimity.

Corona supposed that he had recovered from his annoyance at not being admitted to share the secret for which she was unconsciously sacrificing so much. She had expected this result and was more than usually cheerful. Once old Saracinesca mentioned Gouache, but both Corona and Giovanni hastened to change the subject. This time, however, Giovanni did not look at his wife when the name was pronounced. Those days were over now.

CHAPTER IX

THE excitement which had reigned in Rome for weeks past was destined to end almost as suddenly as it had begun. The events which followed the 22nd of October have been frequently and accurately described; indeed, if we consider the small number of the troops engaged and the promptness with which a very limited body of men succeeded in quelling what at first appeared to be a formidable revolution, we are surprised at the amount of attention which has been accorded to the little campaign. The fact is that although the armies employed on both sides were insignificant, the questions at stake were enormous, and the real powers which found themselves confronted at Monte Rotondo and Mentana were the Kingdom of Italy and the French Empire. Until the ultimatum was presented to Italy by the French Minister on the 19th of October, Italy hoped to take possession of Rome on the pretext of restoring order after allowing it to be subverted by Garibaldi's guerillas. The military cordon formed by the Italian army to prevent Garibaldi's crossing the frontier was a mere show. The arrest of the leader himself, however it was intended by those who ordered it, turned out in effect to be a mere comedy, as he soon found himself at liberty and no one again attempted to seize him. When France interfered the scale turned. She asserted her determination to maintain the Convention of 1864 by force of arms, and Italy was obliged to allow Garibaldi to be defeated, since she was unable to face the perils of a war with her powerful neighbour. If a small body of French troops had not entered Rome on the 30th of the month, the events of 1870 would have occurred three years earlier, though probably with different results.

It being the object of the general commanding the Pope's forces to concentrate a body of men with whom to meet Garibaldi, who was now advancing boldly, the small detachments, of which many had already been sent to the front, were kept back in Rome in the hope of getting together something like an army. Gouache's departure was accordingly delayed from day to day, and it was not until the early morning of the 3rd of November that he actually quitted Rome with the whole available corps of Zouaves. Ten days elapsed, therefore, after the events last described, during which time he was hourly in expectation of orders to march. The service had become so arduous within the city that he could scarcely call a moment his own. It was no time to think of social duties, and he spent the leisure he had in trying to see Faustina Montevarchi as often as possible.

This, however, was no easy matter. It was a provoking fact that his duties kept him busily occupied in the afternoon and evening, and that the hours he could command fell almost always in the morning. To visit the Palazzo Montevarchi on any pretext whatever before one o'clock in the day was out of the question. He had not even the satisfaction of seeing Faustina drive past him in the Corso when she was out with her mother and Flavia, since they drove just at the time when he was occupied. Gouache told himself again and again that the display of ingenuity was in a measure the natural duty of a man in love, but the declaration did not help him very much. He was utterly at a loss for an expedient, and suffered keenly in being deprived of the possibility of seeing Faustina after having seen her so often and so intimately. A week earlier he could have borne it better, but now the separation was intolerable. In time of peace he would have disobeyed orders and thrown up his service for the day, no matter what the consequences turned out to be for himself; but at the present moment, when every man was expected to be at his post, such conduct seemed dishonourable and cowardly. He submitted in silence, growing daily more careworn, and losing much of the inexhaustible gaiety which made him a general favourite with his comrades.

There was but one chance of seeing Faustina, and even that one offered little probability of an interview. He knew that on Sunday mornings she sometimes went to church at an early hour with no one but her maid for a companion. Her mother and Flavia preferred to rise later and attended another mass. Now it chanced that in the year 1867, the 22nd of October, the date of the insurrection, fell on Tuesday. Five days, therefore, must elapse before he could see Faustina on a Sunday, and if he failed to see her then he would have to wait another week.

Unfortunately, Faustina's early expeditions to church were by no means certain or regular, and it would be necessary to convey a message to her before the day arrived. This was no easy matter. To send anything through the post was out of the question, and Gouache knew how hard it would be to find the means of putting a note into her hands through a servant. Hour after hour he cudgelled his brains for an expedient without success, until the idea pursued him and made him nervous. The time approached rapidly and he had as yet accomplished nothing. The wildest schemes suggested themselves to him and were rejected as soon as he thought of them. He met some of his acquaintances during the idle hours of the morning, and it almost drove him mad to think that almost any one of them could see Faustina any day he pleased. He did what he could to obtain leave in the afternoon or evening, but his exertions were fruitless. He was a man who was trusted, and knew it, and the disturbed state of affairs made it necessary that every man should do precisely what was allotted to him, at the risk of causing useless complications in the effort to concentrate and organise the troops which was now going forward. At last he actually went to the Palazzo Montevarchi in the morning and inquired if he could see the princess.

The porter replied that she was not visible, and that the prince had gone out. There was nothing to be done, and he turned to go away. Suddenly he stopped as he stood under the deep arch, facing the blank wall on the opposite side of the street. That same wall was broad and smooth and dark in colour. He only looked at it a moment, and then to excuse his hesitation in the eyes of the porter, he took out a cigarette, and lit it before going out. As he passed through the Piazza Colonna a few minutes later he went into a shop and bought two large tubes of paint with a broad brush. That night, when he was relieved from duty, he went back to the Palazzo Montevarchi. It was very late, and the streets were deserted. He stood before the great closed doors of the palace and then walked straight across the street to the blank wall with his paint and brush in his hands.

On the following morning when the Montevarchi porter opened the gates his eyes were rejoiced by some most extraordinary specimens of calligraphy executed upon the dark stones with red paint of a glaringly vivid hue. The letters A. G. were drawn at least four feet high in the centre, and were repeated in every size at irregular intervals for some distance above, below, and on each side. The words "Domenica," Sunday, and "Messa," mass, were scrawled everywhere in capitals, in roundhand, large and small. Then to give the whole the air of having been designed by a street-boy, there were other words, such as "Viva Pio IX," "Viva il Papa Re," and across these, in a different manner, and in green paint, "Viva Garibaldi," "Morte a Antonelli," and similar revolutionary sentiments. The whole, however, was so disposed that Gouache's initials and the two important words stood out in bold relief from the rest, and could not fail to attract the eye.

Of the many people who came and went that day through the great gate of the Palazzo Montevarchi two only attached any importance to the glaring scrawls on the opposite wall. One of these was Faustina herself, who saw and understood. The other was San Giacinto, who stared at the letters for several seconds, and then smiled faintly as he entered the palace. He, too, knew what the signs meant, and remarked to himself that Gouache was an enterprising youth, but that, in the interest of the whole tribe of Montevarchi, it would be well to put a stop to his love-making as soon as possible. It was now Saturday afternoon and there was no time to be lost.

San Giacinto made a short visit, and, on leaving, went immediately to the Palazzo Saracinesca. He knew that at four o'clock Corona would probably not yet be at home. This turned out to be the case, and having announced his intention of waiting for her return he was ushered into the sitting-room. As soon as the servant was gone he went to Corona's writing-table and took from it a couple of sheets of her paper and two of her envelopes. These latter were stamped with a coronet and her initials. He folded the paper carefully and put the four bits into his pocket-book. He waited ten minutes, but no one came. Then he left the house, telling the servant to say that he had called and would return presently. In a few minutes he was at his lodgings, where he proceeded to write the following note. He had taken two sheets in case the first proved a failure:

> I have understood, but alas! I cannot come. Oh, my beloved! When shall we meet again? It seems years since Tuesday night—and yet I am so watched that I can do nothing. Some one suspects something. I am sure of it. *A trusty person* will bring you this. I love you always—do not doubt it, though I cannot meet you tomorrow.

San Giacinto, who had received a tolerable education and had conscientiously made the best of it, prided himself upon his handwriting. It was small, clear, and delicate, like that of many strong, quiet men, whose nerves do not run away with their fingers. On the present occasion he took pains to make it even more careful than usual, and the result was that it looked not unlike the "copperplate" handwriting a girl would learn at the convent, though an expert would probably have declared it disguised. It had been necessary, in order to deceive Gouache, to write the note on the paper generally used by women of society. As he could not get any of Faustina's own, it seemed the next best thing to take Corona's, since Corona was her most intimate friend.

Gouache had told San Giacinto that he was engaged every afternoon, in hopes that he would in turn chance to mention the fact to Faustina. It was therefore pretty certain that Anastase would not be at home between four and five o'clock. San Giacinto drove to the Zouave's lodgings and asked for him. If he chanced to be in, the note could be given to his old landlady. He was out, however, and San Giacinto asked to be allowed to enter the room on the pretext of writing a word for his friend. The landlady was a dull old creature, who had been warming herself with a pot of coals when San Giacinto rang. In answer to his request she resumed her occupation and pointed to the door of the Zouave's apartment.

San Giacinto entered, and looked about him for a conspicuous place in which to put the letter he had prepared. He preferred not to trust to the memory of the woman, who might forget to deliver it until the next day, especially if Gouache came home late that night, as was very likely. The table of the small sitting-room was littered with letters and papers, books and drawings, so that an object placed in the midst of such disorder would not be likely to attract Gouache's attention. The door beyond was open, and showed a toilet-table in the adjoining chamber, which was indeed the bedroom. San Giacinto went in, and taking the note from his pocket, laid it on an old-fashioned pincushion before the glass. The thing slipped, however, and in order to fasten it firmly he thrust a gold pin that lay on the table through the letter and pinned it to the cushion in a conspicuous position. Then he went out and returned to the Palazzo Saracinesca as he had promised to do.

In doing all this he had no intention of injuring either Gouache or Faustina. He perceived clearly enough that their love affair could not come to any good termination, and as his interests were now very closely bound up with those of the Montevarchi, it seemed wisest to break off the affair by any means in his power, without complicating matters by speaking to Gouache or to Faustina's father or mother. He knew enough of human nature to understand that Gouache would be annoyed at losing the chance of a meeting, and he promised himself to watch the two so carefully as to be able to prevent other clandestine interviews during the next few days. If he could once sow the seeds of a quarrel between the two, he fancied it would be easy to break up the relations. Nothing makes a woman so angry as to wait for a man who has promised to meet her, and if he fails to come altogether her anger will probably be very serious. In the present case he supposed that Faustina would go to the church, but that Gouache, being warned that he was not to come, would not think of keeping the tryst. The scheme, if not profound, was at least likely to produce a good deal of trouble between the lovers.

San Giacinto returned to the Palazzo Saracinesca, but he found only the old prince at home, though he prolonged his visit in the hope of seeing Corona or Sant' Ilario.

"By the bye," he said, as he and his companion sat together in the prince's study, "I remember that you were so good as to say that you would let me see those family papers some day. They must be very interesting and I would be glad to avail myself of your offer."

"Certainly," replied Saracinesca "They are in the Archives in a room of the library. It is rather late now. Do you mind waiting till tomorrow?"

"Not in the least, or as long as you like. To tell the truth, I would like to show them to my future father-in-law, who loves archaeology. I was talking about them with him yesterday. After all, however, I suppose the duplicates are at the Cancelleria, and we can see them there."

"I do not know," said the prince, carelessly, "I never took the trouble to inquire. There is probably some register of them, or something to prove that they are in existence."

"There must be, of course. Things of that importance would not be allowed to go unregistered, unless people were very indifferent in those days."

"It is possible that there are no duplicates. It may be that there is only an official notice of the deed giving the heads of the agreement. You see it was a friendly arrangement, and there was supposed to be no probability whatever that your great-grandfather would ever marry. The papers I have are all in order and legally valid, but there may have been some carelessness about registering them. I cannot be sure. Indeed it is thirty years at least since I looked at the originals."

"If you would have them taken out some time before I am married, I should be glad to see them, but there is no hurry. So all this riot and revolution has meant something after all," added San Giacinto to change the subject "Garibaldi has taken Monte Rotondo, I hear today."

"Yes, and if the French are not quick, we shall have the diversion of a siege," replied Saracinesca rather scornfully. "That same taking of Monte Rotondo was one of those gallant deeds for which Garibaldi is so justly famous. He has six thousand men, and there were only three hundred and fifty soldiers inside. Twenty to one, or thereabouts."

It is unnecessary to detail the remainder of the conversation. Saracinesca went off into loud abuse of Garibaldi, confounding the whole Italian Government with him and devoting all to one common destination, while San Giacinto reserved his judgment, believing that there was probably a wide difference between the real intentions of the guerilla general and of his lawful sovereign, Victor Emmanuel the Second, King of Italy. At last the two men were informed that Corona had returned. They left the study and found her in the sitting-room.

"Where is Giovanni?" she asked as soon as they entered. She was standing before the fireplace dressed as she had come in.

"I have no idea where he is," replied Saracinesca. "I suppose he is at the club, or making visits somewhere. He has turned into a very orderly boy since you married him." The old man laughed a little.

"I have missed him," said Corona, taking no notice of her father-in-law's remark. "I was to have picked him up on the Pincio, and when I got there he was gone. I am so afraid he will think I forgot all about it, for I must have been late. You see, I was delayed by a crowd in the Tritone—there is always a crowd there."

Corona seemed less calm than usual. The fact was, that since the affair which had caused her husband so much annoyance, some small part of which she had perceived, she had been trying to make up to him for his disappointment in not knowing her secret by being with him more than usual and by exerting herself to please him in every way. They did not usually meet during the afternoon, as he generally went out on foot, while she drove, but today they had agreed that she should come to the Pincio and take him for a short drive and bring him home. The plan was part of her fixed intention to be more than usually thoughtful where he was concerned, and the idea that she had kept him waiting and that he had gone away caused her more regret than would have been natural in the ordinary course of events.

In order to explain what now took place, it is necessary to return to Giovanni himself who, as Corona had said, had waited for his wife near the band-stand on the Pincio for some time, until growing weary, he had walked away and left the gardens.

Though he manfully concealed what he felt, the passion that had been sown in his heart had grown apace and in a few days had assumed dominating proportions. He suspected everything and everybody while determined to appear indifferent. Even Corona's efforts to please him, which of late had grown so apparent, caused him suspicion. He asked himself why her manner should have changed, as it undoubtedly had during the last few days. She had always been a good and loving wife to him, and he was well pleased with her gravity and her dignified way of showing her affection. Why should she suddenly think it needful to become so very solicitous for his welfare and happiness during every moment of his life? It was not like her to come into his study early in the morning and to ask what he meant to do during the day. It was a new thing that she should constantly propose to walk with him, to drive with him, to read aloud to him, to make herself not only a part of his heart but a part of his occupations. Had the change come gradually, he would not have distrusted her motives. He liked his wife's company and conversation, but as they each had things to do which could not conveniently be done together, he had made up his mind to the existence which was good enough for his companions in society. Other men did not think of spending the afternoon in their wives' carriages, leaving cards or making visits, or driving round and round the Villa Borghese and the Pincio. To do so was to be ridiculous in the extreme, and besides, though he liked to be with Corona, he detested visiting, and hated of all things to stop a dozen times in the course of a drive in order to send a footman upstairs with cards. He preferred to walk or to lounge in the club or to stay at home and study the problems of his improvements for Saracinesca. Corona's manner irritated him therefore, and made him think more than ever of the subject which he would have done better to abandon from the first.

Nevertheless, he would not show that he was wearied by his wife's attention, still less that he believed her behaviour to be prompted by a desire to deceive him. He was uniformly courteous and gentle, acquiescing in her little plans whenever he could do so, and expressing a suitable degree of regret when he was prevented from joining her by some previous engagement. But the image of the French Zouave was ever present with him. He could not get rid of Gouache's dark, delicate features, even in his dreams; the sound of the man's pleasant voice and of his fluent conversation was constantly in his ears, and he could not look at Corona without fancying how she would look if Anastase were beside her whispering tender speeches.

All the time, he submitted with a good grace to do whatever she proposed, and on this afternoon he found himself waiting for her beside the band-stand. At first he watched the passing carriages indifferently enough, supposing that his own liveries would presently loom up in the long line of high-seated coachmen and lacqueys, and having no especial desire to see them. His position when in Corona's company grew every day more difficult, and he thought as he stood by the stone pillar at the corner that he would on the whole be glad if she did not come. He was egregiously mistaken in himself, however. As the minutes passed he grew uneasy, and watched the advancing carriages with a feverish anxiety, saying to himself that every one must bring Corona, and actually growing pale with emotion as each vehicle turned the distant corner and came into view. The time seemed interminable after he had once yielded to the excitement, and before another quarter of an hour had elapsed, Sant' Ilario turned angrily away and left the Pincio by the stairs that descend near the band-stand towards the winding drive by which the Piazza del Popolo is reached.

It is not easy for a person who is calm to comprehend the workings of a brain over excited with a strong passion. To a man who has lost the sober use of his faculties in the belief that he has been foully betrayed, every circumstance, every insignificant accident, seems a link in the chain of evidence. A week earlier Giovanni would have thought himself mad if the mere idea had suggested itself to him that Corona loved Gouache. Today he believed that she had purposely sent him to wait upon the Pincio, in order that she might be sure of seeing Gouache without fear of interruption. The conviction thrust itself upon him with overwhelming force. He fancied himself the dupe of a common imposition, he saw his magnificent love and trust made the sport of a vulgar trick. The blood mounted to his dark face and as he descended the steps a red mist seemed to be spread between his eyes and all surrounding objects. Though he walked firmly and mechanically, saluting his acquaintances as he passed, he was unconscious of his actions, and moved like a man under the influence of a superior force. Jealousy is that one of all the passions which is most sure to break out suddenly into deeds of violence when long restrained.

Giovanni scarcely knew how he reached the Corso nor how it was that he found himself ascending the dusky staircase which led to Gouache's lodgings. It was less than a quarter of an hour since San Giacinto had been there, and the old woman still held her pot of coals in her hand as she opened the door. As she had pointed to the door when San Giacinto had come, so she now directed Giovanni in the same way. But Giovanni, on hearing that Anastase was out, began to ask questions.

"Has any one been here?" he inquired.

"Eh! There was a gentleman a quarter of an hour ago," replied the woman.

"Has any lady been here?"

"A lady? Macche!" The old creature laughed. "What should ladies do here?"

Giovanni thought he detected some hesitation in the tone. He was in the mood to fancy himself deceived by every one.

"Are you fond of money?" he asked, brutally.

"Eh! I am an old woman. What would you have? Am I crazy that I should not like money? But Signor Gouache is a very good gentleman. He pays well, thank Heaven!"

"What does he pay you for?"

"What for? For his lodging—for his coffee. Bacchus! What should he pay me for? Strange question in truth. Do I keep a shop? I keep lodgings. But perhaps you like the place? It is a fine situation—just in the Corso and only one flight of stairs, a beautiful position for the Carnival. Of course, if you are inclined to pay more than Signor Gouache, I do not say but what—"

"I do not want your lodgings, my good woman," returned Giovanni in gentler tones. "I want to know who comes to see your lodger."

"Who should come? His friends of course. Who else?"

"A lady, perhaps," said Giovanni in a thick voice. It hurt him to say it, and the words almost stuck in his throat. "Perhaps a lady comes sometimes," he repeated, pulling out some loose bank notes.

The old woman's filmy eyes suddenly twinkled in the gloom. The sound of the crisp pieces of paper was delightful to her ear.

"Well," she said after a moment's hesitation, "if a beautiful lady does come here, that is the Signore's affair. It is none of my business."

Giovanni thrust the notes into her palm, which was already wide open to receive them. His heart beat wildly.

"She is beautiful, you say?"

"Oh! As beautiful as you please!" chuckled the hag.

"Is she dark?"

"Of course," replied the woman. There was no mistaking the tone in which the question was asked, for Giovanni was no longer able to conceal anything that he felt.

"And tall, I suppose? Yes. And she was here a quarter of an hour ago, you say? Speak out!" he cried, advancing a step towards the old creature. "If you lie to me, I will kill you! She was here—do not deny it."

"Yes—yes," answered the woman, cowering back in some terror. "Per carita! Don't murder me—I tell you the truth."

With a sudden movement Giovanni turned on his heel and entered Gouache's sitting-room. It was now almost dark in the house and he struck a match and lighted a candle that stood on the stable. The glare illuminated his swarthy features and fiery eyes, and the veins stood out on his forehead and temples like strained and twisted cords. He looked about him in every direction, examining the table, strewn with papers and books, the floor, the furniture, expecting every moment to find something which should prove that Corona had been there. Seeing nothing, he entered the bedroom beyond. It was a small chamber and he had scarcely passed through the door when he found himself before the toilet-table. The note San Giacinto had left was there pinned upon the little cushion with the gold pin, as he had placed it.

Giovanni stared wildly at the thing for several seconds and his face grew deadly white. There was no evidence lacking now, for the pin was Corona's own. It was a simple enough object, made of plain gold, the head being twisted into the shape of the letter C, but there was no mistaking its identity, for Giovanni had designed it himself. Corona used it for fastening her veil.

As the blood sank from his head to his heart Giovanni grew very calm. He set the candle upon the toilet-table and took the note, after putting the pin in his pocket. The handwriting seemed to be feigned, and his lip curled scornfully as he looked at it and then, turning it over, saw that the envelope was one of Corona's own. It seemed to him a pitiable piece of folly in her to distort her writing when there was such abundant proof on all sides to convict her. Without the slightest hesitation he opened the letter and read it, bending down and holding it near the candle. One perusal was enough. He smiled curiously as he read the words, "I am so watched that I can do nothing. Some one suspects something." His attention was arrested by the statement that a trusty person—the words were underlined—would bring the note. The meaning of the emphasis was explained by the pin; the trusty person was herself, who, perhaps by an afterthought, had left the bit of gold as a parting gift in case Gouache marched before they met again.

Giovanni glanced once more round the room, half expecting to find some other convicting piece of evidence. Then he hesitated, holding the candle in one hand and the note in the other. He thought of staying where he was and waiting for Gouache, but the idea did not seem feasible. Nothing which implied waiting could have satisfied him at that moment, and after a few seconds he thrust the note into his pocket and went out. His hand was on the outer door, when he remembered the old woman who sat crouching over her pan of coals, scarcely able to believe her good luck, and longing for Giovanni's departure in order that she might count the crisp notes again. She dared not indulge herself in that pleasure while he was present, lest he should repent of his generosity and take back a part of them, for she had seen how he had taken them from his pocket and saw that he had no idea how much he had given.

"You will say nothing of my coming," said Giovanni, fixing his eyes upon her.
"I, Signore? Do not be afraid! Money is better than words."

"Very good," he answered. "Perhaps you will get twice as much the next time
I want to know the truth."

"God bless you!" chuckled the wrinkled creature. He went out, and the little
bell that was fastened to the door tinkled as the latch sprang back into its place.
Then the woman counted the price of blood, which had so unexpectedly fallen
into her hands. The bank-notes were many and broad, and crisp and new, for
Giovanni had not reckoned the cost. It was long since old Caterina Ranucci had
seen so much money, and she had certainly never had so much of her own.

"Qualche innamorato!" she muttered to herself as she smoothed the notes
one by one and gloated over them and built castles in the air under the light of
her little oil lamp. "It is some fellow in love. Heaven pardon me if I have done
wrong! He seemed so anxious to know that the woman had been here—why
should I not content him? Poveretto! He must be rich. I will always tell him what
he wants to know. Heaven bring him often and bless him."

Then she rocked herself backwards and forwards, hugging her pot of coals
and crooning the words of an ancient Roman ditty:

> "Io vorrei che nella luna
> Ci s'andasse in carrettella
> Per vedere la piu bella
> Delle donne di la su!"

What does the old song mean? Who knows whether it ever meant anything? "I
wish one might drive in a little cart to the moon, to see the most beautiful of the
women up there!" Caterina Ranucci somehow felt as though she could express
her feelings in no better way than by singing the queer words to herself in her
cracked old voice. Possibly she thought that the neighbours would not suspect
her good fortune if they heard her favourite song.

CHAPTER X

SANT' Ilario walked home from Gouache's lodgings. The cool evening air refreshed him and helped him to think over what he had before him in the near future. Indeed the position was terrible enough, and doubly so to a man of his temperament. He would have faced anything rather than this, for there was no point in which he was more vulnerable than in his love for Corona. As he walked her figure rose before him, and her beauty almost dazzled him when he thought of it. But he could no longer think of her without bringing up that other being upon whom his thoughts of vengeance concentrated themselves, until it seemed as though the mere intention must do its object some bodily harm.

The fall was tremendous in itself and in its effects. It must have been a great passion indeed which could make such a man demean himself to bribe an inferior for information against his wife. He himself was so little able to measure the force by which he was swayed as to believe that he had extracted the confession from a reluctant accomplice. He would never have allowed that the sight of the money and the prompting of his own words could have caused the old woman to invent the perfectly imaginary story which he had seemed so fully determined to hear. He did not see that Caterina Ranucci had merely confirmed each statement he had made himself and had taken his bribe while laughing to herself at his folly. He was blinded by something which destroys the mental vision more surely than anger or hatred, or pride, or love itself.

To some extent he was to be pardoned. The chain of circumstantial evidence was consecutive and so convincing that many a just person would have accepted Corona's guilt as the only possible explanation of what had happened. The discoveries he had just made would alone have sufficed to set up a case against her, and many an innocent reputation has been shattered by less substantial proofs. Had he not found a letter, evidently written in a feigned hand and penned upon his wife's own writing-paper, fastened upon Gouache's table with her own pin? Had not the old woman confessed—before he had found the note, too—that a lady had been there but a short time before? Did not these facts agree singularly with Corona's having left him to wait for her during that interval in the public gardens? Above all, did not this conclusion explain at once all those things in her conduct which had so much disturbed him during the past week?

What was this story of Faustina Montevarchi's disappearance? The girl was probably Corona's innocent accomplice. Corona had left the house at one o'clock in the morning with Gouache. The porter had not seen any other woman. The fact that she had entered the Palazzo Montevarchi with Faustina and without Anastase proved nothing, except that she had met the young girl somewhere else, it mattered little where. The story that Faustina had accidentally shut herself into a room in the palace was an invention, for even Corona admitted the fact. That Faustina's flight, however, and the other events of the night of the 22nd had been arranged merely in order that Corona and Gouache might walk in the moonlight for a quarter of an hour, Giovanni did not believe. There was some other mystery here which was yet unsolved. Meanwhile the facts he had collected were enough—enough to destroy his happiness at a single blow. And yet he loved Corona even now, and though his mind was made up clearly enough concerning Gouache, he knew that he could not part from the woman he adored. He thought of the grim old fortress at Saracinesca with its lofty towers and impregnable walls, and when he reflected that there was but one possible exit from the huge mass of buildings, he said to himself that Corona would be safe there for ever.

He had the instincts of a fierce and unforgiving race of men, who for centuries had held the law in their own hands, and were accustomed to wield it as it seemed good in their own eyes. It was not very long since the lords of Saracinesca had possessed the right of life and death over their vassals,[†] and the hereditary traits of character which had been fostered by ages of power had not disappeared with the decay of feudalism. Under the circumstances which seemed imminent, it would not have been thought unnatural if Giovanni had confined his wife during the remainder of her days in his castle among the mountains. The idea may excite surprise among civilised Europeans when it is considered that the events of which I write occurred as recently as 1867, but it would certainly have evoked few expressions of astonishment among the friends of the persons concerned. To Giovanni himself it seemed the only possible conclusion to what was happening, and the determination to kill Gouache and imprison Corona for life appeared in his eyes neither barbarous nor impracticable.

---

†   Until 1870 the right of life and death was still held, so far as actual legality was concerned, by the Dukes of Bracciano, and was attached to the possession of the title, which had been sold and subsequently bought back by the original holders of it.

He did not hasten his pace as he went towards his home. There was something fateful in his regular step and marble face as he moved steadily to the accomplishment of his purpose. The fury which had at first possessed him, and which, if he had then encountered Gouache, would certainly have produced a violent outbreak, had subsided and was lost in the certainty of his dishonour, and in the immensity of the pain he suffered. Nothing remained to be done but to tell Corona that he knew all, and to inflict upon her the consequences of her crime without delay. There was absolutely no hope left that she might prove herself innocent, and in Giovanni's own breast there was no hope either, no hope of ever finding again his lost happiness, or of ever again setting one stone upon another of all that splendid fabric of his life which he had built up so confidently upon the faith of the woman he loved.

As he reached the gates of his home he grew if possible paler than before, till his face was positively ghastly to see, and his eyes seemed to sink deeper beneath his brows, while their concentrated light gleamed more fiercely. No one saw him enter, for the porter was in his lodge, and on reaching the landing of the stairs Giovanni let himself into the apartments with a latch-key.

Corona was in her dressing-room, a high vaulted chamber, somewhat sombrely furnished, but made cheerful by a fire that blazed brightly in the deep old-fashioned chimney-piece. Candles were lighted upon the dressing-table, and a shaded lamp stood upon a low stand near a lounge beside the hearth. The princess was clad in a loose wrapper of some soft cream-coloured material, whose folds fell gracefully to the ground as she lay upon the couch. She was resting before dressing for dinner, and the masses of her blue-black hair were loosely coiled upon her head and held together by a great Spanish comb thrust among the tresses with a careless grace. She held a book in her slender, olive-tinted hand, but she was not reading; her head lay back upon the cushions and the firelight threw her features into strong relief, while her velvet eyes reflected the flashes of the dancing flames as she watched them. Her expression was serene and calm. She had forgotten for the moment the little annoyances of the last few days and was thinking of her happiness, contrasting the peace of her present life with what she had suffered during the five years of her marriage with poor old Astrardente. Could Giovanni have seen her thus his heart might have been softened. He would have asked himself how it was possible that any woman guilty of such enormous misdeeds could lie there watching the fire with a look of such calm innocence upon her face.

But Giovanni did not see her as she was. Even in the extremity of his anger and suffering his courtesy did not forsake him, and he knocked at his wife's door before entering the room. Corona moved from her position, and turned her head to see who was about to enter.

"Come in," she said.

She started when she saw Giovanni's face. Dazzled as she was by the fire, he looked to her like a dead man. She laid one hand upon the arm of the couch as though she would rise to meet him. He shut the door behind him and advanced towards her till only a couple of paces separated them. She was so much amazed by his looks that she sat quite still while he fixed his eyes upon her and began to speak.

"You have wrecked my life," he said in a strange, low voice. "I have come to tell you my decision."

She thought he was raving mad, and, brave as she was, she shrank back a little upon her seat and turned pale.

"You need not be afraid of me," he continued, as he noticed the movement. "I am not going to kill you. I am sorry to say I am fool enough to love you still."

"Giovanni!" cried Corona in an agonised tone. She could find no words, but sprang to her feet and threw her arms about him, gazing imploringly into his face. His features did not relax, for he was prepared for any sort of acting on her part. Without hurting her, but with a strength few men could have resisted, he forced her back to her seat, and then retreated a step before he spoke again. She submitted blindly, feeling that any attempt to thwart him must be utterly useless.

"I know what you have done," he said. "You can have nothing to say. Be silent and listen to me. You have destroyed the greatest happiness the world ever knew. You have dishonoured me and mine. You have dragged my faith in you—God knows how great—into the mire of your infamous life. And worse than that—I could almost have forgiven that, I am so base—you have destroyed yourself—"

Corona uttered a wild cry and sank back upon the cushions, pressing her hands over her ears so that she might not hear the fearful words.

"I will not listen!" she gasped. "You are mad—mad!" Then springing up once more she again clasped him to her breast, so suddenly that he could not escape her. "Oh, my poor Giovanni!" she moaned. "What has happened to you? Have you been hurt? Are you dying? For Heaven's sake speak like yourself!"

He seized her wrists and held her before him so that she was forced to hear what he said. Even then his grasp did not hurt her. His hands were like manacles of steel in which hers could turn though she could not withdraw them.

"I am hurt to death," he said, between his teeth. "I have been to Gouache's rooms and have brought away your letter—and your pin—the pin I gave you, Corona. Do you understand now, or must I say more?"

"My letter?" cried Corona in the utmost bewilderment.

"Yes," he answered, releasing her and instantly producing the note and the gold ornament. "Is that your paper? Is this your pin? Answer me—or no! They answer for themselves. You need say nothing, for you can have nothing to say. They are yours and you know it. If they are not enough there is the woman who let you in, who saw you bring them. What more do you want?"

As long as Giovanni's accusations had been vague and general, Corona had remained horrorstruck, believing that some awful and incomprehensible calamity had befallen her husband and had destroyed his reason. The moment he produced the proof of what he said, her presence of mind returned, and she saw at a glance the true horror of the situation. She never doubted for a moment that she was the victim of some atrocious plot, but having something to face which she could understand her great natural courage asserted itself. She was not a woman to moan and weep helplessly when there was an open danger to be met.

She took the letter and the pin and examined them by the light, with a calmness that contrasted oddly with her previous conduct. Giovanni watched her. He supposed that she had acted surprise until he had brought forward something more conclusive than words, and that she was now exercising her ingenuity in order to explain the situation. His lip curled scornfully, as he fancied he saw the meaning of her actions. After a few seconds she looked up and held out the two objects towards him.

"The paper is mine," she said, "but I did not write the letter. The pin is mine too. I lost it more than a month ago."

"Of course," replied Giovanni, coldly. "I expected that you would say that. It is very natural. But I do not ask you for any explanations. I have them already. I will take you to Saracinesca tomorrow morning and you will have time to explain everything. You will have your whole life to use, until you die, for no other object. I told you I would not kill you."

"Is it possible that you are in earnest?" asked Corona, her voice trembling slightly.

"I am in earnest. Do you think I am a man to jest over such deeds?"

"And do you think I am a woman to do such deeds?"

"Since you have done them—what answer can there be? Not only are you capable of them. You are the woman who has done them. Do lifeless things, like these, lie?"

"No. But men do. I believe you, Giovanni. You found these things in Monsieur Gouache's rooms. You were told I put them there. Whoever told you so uttered the most infamous falsehood that ever was spoken on earth. The person who placed them where they were did so in the hope of ruining me. Can you look back into the past and tell me that you have any other reason for believing in this foul plot?"

"Reasons?" cried Giovanni, fiercely. "Do you want more reasons? We have time. I will give you enough to satisfy you that I know all you have done. Was not this man for ever near you last year, wherever you met, talking with you in low tones, showing by every movement and gesture that he distinguished you with his base love? Were you not together in a corner last Tuesday night just as the insurrection broke out? Did he not kiss your hand when you both thought no one was looking?"

"He kissed my hand before every one," replied Corona, whose wrath was slowly gathering as she saw her husband's determination to prove her guilty.

"There were people in the room," continued Giovanni in a tone of concentrated anger, "but you thought no one was watching you—I could see it in your manner and in your eyes. That same night I came home at one o'clock and you were out. You had gone out alone with that man, expecting that I would not return so soon—though it was late enough, too. You were forced to admit that you were with him, because the porter had seen you and had told me the man was a Zouave."

"I will tell you the story, since you no longer trust me," said Corona, proudly.

"I have no doubt you will tell me some very ingenious tale which will explain why, although you left my house alone, with Gouache, you reached the Palazzo Montevarchi alone with Faustina. But I have not done. He came here the next day. You treated him with unexampled rudeness before me. Half an hour later I found you together in the drawing-room. He was kissing your hand again. You were saying you forgave him and giving him that favourite benediction of yours, which you once bestowed upon me under very similar circumstances. Astrardente was alive and present at that dance in Casa Frangipani. You have me for a husband now and you have found another man whose heart will beat when you bless him. It would be almost better to kill you after all."

"Have you finished?" asked Corona, white with anger.

"Yes. That letter and that pin—left while I, poor fool, was waiting for you this afternoon on the Pincio—those things are my last words. They close the tale very appropriately. I wish I did not love you so—I would not wait for your answer."

"Do you dare to say you love me?"

"Yes—though there is no other man alive who would dare so much, who would dare to love such a woman as you are—for very shame."

"And I tell you," answered Corona in ringing tones, "that, although I can prove to you that every word you say against me is an abominable calumny, so that you shall see how basely you have insulted an innocent woman, yet I shall never love you again—never, never. A man who can believe such things, who can speak such things, is worthy of no woman's love and shall not have mine. And yet you shall hear me tell the truth, that you may know what you have done. You say I have wrecked your life and destroyed your happiness. You have done it for yourself. As there is a God in Heaven—"

"Do not blaspheme," said Giovanni, contemptuously. "I will hear your story."

"Before God, this thing is a lie!" cried Corona, standing at her full height, her eyes flashing with just indignation. Then lowering her voice, she continued speaking rapidly but distinctly. "Gouache loves Faustina, and she loves him. When he left this house that night she followed him out into the street. She reached the Serristori barracks and was stunned by the explosion. Gouache found her there many hours later. When you saw us together a little earlier he was telling me he loved her. He is a man of honour. He saw that the only way to save her good name was to bring her here and let me take her home. He sent me a word by the porter, while she waited in the shadow. I ran down and found her there. We purposely prevented the porter from seeing her. I took her to her father's house, and sent Gouache away, for I was angry with him. I believed he had led an innocent girl into following him—that it was a pre-arranged meeting and that she had gone not realising that there was a revolution. I invented the story of her having lost herself here, in order to shield her. The next day Gouache came. I would not speak to him and went to my room. The servants told me he was gone, but as I was coming back to you I met him. He stopped me and made me believe what is quite true, for Faustina has acknowledged it. She followed him of her own accord, and he had no idea that she was not safe at home. I forgave him. He said he was going to the frontier and asked me to give him a blessing. It was a foolish idea, perhaps, but I did as he wished. If you had come forward like a man instead of listening we would have told you all. But you suspected me even then. I do not know who told you that I had been to his lodging today. The carriage was stopped by a crowd in the Tritone, and I reached the Pincio after you had gone. As for the pin, I lost it a month ago. Gouache may have found it, or it may have been picked up and sold, and he may have chanced to buy it. I never wrote the letter. The paper was either taken from this house or was got from the stationer who stamps it for us. Faustina may have taken it—she may have been here when I was out—it is not her handwriting. I believe it is an abominable plot. But it is as transparent as water. Take the pin and wear it. See Gouache when you have it. He will ask you where you got it, for he has not the slightest idea that it is mine. Are you satisfied? I have told you all. Do you see what you have done, in suspecting me, in accusing me, in treating me like the last of women? I have done. What have you to say?"

"That you have told a very improbable story," replied Giovanni. "You have sunk lower than before, for you have cast a slur upon an innocent girl in order to shield yourself. I would not have believed you capable of that. You can no more prove your innocence than you can prove that this poor child was mad enough to follow Gouache into the street last Tuesday night. I have listened to you patiently. I have but one thing more to do and then there will be nothing left for me but patience. You will send for your servants, and order your effects to be packed for the journey to Saracinesca. If it suits your convenience we will start at eleven o'clock, as I shall be occupied until then. I advise you not to see my father."

Corona stood quite still while he spoke. She could not realise that he paid no attention whatever to her story, save to despise her the more for having implicated Faustina. It was inconceivable to her that all the circumstances should not now be as clear to him as they were to herself. From the state of absolute innocence she could not transfer herself in a moment to the comprehension of all he had suffered, all he had thought, and all he had recalled before accusing her. Even had that been possible, her story seemed to her to give a perfectly satisfactory explanation of all his suspicions. She was wounded, indeed, so deeply that she knew she could never recover herself entirely, but it did not strike her as possible that all she had said should produce no effect at all. And yet she knew his look and his ways, and recognised in the tone of his voice the expression of a determination which it would be hard indeed to change. He still believed her guilty, and he was going to take her away to the dismal loneliness of the mountains for an indefinite time, perhaps for ever. She had not a relation in the world to whom she could appeal. Her mother had died in her infancy; her father, for whom she sacrificed herself in marrying the rich old Duke of Astrardente, was dead long ago. She could turn to no one, unless it were to Prince Saracinesca himself—and Giovanni warned her not to go to his father. She stood for some moments looking fixedly at him as though trying to read his thoughts, and he returned her gaze with unflinching sternness. The position was desperate. In a few hours she would be where there would be no possibility of defence or argument, and she knew the man's character well enough to be sure that where proof failed entreaty would be worse than useless. At last she came near to him and almost gently laid her hand upon his arm.

"Giovanni," she said, quietly, "I have loved you very tenderly and very truly. I swear to you upon our child that I am wholly innocent. Will you not believe me?"

"No," he answered, and the little word fell from his lips like the blow of a steel hammer. His eyes did not flinch; his features did not change.

"Will you not ask some one who knows whether I have not spoken the truth? Will you not let me write—or write yourself to those two, and ask them to come here and tell you their story? It is much to ask of them, but it is life or death to me and they will not refuse. Will you not do it?"

"No, I will not."

"Then do what you will with me, and may God forgive you, for I cannot."

Corona turned from him and crossed the room. There was a cushioned stool there, over which hung a beautiful crucifix. Corona knelt down, as though not heeding her husband's presence, and buried her face in her hands.

Giovanni stood motionless in the middle of the room. His eyes had followed his wife's movements and he watched her in silence for a short time. Convinced, as he was, of her guilt, he believed she was acting a part, and that her kneeling down was merely intended to produce a theatrical effect. The accent of truth in her words made no impression whatever upon him, and her actions seemed to him too graceful to be natural, too dignified for a woman who was not trying all the time to make the best of her appearance. The story she had told coincided too precisely, if possible, with the doings of which he had accused her, while it failed in his judgment to explain the motives of what she had done. He said to himself that he, in her place, would have told everything on that first occasion when she had come home and had found him waiting for her. He forgot, or did not realise, that she had been taken unawares, when she expected to find time to consider her course, and had been forced to make up her mind suddenly. Almost any other woman would have told the whole adventure at once; any woman less wholly innocent of harm would have seen the risk she incurred by asking her husband's indulgence for her silence. He was persuaded that she had played upon his confidence in her and had reckoned upon his belief in her sincerity in order to be bold with half the truth. Suspicion and jealousy had made him so ingenious that he imputed to her a tortuous policy of deception, of which she was altogether incapable.

Corona did not kneel long. She had no intention of making use of the appearance of prayer in order to affect Giovanni's decision, nor in order to induce him to leave her alone. He would, indeed, have quitted the room had she remained upon her knees a few moments longer, but when she rose and faced him once more he was still standing as she had left him, his eyes fixed upon her and his arms folded upon his breast. He thought she was going to renew her defence, but he was mistaken. She came and stood before him, so that a little distance separated him from her, and she spoke calmly, in her deep, musical voice.

"You have made up your mind, then. Is that your last word?"

"It is."

"Then I will say what I have to say. It shall not be much, but we shall not often talk together in future. You will remember some day what I tell you. I am an innocent and defenceless woman. I have no relation to whom I can appeal. You have forbidden me to write to those who could prove me guiltless. For the sake of our child—for the sake of the love I have borne you—I will make no attempt at resistance. The world shall not know that you have even doubted me, the mother of your son, the woman who has loved you. The time will come when you will ask my forgiveness for your deeds. I tell you frankly that I shall never be capable of forgiving you, nor of speaking a kind word to you again. This is neither a threat nor a warning, though it may perhaps be the means of sparing you some disappointment. I only ask two things of your courtesy—that you will inform me of what you mean to do with our child, and that you will then be good enough to leave me alone for a little while."

An evil thought crossed Giovanni's mind. He knew how Corona would suffer if she were not allowed either to see little Orsino or to know what became of him while she was living her solitary life of confinement in the mountains. The diabolical cruelty of the idea fascinated him for a moment, and he looked coldly into her eyes as though he did not mean to answer her. In spite of his new jealousy, however, he was not capable of inflicting this last blow. As he looked at her beautiful white face and serious eyes, he wavered. He loved her still and would have loved her, had the proofs against her been tenfold more convincing than they were. With him his love was a passion apart and by itself. It had been strengthened and made beautiful by the devotion and tenderness and faith which had grown up with it, and had surrounded it as with a wall. But though all these things were swept away the passion itself remained, fierce, indomitable and soul-stirring in its power. It stood alone, like the impregnable keep of a war-worn fortress, beneath whose shadow the outworks and ramparts have been razed to the ground, and whose own lofty walls are battered and dinted by engines of war, shorn of all beauty and of all its stately surroundings, but stern and unshaken yet, grim, massive and solitary.

For an instant Giovanni wavered, unable to struggle against that mysterious power which still governed him and forced him to acknowledge its influence. The effort of resisting the temptation to be abominably cruel carried him back from his main purpose, and produced a sudden revulsion of feeling wholly incomprehensible to himself.

"Corona!" he cried, in a voice breaking with emotion. He threw out his arms wildly and sprang towards her. She thrust him back with a strength of which he would not have believed her capable. Bitter words rose to her lips, but she forced them back and was silent, though her eyes blazed with an anger she had never felt before. For some time neither spoke. Corona stood erect and watchful, one hand resting upon the back of a chair. Giovanni walked to the end of the room, and then came back and looked steadily into her face. Several seconds elapsed before he could speak, and his face was very white.

"You may keep the child," he said at last, in an unsteady tone. Then without another word he left the room and softly closed the door behind him.

When Corona was alone she remained standing as he had last seen her, her gaze fixed on the heavy curtains through which he had disappeared. Gradually her face grew rigid, and the expression vanished from her deep eyes, till they looked dull and glassy. She tottered, lost her hold upon the chair and fell to the floor with an inarticulate groan. There she lay, white, beautiful and motionless as a marble statue, mercifully unconscious, for a space, of all she had to suffer.

Giovanni went from his wife's presence to his father's study. The prince sat at his writing-table, a heap of dusty parchments and papers piled before him. He was untying the rotten strings with which they were fastened, peering through his glasses at the headings written across the various documents. He did not unfold them, but laid them carefully in order upon the table. When San Giacinto had gone away, the old gentleman had nothing to do for an hour or more before dinner. He had accordingly opened a solid old closet in the library which served as a sort of muniment room for the family archives, and had withdrawn a certain box in which he knew that the deeds concerning the cession of title were to be found. He did not intend to look them over this evening, but was merely arranging them for examination on the morrow. He looked up as Giovanni entered, and started from his chair when he saw his son's face.

"Good heavens! Giovannino! What has happened?" he cried, in great anxiety.

"I came to tell you that Corona and I are going to Saracinesca tomorrow," answered Sant' Ilario, in a low voice.

"What? At this time of year? Besides, you cannot get there. The road is full of Garibaldians and soldiers. It is not safe to leave the city! Are you ill? What is the matter?"

"Oh—nothing especial," replied Giovanni with an attempt to assume an indifferent tone "We think the mountain air will be good for my wife, that is all. I do not think we shall really have much difficulty in getting there. Half of this war is mere talk."

"And the other half consists largely of stray bullets," observed the prince, eyeing his son suspiciously from under his shaggy brows. "You will allow me to say, Giovanni, that for thoughtless folly you have rarely had your equal in the world."

"I believe you are right," returned the younger man bitterly. "Nevertheless I mean to undertake this journey."

"And does Corona consent to it? Why are you so pale? I believe you are ill?"

"Yes—she consents. We shall take the child."

"Orsino? You are certainly out of your mind. It is bad enough to take a delicate woman—"

"Corona is far from delicate. She is very strong and able to bear anything."

"Don't interrupt me. I tell you she is a woman, and so of course she must be delicate. Can you not understand common sense? As for the boy, he is my grandson, and if you are not old enough to know how to take care of him, I am. He shall not go. I will not permit it. You are talking nonsense. Go and dress for dinner, or send for the doctor—in short, behave like a human being! I will go and see Corona myself."

The old gentleman's hasty temper was already up, and he strode to the door. Giovanni laid his hand somewhat heavily upon his father's arm.

"Excuse me," he said, "Corona cannot see you now. She is dressing."

"I will talk to her through the door. I will wait in her boudoir till she can see me."

"I do not think she will see you this evening. She will be busy in getting ready for the journey."

"She will dine with us, I suppose?"

"I scarcely know—I am not sure."

Old Saracinesca suddenly turned upon his son. His gray hair bristled on his head, and his black eyes flashed. With a quick movement he seized Giovanni's arms and held him before him as in a vice.

"Look here!" he cried savagely. "I will not be made a fool of by a boy. Something has happened which you are afraid to tell me. Answer me. I mean to know!"

"You will not know from me," replied Sant' Ilario, keeping his temper as he generally did in the face of a struggle. "You will know nothing, because there is nothing to know."

Saracinesca laughed. "Then there can be no possible objection to my seeing Corona," he said, dropping his hold and again going towards the door. Once more Giovanni stopped him.

"You cannot see her now," he said in determined tones.

"Then tell me what all this trouble is about," retorted his father.

But Giovanni did not speak. Had he been cooler he would not have sought the interview so soon, but he had forgotten that the old prince would certainly want to know the reason of the sudden journey.

"Do you mean to tell me or not?"

"The fact is," replied Giovanni desperately, "we have consulted the doctor—Corona is not really well—he advises us to go to the mountains—"

"Giovanni," broke in the old man roughly, "you never lied to me, but you are lying now. There has been trouble between you two, though I cannot imagine what has caused it."

"Pray do not ask me, then. I am doing what I think best—what you would think best if you knew all. I came to tell you that we were going, and I did not suppose you would have anything to say. Since you do not like the idea—well, I am sorry—but I entreat you not to ask questions. Let us go in peace."

Saracinesca looked fixedly at his son for some minutes. Then the anger faded from his face, and his expression grew very grave. He loved Giovanni exceedingly, and he loved Corona for his sake more than for her own, though he admired her and delighted in her conversation. It was certain that if there were a quarrel between husband and wife, and if Giovanni had the smallest show of right on his side, the old man's sympathies would be with him.

Giovanni's sense of honour, on the other hand, prevented him from telling his father what had happened. He did not choose that even his nearest relation should think of Corona as he thought himself, and he would have taken any step to conceal her guilt. Unfortunately for his purpose he was a very truthful man, and had no experience of lying, so that his father detected him at once. Moreover, his pale face and agitated manner told plainly enough that something very serious had occurred, and so soon as the old prince had convinced himself of this his goodwill was enlisted on the side of his son.

"Giovannino," he said at last very gently, "I do not want to pry into your secrets nor to ask you questions which you do not care to answer. I do not believe you are capable of having committed any serious folly which your wife could really resent. If you should be unfaithful to her, I would disown you. If, on the other hand, she has deceived you, I will do all in my power to help you."

Perhaps Giovanni's face betrayed something of the truth at these words. He turned away and leaned against the chimney-piece.

"I cannot tell you—I cannot tell you," he repeated. "I think I am doing what is best. That is all I can say. You may know some day, though I trust not. Let us go away without explanations."

"My dear boy," replied the old man, coming up to him and laying his hand on his shoulder, "you must do as you think best. Go to Saracinesca if you will, and if you can. If not, go somewhere else. Take heart. Things are not always as black as they look."

Giovanni straightened himself as though by an effort, and grasped his father's broad, brown hand.

"Thank you," he said. "Good-bye. I will come down and see you in a few days. Good-bye!"

His voice trembled and he hurriedly left the room. The prince stood still a moment and then threw himself into a deep chair, staring at the lamp and biting his gray moustache savagely, as though to hide some almost uncontrollable emotion. There was a slight moisture in his eyes as they looked steadily at the bright lamp.

The papers and parchments lay unheeded on the table, and he did not touch them again that night. He was thinking, not of his lonely old age nor of the dishonour brought upon his house, but of the boy he had loved as his own soul for more than thirty years, and of a swarthy little child that lay asleep in a distant room, the warm blood tinging its olive cheeks and its little clinched hands thrown back above its head.

For Corona he had no thought but hatred. He had guessed Giovanni's secret too well, and his heart was hardened against the woman who had brought shame and suffering upon his son.

CHAPTER XI

SAN Giacinto had signally failed in his attempt to prevent the meeting between Gouache and Faustina Montevarchi, and had unintentionally caused trouble of a much more serious nature in another quarter. The Zouave returned to his lodging late at night, and of course found no note upon his dressing-table. He did not miss the pin, for he of course never wore it, and attached no particular value to a thing of such small worth which he had picked up in the street and which consequently had no associations for him. He lacked the sense of order in his belongings, and the pin had lain neglected for weeks among a heap of useless little trifles, dingy cotillon favours that had been there since the previous year, stray copper coins, broken pencils, uniform buttons and such trash, accumulated during many months and totally unheeded. Had he seen the pin anywhere else he would have recognised it, but he did not notice its absence. The old woman, Caterina Ranucci, hugged her money and said nothing about either of the visitors who had entered the room during the afternoon. The consequence was that Gouache rose early on the following morning and went towards the church with a light heart. He did not know certainly that Faustina would come there, and indeed there were many probabilities against her doing so, but in the hopefulness of a man thoroughly in love, Gouache looked forward to seeing her with as much assurance as though the matter had been arranged and settled between them.

The parish church of Sant' Agostino is a very large building. The masses succeed each other in rapid succession from seven o'clock in the morning until midday, and a great crowd of parishioners pass in and out in an almost constant stream. It was therefore Gouache's intention to arrive so early as to be sure that Faustina had not yet come, and he trusted to luck to be there at the right time, for he was obliged to visit the temporary barrack of his corps before going to the church, and was also obliged to attend mass at a later hour with his battalion. On presenting himself at quarters he learned to his surprise that Monte Rotondo had not surrendered yet, though news of the catastrophe was expected every moment. The Zouaves were ordered to remain under arms all day in case of emergency, and it was only through the friendly assistance of one of his officers that Anastase obtained leave to absent himself for a couple of hours. He hailed a cab and drove to the church as fast as he could.

In less than twenty minutes after he had stationed himself at the entrance, Faustina ascended the steps accompanied by a servant. The latter was a middle-aged woman with hard features, clad in black, and wearing a handkerchief thrown loosely over her head after the manner of maids in those days. She evidently expected nothing, for she looked straight before her, peering into the church in order to see beforehand at which chapel there was likely to be a mass immediately. Faustina was a lovely figure in the midst of the crowd of common people who thronged the doorway, and whose coarse dark faces threw her ethereal features into strong relief while she advanced. Gouache felt his heart beat hard, for he had not seen her for five days since they had parted on that memorable Tuesday night at the gate of her father's house. Her eyes met his in a long and loving look, and the colour rose faintly in her delicate pale cheek. In the press she managed to pass close to him, and for a moment he succeeded in clasping her small hand in his, her maid being on the other side. He was about to ask a question when she whispered a few words and passed on.

"Follow me through the crowd, I will manage it," was what she said.

Gouache obeyed, and kept close behind her. The church was very full and there was difficulty in getting seats.

"I will wait here," said the young girl to her servant. "Get us chairs and find out where there is to be a mass. It is of no use for me to go through the crowd if I may have to come back again."

The hard-featured woman nodded and went away. Several minutes must elapse before she returned, and Faustina with Gouache behind her moved across the stream of persons who were going out through the door in the other aisle. In a moment they found themselves in a comparatively quiet corner, separated from the main body of the church by the moving people. Faustina fixed her eyes in the direction whence her woman would probably return, ready to enter the throng instantly, if necessary. Even where they now were, so many others were standing and kneeling that the presence of the Zouave beside Faustina would create no surprise.

"It is very wrong to meet you in church," said the girl, a little shy, at first, with that timidity a woman always feels on meeting a man whom she has last seen on unexpectedly intimate terms.

"I could not go away without seeing you," replied Gouache, his eyes intent on her face. "And I knew you would understand my signs, though no one else would. You have made me very happy, Faustina. It would have been agony to march away without seeing your face again—you do not know what these days have been without you! Do you realise that we used to meet almost every afternoon? Did they tell you why I could not come? I told every one I met, in hopes you might hear. Did you? Do you understand?"

Faustina nodded her graceful head, and glanced quickly at his face. Then she looked down, tapping the pavement gently with her parasol. The colour came and went in her cheeks.

"Do you really love me?" she asked in a low voice.

"I think, my darling, that no one ever loved as I love. I would that I might be given time to tell you what my love is, and that you might have patience to hear. What are words, unless one can say all one would? What is it, if I tell you that I love you with all my heart, and soul and thoughts? Do not other men say as much and forget that they have spoken? I would find a way of saying it that should make you believe in spite of yourself—"

"In spite of myself?" interrupted Faustina, with a bright smile while her brown eyes rested lovingly on his for an instant. "You need not that," she added simply, "for I love you, too."

Nothing but the sanctity of the place prevented Anastase from taking her in his arms then and there. There was something so exquisite in her simplicity and earnestness that he found himself speechless before her for a moment. It was something that intoxicated his spirit more than his senses, for it was utterly new to him and appealed to his own loyal and innocent nature as it could not have appealed to a baser man.

"Ah, Faustina!" he said at last. "God made you when he made the violets, on a spring morning in Paradise!"

Faustina blushed again, faintly as the sea at dawn.

"Must you go away?" she asked.

"You would not have me desert at such a moment?"

"Would it be deserting—quite? Would it be dishonourable?"

"It would be cowardly. I should never dare to look you in the face again."

"I suppose it would be wrong," she answered with a bitter little sigh.

"I will come back very soon, dearest. The time will be short."

"So long—so long! How can you say it will be short? If you do not come soon you will find me dead—I cannot bear it many days more."

"I will write to you."

"How can you write? Your letters would be seen. Oh no! It is impossible!"

"I will write to your friend—to the Princess Sant'Ilario. She will give you the letters. She is safe, is she not?"

"Oh, how happy I shall be! It will be almost like seeing you—no, not that! But so much better than nothing. But you do not go at once?"

"It may be today, tomorrow, at any time. But you shall know of it. Ah, Faustina! My own one—"

"Hush! There is my maid. Quick, behind the pillar. I will meet her. Good-bye—good-bye—Oh! Not good-bye—some other word—"

"God keep you, my beloved, and make it not 'good-bye'!"

With one furtive touch of the hand, one long last look, they separated, Faustina to mingle in the crowd, Gouache to follow at a long distance until he saw her kneeling at her chair before one of the side altars of the church. Then he stationed himself where he could see her, and watched through the half hour during which the low mass lasted. He did not know when he should see her again, and indeed it was as likely as not that they should not meet on this side of eternity. Many a gallant young fellow marched out in those days and was picked off by a bullet from a red-shirted volunteer. Gouache, indeed, did not believe that his life was to be cut short so suddenly, and built castles in the air with that careless delight in the future which a man feels who is not at all afraid. But such accidents happened often, and though he might be more lucky than another, it was just as possible that an ounce of lead should put an end to his soldiering, his painting and his courtship within another week. The mere thought was so horrible that his bright nature refused to harbour it, and he gazed on Faustina Montevarchi as she knelt at her devotions, wondering, indeed, what strange chances fate had in store for them both, but never once doubting that she should one day be his. He waited until she passed him in the crowd, and gave him one more look before going away. Then, when he had seen her disappear at the turning of the street, he sprang into his cab and was driven back to the barracks where he must remain on duty all day.

As he descended he was surprised to see Sant' Ilario standing upon the pavement, very pale, and apparently in a bad humour, his overcoat buttoned to his throat, and his hands thrust in the pockets. There was no one in the street, but the sentinel at the doorway, and Giovanni walked quickly up to Gouache as the latter fumbled for the change to pay his driver. Anastase smiled and made a short military salute. Sant' Ilario bowed stiffly and did not extend his hand.

"I tried to find you last night," he said coldly. "You were out. Will you favour me with five minutes' conversation?"

"Willingly," answered the other, looking instinctively at his watch, to be sure that he had time to spare.

Sant' Ilario walked a few yards up the street, before speaking, Gouache keeping close to his side. Then both stopped, and Giovanni turned sharply round and faced his enemy.

"It is unnecessary to enter into any explanations, Monsieur Gouache," he said. "This is a matter which can only end in one way. I presume you will see the propriety of inventing a pretext which may explain our meeting before the world."

Gouache stared at Sant' Ilario in the utmost amazement. When they had last met they had parted on the most friendly terms. He did not understand a word of what his companion was saying.

"Excuse me, prince," he said at length. "I have not the least idea what you mean. As far as I am concerned this meeting is quite accidental. I came here on duty."

Sant' Ilario was somewhat taken aback by the Zouave's polite astonishment. He seemed even more angry than surprised, however; and his black eyebrows bent together fiercely.

"Let us waste no words," he said imperiously. "If I had found you last night, the affair might have been over by this time."

"What affair?" asked Gouache, more and more mystified.

"You are amazingly slow of comprehension, Monsieur Gouache," observed Giovanni. "To be plain, I desire to have an opportunity of killing you. Do you understand me now?"

"Perfectly," returned the soldier, raising his brows, and then breaking into a laugh of genuine amusement. "You are quite welcome to as many opportunities as you like, though I confess it would interest me to know the reason of your good intentions towards me."

If Gouache had behaved as Giovanni had expected he would, the latter would have repeated his request that a pretext should be found which should explain the duel to the world. But there was such extraordinary assurance in the Zouave's manner that Sant' Ilario suddenly became exasperated with him and lost his temper, a misfortune which very rarely happened to him.

"Monsieur Gouache," he said angrily, "I took the liberty of visiting your lodgings yesterday afternoon, and I found this letter, fastened with this pin upon your table. I presume you will not think any further explanation necessary."

Gouache stared at the objects which Sant' Ilario held out to him and drew back stiffly. It was his turn to be outraged at the insult.

"Sir," he said, "I understand that you acted in the most impertinent manner in entering my room and taking what did not belong to you. I understand nothing else. I found that pin on the Ponte Sant' Angelo a month ago, and it was, I believe, upon my table yesterday. As for the letter I know nothing about it. Yes, if you insist, I will read it."

There was a pause during which Gouache ran his eyes over the few lines written on the notepaper, while Giovanni watched him very pale and wrathful.

"The pin is my wife's, and the note is written on her paper and addressed to you, though in a feigned hand. Do you deny that both came from her, were brought by her in person, for yourself?"

"I deny it utterly and categorically," answered Gouache. "Though I will assuredly demand satisfaction of you for entering my rooms without my permission, I give you my word of honour that I could receive no such letter from the princess, your wife. The thing is monstrously iniquitous, and you have been grossly deceived into injuring the good name of a woman as innocent as an angel. Since the pin is the property of the princess, pray return it to her with my compliments, and say that I found it on the bridge of Sant' Angelo. I can remember the very date. It was a quarter of an hour before I was run over by Prince Montevarchi's carriage. It was therefore on the 23rd of September. As for the rest, do me the favour to tell me where my friends can find yours in an hour."

"At my house. But allow me to add that I do not believe a word of what you say."

"Is it a Roman custom to insult a man who has agreed to fight with you?" inquired Gouache. "We are more polite in France. We salute our adversaries before beginning the combat."

Therewith the Zouave saluted Giovanni courteously and turned on his heel, leaving the latter in an even worse humour than he had found him. Gouache was too much surprised at the interview to reason connectedly about the causes which had led to it, and accepted the duel with Sant' Ilario blindly, because he could not avoid it, and because whatever offence he himself had unwittingly given he had in turn been insulted by Giovanni in a way which left him no alternative but that of a resort to arms. His adversary had admitted, had indeed boasted, of having entered Gouache's rooms, and of having taken thence the letter and the pin. This alone constituted an injury for which reparation was necessary, but not content with this, Sant' Ilario had given him the lie direct. Matters were so confused that it was hard to tell which was the injured party; but since the prince had undoubtedly furnished a pretext more than sufficient, the soldier had seized the opportunity of proposing to send his friends to demand satisfaction. It was clear, however, that the duel could not take place at once, since Gouache was under arms, and it was imperatively necessary that he should have permission to risk his life in a private quarrel at such a time. It was also certain that his superiors would not allow anything of the kind at present, and Gouache for his part was glad of the fact. He preferred to be killed before the enemy rather than in a duel for which there was no adequate explanation, except that a man who had been outrageously deceived by a person or persons unknown had chosen to attack him for a thing he had never done. He had not the slightest intention of avoiding the encounter, but he preferred to see some active service in a cause to which he was devoted before being run through the body by one who was his enemy only by mistake. Giovanni's reputation as a swordsman made it probable that the issue would be unfavourable to Gouache, and the latter, with the simple fearlessness that belonged to his character, meant if possible to have a chance of distinguishing himself before being killed.

Half an hour later, a couple of officers of Zouaves called upon Sant' Ilario, and found his representatives waiting for them. Giovanni had had the good fortune to find Count Spicca at home. That melancholy gentleman had been his second in an affair with Ugo del Ferice nearly three years earlier and had subsequently killed one of the latter's seconds in consequence of his dishonourable behaviour in the field. He had been absent in consequence until a few weeks before the present time, when matters had been arranged, and he had found himself free to return unmolested. It had been remarked at the club that something would happen before he had been in Rome many days. He was a very tall and cadaverous man, exceedingly prone to take offence, and exceedingly skilful in exacting the precise amount of blood which he considered a fair return for an injury. He had never been known to kill a man by accident, but had rarely failed to take his adversary's life when he had determined to do so. Spicca had brought another friend, whom it is unnecessary to describe. The interview was short and conclusive.

The two officers had instructions to demand a serious duel, and Spicca and his companion had been told to make the conditions even more dangerous if they could do so. On the other hand, the officers explained that as Rome was in a state of siege, and Garibaldi almost at the gates, the encounter could not take place until the crisis was past. They undertook to appear for Gouache in case he chanced to be shot in an engagement. Spicca, who did not know the real cause of the duel, and was indeed somewhat surprised to learn that Giovanni had quarrelled with a Zouave, made no attempt to force an immediate meeting, but begged leave to retire and consult with his principal, an informality which was of course agreed to by the other side. In five minutes he returned, stating that he accepted the provisions proposed, and that he should expect twenty-four hours' notice when Gouache should be ready. The four gentlemen drew up the necessary "protocol," and parted on friendly terms after a few minutes' conversation, in which various proposals were made in regard to the ground.

Spicca alone remained behind, and he immediately went to Giovanni, carrying a copy of the protocol, on which the ink was still wet.

"Here it is," he said sadly, as he entered the room, holding up the paper in his hand. "These revolutions are very annoying! There is no end to the inconvenience they cause."

"I suppose it could not be helped," answered Giovanni, gloomily.

"No. I believe I have not the reputation of wasting time in these matters. You must try and amuse yourself as best you can until the day comes. It is a pity you have not some other affair in the meanwhile, just to make the time pass pleasantly. It would keep your hand in, too. But then you have the pleasures of anticipation."

Giovanni laughed hoarsely, Spicca took a foil from the wall and played with it, looking along the thin blade, then setting the point on the carpet and bending the weapon to see whether it would spring back properly. Giovanni's eyes followed his movements, watching the slender steel, and then glancing at Spicca's long arms, his nervous fingers and peculiar grip.

"How do you manage to kill your man whenever you choose?" asked Sant' Ilario, half idly, half in curiosity.

"It is perfectly simple, at least with foils," replied the other, making passes in the air. "Now, if you will take a foil, I will promise to run you through any part of your body within three minutes. You may make a chalked mark on the precise spot. If I miss by a hair's-breadth I will let you lunge at me without guarding."

"Thank you," said Giovanni; "I do not care to be run through this morning, but I confess I would like to know how you do it. Could not you touch the spot without thrusting home?"

"Certainly, if you do not mind a scratch on the shoulder or the arm. I will try and not draw blood. Come on—so—in guard—wait a minute! Where will you be hit? That is rather important."

Giovanni, who was in a desperate humour and cared little what he did, rather relished the idea of a bout which savoured of reality. There was a billiard-table in the adjoining room, and he fetched a piece of chalk at once.

"Here," said he, making a small white spot upon his coat on the outside of his right shoulder.

"Very well," observed Spicca. "Now, do not rush in or I may hurt you."

"Am I to thrust, too?" asked Giovanni.

"If you like. You cannot touch me if you do."

"We shall see," answered Sant' Ilario, nettled at Spicca's poor opinion of his skill. "In guard!"

They fell into position and began play. Giovanni immediately tried his special method of disarming his adversary, which he had scarcely ever known to fail. He forgot, however, that Spicca had seen him practise this piece of strategy with success upon Del Ferice. The melancholy duellist had spent weeks in studying the trick, and had completely mastered it. To Giovanni's surprise the Count's hand turned as easily as a ball in a socket, avoiding the pressure, while his point scarcely deviated from the straight line. Giovanni, angry at his failure, made a quick feint and a thrust, lunging to his full reach. Spicca parried as easily and carelessly as though the prince had been a mere beginner, and allowed the latter to recover himself before he replied. A full two seconds after Sant' Ilario had resumed his guard, Spicca's foil ran over his with a speed that defied parrying, and he felt a short sharp prick in his right shoulder. Spicca sprang back and lowered his weapon.

"I think that is the spot," he said coolly, and then came forward and examined Giovanni's coat. The point had penetrated the chalked mark in the centre, inflicting a wound not more than a quarter of an inch deep in the muscle of the shoulder.

"Observe," he continued, "that it was a simple tierce, without a feint or any trick whatever."

On realising his absolute inferiority to such a master of the art, Giovanni broke into a hearty laugh at his own discomfiture. So long as he had supposed that some sort of equality existed between them he had been angry at being outdone; but when he saw with what ease Spicca had accomplished his purpose, his admiration for the skill displayed made him forget his annoyance.

"How in the world did you do it?" he said. "I thought I could parry a simple tierce, even though I might not be a match for you!"

"Many people have thought the same, my friend. There are two or three elements in my process, one of which is my long reach. Another is the knack of thrusting very quickly, which is partly natural, and partly the result of practice. My trick consists in the way I hold my foil. Look here. I do not grasp the hilt with all my fingers as you do. The whole art of fencing lies in the use of the thumb and forefinger. I lay my forefinger straight in the direction of the blade. Of course I cannot do it with a basket or a bell hilt, but no one ever objects to common foils. It is dangerous—yes—I might hurt my finger, but then, I am too quick. You ask the advantage? It is very simple. You and I and every one are accustomed from childhood to point with the forefinger at things we see. The accuracy with which we point is much more surprising than you imagine. We instinctively aim the forefinger at the object to a hair's-breadth of exactness. I only make my point follow my forefinger. The important thing, then, is to grasp the hilt very firmly, and yet leave the wrist limber. I shoot in the same way with a revolver, and pull the trigger with my middle finger. I scarcely ever miss. You might amuse yourself by trying these things while you are waiting for Gouache. They will make the time pass pleasantly."

Spicca, whose main pleasure in life was in the use of weapons, could not conceive of any more thoroughly delightful occupation.

"I will try it," said Giovanni, rubbing his shoulder a little, for the scratch irritated him. "It is very interesting. I hope that fellow will not go and have himself killed by the Garibaldians before I get a chance at him."

"You are absolutely determined to kill him, then?" Spicca's voice, which had grown animated during his exposition of his method, now sank again to its habitually melancholy tone.

Giovanni only shrugged his shoulders at the question, as though any answer were needless. He hung the foil he had used in its place on the wall, and began to smoke.

"You will not have another bout?" inquired the Count, putting away his weapon also, and taking his hat to go.

"Thanks—not today. We shall meet soon, I hope. I am very grateful for your good offices, Spicca. I would ask you to stay to breakfast, but I do not want my father to know of this affair. He would suspect something if he saw you here."

"Yes," returned the other quietly, "people generally do. I am rather like a public executioner in that respect. My visits often precede a catastrophe. What would you have? I am a lonely man."

"You, who have so many friends!" exclaimed Giovanni.

"Bah! It is time to be off," said Spicca, and shaking his friend's hand hastily he left the room.

Giovanni stood for several minutes after he had gone, wondering with a vague curiosity what this man's history had been, as many had wondered before. There was a fatal savour of death about Spicca which everybody felt who came near him. He was dreaded as one of the worst-tempered men and one of the most remarkable swordsmen in Europe. He was always consulted in affairs of honour, and his intimate acquaintance with the code, his austere integrity, and his vast experience, made him invaluable in such matters. But he was not known to have any intimate friends among men or women. He neither gambled nor made love to other men's wives, nor did any of those things which too easily lead to encounters of arms; and yet, in his cold and melancholy way he was constantly quarrelling and fighting and killing his man, till it was a wonder that the police would tolerate him in any European capital. It was rumoured that he had a strange history, and that his life had been embittered in his early youth by some tragic circumstance, but no one could say what that occurrence had been nor where it had taken place. He felt an odd sympathy for Giovanni, and his reference to his loneliness in his parting speech was unique, and set his friend to wondering about him.

Giovanni's mind was now as much at rest as was possible, under conditions which obliged him to postpone his vengeance for an indefinite period. He had passed a sleepless night after his efforts to find Gouache and had risen early in the morning to be sure of catching him. He had not seen his father since their interview of the previous evening, and had hoped not to see him again till the moment of leaving for Saracinesca. The old man had understood him, and that was all that was necessary for the present. He suspected that his father would not seek an interview any more than he did himself. But an obstacle had presented itself in the way of his departure which he had not expected, and which irritated him beyond measure. Corona was ill. He did not know whether her ailment were serious or not, but it was evident that he could not force her to leave her bed and accompany him to the country, so long as the doctor declared that she could not be moved. When Spicca was gone, he did not know what to do with himself. He would not go and see his wife, for any meeting must be most unpleasant. He had nerved himself to conduct her to the mountains, and had expected that the long drive would be passed in a disagreeable silence. So long as Corona was well and strong, he could have succeeded well enough in treating her as he believed that she deserved. Now that she was ill, he felt how impossible it would be for him to take good care of her without seeming to relent, even if he did not relent in earnest; and on the other hand his really noble nature would have prevented him from being harsh in his manner to her while she was suffering.

Until he had been convinced that a duel with Gouache was for the present impossible, his anger had supported him, and had made the time pass quickly throughout the sleepless night and through the events of the morning. Now that he was alone, with nothing to do but to meditate upon the situation, his savage humour forsook him and the magnitude of his misfortune oppressed him and nearly drove him mad. He went over the whole train of evidence again and again, and as often as he reviewed what had occurred, his conviction grew deeper and stronger, and he acknowledged that he had been deceived as man was never deceived before. He realised the boundless faith he had given to this woman who had betrayed him; he recollected the many proofs she had given him of her love; he drew upon the store of his past happiness and tortured himself with visions of what could never be again; he called up in fancy Corona's face when he had led her to the altar and the very look in her eyes was again upon him; he remembered that day more than two years ago when, upon the highest tower of Saracinesca, he had asked her to be his wife, and he knew not whether he desired to burn the memory of that first embrace from his heart, or to dwell upon the sweet recollection of that moment and suffer the wound of today to rankle more hotly by the horror of the comparison. When he thought of what she had been, it seemed impossible that she could have fallen; when he saw what she had become he could not believe that she had ever been innocent. A baser man than Giovanni would have suffered more in his personal vanity, seeing that his idol had been degraded for a mere soldier of fortune—or for a clever artist—whichever Gouache called himself, and such a husband would have forgiven her more easily had she forsaken him for one of his own standing and rank. But Giovanni was far above and beyond the thought of comparing his enemy with himself. He was wounded in what he had held most sacred, which was his heart, and in what had grown to be the mainspring of his existence, his trust in the woman he loved. Those who readily believe are little troubled if one of their many little faiths be shaken; but men who believe in a few things, with the whole strength of their being, are hurt mortally when that on which they build their loyalty is shattered and overturned.

Giovanni was a just man, and was rarely carried away by appearances; least of all could he have shown any such weakness when the yielding to it involved the destruction of all that he cared for in life. But the evidence was overwhelming, and no man could be blamed for accepting it. There was no link wanting in the chain, and the denials made by Corona and Anastase could not have influenced any man in his senses. What could a woman do but deny all? What was there for Gouache but to swear that the accusation was untrue? Would not any other man or woman have done as much? There was no denying it. The only person who remained unquestioned was Faustina Montevarchi. Either she was the innocent girl she appeared to be or not. If she were, how could Giovanni explain to her that she had been duped, and made an instrument in the hands of Gouache and Corona? She would not know what he meant. Even if she admitted that she loved Gouache, was it not clear that he had deceived her too, for the sake of making an accomplice of one who was constantly with Corona? Her love for the soldier could not explain the things that had passed between Anastase and Giovanni's wife, which Giovanni had seen with his own eyes. It could not account for the whisperings, the furtive meeting and tender words of which he had been a witness in his own house. It could not do away with the letter and the pin. But if Faustina were not innocent of assisting the two, she would deny everything, even as they had done.

As he thought of all these matters and followed the cruelly logical train of reasoning forced upon him by the facts, a great darkness descended upon Giovanni's heart, and he knew that his happiness was gone from him for ever. Henceforth nothing remained but to watch his wife jealously, and suffer his ills with the best heart he could. The very fact that he loved her still, with a passion that defied all things, added a terrible bitterness to what he had to bear, for it made him despise himself as none would have dared to despise him.

CHAPTER XII

As Giovanni sat in solitude in his room he was not aware that his father had received a visit from no less a personage than Prince Montevarchi. The latter found Saracinesca very much preoccupied, and in no mood for conversation, and consequently did not stay very long. When he went away, however, he carried under his arm a bundle of deeds and documents which he had long desired to see and in the perusal of which he promised himself to spend a very interesting day. He had come with the avowed object of getting them, and he neither anticipated nor met with any difficulty in obtaining what he wanted. He spoke of his daughter's approaching marriage with San Giacinto, and after expressing his satisfaction at the alliance with the Saracinesca, remarked that his son-in-law had told him the story of the ancient deed, and begged permission to see it for himself. The request was natural, and Saracinesca was not suspicious at any time; at present, he was too much occupied with his own most unpleasant reflections to attach any importance to the incident. Montevarchi thought there was something wrong with his friend, but inasmuch as he had received the papers, he asked no questions and presently departed with them, hastening homewards in order to lose no time in satisfying his curiosity.

Two hours later he was still sitting in his dismal study with the manuscripts before him. He had ascertained what he wanted to know, namely, that the papers really existed and were drawn up in a legal form. He had hoped to find a rambling agreement, made out principally by the parties concerned, and copied with some improvements by the family notary of the time, for he had made up his mind that if any flaw could be discovered in the deed San Giacinto should become Prince Saracinesca, and should have possession of all the immense wealth that belonged to the family. San Giacinto was the heir in the direct line, and although his great-grand-father had relinquished his birthright in the firm expectation of having no children, the existence of his descendants might greatly modify the provisions of the agreement.

Montevarchi's face fell when he had finished deciphering the principal document. The provisions and conditions were short and concise, and were contained upon one large sheet of parchment, signed, witnessed and bearing the official seal and signature which proved that it had been ratified.

It was set forth therein that Don Leone Saracinesca, being the eldest son of Don Giovanni Saracinesca, deceased, Prince of Saracinesca, of Sant' Ilario and of Torleone, Duke of Barda, and possessor of many other titles, Grandee of Spain of the first class and Count of the Holy Roman Empire, did of his own free will, by his own motion and will, make over and convey to, and bestow upon, Don Orsino Saracinesca, his younger and only brother, the principalities of Saracinesca—here followed a complete list of the various titles and estates—including the titles, revenues, seigneurial rights, appanages, holdings, powers and sovereignty attached to and belonging to each and every one, to him, the aforesaid Don Orsino Saracinesca and to the heirs of his body in the male line direct for ever.

Here there was a stop, and the manuscript began again at the top of the other side of the sheet. The next clause contained the solitary provision to the effect that Don Leone reserved to himself the estate and title of San Giacinto in the kingdom of Naples, which at his death, he having no children, should revert to the aforesaid Don Orsino Saracinesca and his heirs for ever. It was further stated that the agreement was wholly of a friendly character, and that Don Leone bound himself to take no steps whatever to reinstate himself in the titles and possessions which, of his own free will, he relinquished, the said agreement being, in the opinion of both parties, for the advantage of the whole house of Saracinesca.

"He bound himself, not his descendants," remarked Montevarchi at last, as he again bent his head over the document and examined the last clause. "And he says 'having no children'—in Latin the words may mean in case he had none, being in the ablative absolute. Having no children, to Orsino and his heirs for ever—but since he had a son, the case is altered. Ay, but that clause in the first part says to Orsino and his heirs for ever, and says nothing about Leone having no children. It is more absolute than the ablative. That is bad."

For a long time he pondered over the writing. The remaining documents were merely transfers of the individual estates, in each of which it was briefly stated that the property in question was conveyed in accordance with the conditions of the main deed. There was no difficulty there. The Saracinesca inheritance depended solely on the existence of this one piece of parchment, and of the copy or registration of it in the government offices. Montevarchi glanced at the candle that stood before him in a battered brass candlestick, and his old heart beat a little faster than usual. To burn the sheet of parchment, and then deny on oath that he had ever seen it—it was very simple. Saracinesca would find it hard to prove the existence of the thing. Montevarchi hesitated, and then laughed at himself for his folly. It would be necessary first to ascertain what there was at the Chancery office, otherwise he would be ruining himself for nothing. That was certainly the most important step at present. He pondered over the matter for some time and then rose from his chair.

As he stood before the table he glanced once more at the sheet. As though the greater distance made it more clear to his old sight, he noticed that there was a blank space, capable of containing three lines of writing like what was above, while still leaving a reasonable margin at the bottom of the page. As the second clause was the shorter, the scribe had doubtless thought it better to begin afresh on the other side.

Montevarchi sat down again, and took a large sheet of paper and a pen. He rapidly copied the first clause to the end, but after the words "in the male line direct for ever" his pen still ran on. The deed then read as follows: "…in the male line direct for ever, provided that the aforesaid Don Leone Saracinesca shall have no son born to him in wedlock, in which case, and if such a son be born, this present deed is wholly null, void and ineffectual."

Montevarchi did not stop here. He carefully copied the remainder as it stood, to the last word. Then he put away the original and read what he had written very slowly and carefully. With the addition it was perfectly clear that San Giacinto must be considered to be the lawful and only Prince Saracinesca.

"How well those few words would look at the bottom of the page!" exclaimed the old man half aloud. He sat still and gloated in imagination over the immense wealth which would thus be brought into his family.

"They shall be there—they must be there!" he muttered at last. "Millions! Millions! After all it is only common justice. The old reprobate would never have disinherited his son if he had expected to have one."

His long thin fingers crooked themselves and scratched the shabby green baize that covered the table, as though heaping together little piles of money, and then hiding them under the palm of his hand.

"Even if there is a copy," he said again under his breath, "the little work will look as prettily upon it as on this—if only the sheets are the same size and there is the same space," he added, his face falling again at the disagreeable reflection that the duplicate might differ in some respect from the original.

The plan was simple enough in appearance, and provided that the handwriting could be successfully forged, there was no reason why it should not succeed. The man who could do it, if he would, was in the house at that moment, and Montevarchi knew it. Arnoldo Meschini, the shrivelled little secretary and librarian, who had a profound knowledge of the law and spent his days as well as most of his nights in poring over crabbed manuscripts, was the very person for such a piece of work. He understood the smallest variations in handwriting which belonged to different periods, and the minutest details of old-fashioned penmanship were as familiar to him as the common alphabet. But would he do it? Would he undertake the responsibility of a forgery of which the success would produce such tremendous responsibilities, of which the failure would involve such awful disgrace? Montevarchi had reasons of his own for believing that Arnoldo Meschini would do anything he was ordered to do, and would moreover keep the secret faithfully. Indeed, as far as discretion was concerned, he would, in case of exposure, have to bear the penalty. Montevarchi would arrange that. If discovered it would be easy for him to pretend that being unable to read the manuscript he had employed his secretary to do so, and that the latter, in the hope of reward, had gratuitously imposed upon the prince and the courts of law before whom the case would be tried.

One thing was necessary. San Giacinto must never see the documents until they were produced as evidence. In the first place it was important that he, who was the person nearest concerned, should be in reality perfectly innocent, and should be himself as much deceived as any one. Nothing impresses judges like real and unaffected innocence. Secondly, if he were consulted, it was impossible to say what view he might take of the matter. Montevarchi suspected him of possessing some of the hereditary boldness of the Saracinesca. He might refuse to be a party in a deception, even though he himself was to benefit by it, a consideration which chilled the old man's blood and determined him at once to confide the secret to no one but Arnoldo Meschini, who was completely in his power.

The early history of this remarkable individual was uncertain. He had received an excellent education and it is no exaggeration to call him learned, for he possessed a surprising knowledge of ancient manuscripts and a great experience in everything connected with this branch of archaeology. It was generally believed that he had been bred to enter the church, but he himself never admitted that he had been anything more than a scholar in a religious seminary. He had subsequently studied law and had practised for some time, when he had suddenly abandoned his profession in order to accept the ill-paid post of librarian and secretary to the father of the present Prince Montevarchi. Probably his love of mediaeval lore had got the better of his desire for money, and during the five and twenty years he had spent in the palace he had never been heard to complain of his condition. He lived in a small chamber in the attic and passed his days in the library, winter and summer alike, perpetually poring over the manuscripts and making endless extracts in his odd, old-fashioned handwriting. The result of his labours was never published, and at first sight it would have been hard to account for his enormous industry and for the evident satisfaction he derived from his work. The nature of the man, however, was peculiar, and his occupation was undoubtedly congenial to him, and far more profitable than it appeared to be.

Arnoldo Meschini was a forger. He was one of that band of manufacturers of antiquities who have played such a part in the dealings of foreign collectors during the last century, and whose occupation, though slow and laborious, occasionally produces immense profits. He had not given up his calling with the deliberate intention of resorting to this method of earning a subsistence, but had drifted into his evil practices by degrees. In the first instance he had quitted the bar in consequence of having been connected with a scandalous case of extortion and blackmailing, in which he had been suspected of constructing forged documents for his client, though the crime had not been proved against him. His reputation, however, had been ruined, and he had been forced to seek his bread elsewhere. It chanced that the former librarian of the Montevarchi died at that time and that the prince was in search of a learned man ready to give his services for a stipend about equal to the wages of a footman. Meschini presented himself and got the place. The old prince was delighted with him and agreed to forget the aforesaid disgrace he had incurred, in consideration of his exceptional qualities. He set himself systematically to study the contents of the ancient library, with the intention of publishing the contents of the more precious manuscripts, and for two or three years he pursued his object with this laudable purpose, and with the full consent of his employer.

One day a foreign newspaper fell into his hands containing an account of a recent sale in which sundry old manuscripts had brought large prices. A new idea crossed his mind, and the prospect of unexpected wealth unfolded itself to his imagination. For several months he studied even more industriously than before, until, having made up his mind, he began to attempt the reproduction of a certain valuable writing dating from the fourteenth century. He worked in his own room during the evening and allowed no one to see what he was doing, for although it was rarely that the old prince honoured the library with a visit, yet Meschini was inclined to run no risks, and proceeded in his task with the utmost secrecy.

Nothing could exceed the care he showed in the preparation and use of his materials. One of his few acquaintances was a starving, but clever chemist, who kept a dingy shop in the neighbourhood of the Ponte Quattro Capi. To this poor man he applied in order to obtain a knowledge of the ink used in the old writings. He professed himself anxious to get all possible details on the subject for a work he was preparing upon mediaeval calligraphy, and his friend soon set his mind at rest by informing him that if the ink contained any metallic parts he would easily detect them, but that if it was composed of animal and vegetable matter it would be almost impossible to give a satisfactory analysis. At the end of a few days Meschini was in possession of a recipe for concocting what he wanted, and after numerous experiments, in the course of which he himself acquired great practical knowledge of the subject, he succeeded in producing an ink apparently in all respects similar to that used by the scribe whose work he proposed to copy. He had meanwhile busied himself with the preparation of parchment, which is by no means an easy matter when it is necessary to give it the colour and consistency of very ancient skin. He learned that the ligneous acids contained in the smoke of wood could be easily detected, and it was only through the assistance of the chemist that he finally hit upon the method of staining the sheets with a thin broth of untanned leather, of which the analysis would give a result closely approaching that of the parchment itself. Moreover, he made all sorts of trials of quill pens, until he had found a method of cutting which produced the exact thickness of stroke required, and during the whole time he exercised himself in copying and recopying many pages of the manuscript upon common paper, in order to familiarise himself with the method of forming the letters.

It was nearly two years before he felt himself able to begin his first imitation, but the time and study he had expended were not lost, and the result surpassed his expectations. So ingeniously perfect was the facsimile when finished that Meschini himself would have found it hard to swear to the identity of the original if he had not been allowed to see either of the two for some time. The minutest stains were reproduced with scrupulous fidelity. The slightest erasure was copied minutely. He examined every sheet to ascertain exactly how it had been worn by the fingers rubbing on the corners and spent days in turning a page thousands of times, till the oft-repeated touch of his thumb had deepened the colour to the exact tint.

When the work was finished he hesitated. It seemed to him very perfect, but he feared lest he should be deceiving himself from having seen the thing daily for so many months. He took his copy one day to a famous collector, and submitted it to him for examination, asking at the same time what it was worth. The specialist spent several hours in examining the writing, and pronounced it very valuable, naming a large sum, while admitting that he was unable to buy it himself.

Arnoldo Meschini took his work home with him, and spent a day in considering what he should do. Then he deliberately placed the facsimile in his employer's library, and sold the original to a learned man who was collecting for a great public institution in a foreign country. His train of reasoning was simple, for he said to himself that the forgery was less likely to be detected in the shelves of the Montevarchi's palace than if put into the hands of a body of famous scientists who naturally distrusted what was brought to them. Collectors do not ask questions as to whence a valuable thing has been taken; they only examine whether it be genuine and worth the money.

Emboldened by his success, the forger had continued to manufacture facsimiles and sell originals for nearly twenty years, during which he succeeded in producing nearly as many copies, and realised a sum which to him appeared enormous and which was certainly not to be despised by any one. Some of the works he sold were published and annotated by great scholars, some were jealously guarded in the libraries of rich amateurs, who treasured them with all the selfish vigilance of the bibliomaniac. In the meanwhile Meschini's learning and skill constantly increased, till he possessed an almost diabolical skill in the art of imitating ancient writings, and a familiarity with the subject which amazed the men of learning who occasionally obtained permission to enter the library and study there. Upon these, too, Meschini now and then experimented with his forgeries, not one of which was ever detected.

Prince Montevarchi saw in his librarian only a poor wretch whose passion for ancient literature seemed to dominate his life and whose untiring industry had made him master of the very secret necessary in the present instance. He knew that such things as he contemplated had been done before and he supposed that they had been done by just such men as Arnoldo Meschini. He knew the history of the man's early disgrace and calculated wisely enough that the fear of losing his situation on the one hand, and the hope of a large reward on the other, would induce him to undertake the job. To all appearances he was as poor as when he had entered the service of the prince's father five and twenty years earlier. The promise of a few hundred scudi, thought Montevarchi, would have immense weight with such a man. In his eagerness to accomplish his purpose, the nobleman never suspected that the offer would be refused by a fellow who had narrowly escaped being convicted of forgery in his youth, and whose poverty was a matter concerning which no doubt could exist.

Montevarchi scarcely hesitated before going to the library. If he paused at all, it was more to consider the words he intended to use than to weigh in his mind the propriety of using them. The library was a vast old hall, surrounded on all sides, and nearly to the ceiling, with carved bookcases of walnut blackened with age to the colour of old mahogany. There were a number of massive tables in the room, upon which the light fell agreeably from high clerestory windows at each end of the apartment. Meschini himself was shuffling along in a pair of ancient leather slippers with a large volume under his arm, clad in very thread-bare black clothes and wearing a dingy skullcap on his head. He was a man somewhat under the middle size, badly made, though possessing considerable physical strength. His complexion was of a muddy yellow, disagreeable to see, but his features rendered him interesting if not sympathetic. The brow was heavy and the gray eyebrows irregular and bushy, but his gray eyes were singularly clear and bright, betraying a hidden vitality which would not have been suspected from the whole impression he made. A high forehead, very prominent in the upper and middle part, contracted below, so that there was very little breadth at the temples, but considerable expanse above. The eyes were near together and separated by the knifelike bridge of the nose, the latter descending in a fine curve of wonderfully delicate outline. The chin was pointed, and the compressed mouth showed little or nothing of the lips. On each side of his head the coarsely-shaped and promi-nent ears contrasted disagreeably with the fine keenness of the face. He stooped a little from the neck, and his shoulders sloped in a way that made them look narrower than they really were.

As the prince closed the door behind him and advanced, Meschini lifted his cap a little and laid down the book he was carrying, wondering inwardly what had brought his employer to see him at that hour of the morning.

"Sit down," said Montevarchi, with more than usual affability, and setting the example by seating himself upon one of the high-backed chairs which were ranged along the tables. "Sit down, Meschini, and let us have a little conversation."

"Willingly, Signor Principe," returned the librarian, obeying the command and placing himself opposite to the prince.

"I have been thinking about you this morning," continued the latter. "You have been with us a very long time. Let me see. How many years? Eighteen? Twenty?"

"Twenty-five years, Excellency. It is a long time, indeed!"

"Twenty-five years! Dear me! How the thought takes me back to my poor father! Heaven bless him, he was a good man. But, as I was saying, Meschini, you have been with us many years, and we have not done much for you. No. Do not protest! I know your modesty, but one must be just before all things. I think you draw fifteen scudi a month? Yes. I have a good memory, you see. I occupy myself with the cares of my household. But you are not so young as you were once, my friend, and your faithful services deserve to be rewarded. Shall we say thirty scudi a month in future? To continue all your life, even if—heaven avert it—you should ever become disabled from superintending the library—yes, all your life."

Meschini bowed as he sat in acknowledgment of so much generosity, and assumed a grateful expression suitable to the occasion. In reality, his salary was of very little importance to him, as compared with what he realised from his illicit traffic in manuscripts. But, like his employer, he was avaricious, and the prospect of three hundred and sixty scudi a year was pleasant to contemplate. He bowed and smiled.

"I do not deserve so much liberality, Signor Principe," he said. "My poor services—"

"Very far from poor, my dear friend, very far from poor," interrupted Montevarchi. "Moreover, if you will have confidence in me, you can do me a very great service indeed. But it is indeed a very private matter. You are a discreet man, however, and have few friends. You are not given to talking idly of what concerns no one but yourself."

"No, Excellency," replied Meschini, laughing inwardly as he thought of the deceptions he had been practising with success during a quarter of a century.

"Well, well, this is a matter between ourselves, and one which, as you will see, will bring its own reward. For although it might not pass muster in a court of law—the courts you know, Meschini, are very sensitive about little things—" he looked keenly at his companion, whose eyes were cast down.

"Foolishly sensitive," echoed the librarian.

"Yes. I may say that in the present instance, although the law might think differently of the matter, we shall be doing a good deed, redressing a great injustice, restoring to the fatherless his birthright, in a word fulfilling the will of Heaven, while perhaps paying little attention to the laws of man. Man, my friend, is often very unjust in his wisdom."

"Very. I can only applaud your Excellency's sentiments, which do justice to a man of heart."

"No, no, I want no praise," replied the prince in a tone of deprecation. "What I need in order to accomplish this good action is your assistance and friendly help. To whom should I turn, but to the old and confidential friend of the family? To a man whose knowledge of the matter on hand is only equalled by his fidelity to those who have so long employed him?"

"You are very good, Signor Principe. I will do my best to serve you, as I have served you and his departed Excellency, the Signor Principe, your father."

"Very well, Meschini. Now I need only repeat that the reward for your services will be great, as I trust that hereafter your recompense may be adequate for having had a share in so good a deed. But, to be short, the best way to acquaint you with the matter is to show you this document which I have brought for the purpose."

Montevarchi produced the famous deed and carefully unfolded it upon the table. Then, after glancing over it once more, he handed it to the librarian. The latter bent his keen eyes upon the page and rapidly deciphered the contents. Then he read it through a second time and at last laid it down upon the table and looked up at the prince with an air of inquiry.

"You see, my dear Meschini," said Montevarchi in suave tones, "this agreement was made by Don Leone Saracinesca because he expected to have no children. Had he foreseen what was to happen—for he has legitimate descendants alive, he would have added a clause here, at the foot of the first page—do you see? The clause he would have added would have been very short—something like this, 'Provided that the aforesaid Don Leone Saracinesca shall have no son born to him in wedlock, in which case, and if such a son be born, this present deed is wholly null, void and ineffectual.' Do you follow me?"

"Perfectly," replied Meschini, with a strange look in his eyes. He again took the parchment and looked it over, mentally inserting the words suggested by his employer. "If those words were inserted, there could be no question about the view the tribunals would take. But there must be a duplicate of the deed at the Cancellaria."

"Perhaps. I leave that to your industry to discover. Meanwhile, I am sure you agree with me that a piece of horrible injustice has been caused by this document; a piece of injustice, I repeat, which it is our sacred duty to remedy and set right."

"You propose to me to introduce this clause, as I understand, in this document and in the original," said the librarian, as though he wished to be quite certain of the nature of the scheme.

Montevarchi turned his eyes away and slowly scratched the table with his long nails.

"I mean to say," he answered in a lower voice, "that if it could be made out in law that it was the intention of the person, of Don Leone—"

"Let us speak plainly," interrupted Meschini. "We are alone. It is of no use to mince matters here. The only way to accomplish what you desire is to forge the words in both parchments. The thing can be done, and I can do it. It will be successful, without a shadow of a doubt. But I must have my price. There must be no misunderstanding. I do not think much of your considerations of justice, but I will do what you require, for money."

"How much?" asked Montevarchi in a thick voice. His heart misgave him, for he had placed himself in the man's power, and Meschini's authoritative tone showed that the latter knew it, and meant to use his advantage.

"I will be moderate, for I am a poor man. You shall give me twenty thousand scudi in cash, on the day the verdict is given in favour of Don Giovanni Saracinesca, Marchese di San Giacinto. That is your friend's name, I believe."

Montevarchi started as the librarian named the sum, and he turned very pale, passing his bony hand upon the edge of the table.

"I would not have expected this of you!" he exclaimed.

"You have your choice," returned the other, bringing his yellow face nearer to his employer's and speaking very distinctly. "You know what it all means. Saracinesca, Sant' Ilario, and Barda to your son-in-law, besides all the rest, amounting perhaps to several millions. To me, who get you all this, a paltry twenty thousand. Or else—" he paused and his bright eyes seemed to penetrate into Montevarchi's soul. The latter's face exhibited a sudden terror, which Meschini understood.

"Or else?" said the prince. "Or else, I suppose you will try and intimidate me by threatening to expose what I have told you?"

"Not at all, Excellency," replied the old scholar with sudden humility. "If you do not care for the bargain let us leave it alone. I am only your faithful servant, Signor Principe. Do not suspect me of such ingratitude! I only say that if we undertake it, the plan will be successful. It is for you to decide. Millions or no millions, it is the same to me. I am but a poor student. But if I help to get them for you—or for your son-in-law—I must have what I asked. It is not one per cent—scarcely a broker's commission! And you will have so much. Not but what your Excellency deserves it all, and is the best judge."

"One per cent?" muttered Montevarchi. "Perhaps not more than half per cent. But is it safe?" he asked suddenly, his fears all at once asserting themselves with a force that bewildered him.

"Leave all that to me," answered Meschini confidently. "The insertion shall be made, unknown to any one, in this parchment and in the one in the Chancery. The documents shall be returned to their places with no observation, and a month or two later the Marchese di San Giacinto can institute proceedings for the recovery of his birthright. I would only advise you not to mention the matter to him. It is essential that he should be quite innocent in order that the tribunal may suspect nothing. You and I, Signor Principe, can stay at home while the case is proceeding. We shall not even see the Signor Marchese's lawyers, for what have we to do with it all? But the Signor Marchese himself must be really free from all blame, or he will show a weak point. Now, when all is ready, he should go to the Cancellaria and examine the papers there for himself. He himself will suspect nothing. He will be agreeably surprised."

"And how long will it take you to do the—the work?" asked Montevarchi in hesitating tones.

"Let me see," Meschini began to make a calculation under his breath. "Ink, two days—preparing parchment for experiments, a week—writing, twice over, two days—giving age, drying and rubbing, three days, at least. Two, nine, eleven, fourteen. A fortnight," he said aloud. "I cannot do it in less time than that. If the copy in the Chancery is by another hand it will take longer."

"But how can you work at the Chancery?" asked the prince, as though a new objection had presented itself.

"Have no fear, Excellency. I will manage it so that no one shall find it out.

Two visits will suffice. Shall I begin at once? Is it agreed?"

Montevarchi was silent for several minutes, and his hands moved uneasily.

"Begin at once," he said at last, as though forcing himself to make a determination. He rose to go as he spoke.

"Twenty thousand scudi on the day the verdict is given in favour of the Signor Marchese. Is that it?"

"Yes, yes. That is it. I leave it all to you."

"I will serve your Excellency faithfully, never fear."

"Do, Meschini. Yes. Be faithful as you have always been. Remember, I am not avaricious. It is in the cause of sound justice that I stoop to assume the appearance of dishonesty. Can a man do more? Can one go farther than to lose one's self-esteem by appearing to transgress the laws of honour in order to accomplish a good object; for the sake of restoring the birthright to the fatherless and the portion to the widow, or indeed to the widower, in this case? No, my dear friend. The means are more than justified by the righteousness of our purpose. Believe me, my good Meschini—yes, you are good in the best sense of the word—believe me, the justice of this world is not always the same as the justice of Heaven. The dispensations of providence are mysterious."

"And must remain so, in this case," observed the librarian with an evil smile.

"Yes, unfortunately, in this case we shall not reap the worldly praise which so kind an action undoubtedly deserves. But we must have patience under these trials. Good-bye, Meschini, good-bye, my friend. I must busy myself with the affairs of my household. Every man must do his duty in this world, you know."

The scholar bowed his employer to the door, and then went back to the parchment, which he studied attentively for more than an hour, keeping a huge folio volume open before him, into which he might slip the precious deed in case he were interrupted in his occupation.

CHAPTER XIII

Sant' Ilario could not realise that the course of events had been brought to a standstill at the very moment when his passions were roused to fury. He could not fight Gouache for the present and Corona was so ill that he could not see her. Had he wished to visit her, the old-fashioned physician would probably have forbidden him to do so, but in reality he was glad to be spared the emotions of a meeting which must necessarily be inconclusive. His first impulse had been to take her away from Rome and force her to live alone with him in the mountains. He felt that no other course was open to him, for he knew that in spite of all that had happened he could not bear to live without her, and yet he felt that he could no longer suffer her to come and go in the midst of society, where she must necessarily often meet the man she had chosen to love. Nor could he keep her in Rome and at the same time isolate her as he desired to do. If the world must talk, he would rather not be where he could hear what it said. The idea of a sudden journey, terminating in the gloomy fortress of Saracinesca, was pleasant to his humour. The old place was ten times more grim and dismal in winter than in summer, and in his savage mood he fancied himself alone with his wife in the silent halls, making her feel the enormity of what she had done, while jealously keeping her a prisoner at his mercy.

But her illness had put a stop to his plans for her safety, while the revolution had effectually interfered with the execution of his vengeance upon Gouache. He could find no occupation which might distract his mind from the thoughts that beset him, and no outlet for the restless temper that craved some sort of action, no matter what, as the expression of what he suffered. He and his father met in silence at their meals, and though Giovanni felt that he had the old man's full sympathy, he could not bring himself to speak of what was nearest to his heart. He remembered that his marriage had been of his own seeking, and his pride kept him from all mention of the catastrophe by which his happiness had been destroyed. Old Saracinesca suffered in his own way almost as much as his son, and it was fortunate that he was prevented from seeing Corona at that time, for it is not probable that he would have controlled himself had he been able to talk with her alone. When little Orsino was brought in to them, the two men looked at each other, and while the younger bit his lip and suppressed all outward signs of his agony, the tears more than once stole into the old prince's eyes so that he would turn away and leave the room. Then Giovanni would take the child upon his knee and look at it earnestly until the little thing was frightened and held out its arms to its nurse, crying to be taken away. Thereupon Sant' Ilario's mood grew more bitter than before, for he was foolish enough to believe that the child had a natural antipathy for him, and would grow up to hate the sight of its father. Those were miserable days, never to be forgotten, and each morning and evening brought worse news of Corona's state, until it was clear, even to Giovanni, that she was dangerously ill. The sound of voices grew rare in the Palazzo Saracinesca and the servants moved noiselessly about at their work, oppressed by the sense of coming disaster, and scarcely speaking to each other.

San Giacinto came daily to make inquiries and spent some time with the two unhappy men without wholly understanding what was passing. He was an astute man, but not possessed of the delicacy of feeling whereby real sympathy sometimes reaches the truth by its own intuitive reasoning. Moreover, he was wholly ignorant of having played a very important part in bringing about the troubles which now beset Casa Saracinesca. No one but himself knew how he had written the note that had caused such disastrous results, and he had no intention of confiding his exploit to any one of his acquaintance. He had of course not been able to ascertain whether the desired effect had been produced, for he did not know at what church the meeting between Faustina and Gouache was to take place, and he was too cunning to follow her as a spy when he had struck so bold a blow at her affection for the artist-soldier. His intellect was keen, but his experience had not been of a high order, and he naturally thought that she would reason as he had reasoned himself, if she chanced to see him while she was waiting for the man she loved. She knew that he was to marry her sister, and that he might therefore be supposed to disapprove of an affair which could only lead to a derogatory match for herself, and he had therefore carefully abstained from following her on that Sunday morning when she had met Anastase.

Nevertheless he could see that something had occurred in his cousin's household which was beyond his comprehension, for Corona's illness was not alone enough to account for the manner of the Saracinesca. It is a social rule in Italy that a person suffering from any calamity must be amused, and San Giacinto used what talents he possessed in that direction, doing all he could to make the time hang less heavily on Giovanni's hands. He made a point of gathering all the news of the little war in order to repeat it in minute detail to his cousins. He even prevailed upon Giovanni to walk with him sometimes in the middle of the day, and Sant' Ilario seemed to take a languid interest in the barricades erected at the gates of the city, and in the arrangements for maintaining quiet within the walls. Rome presented a strange aspect in those days. All who were not Romans kept their national flags permanently hung from their windows, as a sort of protection in case the mob should rise, or in the event of the Garibaldians suddenly seizing the capital. Patrols marched everywhere about the streets and mounted gendarmes were stationed at the corners of the principal squares and at intervals along the main thoroughfares. Strange to say, the numerous flags and uniforms that were to be seen produced an air of festivity strongly at variance with the actual state of things, and belied by the anxious expressions visible in the faces of the inhabitants. All these sights interested San Giacinto, whose active temperament made him very much alive to what went on around him, and even Giovanni thought less of his great sorrow when he suffered himself to be led out of the house by his cousin.

When at last it was known that the French troops were on their way from Civita Vecchia, the city seemed to breathe more freely. General Kanzler, the commander-in-chief of the Pontifical forces, had done all that was humanly possible to concentrate his little army, and the arrival of even a small body of Frenchmen made it certain that Garibaldi could be met with a fair chance of success. Of all who rejoiced at the prospect of a decisive action, there was no one more sincerely delighted than Anastase Gouache.

So long as the state of siege lasted and he was obliged to follow the regular round of his almost mechanical duty, he was unable to take any step in the direction whither all his hopes tended, and he lived in a state of perpetual suspense. It was a small consolation that he found time to reflect upon the difficulties of his situation and to revolve in his mind the language he should use when he went to ask the hand of Montevarchi's daughter. He was fully determined to take this bold step, and though he realised the many objections which the old prince would certainly raise against the match, he had not the slightest doubt of his power to overcome them all. He could not imagine what it would be like to fail, and he cherished and reared what should have been but a slender hope until it seemed to be a certainty. The unexpected quarrel thrust upon him by Sant' Ilario troubled him very little, for he was too hopeful by nature to expect any serious catastrophe, and he more than once laughed to himself when he thought Giovanni was really jealous of him. The feeling of reverence and respectful admiration which he had long entertained for Corona was so far removed from love as to make Giovanni's wrath appear ridiculous. He would far sooner have expected a challenge from one of Faustina's brothers than from Corona's husband, but, since Sant' Ilario had determined to quarrel, there was no help for it, and he must give him all satisfaction as soon as possible. That Giovanni had insulted him by entering his lodgings unbidden, and by taking certain objects away which were practically the artist's property, was a minor consideration, since it was clear that Giovanni had acted all along under an egregious misapprehension. One thing alone puzzled Anastase, and that was the letter itself. It seemed to refer to his meeting with Faustina, but she had made no mention of it when he had seen her in the church. Gouache did not suspect Giovanni of having concocted the note for any purposes of his own, and quite believed that he had found it as he had stated, but the more the artist tried to explain the existence of the letter, the further he found himself from any satisfactory solution of the question. He interrogated his landlady, but she would say nothing about it, for the temptation of Giovanni's money sealed her lips.

The week passed somehow, unpleasantly enough for most of the persons concerned in this veracious history, but Saturday night came at last, and brought with it a series of events which modified the existing situation. Gouache was on duty at the barracks when orders were received to the effect that the whole available force in Rome was to march soon after midnight. His face brightened when he heard the news, although he realised that in a few hours he was to leave behind him all that he held most dear and to face death in a manner new to him, and by no means pleasant to most men.

Between two and three o'clock on Sunday morning Gouache found himself standing in the midst of a corps of fifteen hundred Zouaves, in almost total darkness and under a cold, drizzling November rain. His teeth chattered and his wet hands seemed to freeze to the polished fittings of his rifle, and he had not the slightest doubt that every one of his comrades experienced the same unenviable sensations. From time to time the clear voice of an officer was heard giving an order, and then the ranks closed up nearer, or executed a sidelong movement by which greater space was afforded to the other troops that constantly came up towards the Porta Pia. There was little talking during an hour or more while the last preparations for the march were being made, though the men exchanged a few words from time to time in an undertone. The splashing tramp of feet on the wet road was heard rapidly approaching every now and then, followed by a dead silence when the officers' voices gave the order to halt. Then a shuffling sound followed as the ranks moved into the exact places assigned to them. Here and there a huge torch was blazing and spluttering in the fine rain, making the darkness around it seem only thicker by the contrast, but lighting up fragments of ancient masonry and gleaming upon little pools of water in the open spaces between the ranks. It was a dismal night, and it was fortunate that the men who were to march were in good spirits and encouraged by the arrival of the French, who made the circuit of the city and were to join them upon the road in order to strike the final blow against Garibaldi and his volunteers.

The Zouaves were fifteen hundred, and there were about as many more of the native troops, making three thousand in all. The French were two thousand. The Garibaldians were, according to all accounts, not less than twelve thousand, and were known to be securely entrenched at Monte Rotondo and further protected by the strong outpost of Mentana, which lies nearly on the direct road from Rome to the former place. Considering the relative positions of the two armies, the odds were enormously in favour of Garibaldi, and had he possessed a skill in generalship at all equal to his undoubted personal courage, he should have been able to drive the Pope's forces back to the very gates of Rome. He was, however, under a twofold disadvantage which more than counterbalanced the numerical superiority of the body he commanded. He possessed little or no military science, and his men were neither confident nor determined. His plan had been to create a revolution in Rome and to draw out the papal army at the same time, in order that the latter might find itself between two fires. His men had expected that the country would rise and welcome them as liberators, whereas they were received as brigands and opposed with desperate energy at every point by the peasants themselves, a turn of affairs for which they were by no means prepared. Monte Rotondo, defended by only three hundred and fifty soldiers, resisted Garibaldi's attacking force of six thousand during twenty-seven hours, a feat which must have been quite impracticable had the inhabitants themselves not joined in the defence. The revolution in Rome was a total failure, the mass of the people look-ing on with satisfaction, while the troops shot down the insurgents, and at times even demanding arms that they might join in suppressing the disturbance.

The Rome of 1867 was not the Rome of 1870, as will perhaps be understood hereafter. With the exception of a few turbulent spirits, the city contained no revolutionary element, and very few who sympathised with the ideas of Italian Unification.

But without going any further into political considerations for the present, let us follow Anastase Gouache and his fifteen hundred comrades who marched out of the Porta Pia before dawn on the third of November. The battle that followed merits some attention as having been the turning-point of a stirring time, and also as having produced certain important results in the life of the French artist, which again reacted in some measure upon the family history of the Saracinesca.

Monte Rotondo itself is sixteen miles from Rome, but Mentana, which on that day was the outpost of the Garibaldians and became the scene of their defeat, is two miles nearer to the city. Most people who have ridden much in the Campagna know the road which branches to the left about five miles beyond the Ponte Nomentano. There is perhaps no more desolate and bleak part of the undulating waste of land that surrounds the city on all sides. The way is good as far as the turning, but after that it is little better than a country lane, and in rainy weather is heavy and sometimes almost impassable. As the rider approaches Mentana the road sinks between low hills and wooded knolls that dominate it on both sides, affording excellent positions from which an enemy might harass and even destroy an advancing force. Gradually the country becomes more broken until Mentana itself appears in view, a formidable barrier rising upon the direct line to Monte Rotondo. On all sides are irregular hillocks, groups of trees growing upon little elevations, solid stone walls surrounding scattered farmhouses and cattle-yards, every one of which could be made a strong defensive post. Mentana, too, possesses an ancient castle of some strength, and has walls of its own like most of the old towns in the Campagna, insignificant perhaps, if compared with modern fortifications, but well able to resist for many hours the fire of light field-guns.

It was past midday when Gouache's column first came in view of the enemy, and made out the bright red shirts of the Garibaldians, which peeped out from among the trees and from behind the walls, and were visible in some places massed in considerable numbers. The intention of the commanding officers, which was carried out with amazing ease, was to throw the Zouaves and native troops in the face of the enemy, while the French chasseurs, on foot and mounted, made a flanking movement and cut off Garibaldi's communication with Monte Rotondo, attacking Mentana at the same time from the opposite side.

Gouache experienced an odd sensation when the first orders were given to fire. His experience had hitherto been limited to a few skirmishes with the outlaws of the Samnite hills, and the idea of standing up and deliberately taking aim at men who stood still to be shot at, so far as he could see, was not altogether pleasant. He confessed to himself that though he wholly approved of the cause for which he was about to fire his musket, he felt not the slightest hatred for the Garibaldians, individually or collectively. They were extremely picturesque in the landscape, with their flaming shirts and theatrical hats. They looked very much as though they had come out of a scene in a comic opera, and it seemed a pity to destroy anything that relieved the dismal grayness of the November day. As he stood there he felt much more like the artist he was, than like a soldier, and he felt a ludicrously strong desire to step aside and seat himself upon a stone wall in order to get a better view of the whole scene.

Presently as he looked at a patch of red three or four hundred yards distant, the vivid colour was obscured by a little row of puffs of smoke. A rattling report followed, which reminded him of the discharges of the tiny mortars the Italian peasants love to fire at their village festivals. Then almost simultaneously he heard the curious swinging whistle of a dozen bullets flying over his head. This latter sound roused him to an understanding of the situation, as he realised that any one of those small missiles might have ended its song by coming into contact with his own body. The next time he heard the order to fire he aimed as well as he could, and pulled the trigger with the best possible intention of killing an enemy.

For the most part, the Garibaldians retired after each round, reappearing again to discharge their rifles from behind the shelter of walls and trees, while the Zouaves slowly advanced along the road, and began to deploy to the right and left wherever the ground permitted such a movement. The firing continued uninterruptedly for nearly half an hour, but though the rifles of the papal troops did good execution upon the enemy, the bullets of the latter seldom produced any effect.

Suddenly the order was given to fix bayonets, and immediately afterwards came the command to charge. Gouache was all at once aware that he was rushing up hill at the top of his speed towards a small grove of trees that crowned the eminence. The bright red shirts of the enemy were visible before him amongst the dry underbrush, and before he knew what he was about he saw that he had run a Garibaldian through the calf of the leg. The man tumbled down, and Gouache stood over him, looking at him in some surprise. While he was staring at his fellow-foe the latter pulled out a pistol and fired at him, but the weapon only snapped harmlessly.

"As the thing won't go off," said the man coolly, "perhaps you will be good enough to take your bayonet out of my leg."

He spoke in Italian, with a foreign accent, but in a tone of voice and with a manner which proclaimed him a gentleman. There was a look of half comic discomfiture in his face that amused Gouache, who carefully extracted the steel from the wound, and offered to help his prisoner to his feet. The latter, however, found it hard to stand.

"Circumstances point to the sitting posture," he said, sinking down again. "I suppose I am your prisoner. If you have anything to do, pray do not let me detain you. I cannot get away and you will probably find me here when you come back to dinner. I will occupy myself in cursing you while you are gone."

"You are very kind," said Gouache, with a laugh. "May I offer you a cigarette and a little brandy?"

The stranger looked up in some astonishment as he heard Gouache's voice, and took the proffered flask in silence, as well as a couple of cigarettes from the case.

"Thank you," he said after a pause. "I will not curse you quite as heartily as I meant to do. You are very civil."

"Do not mention it," replied Gouache. "I wish you a very good morning, and I hope to have the pleasure of your company at dinner tonight."

Thereupon the Zouave shouldered his rifle and trotted off down the hill. The whole incident had not occupied more than three minutes and his comrades were not far off, pursuing the Garibaldians in the direction of a large farmhouse, which afforded the prospect of shelter and the means of defence. Half a dozen killed and wounded remained upon the hill besides Gouache's prisoner.

The Vigna di Santucci, as the farmhouse was called, was a strong building surrounded by walls and fences. A large number of the enemy had fallen back upon this point and it now became evident that they meant to make a determined resistance. As the Zouaves came up, led by Charette in person, the Reds opened a heavy fire upon their advancing ranks. The shots rattled from the walls and windows in rapid succession, and took deadly effect at the short range. The Zouaves blazed away in reply with their chassepots, but the deep embrasures and high parapets offered an excellent shelter for the riflemen, and it was no easy matter to find an aim. The colonel's magnificent figure and great fair beard were conspicuous as he moved about the ranks, encouraging the men and searching for some means of scaling the high walls. Though anxious for the safety of his troops, he seemed as much at home as though he were in a drawing-room, and paid no

more attention to the whistling bullets than if they had been mere favours showered upon him in an afternoon's carnival. The firing grew hotter every moment
and it was evident that unless the place could be carried by assault at once, the
Zouaves must suffer terrible losses. The difficulty was to find a point where the
attempt might be made with a good chance of success.

"It seems to me," said Gouache, to a big man who stood next to him, "that if
we were in Paris, and if that were a barricade instead of an Italian farmhouse, we
should get over it."

"I think so, too," replied his comrade, with a laugh.

"Let us try," suggested the artist quietly. "We may as well have made the
attempt, instead of standing here to catch cold in this horrible mud. Come
along," he added quickly, "or we shall be too late. The colonel is going to order the
assault—do you see?"

It was true. A loud voice gave a word of command which was echoed and
repeated by a number of officers. The men closed in and made a rush for the
farmhouse, trying to scramble upon each other's shoulders to reach the top of the
wall and the windows of the low first story. The attempt lasted several minutes,
during which the enemies' rifles poured down a murderous fire upon the struggling soldiers. The latter fell back at last, leaving one man alone clinging to the
top of the wall.

"It is Gouache!" cried a hundred voices at once. He was a favourite with
officers and men and was recognised immediately.

He was in imminent peril of his life. Standing upon the shoulders of the
sturdy comrade to whom he had been speaking a few minutes before he had
made a spring, and had succeeded in getting hold of the topmost stones. Taking
advantage of the slight foothold afforded by the crevices in the masonry, he drew
himself up with catlike agility till he was able to kneel upon the narrow summit.
He had chosen a spot for his attempt where he had previously observed that no
enemy appeared, rightly judging that there must be some reason for this peculiarity, of which he might be able to take advantage. This proved to be the case,
for he found himself immediately over a horse pond, which was sunk between
two banks of earth that followed the wall on the inside up to the water, and upon
which the riflemen stood in safety behind the parapet. The men so stationed had
discharged their pieces during the assault, and were busily employed in reloading
when they noticed the Zouave perched upon the top of the wall. One or two who

had pistols fired them at him, but without effect. One or two threw stones from the interior of the vineyard.

Gouache threw himself on his face along the wall and began quickly to throw down the topmost stones. The mortar was scarcely more solid than dry mud, and in a few seconds he had made a perceptible impression upon the masonry. But the riflemen had meanwhile finished reloading and one of them, taking careful aim, fired upon the Zouave. The bullet hit him in the fleshy part of the shoulder, causing a stinging pain and, what was worse, a shock that nearly sent him rolling over the edge. Still he clung on desperately, loosening the stones with a strength one would not have expected in his spare frame. A minute longer, during which half a dozen more balls whizzed over him or flattened themselves against the stones, and then his comrades made another rush, concentrating their force this time at the spot where he had succeeded in lowering the barrier. His left arm was almost powerless from the flesh-wound in his shoulder, but with his right he helped the first man to a footing beside him. In a moment more the Zouaves were swarming over the wall and dropping down by scores into the shallow pool on the other side.

The fight was short but desperate. The enemy, driven to bay in the corners of the yard and within the farmhouse, defended themselves manfully, many of them being killed and many more wounded. But the place was carried and the great majority fled precipitately through the exits at the back and made the best of their way towards Mentana.

An hour later Gouache was still on his legs, but exhausted by his efforts in scaling the wall and by loss of blood from his wound, he felt that he could not hold out much longer. The position at that time was precarious. It was nearly four o'clock and the days were short. The artillery was playing against the little town, but the guns were light field-pieces of small calibre, and though their position was frequently changed they made but little impression upon the earthworks thrown up by the enemy. The Garibaldians massed themselves in large numbers as they retreated from various points upon Mentana, and though their weapons were inferior to those of their opponents their numbers made them still formidable. The Zouaves, gendarmes, and legionaries, however, pressed steadily though slowly onward. The only question was whether the daylight would last long enough. Should the enemy have the advantage of the long night in which to bring up reinforcements from Monte Rotondo and repair the breaches in their defences the attack might last through all the next day.

The fortunes of the little battle were decided by the French chasseurs, who had gradually worked out a flanking movement under cover of the trees and the broken country. Just as Gouache felt that he could stand no longer, a loud shout upon the right announced the charge of the allies, and a few minutes later the day was practically won. The Zouaves rushed forward, cheered and encouraged by the prospect of immediate success, but Anastase staggered from the ranks and sank down under a tree unable to go any farther. He had scarcely settled himself in a comfortable position when he lost consciousness and fainted away.

Mentana was not taken, but it surrendered on the following morning, and as Monte Rotondo had been evacuated during the night and most of the Garibaldians had escaped over the frontier, the fighting was at an end, and the campaign of twenty-four hours terminated in a complete victory for the Roman forces.

When Gouache came to himself his first sensation was that of a fiery stream of liquid gurgling in his mouth and running down his throat. He swallowed the liquor half unconsciously, and opening his eyes for a moment was aware that two men were standing beside him, one of them holding a lantern in his hand, the rays from which dazzled the wounded Zouave and prevented him from recognising the persons.

"Where is he hurt?" asked a voice that sounded strangely familiar in his ears.

"I cannot tell yet," replied the other man, kneeling down again beside him and examining him attentively.

"It is only my shoulder," gasped Gouache. "But I am very weak. Let me sleep, please." Thereupon he fainted again, and was conscious of nothing more for some time.

The two men took him up and carried him to a place near, where others were waiting for him. The night was intensely dark, and no one spoke a word, as the little party picked its way over the battle-field, occasionally stopping to avoid treading upon one of the numerous prostrate bodies that lay upon the ground. The man who had examined Gouache generally stooped down and turned the light of his lantern upon the faces of the dead men, expecting that some one of them might show signs of life. But it was very late, and the wounded had already been carried away. Gouache alone seemed to have escaped observation, an accident probably due to the fact that he had been able to drag himself to a sheltered spot before losing his senses.

During nearly an hour the men trudged along the road with their burden, when at last they saw in the distance the bright lamps of a carriage shining through the darkness. The injured soldier was carefully placed among the cushions, and the two gentlemen who had found him got in and closed the door.

Gouache awoke in consequence of the pain caused by the jolting of the vehicle. The lantern was placed upon one of the vacant seats and illuminated the faces of his companions, one of whom sat behind him and supported his weight by holding one arm around his body. Anastase stared at this man's face for some time in silence and in evident surprise. He thought he was in a dream, and he spoke rather to assure himself that he was awake than for any other reason.

"You were anxious lest I should escape you after all," he said. "You need not be afraid. I shall be able to keep my engagement."

"I trust you will do nothing of the kind, my dear Gouache," answered Giovanni Saracinesca.

CHAPTER XIV

ON the Saturday afternoon preceding the battle of Mentana, Sant' Ilario was alone in his own room, trying to pass the weary hours in the calculation of certain improvements he meditated at Saracinesca. He had grown very thin and careworn during the week, and he found it hard to distract his mind even for a moment from the thought of his misfortunes. Nothing but a strong mental effort in another direction could any longer fix his attention, and though any kind of work was for the present distasteful to him, it was at least a temporary relief from the contemplation of his misfortunes.

He could not bring himself to see Corona, though she grew daily worse, and both the physicians and the attendants who were about her looked grave. His action in this respect did not proceed from heartlessness, still less from any wish to add to her sufferings; on the contrary, he knew very well that, since he could not speak to her with words of forgiveness, the sight of him would very likely aggravate her state. He had no reason to forgive her, for nothing had happened to make her guilt seem more pardonable than before. Had she been well and strong as usual he would have seen her often and would very likely have reproached her again and again most bitterly with what she had done. But she was ill and wholly unable to defend herself; to inflict fresh pain at such a time would have been mean and cowardly. He kept away and did his best not to go mad, though he felt that he could not bear the strain much longer.

As the afternoon light faded from his chamber he dropped the pencil and paper with which he had been working and leaned back in his chair. His face was haggard and drawn, and sleepless nights had made dark circles about his deep-set eyes, while his face, which was naturally lean, had grown suddenly thin and hollow. He was indeed one of the most unhappy men in Rome that day, and so far as he could see his misery had fallen upon him through no fault of his own. It would have been a blessed relief, could he have accused himself of injustice, or of any misdeed which might throw the weight and responsibility of Corona's actions back upon his own soul. He loved her still so well that he could have imagined nothing sweeter than to throw himself at her feet and cry aloud that it was he who had sinned and not she. He tortured his imagination for a means of proving that she might be innocent. But it was in vain. The chain of circumstantial evidence was complete and not a link was missing, not one point uncertain. He would have given her the advantage of any doubt which could be thought to exist, but the longer he thought of it all, the more sure he grew that there was no doubt whatever.

He sat quite still until it was nearly dark, and then with a sudden and angry movement quite unlike him, he sprang to his feet and left the room. Solitude was growing unbearable to him, and though he cared little to see any of his associates, the mere presence of other living beings would, he thought, be better than nothing. He was about to go out of the house when he met the doctor coming from Corona's apartments.

"I do not wish to cause you unnecessary pain," said the physician, "but I think it would be better that you should see the princess."

"Has she asked for me?" inquired Giovanni, gloomily.

"No. But I think you ought to see her."

"Is she dying?" Sant' Ilario spoke under his breath, and laid his hand on the doctor's arm.

"Pray be calm, Signor Principe. I did not say that. But I repeat—"

"Be good enough to say what you mean without repetition," answered Giovanni almost savagely.

The physician's face flushed with annoyance, but as Giovanni was such a very high and mighty personage he controlled his anger and replied as calmly as he could.

"The princess is not dying. But she is very ill. She may be worse before morning. You had better see her now, for she will know you. Later she may not."

Without waiting for more Giovanni turned on his heel and strode towards his wife's room. Passing through an outer chamber he saw one of her women sitting in a corner and shedding copious tears.

She looked up and pointed to the door in a helpless fashion. In another moment Giovanni was at Corona's bedside.

He would not have recognised her. Her face was wasted and white, and looked ghastly by contrast with the masses of her black hair which were spread over the broad pillow. Her colourless lips were parted and a little drawn, and her breath came faintly. Only her eyes retained the expression of life, seeming larger and more brilliant than he had ever seen them before.

Giovanni gazed on her in horror for several seconds. In his imagination he had supposed that she would look as when he had seen her last, and the shock of seeing her as she was, unstrung his nerves. For an instant he forgot everything that was past in the one strong passion that dominated him in spite of himself. His arms went round her and amidst his blinding tears he showered hot kisses on her death-like face. With a supreme effort, for she was so weak as to be almost powerless, she clasped her hands about his neck and pressed her to him, or he pressed her. The embrace lasted but a moment and her arms fell again like lead.

"You know the truth at last, Giovanni," she said, feebly. "You know that I am innocent or you would not—"

He did not know whether her voice failed her from weakness, or whether she was hesitating. He felt as though she had driven a sharp weapon into his breast by recalling all that separated them. He drew back a little, and his face darkened.

What could he do? She was dying and it would be diabolically cruel to undeceive her. In that moment he would have given his soul to be able to lie, to put on again the expression that was in his face when he had kissed her a moment before. But the suffering of which she reminded him was too great, the sin too enormous, and though he tried bravely he could not succeed. But he made the effort. He tried to smile, and the attempt was horrible. He spoke, but there was no life in his words.

"Yes, dear," he said, though the words choked him like hot dust, "I know it was all a mistake. How can I ever ask your forgiveness?"

Corona saw that it was not the truth, and with a despairing cry she turned away and hid her face in the pillow. Giovanni felt an icy chill of horror descending to his heart. A more terrible moment could scarcely be imagined. There he stood beside his dying wife, the conviction of her sin burnt in upon his heart, but loving her fiercely still, willing in that supreme crisis to make her think she was forgiven, striving to tell the kind lie that nevertheless would not be told, powerless to deceive her who had so horribly betrayed him.

Once more he bent over her and laid his hand on hers. The touch of her wasted fingers brought the tears to his eyes again, but the moment of passion was past. He bent down and would have comforted her had he known how, but not a word would form itself upon his lips. Her face was turned away and he could see that she was determined not to look at him. Only now and then a passionate sob shook her and made her tremble, like a thing of little weight shaken by the wind.

Giovanni could bear it no longer. Once more he kissed her heavy hair and then quickly went out, he knew not whither. When he realised what he was doing he found himself leaning against a damp wall in the street. He pulled himself together and walked away at a brisk pace, trying to find some relief in rapid motion. He never knew how far he walked that night, haunted by the presence of Corona's deathly face and by the sound of that despairing cry which he had no power to check. He went on and on, challenged from time to time by the sentinels to whom he mechanically showed his pass. Striding up hill and down through the highways and through the least frequented streets of the city, it was all the same to him in his misery, and he had no consciousness of what he saw or heard. At eight o'clock in the evening he was opposite Saint Peter's; at midnight he was standing alone at the desolate cross-roads before Santa Croce in Gerusalemme, beyond the Lateran, and only just within the walls. From place to place he wandered, feeling no fatigue, but only a burning fever in his head and an icy chill in his heart. Sometimes he would walk up and down some broad square twenty or thirty times; then again he followed a long thoroughfare throughout its whole length, and retraced his steps without seeing that he passed twice through the same street.

At last he found himself in a great crowd of people. Had he realised that it was nearly three o'clock in the morning the presence of such a concourse would have astonished him. But if he was not actually ill and out of his mind, he was at all events in such a confused state that he did not even ask himself what was the meaning of the demonstration.

The tramp of marching troops recalled the thought of Gouache, and suddenly he understood what was happening. The soldiers were leaving Rome to attack the Garibaldians, and he was near one of the gates. By the light of flaring torches he recognised at some distance the hideous architecture of the Porta Pia. He caught sight of the Zouave uniform under the glare and pressed forward instinctively, trying to see the faces of the men. But the crowd was closely packed and he could not obtain a view, try as he might, and the darkness was so thick that the torches only made the air darker around them.

He listened to the tramp of feet and the ring of steel arms and accoutrements like a man in an evil dream. Instead of passing quickly, the time now seemed interminable, for he was unable to move, and the feeling that among those thousands of moving soldiers there was perhaps that one man for whose blood he thirsted, was intolerable. At last the tramping died away in the distance and the crowd loosened itself and began to break up. Giovanni was carried with the stream, and once more it became indifferent to him whither he went. All at once he was aware of a very tall man who walked beside him, a man so large that he looked up, sure that the giant could be none but his cousin San Giacinto.

"Are you here, too?" asked the latter in a friendly voice, as he recognised Giovanni by the light of a lamp, under which they were passing.

"I came to see them off," replied Sant' Ilario, coldly. It seemed to him as though his companion must have followed him.

"So did I," said San Giacinto. "I heard the news late last night, and only lay down for an hour or two."

"What time is it?" asked Giovanni, who supposed it was about midnight.

"Five o'clock. It will be daylight, or dawn at least, in an hour."

Giovanni was silent, wondering absently where he had been all night. For some time the two walked on without speaking.

"You had better come and have coffee with me," said San Giacinto as they passed through the Piazza Barbarini. "I made my man get up so that I might have some as soon as I got home."

Giovanni assented. The presence of some one with whom he could speak made him realise that he was almost exhausted for want of food. It was morning, and he had eaten nothing since the preceding midday, and little enough then. In a few minutes they reached San Giacinto's lodging. There was a lamp burning brightly on the table of the sitting-room, and a little fire was smouldering on the hearth. Giovanni sank into a chair, worn out with hunger and fatigue, while the servant brought the coffee and set it on the table.

"You look tired," remarked San Giacinto. "One lump or two?"

Giovanni drank the beverage without tasting it, but it revived him, and the warmth of the room comforted his chilled and tired limbs. He did not notice that San Giacinto was looking hard at him, wondering indeed what could have produced so strange an alteration in his appearance and manner.

"How is the princess?" asked the big man in a tone of sympathy as he slowly stirred the sugar in his coffee.

"Thank you—she is very well," answered Giovanni, mechanically. In his mind the secret which he must conceal was so closely connected with Corona's illness that he almost unconsciously included her state among the things of which he would not speak. But San Giacinto looked sharply at him, wondering what he meant.

"Indeed? I thought she was very ill."

"So she is," replied Sant' Ilario, bluntly. "I forgot—I do not know what I was thinking of. I fear she is in a very dangerous condition."

He was silent again, and sat leaning upon the table absently looking at the objects that lay before him, an open portfolio and writing materials, a bit of seal-ingwax, a small dictionary, neatly laid in order upon the dark red cloth. He did not know why he had allowed himself to be led to the place, but he felt a sense of rest in sitting there quietly in silence. San Giacinto saw that there was something wrong and said nothing, but lighted a black cigar and smoked thoughtfully.

"You look as though you had been up all night," he remarked after a long pause.

Giovanni did not answer. His eyes did not look up from the red blotting-paper in the open portfolio before him. As he looked down San Giacinto almost believed he was asleep, and shook the table a little to see whether his cousin would notice it. Instantly Giovanni laid his hand upon the writing book, to steady it before him. But still he did not look up.

"You seem to be interested," said San Giacinto, with a smile, and he blew a cloud of smoke into the air.

Giovanni was indeed completely absorbed in his studies, and only nodded his head in answer. After a few minutes more he rose and took the portfolio to a dingy mirror that stood over the chimney-piece of the lodging, and held up the sheet of red blotting-paper before the reflecting surface. Apparently not satisfied with this, he brought the lamp and set it upon the shelf, and then repeated the process.

"You are an infernal scoundrel," he said in a low voice, that trembled with wrath, as he turned and faced San Giacinto.

"What do you mean?" inquired the latter with a calmness that would have staggered a less angry man.

Giovanni drew from his pocket-book the note he had found in Gouache's room. For a week he had kept it about him. Without paying any further attention to San Giacinto he held it in one hand and again placed the blotting-paper in front of the mirror. The impression of the writing corresponded exactly with the original. As it consisted of but a very few words and had been written quickly, almost every stroke had been reproduced upon the red paper in a reversed fac-simile. Giovanni brought the two and held them before San Giacinto's eyes. The latter looked surprised but did not betray the slightest fear.

"Do you mean to tell me that you did not write this note?" asked Giovanni, savagely.

"Of course I wrote it," replied the other coolly.

Giovanni's teeth chattered with rage. He dropped the portfolio and the letter and seized his cousin by the throat, burying his fingers in the tough flesh with the ferocity of a wild animal. He was very strong and active and had fallen upon his adversary unawares, so that he had an additional advantage. But for all that he was no match for his cousin's giant strength. San Giacinto sprang to his feet and his great hands took hold of Giovanni's arms above the elbow, lifting him from the ground and shaking him in the air as easily as a cat worries a mouse. Then he thrust him into his chair again and stood holding him so that he could not move.

"I do not want to hurt you," he said, "but I do not like to be attacked in this way. If you try it again I will break some of your bones."

Giovanni was so much astonished at finding himself so easily overmatched that he was silent for a moment. The ex-innkeeper relinquished his hold and picked up his cigar, which had fallen in the struggle.

"I do not propose to wrestle with you for a match," said Giovanni at last. "You are stronger than I, but there are other weapons than those of brute strength. I repeat that you are an infernal scoundrel."

"You may repeat it as often as you please," replied San Giacinto, who had recovered his composure with, marvellous rapidity. "It does not hurt me at all."

"Then you are a contemptible coward," cried Giovanni, hotly.

"That is not true," said the other. "I never ran away in my life. Perhaps I have not much reason to avoid a fight," he added, looking down at his huge limbs with a smile.

Giovanni did not know what to do. He had never had a quarrel with a man who was able to break his neck, but who would not fight like a gentleman. He grew calmer, and could have laughed at the situation had it been brought about by any other cause.

"Look here, cousin," said San Giacinto, suddenly and in a familiar tone, "I am as good a gentleman as you, though I have kept an inn. If it is the custom here to play with swords and such toys I will take a few lessons and we will have it out. But I confess that I would like to know why you are so outrageously angry. How did you come by that letter? It was never meant for you, nor for any of yours. I pinned it upon Gouache's dressing-table with a pin I found there. I took the paper from your wife's table a week ago yesterday. If you want to know all about it I will tell you."

"And whom did you intend for the author of the letter? Whom but my wife?"

"Your wife!" cried San Giacinto in genuine astonishment. "You are out of your mind. Gouache was to meet Faustina Montevarchi on Sunday morning at a church, and I invented the note to prevent the meeting, and put it on his table during the previous afternoon. I am going to marry Donna Flavia, and I do not mean to allow a beggarly Zouave to make love to my future sister-in-law. Since you took the note they must have met after all. I wish you had left it alone."

Giovanni sank into a chair before the table and buried his face in his hands. San Giacinto stood looking at him in silence, beginning to comprehend what had happened, and really distressed that his comparatively harmless stratagem should have caused so much trouble. He looked at things from a lower point of view than Giovanni, but he was a very human man, after all. It was hard for him to believe that his cousin could have really suspected Corona of loving Gouache; but Giovanni's behaviour left no other explanation. On the other hand, he felt that whatever might be thought of his own part in the affair, it was Giovanni's own fault that things had turned out as they had, seeing that he had been guilty of a very serious indiscretion in entering Gouache's rooms unbidden and in reading what was meant for the Zouave.

Giovanni rose and his face was pale again, but the expression had utterly changed in the course of a few seconds. He suffered horribly, but with a pain more easy to bear than that which had tortured him during the past week. Corona was innocent, and he knew it. Every word she had spoken a week ago, when he had accused her, rang again in his ears, and as though by magic the truth of her statement was now as clear as the day. He could never forgive himself for having doubted her. He did not know whether he could ever atone for the agony he must have caused her. But it was a thousand times better that he should live long years of bitter self-reproach, than that the woman he so loved should have fallen. He forgot San Giacinto and the petty scheme which had brought about such dire consequences. He forgot his anger of a moment ago in the supreme joy of knowing that Corona had not sinned, and in the bitter contrition for having so terribly wronged her. If he felt anything towards San Giacinto it was gratitude, but he stood speechless under his great emotion, not even thinking what he should say.

"If you doubt the truth of my explanation," said San Giacinto, "go to the Palazzo Montevarchi. Opposite the entrance you will see some queer things painted on the wall. There are Gouache's initials scrawled a hundred times, and the words 'Sunday' and 'Mass' very conspicuous. A simple way, too, would be to ask him whether he did not actually meet Faustina last Sunday morning. When a man advertises his meetings with his lady-love on the walls of the city, no one can be blamed for reading the advertisement."

He laughed at the conceit and at his own astuteness; but Giovanni scarcely heeded him or his words.

"Good-bye," said the latter, holding out his hand.

"You do not want to fight any more, then?" asked San Giacinto.

"Not unless you do. Good-bye."

Without another word he left the room and descended into the street. The cold gray dawn was over everything and the air was raw and chilly. There is nothing more dismal than early dawn in a drizzling rain when a man has been up all night, but Giovanni was unconscious of any discomfort, and there were wings under his feet as he hastened homeward along the slippery pavements.

The pallor in his face had given way to a slight flush that gave colour and animation to his cheeks, and though his eyes were bright their expression was more natural than it had been for many days. He was in one of the strangest humours which can have sway over that unconsciously humorous animal, man. In the midst of the deepest self-abasement his heart was overflowing with joy. The combination of sorrow and happiness is a rare one, not found every day, but the condition of experiencing both at the same time and in the highest degree is very possible.

Giovanni, indeed, could not feel otherwise than he did. Had he suspected Corona and accused her on grounds wholly frivolous and untenable, in the unreasoning outbreak of a foolish jealousy, he could not have been so persuaded of her guilt as to feel the keenest joy on finding her innocent. In that case his remorse would have outweighed his satisfaction. Had he, on the other hand, suspected her without making the accusation, he would have been happy on discovering his mistake, but could have felt little or no remorse. As it was, he had accused her upon evidence which most tribunals would have thought sufficient for a conviction, and on seeing all doubt cleared away he realised with terrible force the extent of the pain he had inflicted. While he had still believed that she had fallen, he had still so loved her as to wish that he could take the burden of her guilt upon his own shoulders. Now that her innocence was proved beyond all doubt, he had no thought but to ask her forgiveness.

He let himself in with a latch-key and ran up the dim stairs. A second key opened the polished door into the dark vestibule, and in a moment more he was in the ante-chamber of Corona's apartment. Two or three women, pale with watching, were standing round a table, upon which something was heating over a spirit lamp. Giovanni stopped and spoke to them.

"How is she?" he asked, his voice unsteady with anxiety.

The women shook their heads, and one of them began to cry. They loved their mistress dearly and had little hope of her recovery. They had been amazed, too, at Giovanni's apparent indifference during the whole week, and seemed surprised when he went towards the door. One motioned to him to make no noise. He turned the latch very gently and advanced into the darkened chamber.

Corona was lying as he had seen her on the previous evening, and there seemed to be little or no change in her state. Her eyes were closed and her breathing was scarcely perceptible. A nurse was nodding in a chair near the night light and looked up as Giovanni entered. He pointed to the door and she went out.

All was so exactly as it had been twelve hours earlier that he could hardly realise the immense change that had taken place in his own heart during the interval. He stood looking at his wife, scarcely breathing for fear of disturbing her and yet wishing that she might wake to hear what he had to say. But she did not move nor show any signs of consciousness. Her delicate, thin hand lay upon the coverlet. He stooped down very slowly and cautiously, and kissed the wasted fingers. Then he drew back quickly and noiselessly as though he had done something wrong. He thought she must be asleep, and sat down in the chair the nurse had vacated. The stillness was profound. The little night light burned steadily without flickering and cast queer long shadows from the floor upwards over the huge tapestries upon the wall. The quaint figures of heroes and saints, that had seen many a Saracinesca born and many a one die in the ancient vaulted room, seemed to take the expressions of old friends watching over the suffering woman. A faint odour like that of ether pervaded the still air, an odour Giovanni never forgot during his life. Everything was so intensely quiet that he almost thought he could hear the ticking of his watch in his pocket.

Corona stirred at last, and slowly opening her eyes, turned them gradually till they met her husband's gaze. At the first movement she made he had risen to his feet and now stood close beside her.

"Did you kiss my hand—or did I dream it?" she asked faintly.

"Yes, darling." He could not at once find words to say what he wanted.

"Why did you?"

Giovanni fell on his knees by the bedside and took her hand in both his own.

"Corona, Corona—forgive me!" The cry came from his heart, and was uttered with an accent of despair that there was no mistaking. She knew, faint and scarcely conscious though she was, that he was not attempting to deceive her this time. But he could say no more. Many a strong man would in that moment have sobbed aloud and shed tears, but Giovanni was not as other men. Under great emotion all expression was hard for him, and the spontaneity of tears would have contradicted his nature.

Corona wondered what had happened, and lay quite still, looking at his bent head and feeling the trembling touch of his hands on hers. For several seconds the stillness was almost as profound as it had been before. Then Giovanni spoke out slowly and earnestly.

"My beloved wife," he said, looking up into her face, "I know all the truth now. I know what I have done. I know what you have suffered. Forgive me if you can. I will give my whole life to deserve your pardon."

For an instant all Corona's beauty returned to her face as she heard his words. Her eyes shone softly, the colour mounted to her pale cheeks, and she breathed one happy sigh of relief and gladness. Her fingers contracted and closed round his with a tender pressure.

"It is true," she said, scarcely audibly. "You are not trying to deceive me in order to keep me alive?"

"It is true, darling," he answered. "San Giacinto wrote the letter. It was not even meant to seem to come from you. Oh, Corona—can you ever forgive me?"

She turned so as to see him better, and looked long into his eyes. The colour slowly faded again from her face, and her expression changed, growing suddenly sad.

"I will forgive you. I will try to forget it all, Giovanni. You should have believed me, for I have never lied to you. It will be long before I am strong again, and I shall have much time to think of it."

Giovanni rose to his feet, still clasping her hand. Something told him that she was not a woman who could either forgive or forget such an injury, and her tone was colder than he had hoped. The expiation had begun and he was already suffering the punishment of his unbelief. He bore the pain bravely. What right had he to expect that she would suddenly become as she had been before? She had been, and still was, dangerously ill, and her illness had been caused by his treatment of her. It would be long before their relations could be again what they had once been, and it was not for him to complain. She might have sent him away in anger; he would not have thought her too unkind. But when he remembered her love, he trembled at the thought of living without it. His voice was very gentle as he answered her, after a short pause.

"You shall live to forget it all, Corona. I will make you forget it. I will undo what I have done."

"Can you, Giovanni? Is there no blood upon your hands?" She knew her husband well, and could hardly believe that he had refrained from taking vengeance upon Gouache.

"There is none, thank God," replied Giovanni. "But for a happy accident I should have killed the man a week ago. It was all arranged."

"You must tell him that you have been mistaken," said Corona simply.

"Yes, I will."

"Thank you. That is right."

"It is the least I can do."

Giovanni felt that words were of very little use, and even had he wished to say more he would not have known how to speak. There was that between them which was too deep for all expression, and he knew that henceforth he could only hope to bring back Corona's love by his own actions. Besides, in her present state, he guessed that it would be wiser to leave her, than to prolong the interview.

"I will go now," he said. "You must rest, darling, and be quite well tomorrow."

"Yes. I can rest now."

She said nothing about seeing him again. With a humility almost pathetic in such a man, he bent down and touched her hand with his lips. Then he would have gone away, but she held his fingers and looked long into his eyes.

"I am sorry for you, dear," she said, and paused, not taking her eyes from his. "Kiss me," she added at last, with a faint smile.

A moment later, he was gone. She gazed long at the door through which he had left the room, and her expression changed more than once, softening and hardening again as the thoughts chased each other through her tired brain. At last she closed her eyes, and presently fell into a peaceful sleep.

Giovanni waited in his room until his father was awake and then went to tell him what had happened. The old gentleman looked weary and sad, but his keen sight noticed the change in his son's manner.

"You look better," he said.

"I have been undeceived," answered Giovanni. "I have been mistaken, misled by the most extraordinary set of circumstances I have ever heard of."

Saracinesca's eyes suddenly gleamed angrily and his white beard bristled round his face.

"You have made a fool of yourself," he growled. "You have made your wife ill and yourself miserable in a fit of vulgar jealousy. And now you have been telling her so."

"Exactly. I have been telling her so."

"You are an idiot, Giovanni. I always knew it."

"I have only just found it out," answered the younger man.

"Then you are amazingly slow at discovery. Why do you stand there staring at me? Do you expect any sympathy? You will not get it. Go and say a litany outside

your wife's door. You have made me spend the most horrible week I ever remember, just because you are not good enough for her. How could you ever dare to
suspect that woman? Go away. I shall strangle you if you stay here!"

"That consideration would not have much weight," replied Giovanni. "I
know how mad I have been, much better than you can tell me. And yet, I doubt
whether any one was ever so strangely mistaken before."

"With your intelligence the wonder is that you are not always mistaken.
Upon my soul, the more I think of it, the more I am amazed at your folly. You
acted like a creature in the theatre. With your long face and your mystery and
your stage despair, you even made a fool of me. At all events, I shall know what
to expect the next time it happens. I hope Corona will have the sense to make
you do penance."

To tell the truth Giovanni had not expected any better treatment from his
father than he actually received, and he was not in a humour to resent reproaches
which he knew to be well deserved. He had only intended to tell the prince the
result of what had occurred, and he relaxed nothing of his determination, even
though he might have persuaded the old gentleman that the accumulated evidence had undoubtedly justified his doubts. With a short salutation he left the
room and went out, hoping that Gouache had not accompanied the expedition
to Mentana, improbable as that seemed.

He was, of course, disappointed, for while he was making inquiries Gouache
was actually on the way to the battle with his corps, as has been already seen.
Giovanni spent most of the day in the house, constantly inquiring after Corona,
and trying to occupy his mind in reading, though with little success. The idea that
Gouache might be killed without having learned the truth began to take possession of him and caused him an annoyance he could not explain. It was not that he
felt any very profound remorse for having wronged the man. His nature was not
so sensitive as that. It was rather, perhaps, because he regarded the explanation
with Anastase as a part of what he owed Corona, that he was so anxious to meet
him alive. Partly, too, his anxiety arose from his restlessness and from the desire
for action of some sort in which to forget all he had suffered, and all he was still
suffering.

Towards evening he went out and heard news of the engagement. It was
already known that the enemy had fallen back upon Mentana, and no one
doubted the ultimate result of the day's fighting. People were already beginning

to talk of going out to take assistance to the wounded. The idea struck Giovanni as plausible and he determined to act upon it at once. He took a surgeon and several men with him, and drove out across the Campagna to the scene of the battle.

As has been told, he found Gouache at last, after a long and difficult search. The ground was so broken and divided by ditches, walls and trees, that some of the wounded were not found until the middle of the next day. Unless Giovanni had undertaken the search Anastase might have escaped notice for a long time, and it was no wonder if he expressed astonishment on waking up to find himself comfortably installed in Saracinesca's carriage, tended by the man who a few days earlier had wanted to take his life.

CHAPTER XV

GOUACHE'S wound was by no means dangerous, and when he had somewhat recovered from the combined effects of loss of blood and excessive fatigue he did not feel much the worse for having a ball in his shoulder. Giovanni and the doctor gave him food and a little wine in the carriage, and long before they reached the gates of the city the Zouave was well enough to have heard Sant' Ilario's explanation. The presence of the surgeon, however, made any intimate conversation difficult.

"I came to find you," said Giovanni in a low voice, "because everything has been set right in your absence, and I was afraid you might be killed at Mentana without receiving my apology."

Gouache looked at his companion in some surprise. He knew very well that Sant' Ilario was not a man to make excuses without some very extraordinary reasons for such a step. It is a prime law of the code of honour, however, that an apology duly made must be duly accepted as putting an end to any quarrel, and Anastase saw at once that Giovanni had relinquished all intention of fighting.

"I am very glad that everything is explained," answered Gouache. "I confess that I was surprised beyond measure by the whole affair."

"I regret having entered your rooms without your permission," continued Giovanni who intended to go to the end of what he had undertaken. "The pin was my wife's, but the letter was written by another person with a view to influencing your conduct. I cannot explain here, but you shall know whatever is necessary when we are alone. Of course, if you still desire any satisfaction, I am at your service."

"Pray do not suggest such a thing. I have no further feeling of annoyance in the matter."

Gouache insisted on being taken to his own lodgings, though Sant' Ilario offered him the hospitality of the Palazzo Saracinesca. By four o'clock in the morning the ball was extracted and the surgeon took his leave, recommending sleep and quiet for his patient. Gouache, however, would not let Giovanni go without hearing the end of the story.

"The facts are very few," said the latter after a moment's hesitation. "It appears that you had arranged to meet a lady on Sunday morning. A certain person whom I will not name discovered your intention, and conceived the idea of preventing the meeting by sending you a note purporting to come from the lady. As he could get none of her note-paper he possessed himself of some of my wife's. He pinned the note on your table with the pin you had chanced to find. I was foolish enough to enter your room and I recognised the pin and the paper. You understand the rest."

Gouache laughed merrily.

"I understand that you did me a great service. I met the lady after all, but if I had received the note I would not have gone, and she would have waited for me. Do you mind telling me the name of the individual who tried to play me the trick?"

"If you will excuse my discretion, I would rather not. He knows that his plan failed. I should not feel justified in telling you his name, from other motives."

"As you please," said Gouache. "I daresay I shall find him out."

So the interview ended and Giovanni went home to rest at last, almost as much worn out as Gouache himself. He was surprised at the ease with which everything had been arranged, but he was satisfied with the result and felt that a weight had been taken from his mind. He slept long and soundly and awoke the next morning to hear that Corona was much better.

The events of Saturday and Sunday had to all appearances smoothed many difficulties from the lives of those with whom my history is concerned. Corona and Giovanni were once more united, though the circumstances that had produced so terrible a breach between them had left a shadow on their happiness. Gouache had fought his battle and had returned with a slight wound so that as soon as he could go out he would be able to renew his visits at the Palazzo Montevarchi and see Faustina without resorting to any more ingenious stratagems. San Giacinto had failed to produce the trouble he had planned, but his own prospects were brilliant enough. His marriage with Flavia was to take place on the last of the month and the preliminaries were being arranged as quickly as possible. Flavia herself was delighted with the new dignity she assumed in the family, and if she was not positively in love with San Giacinto, was enough attracted by him to look forward with pleasure upon the prospect of becoming his wife. Old Montevarchi alone seemed preoccupied and silent, but his melancholy mood was relieved by occasional moments of anticipated triumph, while he made frequent visits to the library and seemed to find solace in the conversation of the librarian, Arnoldo Meschini.

In the future of each of these persons there was an element of uncertainty which most of them disregarded. As Corona recovered, Giovanni began to think that she would really forget as well as forgive all he had made her suffer. Gouache on his part entertained the most sanguine hopes of marrying Faustina. Montevarchi looked forward with assurance to the success of his plot against the Saracinesca. San Giacinto and Flavia were engaged, indeed, but were not yet married. And yet the issue of none of these events was absolutely sure.

The first matter with which we are concerned is the forgery of the clauses in the documents, which Meschini had undertaken to accomplish and actually finished in less than three weeks. It was indeed an easy task for a man so highly skilled in the manufacture of chirographic antiquities, but he had found himself unexpectedly balked at the outset, and the ingenuity he displayed in overcoming the difficulties he met with is worth recording.

It was necessary in the first place to ascertain whether there was a copy of the principal deed at the Chancery. He had no trouble in finding that such a copy existed, and was indeed fully prepared for the contingency. But when the parchment was produced, his face fell. It was a smaller sheet than the first and the writing was a little wider, so that the space at the foot of the first page was considerably less than in the original. He saw at once that it would be impossible to make the insertion, even if he could get possession of the document for a time long enough to execute the work. Moreover, though he was not actually watched while he read it, he could see that it would be almost impracticable to use writing materials in the office of the Chancery without being observed. He was able, however, to take out the original which he carried with him and to compare it with the copy. Both were by one hand, and the copy was only distinguished by the seal of the government office. It was kept, like all such documents, in a dusty case upon which were written the number and letter of the alphabet by which it was classified.

Meschini hesitated only a moment, and then decided to substitute the original for the copy. Should the keeper of the archives chance to look at the parchment and discover the absence of the seal, Meschini could easily excuse himself by saying that he had mistaken the two, and indeed with that one exception they were very much alike. The keeper, however, noticed nothing and Arnoldo had the satisfaction of seeing him unsuspiciously return the cardboard case to its place on the shelves. He went back to his room and set to work.

The longer he looked at the sheet the more clearly he saw that it would be impossible to make the insertion. There was nothing to be done but to forge a new document with the added words. He did not like the idea, though he believed himself fully able to carry it out. There was a risk, he thought, which he had not meant to undertake; but on the other hand the reward was great. He put forth all his skill to produce the imitation and completed it in ten days to his entire satisfaction. He understood the preparation of seals as well as the rest of his art, and had no difficulty in making a die which corresponded precisely with the wax. In the first place he took off the impression carefully with kneaded bread. From this with a little plaster of Paris he reproduced the seal, which he very carefully retouched with a fine steel instrument until it was quite perfect. Over this again he poured melted lead, thus making a hard die with which he could stamp the wax without danger of breaking the instrument. Once more he retouched the lead with a graving tool, using a lens for the work and ultimately turning out an absolutely accurate copy of the seal used in the Chancery office. He made experiments as he proceeded, and when he was at last satisfied he turned to the actual forgery, which was a longer matter and required greater skill and patience. Nothing was omitted which could make the fraud complete. The parchment assumed the exact shade under his marvellous manipulation. The smallest roughness was copied with faultless precision, and then by many hours of handling and the use of a little dust collected among the books in the

library, he imparted to the whole the appearance of age which was indispensable. When he had finished he showed his work to old Montevarchi, but by an
inherent love of duplicity did not tell him that the whole document was forged,
merely pointing to the inserted clause as a masterpiece of imitation. First, however, he pretended that the copy had actually contained the inserted words, and
the prince found it hard to believe that this was not the case. Meschini was
triumphant.

Again he returned to the Chancery and substituted what he had written for
the first original upon which he had now to make the insertion. There was no
difficulty here, and yet he hesitated before beginning. It seemed to him safer after
all to forge the whole of the second as he had done the first. A slip of the pen, an
unlucky drop of ink might mar the work and excite suspicion, whereas if he made
a mistake upon a fresh sheet of parchment he could always begin again. There was
only one danger. The Saracinesca might have made some private mark upon the
original which should elude even his microscopic examination. He spent nearly a
day in examining the sheet with a lens but could discover nothing. Being satisfied
of the safety of the proceeding he executed the forgery with the same care he had
bestowed upon the first, and showed it to his employer. The latter could scarcely
believe his eyes, and was very far from imagining that the two originals were
intact and carefully locked up in Meschini's room. The prince took the document
and studied its contents again during many hours before he finally decided to
return it to old Saracinesca.

It was a moment of intense excitement. He hesitated whether he should
take the manuscripts back himself or send them by a messenger. Had he been
sure of controlling himself, he would have gone in person, but he knew that if
Saracinesca should chance to look over the writing when they were together, it
would be almost impossible to conceal emotion under such a trial of nerve. What
he really hoped was that the prince would think no more of the matter, and put
away the parcel without examining the contents.

Montevarchi pondered long over the course he should pursue, his eyes
gleaming now and then with a wild triumph, and then growing dull and glassy at
the horrible thought of discovery. Then again the consciousness that he was committing a great crime overcame him, and he twisted his fingers nervously. He had
embarked upon the undertaking, however, and he fully believed that it would be
impossible to draw back even had he wished to do so. The insertions were made

and could not be erased. It is possible that at one moment, had Montevarchi known the truth, he would have drawn back; but it is equally sure that if he had done so he would sooner or later have regretted it, and would have done all in his power to recover lost ground and to perpetrate the fraud. The dominant passion for money, when it is on the point of being satisfied, is one of the strongest incentives to evil deeds, and in the present case the stake was enormous. He would not let it slip through his fingers. He rejoiced that the thing was done and that the millions of the Saracinesca were already foredoomed to be his.

It is doubtful whether he was able to form a clear conception of what would take place after the trial was over and the property awarded to his son-in-law. It was perhaps enough for his ambition that his daughter should be Princess Saracinesca, and he did not doubt his power to control some part of the fortune. San Giacinto, who was wholly innocent in the matter, would, he thought, be deeply grateful for having been told of his position, and would show his gratitude in a befitting manner. Moreover, Montevarchi's avarice was on a grand scale, and it was not so much the possession of more money for himself that he coveted, as the aggrandisement of his children and grandchildren. The patriarchal system often produces this result. He would scarcely have known what to do with a greater fortune than he possessed, but he looked forward with a wild delight to seeing his descendants masters of so much wealth. The fact that he could not hope to enjoy his satisfaction very long did not detract from its reality or magnitude. The miser is generally long-lived, and does not begin to anticipate death until the catastrophe is near at hand. Even then it is a compensation to him to feel that the heirs of his body are to be made glorious by what he has accumulated, and his only fear is that they will squander what he has spent his strength in amassing. He educates his children to be thrifty and rejoices when they spend no money, readily believing them to be as careful as himself, and seldom reflecting that, if he furnished them with the means, their true disposition might turn out to be very different. It is so intensely painful to him to think of wealth being wasted that he cultivates the belief in the thriftiness of those who must profit by his death. If he has been born to worldly state as well as to a great inheritance, he extends the desire of accumulation to the fortunes of his relations and descendants, and shows a laudable anxiety that they should possess all that he can get for them, provided it is quite impossible that he should get it for himself. The powers of the world have been to a great extent built up on this principle, and it is a maxim in many a great family that there is no economy like enriching one's relatives to the third and fourth generation.

The struggle in Montevarchi's mind was so insignificant and lasted so short a time, that it might be disregarded altogether, were it not almost universally true that the human mind hesitates at the moment of committing a crime. That moment of hesitation has prevented millions of frightful deeds, and has betrayed thousands of carefully plotted conspiracies whose success seemed assured, and it is amazing to think what an influence has been exerted upon the destinies of the human race by the instinctive fear of crossing the narrow boundary between right and wrong. The time occupied in such reflection is often only infinitesimal. It has been called the psychological moment, and if the definition means that it is the instant during which the soul suggests, it is a true one. It is then that our natural repulsion for evil asserts itself; it is then that the consequences of what we are about to do rise clearly before us as in a mirror; it is then that our courage is suddenly strengthened to do the right, or deserts us and leaves us mere instruments for the accomplishment of the wrong. If humanity had not an element of good in it, there would be no hesitation in the perpetration of crime, any more than a wild beast pauses before destroying a weaker creature. Perhaps there is no clearer proof of the existence of a divine soul in man, than his intuitive reluctance to do what in the lower animals would be most natural. Circumstances, education, the accidents of life, all tend to make this psychologic moment habitually shorter or longer. The suspense created in the conscience, during which the intelligence is uncertain how to act, may last a week or a second, a year or a quarter of an hour; but it is a stage through which all must pass, both the professional criminal and the just man who is perhaps tempted to commit a crime but once during his life.

Old Lotario Montevarchi had never been guilty of any misdeed subject to the provisions of the penal code; but he had done most things in his love of money which were not criminal only because the law had not foreseen the tortuous peculiarities of his mind. Even now he persuaded himself that the end was a righteous one, and that his course was morally justifiable. He had that power of deceiving himself which characterises the accomplished hypocrite, and he easily built up for San Giacinto a whole edifice of sympathy which seemed in his own view very real and moral. He reflected with satisfaction upon the probable feelings of the old Leone Saracinesca, when, after relinquishing his birthright, he found himself married and the father of a son. How the poor man must have cursed his folly and longed for some means of undoing the deed! It was but common justice after all—it was but common justice, and it was a mere accident of fate that Leone's great-grandson, who was now to be reinstated in all the glories of his princely possessions, was also to marry Flavia Montevarchi.

The prospect was too alluring and the suspense lasted but a moment, though he believed that he spent much time in considering the situation. The thoughts that really occupied him were not of a nature to hinder the accomplishment of his plan, and he was not at all surprised with himself when he finally tied up the packet and rang for a messenger. Detection was impossible, for by Meschini's skilful management, the original and the official copy corresponded exactly and were such marvellous forgeries as to defy discovery. When it is considered that the greatest scientists and specialists in Europe have recently disagreed concerning documents which are undoubtedly of modern manufacture, and which were produced by just such men as Arnoldo Meschini, it need not appear surprising that the latter should successfully impose upon a court of law. The circumstances of the Saracinesca family history, too, lent an air of probability to the alleged facts. The poverty and temporary disappearance of Leone's descendants explained why they had not attempted to recover their rights. Nay, more, since Leone had died when his son was an infant, and since there was no copy of the document among his papers, it was more than probable that the child on growing up had never known the nature of the deed, and would not have been likely to suspect what was now put forward as the truth, unless his attention were called to it by some person possessed of the necessary knowledge.

The papers were returned to Prince Saracinesca in the afternoon with a polite note of thanks. It will be remembered that the prince had not read the documents, as he had meant to do, in consequence of the trouble between Giovanni and Corona which had made him forget his intention. He had not looked over them since he had been a young man and the recollection of their contents was far from clear. Having always supposed the collateral branch of his family to be extinct, it was only natural that he should have bestowed very little thought upon the ancient deeds which he believed to have been drawn up in due form and made perfectly legal.

When he came home towards evening, he found the sealed packet upon his table, and having opened it, was about to return the papers to their place in the archives. It chanced that he had a letter to write, however, and he pushed the documents aside before taking them to the library. While he was writing, Giovanni entered the room.

As has been seen, the prince had been very angry with his son for having allowed himself to doubt Corona, and though several days had elapsed since the matter had been explained, the old man's wrath had not wholly subsided. He still felt considerable resentment against Giovanni, and his intercourse with the latter had not yet regained its former cordiality. As Sant' Ilario entered the room, Saracinesca looked up with an expression which showed clearly that the interruption was unwelcome.

"Do I disturb you?" asked Giovanni, noticing the look.

"Do you want anything?"

"No—nothing especial."

Saracinesca's eye fell upon the pile of manuscripts that lay on the table. It struck him that Giovanni might occupy himself by looking them over, while he himself finished the letter he had begun.

"There are those deeds relating to San Giacinto," he said, "you might look through them before they are put away. Montevarchi borrowed them for a day or two and has just sent them back."

Giovanni took the bundle and established himself in a comfortable chair beside a low stand, where the light of a lamp fell upon the pages as he turned them. He made no remark, but began to examine the documents, one by one, running his eye rapidly along the lines, as he read on mechanically, not half comprehending the sense of the words. He was preoccupied by thoughts of Corona and of what had lately happened, so that he found it hard to fix his attention. The prince's pen scratched and spattered on the paper, and irritated Giovanni, for the old gentleman wrote a heavy, nervous handwriting, and lost his temper twenty times in five minutes, mentally cursing the ink, the paper and the pen, and wishing he could write like a shopman or a clerk.

Giovanni's attention was arrested by the parchment on which the principal deed was executed, and he began to read the agreement with more care than he had bestowed upon the other papers. He understood Latin well enough, but the crabbed characters puzzled him from time to time. He read the last words on the first page without thinking very much of what they meant: "*Eo tamen pacto, quod si praedicto Domino Leoni ex legitimo matrimonio heres nasceretur, instrumentum hoc nullum, vanum atque plane invalidum fiat.*"

Giovanni smiled at the quaint law Latin, and then read the sentence over again. His face grew grave as he realised the tremendous import of those few words. Again and again he translated the phrase, trying to extract from it some other meaning than that which was so unpleasantly clear. No other construction, however, could be put upon what was written, and for some minutes Giovanni sat staring at the fire, bewildered and almost terrified by his discovery.

"Have you ever read those papers?" he asked at last, in a voice that made his father drop his pen and look up.

"Not for thirty years."

"Then you had better read them at once. San Giacinto is Prince Saracinesca and you and I are nobody."

Saracinesca uttered a fierce oath and sprang from his chair.

"What do you mean?" he asked, seizing Giovanni's arm violently with one hand and taking the parchment with the other.

"Read for yourself. There—at the foot of the page, from 'eo tamen pacto.' It is plain enough. It says, 'On the understanding that if an heir be born to the aforesaid Don Leone, in lawful wedlock, the present instrument shall be wholly null, void and inefficacious.' An heir was born, and San Giacinto is that heir's grandson. You may tear up the document. It is not worth the parchment it is written upon, nor are we either."

"You are mad, Giovannino!" exclaimed the prince, hoarsely, "that is not the meaning of the words. You have forgotten your Latin."

"I will get you a dictionary—or a lawyer—whichever you prefer."

"You are not in earnest, my boy. Look here—*eo tamen pacto*—that means 'by this agreement'—does it not? I am not so rusty as you seem to think."

"It means 'on this understanding, however.' Go on. *Quod si*, that if—*prae-dicto Domino Leoni*, to the aforesaid Don Leone—*ex legitimo matrimonio*, from a lawful marriage—*heres nasceretur*, an heir should be born—*hoc instrumentum*, this deed—shall be null, worthless and invalid. You cannot get any other sense out of it. I have tried for a quarter of an hour. You and I are beggars. Saracinesca, Torleone, Barda, and all the rest belong to San Giacinto, the direct descendant of your great-grandfather's elder brother. You are simple Don Leone, and I am plain Don Giovanni. That is what it means."

"Good God!" cried the old man in extreme horror. "If you should be right—"

"I am right," replied Giovanni, very pale.

With wild eyes and trembling hands the prince spread the document upon the table and read it over again. He turned it and went on to the end, his excitement bringing back in the moment such scholarship as he had once possessed and making every sentence as clear as the day.

"Not even San Giacinto—not even a title!" he exclaimed desperately. He fell back in his chair, crushed by the tremendous blow that had fallen so unexpectedly upon him in his old age.

"Not even San Giacinto," repeated Giovanni, stupidly. His presence of mind began to forsake him, too, and he sank down, burying his face in his hands. As in a dream he saw his cousin installed in the very chair where his father now sat, master of the house in which he, Giovanni, had been born, like his father before him, master of the fortresses and castles, the fair villas and the broad lands, the palaces and the millions to which Giovanni had thought himself heir, lord over the wealth and inheritances of his race, dignified by countless titles and by all the consideration that falls to the lot of the great in this world.

For a long time neither spoke, for both were equally overwhelmed by the magnitude of the disaster that hung over their heads. They looked furtively at each other, and each saw that his companion was white to the lips. The old man was the first to break the silence.

"At all events, San Giacinto does not know how the deed stands," he said.

"It will make it all the harder to tell him," replied Giovanni.

"To tell him? You would not be so mad—"

"Do you think it would be honourable," asked the younger man, "for us to remain in possession of what clearly does not belong to us? I will not do it."

"We have been in possession for more than a century."

"That is no reason why we should continue to steal another man's money," said Giovanni. "We are men. Let us act like men. It is bitter. It is horrible. But we have no other course. After all, Corona has Astrardente. She will give you a home. She is rich."

"Me? Why do you say me? Us both."

"I will work for my living," said Giovanni, quietly. "I am young. I will not live on my wife."

"It is absurd!" exclaimed the prince. "It is Quixotic. San Giacinto has plenty of money without ruining us. Even if he finds it out I will fight the case to the end. I am master here, as my father and my father's father were before me, and

I will not give up what is mine without a struggle. Besides, who assures us that he is really what he represents himself to be? What proves that he is really the descendant of that same Leone?"

"For that matter," answered Giovanni, "he will have to produce very positive proofs, valid in law, to show that he is really the man. I will give up everything to the lawful heir, but I will certainly not turn beggar to please an adventurer. But I say that, if San Giacinto represents the elder branch of our house, we have no right here. If I were sure of it I would not sleep another night under this roof."

The old man could not withhold his admiration. There was something supremely noble and generous about Giovanni's readiness to sacrifice everything for justice which made his old heart beat with a strange pride. If he was reluctant to renounce his rights it was after all more on Giovanni's account, and for the sake of Corona and little Orsino. He himself was an old man and had lived most of his life out already.

"You have your mother's heart, Giovannino," he said simply, but there was a slight moisture in his eyes, which few emotions had ever had the power to bring there.

"It is not a question of heart," replied Giovanni. "We cannot keep what does not belong to us."

"We will let the law decide what we can keep. Do you realise what it would be like, what a position we should occupy if we were suddenly declared beggars? We should be absolute paupers. We do not own a foot of land, a handful of money that does not come under the provisions of that accursed clause."

"Wait a minute," exclaimed Giovanni, suddenly recollecting that he possessed something of his own, a fact he had wholly forgotten in the excitement of his discovery. "We shall not be wholly without resources. It does not follow from this deed that we must give to San Giacinto any of the property our branch of the family has acquired by marriage, from your great grandfather's time to this. It must be very considerable. To begin with me, my fortune came from my mother. Then there was your mother, and your father's mother, and so on. San Giacinto has no claim to anything not originally the property of the old Leone who made this deed."

"That is true," replied the prince, more hopefully. "It is not so bad as it looked. You must be right about that point."

"Unless the courts decide that San Giacinto is entitled to compensation and interest, because four generations have been kept out of the property."

Both men looked grave. The suggestion was unpleasant. Such judgments had been given before and might be given again.

"We had better send for our lawyer," said the prince, at last. "The sooner we know the real value of that bit of parchment the better it will be for us. I cannot bear the suspense of waiting a day to know the truth. Imagine that the very chair I am sitting upon may belong to San Giacinto. I never liked the fellow, from the day when I first found him in his inn at Aquila."

"It is not his fault," answered Giovanni, quietly. "This is a perfectly simple matter. We did not know what these papers were. Even if we had known, we should have laughed at them until we discovered that we had a cousin. After all we shall not starve, and what is a title? The Pope will give you another when he knows what has happened. I would as soon be plain Don Giovanni as Prince of Sant' Ilario."

"For that matter, you can call yourself Astrardente."

"I would rather not," said Giovanni, with something like a laugh. "But I must tell Corona this news."

"Wait till she is herself again. It might disturb her too much."

"You do not know her!" Giovanni laughed heartily this time. "If you think she cares for such things, you are very much mistaken in her character. She will bear the misfortune better than any of us. Courage, padre mio! Things are never so black as they look at first."

"I hope not, my boy, I hope not! Go and tell your wife, if you think it best. I would rather be alone."

Giovanni left the room, and Saracinesca was alone. He sank back once more in his chair and folded his strong brown hands together upon the edge of the table before him. In spite of all Giovanni could say, the old man felt keenly the horror of his position. Only those who, having been brought up in immense wealth and accustomed from childhood to the pomp and circumstance of a very great position, are suddenly deprived of everything, can understand what he felt.

He was neither avaricious nor given to vanity. He had not wasted his fortune, though he had spent magnificently a princely income. He had not that small affection for greatness which, strange to say, is often found in the very great. But his position was part of himself, so that he could no more imagine himself plain Don Leone Saracinesca, than he could conceive himself boasting of his ancient titles. And yet it was quite plain to him that he must either cease to be a prince altogether, or accept a new title as a charity from his sovereign. As for his fortune, it was only too plain that the greater part of it had never been his.

To a man of his temperament the sensation of finding himself a mere impostor was intolerable. His first impulse had of course been to fight the case, and had the attack upon his position come from San Giacinto, he would probably have done so. But his own son had discovered the truth and had put the matter clearly before him, in such a light as to make an appeal to his honour. He had no choice but to submit. He could not allow himself to be outdone in common honesty by the boy he loved, nor could he have been guilty of deliberate injustice, for his own advantage, after he had been convinced that he had no right to his possessions. He belonged to a race of men who had frequently committed great crimes and done atrocious deeds, notorious in history, from motives of personal ambition, for the love of women or out of hatred for men, but who had never had the reputation of loving money or of stooping to dishonour for its sake. As soon as he was persuaded that everything belonged to San Giacinto, he felt that he must resign all in favour of the latter.

One doubt alone remained to be solved. It was not absolutely certain that San Giacinto was the man he represented himself to be. It was quite possible that he should have gained possession of the papers he held, by some means known only to himself; such things are often sold as curiosities, and as the last of the older branch of whom there was any record preserved in Rome had died in obscurity, it was conceivable that the ex-innkeeper might have found or bought the documents he had left, in order to call himself Marchese di San Giacinto. Saracinesca did not go so far as to believe that the latter had any knowledge whatsoever of the main deed which was about to cause so much trouble, unless he had seen it in the hands of Montevarchi, in which case he could not be blamed if he brought a suit for the recovery of so much wealth.

CHAPTER XVI

GIOVANNI was quite right in his prediction concerning Corona's conduct. He found her in her dressing-room, lying upon the couch near the fire, as he had found her on that fatal evening three weeks earlier. He sat down beside her and took her hand in his. She had not wholly recovered her strength yet, but her beauty had returned and seemed perfected by the suffering through which she had passed. In a few words he told her the whole story, to which she listened without showing any great surprise. Once or twice, while he was speaking, her dark eyes sought his with an expression he did not fully understand, but which was at least kind and full of sympathy.

"Are you quite sure of all the facts?" she asked when he had finished. "Are you certain that San Giacinto is the man? I cannot tell why, but I have always distrusted him since he first came to us."

"That is the only point that remains to be cleared up," answered Giovanni. "If he is not the man he will not venture to take any steps in the matter, lest he should be exposed and lose what he has."

"What will you do?"

"I hardly know. If he is really our cousin, we must give up everything without a struggle. We are impostors, or little better. I think I ought to tell him plainly how the deed is made out, in order that he may judge whether or not he is in a position to prove his identity."

"Do you imagine that he does not know all about it as well as we ourselves?"

"Probably not—otherwise he would have spoken."

"The papers came back from Montevarchi today," said Corona. "It is gratuitous to suppose that the old man has not told his future son-in-law what they contain. Yes—you see it yourself. Therefore San Giacinto knows. Therefore, also, if he is the man he pretends to be, he will let you know his intentions soon enough. I fancy you forgot that in your excitement. If he says nothing, it is because he cannot prove his rights."

"It is true," replied Giovanni, "I did not think of that. Nevertheless I would like to be beforehand. I wish him to know that we shall make no opposition. It is a point of honour."

"Which a woman cannot understand, of course," added Corona, calmly.

"I did not say that. I do not mean it."

"Well—do you want my advice?"

"Always."

The single word was uttered with an accent implying more than mere trust, and was accompanied by a look full of strong feeling. But Corona's expression did not change. Her eyes returned the glance quietly, without affectation, neither lovingly nor unlovingly, but indifferently. Giovanni felt a sharp little pain in his heart as he realised the change that had taken place in his wife.

"My advice is to do nothing in the matter. San Giacinto may be an impostor; indeed, it is not at all unlikely. If he is, he will take advantage of your desire to act generously. He will be forewarned and forearmed and will have time to procure all the proofs he wants. What could you say to him? 'If you can prove your birth, I give you all I possess.' He will at once see that nothing else is necessary, and if he is a rogue he will succeed. Besides, as I tell you, he knows what that deed contains as well as you do, and if he is the man he will bring an action against your father in a week. If he does not, you gain the advantage of having discovered that he is an impostor without exposing yourself to be robbed."

"It goes against the grain," said Giovanni. "But I suppose you are right."

"You will do as you think best. I have no power to make you follow my advice."

"No power? Ah, Corona, do not say that!"

A short silence followed, during which Corona looked placidly at the fire, while Giovanni gazed at her dark face and tried to read the thoughts that were passing in her mind. She did not speak, however, and his guesswork was inconclusive. What hurt him most was her indifference, and he longed to discover by some sign that it was only assumed.

"I would rather do as you think best," he said at last.

She glanced at him and then looked back at the blazing logs.

"I have told you what I think," she answered. "It is for you to judge and to decide. The whole matter affects you more than it does me."

"Is it not the same?"

"No. If you lose the Saracinesca titles and property we shall still be rich enough. You have a fortune of your own, and so have I. The name is, after all, an affair which concerns you personally. I should have married you as readily had you been called anything else."

The reference to the past made Giovanni's heart leap, and the colour came quickly to his face. It was almost as though she had said that she would have loved him as well had he borne another name, and that might mean that she loved him still. But her calmness belied the hasty conclusion he drew from her words. He thought she looked like a statue, as she lay there in her magnificent rest, her hands folded upon her knees before her, her eyes so turned that he could see only the drooping lids.

"A personal affair!" he exclaimed suddenly, in a bitter tone. "It was different once, Corona."

For the first time since they had been talking her face betrayed some emotion. There was the slightest possible quiver of the lip as she answered.

"Your titles were never anything but a personal affair."

"What concerns me concerns you, dear," said Giovanni, tenderly.

"In so much that I am very sorry—sincerely sorry, when anything troubles you." Her voice was kind and gentle, but there was no love in the words. "Believe me, Giovanni, I would give all I possess to spare you this."

"All you possess—is there not a little love left in your all?"

The cry came from his heart. He took her hand in both of his, and leaned forward towards her. Her fingers lay passively in his grasp, and the colour did not change in her dark cheeks. A moment ago there had been in her heart a passionate longing for the past, which had almost betrayed itself, but when he spoke of present love his words had no power to rouse a responsive echo. And yet she could not answer him roughly, for he was evidently in earnest. She said nothing, therefore, but left her hand in his. His love, which had been as fierce and strong as ever, even while he had doubted her faith, began to take new proportions of which he had never dreamt. He felt like a man struggling with death in some visible and tangible shape.

"Is it all over? Will you never love me again?" he asked hoarsely.

Her averted face told no tale, and still her fingers lay inert between his broad hands. She knew how he suffered, and yet she would not soothe him with the delusive hope for which he longed so intensely.

"For God's sake, Corona, speak to me! Is there never to be any love again? Can you never forgive me?"

"Ah, dear, I have forgiven you wholly—there is not an unkind thought left in my heart for you!" She turned and laid the hand that was free upon his shoulder, looking into his face with an expression that was almost imploring. "Do not think it is that, oh, not that! I would forgive you again, a thousand times—"

"And love me?" he cried, throwing his arms round her neck, and kissing her passionately again and again. But suddenly he drew back, for there was no response to his caresses. He turned very pale as he saw the look in her eyes. There were tears there, for the love that had been, for his present pain, perhaps, but there was not one faint spark of the fire that had burned in other days.

"I cannot say it!" she answered at last. "Oh, do not make me say it, for the sake of all that was once!"

In his emotion Giovanni slipped from the low chair and knelt beside his wife, one arm still around her. The shock of disappointment, in the very moment when he thought she was yielding, was almost more than he could bear. Had not her heart grown wholly cold, the sight of his agonised face would have softened her. She was profoundly moved and pitied him exceedingly, but she could not do more.

"Giovanni—do not look at me so! If I could! If I only could—"

"Are you made of stone?" he asked, in a voice choking with pain.

"What can I do!" she cried in despair, sinking back and hiding her face in her hands. She was in almost as great distress as he himself.

"Love me, Corona! Only love me, ever so little! Remember that you loved me once—"

"God knows how dearly! Could I forget it, I might love you now—"

"Oh, forget it then, beloved! Let it be undone. Let the past be unlived. Say that you never loved me before, and let the new life begin today—can you not? Will you not? It is so little I ask, only the beginning. I will make it grow till it shall fill your heart. Sweet love, dear love! Love me but enough to say it—"

"Do you think I would not, if I could? Ah, I would give my whole life to bring back what is gone, but I cannot. It is dead. You—no, not you—some evil thing has killed it. Say it? Yes, dear, I would say it—I will say it if you bid me. Giovanni, I love you—yes, those are the words. Do they mean anything? Can I make them sound true? Can I make the dead alive again? Is it anything but the breath of my lips? Oh, Giovanni, my lost love, why are you not Giovanni still?"

Again his arms went round her and he pressed her passionately to his heart. She turned pale, and though she tried to hide it, she shrank from his embrace, while her lips quivered and the tears of pain started in her eyes. She suffered horribly, in a way she had never dreamed of as possible. He saw what she felt and let her fall back upon the cushions, while he still knelt beside her. He saw that his mere touch was repugnant to her, and yet he could not leave her. He saw how bravely she struggled to bear his kisses, and how revolting they were to her, and yet the magic of her beauty held his passionate nature under a spell, while the lofty dignity of her spirit enthralled his soul. She was able to forgive, though he had so injured her, she was willing to love him, if she could, though he had wounded her so cruelly; it was torture to think that she could go no further, that he should never again hear the thrill of passion in her voice, nor see the whole strength of her soul rise in her eyes when his lips met hers.

There was something grand and tragic in her suffering, in her realisation of all that he had taken from her by his distrust. She sank back on her couch, clasping her hands together so tightly that the veins showed clearly beneath the olive skin. As she tried to overcome her emotion, the magnificent outline of her face was ennobled by her pain, the lids closed over her dark eyes, and the beautiful lips set themselves sternly together, as though resolved that no syllable should pass them which could hurt him, even though they could not formulate the words he would have given his soul to hear.

Giovanni knelt beside her, and gazed into her face. He knew she had not fainted, and he was almost glad that for a moment he could not see her eyes. Tenderly, timidly, he put out his hand and laid it on her clasped fingers, then drew it back again very quickly, as though suddenly remembering that the action might pain her. Her heavy hair was plaited into a thick black coil that fell upon the arm of the couch. He bent lower and pressed his lips upon the silken tress, noiselessly, fearing to disturb her, fearing lest she should even notice it. He had lost all his pride and strength and dominating power of character and he felt himself unworthy to touch her.

But he was too strong a man to continue long in such a state. Before Corona opened her eyes, he had risen to his feet and stood at some distance from her, resting his arm upon the chimney-piece, watching her still, but with an expression which showed that a change had taken place in him, and that his resolute will had once more asserted itself.

"Corona!" he said at last, in a voice that was almost calm.

Without changing her position she looked up at him. She had been conscious that he had left her side, and she experienced a physical sensation of relief.

"Corona," he repeated, when he saw that she heard him, "I do not complain. It is all my fault and my doing. Only, let it not be hate, dear. I will not touch you, I will not molest you. I will pray that you may love me again. I will try and do such things as may make you love me as you did once. Forgive me, if my kisses hurt you. I did not know they would, but I have seen it. I am not a brute. If I were, you would put something of the human into my heart. It shall never happen again, that I forget. Our life must begin again. The old Giovanni was your husband, and is dead. It is for me to win another love from you. Shall it be so, dear? Is it not to be all different—even to my very name?"

"All, all different," repeated Corona in a low voice. "Oh, how could I be so unkind! How could I show you what I felt?"

Suddenly, and without the least warning, she sprang to her feet and made two steps towards him. The impulse was there, but the reality was gone. Her arms were stretched out, and there was a look of supreme anguish in her eyes. She stopped short, then turned away once more, and as she sank upon the couch, burying her face in the cushions, the long restrained tears broke forth, and she sobbed as though her heart must break.

Giovanni wished that his own suffering could find such an outlet, but there was no such relief possible for his hardy masculine nature. He could not bear the sight of her grief, and yet he knew that he could not comfort her, that to lay his hand upon her forehead would only add a new sting to the galling wound. He turned his face away and leaned against the heavy chimney-piece, longing to shut out the sound of her sobs from his ears, submitting to a torture that might well have expiated a greater misdeed than his. The time was past when he could feel that an unbroken chain of evidence had justified him in doubting and accusing Corona. He knew the woman he had injured better now than he had known her then, for he understood the whole depth and breadth of the love he had so ruthlessly destroyed. It was incredible to him, now, that he should ever have mistrusted a creature so noble, so infinitely grander than himself. Every tear she shed fell like molten fire upon his heart, every sob that echoed through the quiet room was a reproach that racked his heart-strings and penetrated to the secret depths of his soul. He could neither undo what he had done nor soothe the pain inflicted by his actions. He could only stand there, and submit patiently to the suffering of his expiation.

The passionate outburst subsided at last, and Corona lay pale and silent upon her cushions. She knew what he felt, and pitied him more than herself.

"It is foolish of me to cry," she said presently. "It cannot help you."

"Help me?" exclaimed Giovanni, turning suddenly. "It is not I, it is you. I would have died to save you those tears."

"I know it—would I not give my life to spare you this? And I will. Come and sit beside me. Take my hand. Kiss me—be your own self. It is not true that your kisses hurt me—it shall not be true—"

"You do not mean it, dear," replied Giovanni, sadly. "I know how true it is."

"It shall not be true. Am I a devil to hurt you so? Was it all your fault? Was I not wrong too? Indeed—"

"No, my beloved. There is nothing wrong in you. If you do not love me—"

"I do. I will, in spite of myself."

"You mean it, darling—I know. You are good enough, even for that. But you cannot. It must be all my doing, now."

"I must," cried Corona, passionately. "Unless I love you, I shall die. I was wrong, too, you shall let me say it. Was I not mad to do the things I did? What man would not have suspected? Would a man be a man at all, if he did not watch the woman he loves? Would love be love without jealousy when there seems to be cause for it? Should I have married you, had I thought that you would be so careless as to let me do such things without interfering? Was it not my fault when I came back that night and would not tell you what had happened? Was it not madness to ask you to trust me, instead of telling you all? And yet," she turned her face away, "and yet, it hurt me so!"

"You shall not blame yourself, Corona. It was all my fault."

"Come and sit here, beside me. There—take my hand. Does it tremble? Do I draw it away? Am I not glad that it should rest in yours? Look at me—am I not glad? Giovanni—dear husband—true love! Look into my eyes. Do you not see that I love you? Why do you shake your head and tremble? It is true, I tell you."

Suddenly the forced smile faded from her face, the artificial expression she tried so pathetically to make real, disappeared, and gave place to a look of horror and fear. She drew back her hand and turned desperately away.

"I am lying, lying—and to you!" she moaned. "Oh God! Have mercy, for I am the most miserable woman in the world!"

Giovanni sat still, resting his chin upon his hand and staring at the fire. His hopes had risen for a moment, and had fallen again, if possible more completely than before. Every line of his strongly-marked face betrayed the despair that overwhelmed him. And yet he was no longer weak, as he had been the first time. He was wondering at the hidden depths of Corona's nature which had so suddenly become visible. He comprehended the magnitude of a passion which in being extinguished could leave such emotions behind, and he saw with awful distinctness the beauty of what he had lost and the depth of the abyss by which he was separated from it. Only a woman who had loved to distraction could make such desperate efforts to revive an affection that was dead; only a woman capable of the most lofty devotion could sink her pride and her own agony, in the attempt to make the man she had loved forgive himself. He could have borne her reproaches more easily than the sight of her anguish, but she would not reproach him. He could have borne her hatred almost better than such unselfish forgive-ness, and yet she had forgiven him. For the first time in his life he wished that he might die—he, who loved life so dearly. Perhaps it would be easier for her to see him dead at her feet than to feel that he must always be near her and that she could not love him.

"It is of no use, dear," he said, at last. "I was right. The old Giovanni is dead. We must begin our life again. Will you let me try? Will you let me do my best to live for you and to raise up a new love in your heart?"

"Can you? Can we go back to the old times when we first met? Can you? Can I?"

"If you will—"

"If I will? Is there anything I would not do to gain that?"

"Our lives may become so different from what they now are, as to make it more easy," said Giovanni. "Do you realise how everything will be changed when we have given up this house? Perhaps it is better that it should be so, after all."

"Yes—far better. Oh, I am so sorry for you!"

"Who pities, may yet love," he said in low tones.

Corona did not make any answer, but for many minutes lay watching the dancing flames. Giovanni knew that it would be wiser to say nothing more which could recall the past, and when he spoke again it was to ask her opinion once more concerning the best course to pursue in regard to the property.

"I still think," answered Corona, "that you had better do nothing for the present. You will soon know what San Giacinto means to do. You may be sure that if he has any rights he will not forget to press them. If it comes to the worst and you are quite sure that he is the man you—that is to say, your father—can give up everything without a suit. It is useless to undertake the consequences of a misfortune which may never occur. It would be reckless to resign your inheri-tance without a struggle, when San Giacinto, if he is an honest man, would insist upon the case being tried in law."

"That is true. I will take your advice. I am so much disturbed about other things that I am inclined to go to all extremes at once. Will you dine with us this evening?"

"I think not. Give me one more day. I shall be stronger tomorrow."

"I have tired you," exclaimed Giovanni in a tone of self-reproach. Corona did not answer the remark, but held out her hand with a gentle smile.

"Good night, dear," she said.

An almost imperceptible expression of pain passed quickly over Giovanni's face as he touched her fingers with his lips. Then he left the room without speaking again.

In some respects he was glad that he had induced Corona to express herself. He had no illusions left, for he knew the worst and understood that if his wife was ever to love him again there must be a new wooing. It is not necessary to dwell upon what he felt, for in the course of the conversation he had not been able to conceal his feelings. Disappointment had come upon him very suddenly, and might have been followed by terrible consequences, had he not foreseen, as in a dream of the future, a possibility of winning back Corona's love. The position in which they stood with regard to each other was only possible because they were exceptional people and had both loved so well that they were willing to do anything rather than forego the hope of loving again. Another man would have found it hard to own himself wholly in the wrong; a woman less generous would have either pretended successfully that she still loved, or would not have acknowledged that she suffered so keenly in finding her affection dead. Perhaps, too, if there had been less frankness there might have been less difficulty in reviving the old passion, for love has strange ways of hiding himself, and sometimes shows himself in ways even more unexpected.

A profound student of human nature would have seen that a mere return to the habit of pleasant intercourse could not suffice to forge afresh such a bond as had been broken, where two such persons were concerned. Something more was necessary. It was indispensable that some new force should come into play, to soften Corona's strong nature and to show Giovanni in his true light. Unfortunately for them such a happy conclusion was scarcely to be expected. Even if the question of the Saracinesca property were decided against them, an issue which, at such a time, was far from certain, they would still be rich. Poverty might have drawn them together again, but they could not be financially ruined.

Corona would have all her own fortune, while Giovanni was more than well provided for by what his mother had left him. The blow would tell far more heavily upon Giovanni's pride than upon his worldly wealth, severe as the loss must be in respect of the latter. It is impossible to say whether Corona might not have suffered as much as Giovanni himself, had the prospect of such a catastrophe presented itself a few weeks earlier. At present it affected her very little. The very name of Saracinesca was disagreeable to her hearing, and the house she lived in had lost all its old charm for her. She would willingly have left Rome to travel for a year or two rather than continue to inhabit a place so full of painful recollections; she would gladly have seen another name upon the cards she left at her friends' houses—even the once detested name of Astrardente. When she had married Giovanni she had not been conscious that she became richer than before. When one had everything, what difference could a few millions more bring into life? It was almost a pity that they could not become poor and be obliged to bear together the struggles and privations of poverty.

CHAPTER XVII

SAN Giacinto and Flavia were married on Saturday the thirtieth of November, thereby avoiding the necessity of paying a fee for being united during Advent, much to the satisfaction of Prince Montevarchi. The wedding was a brilliant affair, and if the old prince's hospitality left something to be desired, the display of liveries, coaches and family silver was altogether worthy of so auspicious an occasion. Everybody was asked, and almost everybody went, from the Saracinesca to Anastase Gouache, from Valdarno to Arnoldo Meschini. Even Spicca was there, as melancholy as usual, but evidently interested in the proceedings. He chanced to find himself next to Gouache in the crowd.

"I did not expect to see you here," he remarked.

"I have been preserved from a variety of dangers in order to assist at the ceremony," answered the Zouave, with a laugh. "At one time I thought it more likely that I should be the person of importance at a funeral."

"So did I. However, it could not be helped." Spicca did not smile.

"You seem to regret it," observed Gouache, who knew his companion's eccentric nature.

"Only on general principles. For the rest, I am delighted to see you. Come and breakfast with me when this affair is over. We will drink to the happiness of two people who will certainly be very unhappy before long."

"Ourselves?"

"No. The bride and bridegroom. 'Ye, who enter, leave all hope behind!' How can people be so foolish as to enter into an engagement from which there is no issue? The fools are not all dead yet."

"I am one of them," replied Gouache.

"You will probably have your wish. Providence has evidently preserved you from sudden death in order to destroy you by lingering torture. Is the wedding day fixed?"

"I wish it were."

"And the bride?"

"How can I tell?"

"Do you mean to say that, as an opinion, you would rather be married than not? The only excuse for the folly of marrying is the still greater folly of loving a woman enough to marry her. Of course, a man who is capable of that, is capable of anything. Here comes the bride with her father. Think of being tied to her until a merciful death part you. Think of being son-in-law to that old man, until heaven shall be pleased to remove him. Think of calling that stout English lady, mother-in-law, until she is at last overtaken by apoplexy. Think of calling all those relations brothers and sisters, Ascanio, Onorato, Andrea, Isabella, Bianca, Faustina! It is a day's work to learn their names and titles. She wears a veil—to hide her satisfaction—a wreath of orange flowers, artificial, too, made of paper and paste and wire, symbols of innocence, of course, pliable and easily patched together. She looks down, lest the priest should see that her eyes are laughing. Her father is whispering words of comfort and encouragement into her ear. 'Mind your expression,' he is saying, no doubt—'you must not look as though you were being sacrificed, nor as though you were too glad to be married, for everybody is watching you. Do not say, I will, too loudly nor inaudibly either, and remember that you are my daughter.' Very good advice. Now she kneels down and he crosses to the other side. She bends her head very low. She is looking under her elbow to see the folds of her train. You see—she moves her heel to make the gown fall better—I told you so. A pretty figure, all in white, before the great altar with the lights, and the priest in his robes, and the organ playing, and that Hercules in a black coat for a husband. Now she looks up. The rings are there on the gold salver upon the altar. She has not seen hers, and is wondering whether it is of plain gold, or a band of diamonds, like the Princess Valdarno's. Now then—*ego conjungo vos*—the devil, my friend, it is an awful sight!"

"Cynic!" muttered Gouache, with a suppressed laugh.

"There—it is done now, and she is already thinking what it will be like to dine alone with him this evening, and several thousand evenings hereafter. Cynic, you say? There are no more cynics. They are all married, and must turn stoics if they can. Let us be off. No—there is mass. Well then, go down on your knees and pray for their souls, for they are in a bad case. Marriage is Satan's hot-house for poisonous weeds. If anything can make a devil of an innocent girl it is marriage. If anything can turn an honest man into a fiend it is matrimony. Pray for them, poor creatures, if there is any available praying power left in you, after attending to the wants of your own soul, which, considering your matrimonial intentions, I should think very improbable."

Gouache looked at his companion curiously, for Spicca's virulence astonished him. He was not at all intimate with the man and had never heard him express his views so clearly upon any subject. Unlike most people, he was not in the least afraid of the melancholy Italian.

"From the way you talk," he remarked, "one might almost imagine that you had been married yourself."

Spicca looked at him with an odd expression, in which there was surprise as well as annoyance, and instead of making any answer, crossed himself and knelt down upon the marble pavement. Gouache followed his example instinctively.

Half an hour later the crowd moved slowly out of the church, and those who had carriages waited in the huge vestibule while the long line of equipages moved up to the gates. Gouache escaped from Spicca in the hope of getting a sight of Faustina before she drove away with her mother in one of the numerous Montevarchi coaches. Sant' Ilario and Corona were standing by one of the pillars, conversing in low tones.

"Montevarchi looked as though he knew it," said Giovanni.

"What?" asked Corona, quietly.

"That his daughter is the future Princess Saracinesca."

"It remains to be seen whether he is right."

Gouache had been pushed by the crowd into one of the angles of the pilaster while the two speakers stood before one of the four pillars of which it was built up. The words astonished him so much that he forced his way out until he could see the Princess of Sant' Ilario's beautiful profile dark against the bright light of the street. She was still speaking, but he could no longer hear her voice, some acoustic peculiarity of the columns had in all probability been the means of conveying to him the fragment of conversation he had overheard. Avoiding recognition, he slipped away through an opening in the throng and just succeeded in reaching the gate as the first of the Montevarchi carriages drew up. The numerous members of the family were gathered on the edge of the crowd, and Gouache managed to speak a few words with Faustina.

The girl's delicate face lighted up when she was conscious of his presence, and she turned her eyes lovingly to his. They met often now in public, though San Giacinto did his best to keep them apart.

"Here is a secret," said Gouache in a quick whisper. "I have just heard Sant' Ilario telling his wife that your sister is the future Princess Saracinesca. What does it mean?"

Faustina looked at him in the utmost astonishment. It was clear that she knew nothing of the matter at present.

"You must have heard wrong," she answered.

"Will you come to early mass tomorrow?" he asked hurriedly, for he had no time to lose.

"I will try—if it is possible. It will be easier now that San Giacinto is to be away. He knows everything, I am sure."

"San Giacinto?" It was Gouache's turn to be astonished. But explanations were impossible in such a crowd, and Faustina was already moving away.

"Say nothing about what I have told you," Anastase whispered as she left him. She bowed her lovely head in silence and passed on.

And so the Marchese di San Giacinto took Flavia Montevarchi for his wife, and all Rome looked on and smiled, and told imaginary stories of his former life, acknowledging, nevertheless, that Flavia had done very well—the stock phrase— since there was no doubt whatever but that the gigantic bridegroom was the cousin of the Saracinesca, and rich into the bargain. Amidst all the gossip and small talk no one, however, was found who possessed enough imagination to foretell what in reality was very imminent, namely, that the Marchese might turn out to be the prince.

The last person to suspect such a revelation was San Giacinto himself. He had indeed at one time entertained some hopes of pushing forward a claim which was certainly founded upon justice if not upon good law, but since Montevarchi had kept the documents relating to the case for many days, and had then returned them without mentioning the subject to his future son-in-law, the latter had thought it wiser to let the matter rest for the present, shrewdly suspecting that such a man as Montevarchi would not readily let such an opportunity of enriching his own daughter slip through his fingers. It has been already seen that Montevarchi purposely prevented San Giacinto from seeing the papers in order that he might be in reality quite innocent of any complicity in the matter when the proceedings were instituted, a point very important for the success of the suit.

Half an hour afterwards San Giacinto was closeted with the old prince in the latter's study, which looked more than usually dismal by contrast with the brilliant assemblage in the drawing-rooms.

"Now that we are alone, my dear son," began Montevarchi, who for a wonder had not changed his coat since the ceremony, "now that you are really my son, I have an important communication to make."

San Giacinto sat down and any one might have seen from the expression of his square jaw and determined mouth that he was prepared for battle. He did not trust his father-in-law in the least, and would not have been surprised if he had made an attempt to get back the money he had paid into the lawyer's hands as Flavia's dowry. But San Giacinto had taken all precautions and knew very well that he could not be cheated. Montevarchi continued in a bland voice.

"I have kept the matter as a surprise for you," he said. "You have of course been very busy during these last weeks in making your preparations for the solemn ceremony at which we have just assisted. It was therefore impossible for you to attend to the multifarious details which it has been my care, my privilege, to sift and examine. For it is a privilege we should value highly to labour for those we love, for those with whom we share our dearest affections. I am now about to communicate to you an affair of the highest importance, which, when brought to a successful termination will exercise a tremendous influence over all your life. Let me say beforehand, however, and lest you should suspect me of any unworthy motives, that I expect no thanks, nor any share in the immense triumph in store for you. Do not be surprised if I use somewhat strong language on such an occasion. I have examined everything, preserved everything, taken the best legal advice, and consulted those without whose spiritual counsel I enter upon no weighty undertaking. My dear son, you, and none other, are the real and rightful Prince Saracinesca."

The climax to the long preamble was so unexpected that San Giacinto uttered a loud exclamation of surprise.

"Do not be amazed at what I have told you," said Montevarchi. "The documents upon which the claims of the Saracinesca rest were drawn up by a wise man. Although he had not at that time any intention of marrying, he was aware that with heaven all things are possible, and introduced a clause to the effect that if he should marry and leave heirs direct of his body, the whole deed was to be null, void and ineffectual. I do not know enough of your family history to understand why neither he nor his son nor his grandson ever made any attempt to recover their birthright, but I know enough of law to affirm that the clause is still good. It is identical"—the prince smiled pleasantly—"it is identical in the original and in the copy preserved in the Chancery archives. In my opinion you have only to present the two documents before a competent court, in order to obtain a unanimous verdict in your favour."

San Giacinto looked hard from under his overhanging brows at the old man's keen face. Then, suddenly, he stuck his heavy fist into the palm of his left hand, and rose from his chair, a gleam of savage triumph in his eyes. For some time he paced the room in silence.

"I wish Giovanni no ill, nor his father either," he said at last.

"Heaven forbid!" exclaimed Montevarchi, crossing himself. "And besides, as the property is all yours, that would be of no use."

San Giacinto stared a minute, and then his deep voice rang out in a hearty laugh. He had an intimate conviction that his devout father-in-law was quite capable, not only of wishing evil to his neighbour, but of putting his wishes into execution if his interests could be advanced thereby.

"No," he said, when his merriment had subsided, "I wish them no evil. But, after all, they must know what is contained in the papers they have in their possession, and they must know that I am the prince, and that they have kept me out of my inheritance. I will go and tell them so. Since there is no doubt about the case, I do not see why I should wait."

"Nor I," answered Montevarchi, with the air of a man who has done his part and expects others to finish what he has begun.

"It is fortunate that we have decided to go to Frascati instead of making a journey to the end of Europe. Not but that, as I have never seen Paris, I would have liked the trip well enough."

"You will find Paris pleasanter when you are Prince Saracinesca."

"That is true," replied San Giacinto, thoughtfully. There was the deep light of anticipated triumph in his eyes. "Will you see that the proper preliminary steps are taken?" he asked presently.

"I will engage lawyers for you. But you will have to do the rest yourself. The lawyers might go out and talk it over with you in Frascati. After all, you are a young man of good sense, and will not have any sentiment about being alone with your wife."

"For the matter of that, I anticipate much pleasure in the society of my wife, but when there is so much meat boiling, somebody must watch the pot, as we used to say in Naples. I am a practical man, you know."

"Ah, that is a great quality, one of the very greatest! If I had spent my life in a perpetual honeymoon with the princess, Casa Montevarchi would not be what it is, my son. I have always given my best attention to the affairs of my household, and I expect that you will continue the tradition."

"Never fear! If, by continuing the tradition, you mean that I should get what is mine, I will not disappoint you. Can you tell me when the case can be tried, and in what court it will be heard?"

"With my influence," replied Montevarchi, "the case may be put through at once. A month will suffice for the preliminaries, a day for the hearing. Everything is settled at once by the exhibition of the documents which provide for you in the most explicit terms. You can come in from the country and see them for yourself if you please. But I consider that quite unnecessary. The lawyers will settle everything."

"Pardon my curiosity, but I would like to know why you thought it best not to tell me anything of the matter until now."

"My dear son, you were so busy with the preparations for your marriage, and the questions involved seemed at first so doubtful that I thought it best not to trouble you with them. Then, when I knew the whole truth the time was so near that I preferred to give you the information as a sort of wedding present."

"A magnificent one indeed, for which I cannot find words to express my gratitude."

"No, no! Do not talk of gratitude. I feel that I am fulfilling a sacred duty in restoring to the fatherless his birthright. It is an act of divine justice for the execution of which I have been chosen as the humble instrument. Do your duty by my dear daughter, and render your gratitude to heaven—*quoe sunt Coesaris, Coesari, et quoe sunt Dei, Deo!* Would that we could all live by that rule!"

"To Saracinesca what is his, and to San Giacinto that which belongs to him—that is what you mean?"

"Yes, my good son. I am glad to see that you understand Latin. It does you credit that amidst the misfortunes of your early life you should have so improved yourself as to possess the education necessary to the high rank you are about to assume. I tell you frankly that, in spite of your personal qualities, in spite of the great name and possessions which will soon be yours, if I had not distinguished in you that refinement and instruction without which no gentleman is worthy of the name, I would not have bestowed upon you the hand of that sweet creature whom I have cherished as a flower in the house of my old age."

San Giacinto had made a study of old Montevarchi during a month past, and was not in the least deceived by his rounded periods and well expressed moral sentiments. But he smiled and bowed, enjoying the idea of attributing such flattery to himself in proportion as he felt that he was unworthy of it. He had indeed done his best to acquire a certain amount of instruction, as his father-in-law called it, and his tastes were certainly not so coarse as might have been expected, but he was too strong a man to be easily deceived concerning his own powers, and he knew well enough that he owed his success to his fortune. He saw, too, that Montevarchi, in giving him Flavia, had foreseen the possibility of his claiming the rights of his cousins, and if he had not been thoroughly satisfied with his choice he would have now felt that he had been deceived. He had no regrets, however, for he felt that even had he already enjoyed the titles and wealth he was so soon to claim, he would nevertheless have chosen Flavia for his wife. Of all the young girls he had seen in Rome she was the only one who really attracted him; a fact due, perhaps, to her being more natural than the rest, or at least more like what he thought a woman should naturally be. His rough nature would not have harmonised with Faustina's character; still less could he have understood and appreciated a woman like Corona, who was indeed almost beyond the comprehension of Giovanni, her own husband. San Giacinto was almost a savage, compared with the young men of the class to which he now belonged, and there was something wild and half-tamed in Flavia Montevarchi which had fascinated him from the first, and held him by that side of his temperament by which alone savages are governed.

Had the bringing of the suit been somewhat hastened it is not impossible that San Giacinto and his wife might have driven up to the ancient towers of Saracinesca on that Saturday afternoon, as Giovanni and Corona had done on their wedding day two years and a half earlier. As it was, they were to go out to Frascati to spend a week in Montevarchi's villa, as the prince and princess and all their married children had done before them.

"Eh! What a satisfaction!" exclaimed Flavia, with a sigh of relief as the carriage rolled out of the deep archway under the palace. Then she laughed a little and looked up at her husband out of the corners of her bright black eyes, after which she produced a very pretty silver scent-bottle which her mother had put into her hand as a parting gift. She looked at it, turned it round, opened it and at last smelled the contents.

"Ugh!" she cried, shutting it up quickly and making a wry face. "It is full of salts—horrible! I thought it was something good to smell! Did she think I was going to faint on the way?"

"You do not look like fainting," remarked San Giacinto, who looked gigantic in a wide fur pelisse. He put out his great hand, which closed with a sort of rough tenderness over hers, completely hiding it as well as the smelling-bottle she held. "So it is a satisfaction, is it?" he asked, with a gleam of pleasure in his deep-set eyes.

"If you had been educated under the supervision of the eccellentissima casa Montevarchi, you would understand what a blessed institution marriage is! You—what shall I call you—your name is Giovanni, is it not?"

"Yes—Giovanni. Do you like the name?"

"No—it reminds me of the head of John the Baptist. I will call you—let me see—Nino. Yes—that sounds so small, and you are so immensely big. You are Nino, in future. I am glad you are big. I do not like little men." She nestled close to the giant, with a laugh that pleased him.

San Giacinto suddenly found that he was very much more in love than he had supposed. His life had been very full of contrasts, but this was the greatest which had yet presented itself. He remembered a bright summer's morning a few years earlier, when he had walked back from the church in Aquila with Felice Baldi by his side. Poor Felice! She had worn a very pretty black silk frock with a fine gold chain around her neck, and a veil upon her head, for she was not of the class "that wear hats," as they say in Rome. But she had forced her stout hands into gloves, and Giovanni the innkeeper had been somewhat proud of her ladylike appearance. Her face was very red and there were tears of pleasure and timidity in her eyes, which he remembered very well. It was strange that she, too, should have been proud of her husband's size and strength. Perhaps all women were very much alike. How well he remembered the wedding collation, the little yellow cakes with a drop of hard pink sugar in the middle of each, the bottles of sweet cordial of various flavours, cinnamon, clove, aniseed and the like, the bright red japanned tray, and the cheaply gaudy plates whereon were painted all manner of impossible flowers.

Felice was dead, buried in the campo santo of Aquila, with its whitewashed walls of enclosure and its appalling monuments and mortuary emblems. Poor Felice! She had been a good wife, and he had been a good husband to her. She was such a simple creature that he could almost fancy her spirit shedding tears of satisfied pride at seeing her Giovanni married to a princess, rich and about to be metamorphosed into a prince himself. She had known that he was a Marchese of a great family, and had often begged him to let her be called the Signora Marchesa. But he had always told her that for people in their position it was absurd. They were not poor for their station; indeed, they were among the wealthiest of their class in Aquila. He had promised to assert his title when they should be rich enough, but poor Felice had died too soon. Then had come that great day when Giovanni had won in the lottery—Giovanni who had never played before and had all his life called it a waste of money and a public robbery. But, playing once, he had played high, and all his numbers had appeared on the following Saturday. Two hundred thousand francs in a day! Such luck only falls to the lot of men who are born under destiny. Giovanni had long known what he should do if he only possessed the capital. The winnings were paid in cash, and in a fortnight he had taken up a government contract in the province of Aquila. Then came another and another. Everything turned to gold in his hands, and in two years he was a rich man.

Alone in the world, with his two little boys, and possessed of considerable wealth, the longing had come over him to take the position to which he had a legitimate right, a position which, he supposed, would not interfere with his increasing his fortune if he wished to do so. He had left the children under the supervision of old Don Paolo, the curate, and had come to Rome, where he had lodged in an obscure hotel until he had fitted himself to appear before his cousins as a gentleman. His grave temper, indomitable energy, and natural astuteness had done the rest, and fortune had crowned all his efforts. The old blood of the Saracinesca had grown somewhat coarse by the admixture of a stream very far from blue; but if it had lost in some respects it had gained in others, and the type was not wholly low. The broad-shouldered, dark-complexioned giant was not altogether unworthy of the ancient name, and he knew it as his wife nestled to his side. He loved the wild element in her, but most of all he loved the thoroughbred stamp of her face, the delicacy of her small hands, the aristocratic ring of her laughter, for these all told him that, after three generations of obscurity he had risen again to the level whence his fathers had fallen.

The change in his life became very clear to him, as all these things passed quickly through his mind; and with the consciousness of vivid contrast came the certainty that he loved Flavia far better than he had believed possible.

"And what shall I call you?" he asked, rather bluntly. He did not quite know whether it would be wise to use any term of endearment or not. Indeed, this was the weak point in his experience, but he supplemented the deficiency by a rough tenderness which was far from disagreeable to Flavia.

"Anything you like, dear," she answered. San Giacinto felt the blood rush to his head with pleasure as he heard the epithet.

"Anything?" he asked, with a very unwonted tremour in his voice.

"Anything—provided you will love me," she replied. He thought he had never seen such wicked, fascinating eyes. He drew her face to his and looked into them a moment, his own blazing suddenly with a passion wholly new to him.

"I will not call you anything—instead of calling you, I will kiss you—so—is it not better than any name?"

A deep blush spread over Flavia's face and then subsided suddenly, leaving her very pale. For a long time neither spoke again.

"Did your father tell you the news before we left?" asked San Giacinto at last, when they were rolling over the Campagna along the Via Latina.

"No—what?"

"It is somewhat remarkable news. If you are afraid of fainting," he added, with rough humour, "hold your bottle of salts ready."

Flavia looked up uneasily, wondering whether there were anything wrong about San Giacinto. She knew very well that her father had been glad to get rid of her.

"I am not San Giacinto after all," he said quietly. Flavia started and drew back.

"Who are you then?" she asked quickly.

"I am Prince Saracinesca, and you are the princess." He spoke very calmly, and watched her face to see the effect of the news.

"I wish you were!" she exclaimed nervously. She wondered whether he was going mad.

"There seems to be no doubt about it," he answered, "your father informed me of the fact as a wedding present. He has examined all the papers and will send the lawyers out to Frascati to prepare the case with me."

He told her the whole story in detail. As he proceeded, a singular expression came into Flavia's face, and when he had finished she broke out into voluble expressions of joy.

"I always knew that I was born to be a princess—I mean a real one! How could I be anything else? Oh! I am so happy, and you are such a darling to be a prince! And to think that if papa had not discovered the papers, those horrid Sant' Ilario people would have had everything. Princess Saracinesca! Eh, but how it sounds! Almost as good as Orsini, and much nicer with you, you great big, splendid lion! Why did they not call you Leone? It is too good to be true! And I always hated Corona, ever since I was a little girl and she was the Astrardente, because she used to say I did not behave well and that Faustina was much prettier—I heard her say so when I was behind the curtains. Why did you not find it out ever so long ago? Think what a wedding we should have had, just like Sant' Ilario's! But it was very fine after all, and of course there is nothing to complain of. Evviva! Evviva! Do give me one of those cigarettes—I never smoked in my life, and I am so happy that I know it will not hurt me!"

San Giacinto had his case in his hand, and laughed as he presented it to her. Quiet as he was in his manner he was far the happier of the two, as he was far more capable of profound feeling than the wild girl who was now his wife. He was glad, too, to see that she was so thoroughly delighted, for he knew well enough that even after he had gained the suit he would need the support of an ambitious woman to strengthen his position. He did not believe that the Saracinesca would submit tamely to such a tremendous shock of fortune, and he foresaw that their resentment would probably be shared by a great number of their friends.

Flavia looked prettier than ever as she put the bit of rolled paper between her red lips and puffed away with an energy altogether unnecessary. He would not have believed that, being already so brilliant and good to see, a piece of unexpected good news could have lent her expression so much more brightness. She was positively radiant, as she looked from his eyes at her little cigarette, and then, looking back to him again, laughed and snapped her small gloved fingers.

"Do you know," she said presently, with a glance that completed the conquest of San Giacinto's heart, "I thought I should be dreadfully shy with you—at first—and I am not in the least! I confess, at the very moment when you were putting the ring on my finger I was wondering what we should talk about during the drive."

"You did not think we should have such an agreeable subject of conversation, did you?"

"No—and it is such a pretty ring! I always wanted a band of diamonds—plain gold is so common. Did you think of it yourself or did some one else suggest the idea?"

"Castellani said it was old-fashioned," answered San Giacinto, "but I preferred it."

"Would you have liked one, too?"

"No. It would be ridiculous for a man."

"You have very good taste," remarked Flavia, eyeing him critically. "Where did you get it? You used to keep a hotel in Aquila, did you not?"

San Giacinto had long been prepared for the question and did not wince nor show the slightest embarrassment. He smiled calmly as he answered her.

"You would hardly have called it a hotel, it was a country inn. I daresay I shall manage Saracinesca all the better for having kept a hostelry."

"Of course. Oh, I have such a delightful idea! Let us go to Aquila and keep the hotel together. It would be such fun! You could say you had married a little shop-keeper's daughter in Rome, you know. Just for a month, Nino—do let us do it! It would be such a change after society, and then we would go back for the Carnival. Oh, do!"

"But you forget the lawsuit—"

"That is true. Besides, it will be just as much of a change to be Princess

Saracinesca. But we can do it another time. I would like so much to go about in an apron with a red cotton handkerchief on my head and see all the queer people! When are the lawyers coming?"

"During the week, I suppose."

"There will be a fight," said Flavia, her face growing more grave. "What will Sant' Ilario and his father say and do? I cannot believe that it will all go so smoothly as you think. They do not look like people who would give up easily what they have had so long. I suppose they will be quite ruined."

"I do not know. Corona is rich in her own right, and Sant' Ilario has his mother's fortune. Of course, they will be poor compared with their present wealth. I am sorry for them—"

"Sorry?" Flavia looked at her husband in some astonishment. "It is their own fault. Why should you be sorry?"

"It is not exactly their fault. I could hardly have expected them to come to me and inform me that a mistake had been made in the last century, and that all they possessed was mine."

"All they possessed!" echoed Flavia, thoughtfully. "What a wonderful idea it is!"

"Very wonderful," assented San Giacinto, who was thinking once more of his former poverty.

The carriage rolled on and both were silent for some time, absorbed in dreaming of the greatness which was before them in the near future, San Giacinto enumerating in his mind the titles and estates which were soon to be his, while Flavia imagined herself in Corona's place in Rome, grown suddenly to be a central figure in society, leading and organising the brilliant amusements of her world, and above all, rejoicing in that lavish use of abundant money which had always seemed to her the most desirable of all enjoyments.

CHAPTER XVIII

FAUSTINA Montevarchi was delighted when her sister was at last married and out of the house. The two had always been very good friends, but Faustina felt that she had an enemy in San Giacinto and was relieved when he was gone. She had no especial reason for her suspicions, since he treated her with the same quiet and amicable politeness which he showed to the rest of the household; but her perceptions were extraordinarily true and keen, and she had noticed that he watched her whenever Gouache was in the room, in a way that made her very uncomfortable. Moreover, he had succeeded of late in making Flavia accompany her to early mass on Sunday mornings on pretence of his wishing to see Flavia without the inevitable supervision of the old princess. The plan was ingenious; for Faustina, instead of meeting Gouache, was thus obliged to play chaperon while her sister and San Giacinto talked to their hearts' content. He was a discreet man, however, and Flavia was ignorant of the fact that Faustina and Anastase had sometimes met in the same way, and would have met frequently had they not been prevented. The young girl was clever enough to see why San Giacinto acted as he did; she understood that he was an ambitious man, and that, as he was about to ally himself with her family, he would naturally disapprove of her attachment to Gouache. Now that he was gone, she wondered whether he had devised any steps which would take effect after his departure.

Faustina was quite as much in love as Gouache himself, and spent much time in calculating the chances of a favourable issue from the situation in which she found herself. Life without Anastase was impossible, but the probabilities of her becoming his wife in the ordinary course of events were very few, as far as she was able to judge, and she had moments of extreme depression, during which she despaired of everything. The love of a very young girl may in itself be both strong and enduring, but it generally has the effect of making her prone to extremes of hope and fear, uncertain of herself, vacillating in her ideas, and unsteady in the pursuit of the smaller ends of life. Throw two equal weights into the scales of a perfectly adjusted balance, the arm will swing and move erratically many times before it returns to its normal position, although there is a potential equilibrium in the machine which will shortly assert itself in absolute tranquillity.

Love in a very young person is rarely interesting, unless it is attended by heroic or tragic circumstances. Human life is very like the game of chess, of which the openings are so limited in number that a practised player knows them all by heart, whereas the subsequent moves are susceptible of infinite variation. Almost all young people pass through the early stages of existence by some known gambit, which, has always a definite influence upon their later lives, but never determines the latter entirely. The game is played between humanity on the one side and the unforeseen on the other; but that which can really not be foretold in some measure rarely presents itself until the first effects of love have been felt, a period which, to continue the simile, may be compared in chess to the operation of castling. Then comes the first crisis, and the merest tyro knows how much may depend upon whether he castles on the king's side or on the queen's.

Now the nature of Faustina's first love was such as to make it probable that it would end in some uncommon way. There was something fatal in the suddenness with which her affection had grown and had upset the balance of her judgment. It is safe to say that not one young girl in a million would have behaved as she had done on the night of the insurrection in Rome; not one in a hundred thousand would, in her position, have fallen in love with Gouache.

The position of the professional artist and of the professional man of letters in modern European society is ill defined. As a man who has been brought up in a palace would undoubtedly betray his breeding sooner or later if transported to live amongst a gang of thieves, so a man who has grown to years of discretion in the atmosphere of studios or in the queer company from which most literary men have sprung, will inevitably, at one time or another, offend the susceptibilities of that portion of humanity which calls itself society. It is impossible that it should be otherwise. Among a set of people whose profession it is to do always, and in all things, precisely what their neighbours do, the man who makes his living by doing what other people cannot do, must always be a marked figure. Look at modern society. It cannot toil nor spin; it can hardly put together ten words in a grammatical sequence. But it can clothe itself. The man of letters can both toil and write good English, but his taste in tailoring frequently leaves much to be desired. If he would put himself in the hands of Poole, and hold his tongue, he might almost pass for a member of society. But he must needs talk, and his speech betrayeth him for a Galilean. There are wits in society, both many and keen, who can say something original, cutting and neatly turned, upon almost any subject, with an easy superiority which makes the hair of the learned man stand erect upon his head. The chief characteristic of him who lives by his brains is that he is not only able to talk consecutively upon some subject, but that he actually does so, which, in society, is accounted a monstrous crime against manners. Let him write what he wants to say, and print it; society will either not understand him at all, or will read his works with a dictionary in the secrecy of its own chamber. But if he will hold his tongue in public, society will give him a cup of tea and treat him almost like a human being for the sake of being said to patronise letters. Any one who likes society's tea may drink his fill of it in consideration of wearing a good coat and keeping his wits to himself, but he will not succeed in marrying any of society's sisters, cousins or aunts without a severe struggle.

Anastase Gouache did not quite understand this. He sometimes found himself amidst a group of people who were freely discussing some person unknown to him. On such occasions he held his peace, innocently supposing that his ignorance was without any importance whatsoever, among a set of men and women with whom not to know every detail concerning every one else is to be little better than an outcast.

"Now do tell me all about the Snooks and Montmorency divorce," says Lady Smyth-Tompkins with a sweetly engaging smile, as she holds out her hand.

"I did not know there was such a case—I don't know the people," you answer.

"Oh! I thought, of course, you knew all about it," Lady Smyth-Tompkins replies, and her features turn to stone as she realises that you do not know everybody, and leaves you to your own reflections.

O Thackeray, snobissme maxime! How well you knew them!

There are no snobs among the Latin races, but there is a worse animal, the sycophant, descended directly from the dinner-tables of ancient Rome. In old-fashioned houses there are often several of them, headed invariably by the "giornale ambulante," the walking newspaper, whose business it is to pick up items of news during the day in order to detail them to the family in the evening. There is a certain old princess who sits every evening with her needlework at the head of a long table in the dismal drawing-room of a gigantic palace. On each side of the board are seated the old parasites, the family doctor, the family chaplain, the family lawyer, the family librarian, the peripatetic news-sheet and the rest.

"I have been out today," says her excellency.

"Oh! Ah! Dear me! In this weather! Hear what the princess says! The princess has been out!" The chorus comes up the table, all the answers reaching her ears at once.

"And I saw, as I drove by, the new monument! What a ridiculous thing it is."

"Ho! ho! ho! Hah! hah! hah! Dear me! What a monument! What fine taste the princess has! Hear what the princess thinks of the monument!"

"If you will believe it, the bronze horse has a crooked leg." "He! he! he! Hi! hi! hi! Dear me! A crooked leg! How the princess understands horses! The princess saw that he had a crooked leg!"

And so on, for a couple of hours, in the cold, dimly-lighted room until her excellency has had enough of it and rises to go to bed, when the parasites all scuttle away and quarrel with each other in the street as they walk home. Night after night, to decades of years, the old lady recounts the little journal of her day to the admiring listeners, whose chorus of approval is performed daily with the same unvarying regularity. The times are changing now; the prince is not so easily amused, and the sycophant has accordingly acquired the art of amusing, but there still survive some wonderful monuments of the old school.

Anastase Gouache was a man of great talent and of rising fame, but like other men of his stamp he preferred to believe that he was received on a friendly footing for his own sake rather than on account of his reputation. In his own eyes, he was, as a man, as good as those with whom he associated, and had as much right to make love to Faustina Montevarchi as the young Frangipani, for whom her father destined her. Faustina, on her part, was too young to appreciate the real strength of the prejudices by which she was surrounded. She could not understand that, although the man she loved was a gentleman, young, good-looking, successful, and not without prospects of acquiring a fortune, he was yet wholly ineligible as a husband. Had she seen this ever so clearly it might have made but little difference in her feelings; but she did not see it, and the disparaging remarks about Anastase, which she occasionally heard in her own family, seemed to her utterly unjust as well as quite unfounded. The result was that the two young people were preparing for themselves one of those terrible disappointments of which the consequences are sometimes felt during a score of years. Both, however, were too much in love to bear suspense very long without doing something to precipitate the course of events, and whenever they had the chance they talked the matter over and built wonderful castles in the air.

About a fortnight after the marriage of San Giacinto they were seated together in a room full of people, late in the afternoon. They had been talking for some time upon indifferent subjects. When two persons meet who are very much in love with each other, and waste their time in discussing topics of little importance, it may be safely predicted that something unusual is about to occur.

"I cannot endure this suspense any longer," said Gouache at last.

"Nor I," answered Faustina.

"It is of no use to wait any more. Either your father will consent or he will not. I will ask him and know the worst."

"And if it is the worst—what then?" The young girl turned her eyes towards Anastase with a frightened look.

"Then we must manage without his consent."

"How is that possible?"

"It must be possible," replied Gouache. "If you love me it shall be possible. It is only a question of a little courage and good-will. But, after all, your father may consent. Why should he not?"

"Because—" she hesitated a little.

"Because I am not a Roman prince, you mean." Anastase glanced quickly at her.

"No. He wants me to marry Frangipani."

"Why did you never tell me that?"

"I did not know it when we last met. My mother told me of it last night."

"Is the match settled?" asked Gouache. He was very pale.

"I think it has been spoken of," answered Faustina in a low voice. She shivered a little and pressed her hands together. There was a short silence, during which Anastase did not take his eyes from her, while she looked down, avoiding his look.

"Then there is no time to be lost," said Gouache at last. "I will go to your father tomorrow morning."

"Oh—don't, don't!" cried Faustina, suddenly, with an expression of intense anxiety.

"Why not?" The artist seemed very much surprised.

"You do not know him! You do not know what he will say to you! You will be angry and lose your temper—he will be cruel and will insult you, and you will resent it—then I shall never see you again. You do not know—"

"This is something new," said Gouache. "How can you be sure that he will receive me so badly? Have your people talked about me? After all, I am an honest man, and though I live by my profession I am not poor. It is true, I am not such a match for you as Frangipani. Tell me, do they abuse me at your house?"

"No—what can they say, except that you are an artist? That is not abuse, nor calumny."

"It depends upon how it is said. I suppose it is San Giacinto who says it." Gouache's face darkened.

"San Giacinto has guessed the truth," answered Faustina, shaking her head. "He knows that we love each other, and just now he is very powerful with my father. It will be worse if he wins the suit and is Prince Saracinesca."

"Then that is another reason for acting at once. Faustina—you followed me once—will you not go with me, away, out of this cursed city? I will ask for you first. I will behave honourably. But if he will not consent, what is there left for us to do? Can we live apart? Can you marry Frangipani? Have not many people done before what we think of doing? Is it wrong? Heaven knows, I make no pretence to sanctity. But I would not have you do anything—what shall I say? Anything against your conscience." There was a shade of bitterness in the laugh that accompanied the last words.

"You do not know what things he will say," repeated Faustina, in despairing tones.

"This is absurd," said Gouache. "I can bear anything he can say well enough. He is an old man and I am a young one, and have no intention of taking offence. He may say what he pleases, call me a villain, a brigand—that is your favourite Italian expression—a thief, a liar, anything he pleases. I will not be angry. There shall be no violence. But I cannot endure this state of things any longer. I must try my luck."

"Wait a little longer," answered Faustina, in an imploring tone. "Wait until the suit is decided."

"In order to let San Giacinto get even more influence than he has now? It would be a mistake—you almost said so yourself a moment ago. Besides, the suit may for years."

"It will not last a fortnight."

"Poor Sant' Ilario!" exclaimed Gouache. "Does everybody know about it?"

"I suppose so. But nobody speaks of it. We all feel dreadfully about it, except my father and San Giacinto and Flavia."

"If he is in a good humour this is the very time to go to him."

"Please, please do not insist!" Faustina was evidently very much in earnest. With the instinct of a very young woman, she clung to the half-happiness of the present which was so much greater than anything she had known before in her life. But Gouache would not be satisfied.

"I must know the worst," he said again, as they parted.

"But this is so much, better than the worst," answered Faustina, sadly.

"Who risks nothing, wins nothing," retorted the young man with a bright smile.

In spite of his hopefulness, however, he had received a severe shock on hearing the news of the intended match with young Frangipani. He had certainly never expected to find himself the rival of such a suitor, and his sense of possibility, if man may be said to possess such a faculty, was staggered by the idea. He suddenly awakened to a true understanding of his position in Roman society, and when he contemplated his discovery in all its bearings, his nerve almost forsook him. When he remembered his childhood, his youth, and the circumstances in which he had lived up to a recent time, he found it hard to realise that he was trying to marry such a girl, in spite of her family and in opposition to such a man as was now brought forward as a match for her. It was not in his nature, however, to be discouraged in the face of difficulties. He was like a brave man who has received a stunning blow, but who continues to fight until he has gradually regained his position. Gouache could no more have relinquished Faustina than he could have abandoned a half-finished picture in which he believed, any more than he had given up the attempt to break away the stones at the Vigna Santucci after he had received the bullet in his shoulder. He had acquired his position in life by indomitable perseverance and hopefulness, and those qualities would not now fail him, in one of the most critical situations through which he had ever passed. In spite of Faustina's warning and, to some extent, in spite of his own better judgment, he determined to face the old prince at once and to ask him boldly for his daughter.

He had spoken confidently to Faustina of being married against the will of her father, but when he thought over this alternative he recollected a fact he had almost completely forgotten in considering his matrimonial projects. He was a soldier and had enlisted in the Zouaves for a term of years. It was true that by using the influence he possessed he might hope to be released from his engagement, but such a course was most repugnant to him. Before Mentana it would have been wholly impossible, for it would have seemed cowardly. Now that he had distinguished himself and had been wounded in the cause, the thing might be done without dishonour, but it would involve a species of self-abasement to which he was not prepared to submit. On the other hand, to wait until his term of service should have expired was to risk losing Faustina altogether. He knew that she loved him, but he was experienced enough to know that a young girl is not always able to bear the pressure exercised upon her when marriage is concerned. In Rome, and especially at that time, it was in the power of parents to use the most despotic means for subduing the will of their children. There was even a law by which a disobedient son or daughter could be imprisoned for a considerable length of time, provided that the father could prove that his child had rebelled against his just will. Though Gouache was not aware of this, the fact that a similar institution existed in his own country made him suspect that it was to be found in Rome also. Supposing that Montevarchi refused to accept him for a son-in-law, and that Faustina, on the other hand, refused to marry young Frangipani, it was only too probable that she might be locked up—in a luxuriously furnished cell of course—to reflect upon the error of her ways. It was by no means certain that in the face of such humiliation and suffering Faustina would continue her resistance; indeed, she could hardly be blamed if she yielded in the end. Gouache believed in the sincerity of her love because the case was his own; had he heard of it in the life of another man he would have laughed at the idea that a girl of eighteen could be capable of a serious passion.

It is not necessary, however, to enter into an analysis of the motives and feelings of either Faustina or Anastase. Their connection with the history of the Saracinesca arose from what they did, and not from the thoughts which prompted their actions. It is sufficient to say that Gouache conceived the mad idea of asking Montevarchi's consent to his marriage and to explain the immediate consequences of the step he took.

Matters were rapidly approaching a climax. San Giacinto had seen the lawyers at Frascati, and he had brought his wife back to Rome very soon in order to be on the spot while the case was being prepared. The men of the law declared that the matter was a very simple one and that no court could withhold its decision a single day after seeing the documents which constituted the claim. The only point about which any argument could arise related to the identity of San Giacinto himself, and no difficulty was found in establishing substantial proof that he was Giovanni Saracinesca and not an impostor. His father and grandfather had jealously kept all the records of themselves which were necessary, from the marriage certificate of the original Don Leone, who had signed the deed, to the register of San Giacinto's own birth. Copies were obtained, properly drawn up and certified, of the parish books and of the few government documents which were officially preserved in the kingdom of Naples before 1860, and the lawyers declared themselves ready to open the case. Up to this time the strictest secrecy was preserved, at the request of San Giacinto himself. He said that in such an important matter he wished nothing to transpire until he was ready to act; more especially as the Saracinesca themselves could not be ignorant of the true state of the case and had no right to receive notice of the action beforehand. As Corona had foreseen, San Giacinto intended to obtain the decision by means of a perfectly legal trial, and was honestly ready to court enquiry into the rights he was about to assert. When the moment came and all was ready, he went to the Palazzo Saracinesca and asked for the prince, who received him in the same room in which the two had met when the ex-innkeeper had made his appearance in Rome nearly three months earlier. As San Giacinto entered he felt that he had not wasted his time during that short interval.

"I have come to talk with you upon a business which must be unpleasant to you," he began. "Unfortunately it cannot be avoided. I beg you to believe that it is my wish to act loyally and fairly."

"I hope so," said Saracinesca, bending his bushy gray eyebrows and fixing his keen old eyes upon his visitor.

"You need not doubt it," replied San Giacinto rather proudly. "You are doubtless acquainted with the nature of the deed by which our great-grandfathers agreed to transfer the titles and property to the younger of the two. When we first spoke of the matter I was not aware of the existence of a saving clause. I cannot suppose you ignorant of it. That clause provided that if Leone Saracinesca married and had a lawful heir, the deed should be null and void. He did marry, as you know. I am his direct descendant, and have children of my own by my first marriage. I cannot therefore allow the clause in question to remain in abeyance any longer. With all due respect to you, I am obliged to tell you quite frankly that, in law, I am Prince Saracinesca."

Having thus stated his position as plainly as possible, San Giacinto folded his great hands upon his knee and leaned against the back of his chair. Saracinesca looked as though he were about to make some hasty answer, but he controlled his intention and rose to his feet. After walking twice up and down the room, he came and stood in front of his cousin.

"Let us be plain in what we say," he began. "I give you my word that, until

Montevarchi sent back those papers the other day, I did not know what they contained. I had not read them for thirty years, and at that time the clause escaped me. I do not remember to have noticed it. This may have been due to the fact that I had never heard that Leone had any living descendants, and should therefore have attached no importance to the words if I had seen them."

"I believe you," said San Giacinto, calmly. The old man's eyes flashed.

"I always take it for granted that I am believed," he answered. "Will you give me your word that you are what you assert yourself to be, Giovanni Saracinesca, the great-grandson and lawful heir of Leone?"

"Certainly. I pledge my honour that I am; and I, too, expect to be believed by you."

There was something in the tone of the answer that struck a sympathetic chord in Saracinesca's nature. San Giacinto had risen to his feet, and there was something in the huge, lean strength of him, in the bold look of his eyes, in the ring of his deep voice, that inspired respect. Rough he was, and not over refined or carefully trained in the ways of the world, cruel perhaps, and overbearing too; but he was every inch a Saracinesca, and the old man felt it.

"I believe you," answered the prince. "You may take possession when you please. I am Don Leone, and you are the head of the house."

He made a gesture full of dignity, as though resigning then and there his name and the house in which he lived, to him who was lawfully entitled to both. The action was magnificent and worthy of the man. There was a superb disregard of consequences in his readiness to give up everything rather than keep for a moment what was not his, which affected San Giacinto strangely. In justice to the latter it must be remembered that he had not the faintest idea that he was the instrument of a gigantic fraud from which he was to derive the chief advantage. He instinctively bowed in acknowledgment of his cousin's generous conduct.

"I shall not take advantage of your magnanimity," he said, "until the law has sanctioned my doing so."

"As you please," answered the other. "I have nothing to conceal from the law, but I am prejudiced against lawyers. Do as you think best. A family council can settle the matter as well as the courts."

"Your confidence in me is generous and noble. I prefer, however, that the tribunal should examine the matter."

"As you please," repeated Saracinesca. There was no reason for prolonging an interview which could not be agreeable to either party. The old man remained standing. "No opposition will be made to the suit," he said. "You will simply produce your papers in proper form, and I will declare myself satisfied." He held out his hand.

"I trust you will bear me no ill-will," said San Giacinto rather awkwardly.

"For taking what is yours and not mine? Not in the least. Good evening."

San Giacinto left the room. When he was gone, Saracinesca stood still for a moment, and then sank into a chair. His strong nature had sustained him through the meeting and would sustain him to the end, but he was terribly shaken, and felt a strange sensation of numbness in the back of his head, which was quite new to him. For some minutes he sat still as though dazed and only half conscious. Then he rose again, shook himself as though to get rid of a bad dream and rang the bell. He sent for Giovanni, who appeared immediately.

"San Giacinto has been here," he said quickly. "He is the man. You had better tell your wife, as she will want to collect her things before we leave the house."

Giovanni was staggered by his father's impetuosity. He had realised that the danger existed, but it had always seemed indefinitely far removed.

"I suppose there will be some legal proceedings before everything is settled," he said with more calmness than he felt.

"What is that to us? We must go, sooner or later."

"And if the courts do not decide in his favour, what then?"

"There is no doubt about it," answered the prince, pacing the room as his excitement returned. "You and I are nobody. We had better go and live in an inn. That man is honest. I hate him, but he is honest. Why do you stand there staring at me? Were you not the first to say that if we are impostors we should give up everything of our own free-will? And now you seem to think that I will fight the suit! That is your logic! That is all the consistency you have acquired in your travels! Go and tell your wife that you are nobody, that I am nobody! Go and tell her to give you a title, a name for men to call you by! Go into the market and see whether you can find a name for your father! Go and hire a house for us to live in, when that Neapolitan devil has brought Flavia Montevarchi to live in the palace where your mother died, where you were born—poor Giovanni! Not that I pity you any more than I pity myself. Why should I? You are young and have done this house the honour to spend most of your life out of it. But after all—poor Giovanni!"

Saracinesca seized his son's hand and looked into his eyes. The young man's face was perfectly calm, almost serene in its expression of indifference to misfortune. His whole soul was preoccupied by greater and nobler emotions than any which could be caused by worldly loss. He had been with Corona again, had talked with her and had seen that look in her face which he had learned to dread more than he had ever dreaded anything in his life. What was life itself without that which her eyes refused?

CHAPTER XIX

PRINCE Montevarchi was very much surprised when he was told that Anastase Gouache wished to see him, and as he was very much occupied with the details of the suit his first impulse was to decline the visit. Although he had no idea that matters had already gone so far between the Zouave and Faustina, he was not, however, so blind as the young girl had supposed him to be. He was naturally observant, like most men who devote their lives to the pursuit of their own interests, and it had not escaped him that Faustina and Gouache were very often to be seen talking together in the world. Had he possessed a sense of humour he might possibly have thought that it would be inexpressibly comical if Gouache should take it into his head to fall in love with the girl; but the Italians are not a humorous people, and the idea did not suggest itself to the old gentleman. He consented to receive Gouache because he thought the opportunity would be a good one for reading the young man a lecture upon the humility of his station, and upon the arrogance he displayed in devoting himself thus openly to the daughter of Casa Montevarchi.

"Good day, Monsieur Gouache," he said solemnly, as Anastase entered. "Pray be seated. To what do I owe the honour of your visit?"

Anastase had put on a perfectly new uniform for the interview, and his movements were more than usually alert and his manners a shade more elaborate and formal than on ordinary occasions. He felt and behaved as young men of good birth do who are serving their year in the army, and who, having put on their smartest tunic, hope that in a half light they may be taken for officers.

"Will you allow me to explain my position in the first place?" he asked, seating himself and twisting his cap slowly in his hands.

"Your position? By all means, if you desire to do so. It is an excellent rule in all discourses to put the definition before the argument. Nevertheless, if you would inform me of the nature of the affair, it might help me to understand you better."

"It is very delicate—but I will try to be plain. What I am, I think you know already. I am a painter and I have been successful. For the present, I am a Zouave, but my military service does not greatly interfere with my profession. We have a good deal of time upon our hands. My pictures bring me a larger income than I can spend."

"I congratulate you," observed Montevarchi, opening his small eyes in some astonishment. "The pursuit of the fine arts is not generally very lucrative. For myself, I confess that I am satisfied with those treasures which my father has left me. I am very fond of pictures, it is true; but you will understand that, when a gallery is filled, it is full. You comprehend, I am sure? Much as I might wish to own some of the works of the modern French school, the double disadvantage of possessing already so many canvases, and the still stronger consideration of my limited fortune—yes, limited, I assure you—"

"Pardon me," interrupted Gouache, whose face reddened suddenly, "I had no intention of proposing to sell you a picture. I am not in the habit of advertising myself nor of soliciting orders for my work."

"My dear sir!" exclaimed the prince, seeing that he was on a wrong tack, "have I suggested such a thing? If my words conveyed the idea, pray accept all my excuses. Since you had mentioned the subject of art, my thoughts naturally were directed to my gallery of pictures. I am delighted to hear of your success, for you know how much interest we all feel in him who was the victim of such an unfortunate accident, due doubtless to the carelessness of my men."

"Pray do not recall that! Your hospitality more than repaid me for the little I suffered. The matter concerning which I wish to speak to you is a very serious one, and I hope you will believe that I have considered it well before taking a step which may at first surprise you. To be plain, I come to ask you to confer upon me the honour of Donna Faustina Montevarchi's hand."

Montevarchi leaned back in his chair, speechless with amazement. He seemed to gasp for breath as his long fingers pressed the green table-cover before him. His small eyes were wide open, and his toothless jaw dropped. Gouache feared that he was going to be taken ill.

"You!" cried the old man in a cracked voice, when he had recovered himself enough to be able to speak.

"Yes," answered Anastase, who was beginning to feel very nervous as he observed the first results of his proposal. He had never before quite realised how utterly absurd the match would seem to Montevarchi. "Yes," he repeated. "Is the idea so surprising? Is it inconceivable to you that I should love your daughter? Can you not understand—"

"I understand that you are wholly mad!" exclaimed the prince, still staring at his visitor in blank astonishment.

"No, I am not mad. I love Donna Faustina—"

"You! You dare to love Faustina! You, a painter, a man with a profession and with nothing but what you earn! You, a Zouave, a man without a name, without—"

"You are an old man, prince, but the fact of my having made you an honourable proposition does not give you the right to insult me." The words were spoken in a sharp, determined voice, and brought Montevarchi to his senses. He was a terrible coward and would rather go to a considerable expense than face an angry man.

"Insult you, my dear sir? I would not think of it!" he answered in a very different tone. "But my dear Monsieur Gouache, I fear that this is quite impossible! In the first place, my daughter's marriage is already arranged. The negotiations have been proceeding for some time—she is to marry Frangipani—you must have heard it. And, moreover, with all due respect for the position you have gained by your immense talent—immense, my dear friend, I am the first to say it—the instability of human affairs obliges me to seek for her a fortune, which depends upon the vulgar possession of wealth rather than upon those divine gifts of genius with which you are so richly endowed."

The change from anger to flattery was so sudden that Gouache was confounded and could not find words in which to answer what was said to him. Montevarchi's eyes had lost their expression of astonishment, and a bland smile played about the corners of his sour mouth, while he rubbed his bony hands slowly together, nodding his head at every comma of his elaborate speech. Anastase saw, however, that there was not the slightest hope that his proposal would ever be entertained, and by his own sensations he knew that he had always expected this result. He felt no disappointment, and it seemed to him that he was in the same position in which he had been before he had spoken. On the other hand he was outraged by the words that had fallen from Montevarchi's lips in the first moments of anger and astonishment. A painter, a man with a profession, without a name! Gouache was too human not to feel the sting of each truth as it was uttered. He would have defined himself in very much the same way without the least false pride, but to hear his own estimate of himself, given by another person as the true one, was hard to bear. A painter, yes—he was proud of it. A man with a profession, yes—was it not far nobler to earn money by good work than to inherit what others had stolen in former times? A man without a name—was not his own beginning to be famous, and was it not better to make the name Gouache glorious by his own efforts than to be called Orsini because one's ancestors had been fierce and lawless as bears, or Sciarra because one's progenitor had slapped the face of a pope? Doubtless it was a finer thing to be great by one's own efforts in the pursuit of a noble art than to inherit a greatness originally founded upon a superior rapacity, and a greater physical strength than had characterised the ordinary men of the period. Nevertheless, Gouache knew with shame that at that moment he wished that his name could be changed to Frangipani, and the fabric of his independence, of which he had so long been proud, was shaken to its foundations as he realised that in spite of all fame, all glory, all genius, he could never be what the miserly, cowardly, lying old man before him was by birth—a Roman prince. The conclusion was at once inexpressibly humiliating and supremely ludicrous. He felt himself laughable in his own eyes, and was conscious that a smile was on his face, which Montevarchi would not understand. The old gentleman was still talking.

"I cannot tell you," he was saying, "how much I regret my total inability to comply with a request which evidently proceeds from the best motives, I might almost say from the heart itself. Alas, my dear friend, we are not all masters of our actions! The cares of a household like mine require a foresight, an hourly attention, an unselfish devotion which we can only hope to obtain by constant—"

He was going to say "by constant recourse to prayer," but he reflected that Gouache was probably not of a religious turn of mind, and he changed the sentence.

"—by constant study of the subject. Situated as I am, a Roman in the midst of Romans, I am obliged to consider the traditions of my own people in respect of all the great affairs of life. Believe me, I entreat you, that, far from having any prejudice against yourself, I should rejoice sincerely could I take you by the hand and call you my son. But how can I act? What can I do? Go to your own country, dear Monsieur Gouache, think no more of us, or of our daughters, marry a woman of your own nation, and you will not be disappointed in your dreams of matrimonial felicity!"

"In other words, you refuse altogether to listen to my proposal?" By this time Gouache was able to put the question calmly.

"Alas, yes!" replied the prince with an air of mock regret that exasperated the young man beyond measure. "I cannot think of it, though you are indeed a most sympathetic young man."

"In that case I will not trespass upon your time any longer," said Gouache, who was beginning to fear lest his coolness should forsake him.

As he descended the broad marble stairs his detestation of the old hypocrite overcame him, and his wrath broke out.

"You shall pay me for this some day, you old scoundrel!" he said aloud, very savagely.

Montevarchi remained in his study after Gouache had gone. A sour smile distorted his thin lips, and the expression became more and more accented until the old man broke into a laugh that rang drily against the vaulted ceiling. Some one knocked at the door, and his merriment disappeared instantly. Arnoldo Meschini entered the room. There was something unusual about his appearance which attracted the prince's attention at once.

"Has anything happened?"

"Everything. The case is won. Your Excellency's son-in-law is Prince Saracinesca."

The librarian's bright eyes gleamed with exultation and there was a slight flush in his cheeks that contrasted oddly with his yellow skin. A disagreeable smile made his intelligent face more ugly than usual. He stood half-way between the door and his employer, his long arms hanging awkwardly by his sides, his head thrust forward, his knees a little bent, assuming by habit a servile attitude of attention, but betraying in his look that he felt himself his master's master.

Montevarchi started as he heard the news. Then he leaned eagerly across the table, his fingers as usual slowly scratching the green cloth.

"Are you quite sure of it?" he asked in a trembling voice. "Have you got the verdict?"

Meschini produced a tattered pocket-book, and drew from it a piece of stamped paper, which he carefully unfolded and handed to the prince.

"There is an attested note of it. See for yourself."

Montevarchi hastily looked over the small document, and his face flushed slowly till it was almost purple, while the paper quivered in his hold. It was clear that everything had succeeded as he had hoped, and that his most sanguine expectations were fully realised. His thoughts suddenly recurred to Gouache, and he laughed again at the young man's assurance.

"Was Saracinesca in the court?" he asked presently.

"No. There was no one connected with the case except the lawyers on each side. It did not amount to a trial. The Signor Marchese's side produced the papers proving his identity, and the original deed was submitted. The prince's side stated that his Excellency was convinced of the justice of the claim and would make no opposition. Thereupon the court granted an order to the effect that the Signor Marchese was the heir provided for in the clause and was entitled to enjoy all the advantages arising from the inheritance; but that, as there was no opposition made by the defendants, the subsequent transactions would be left in the hands of the family, the court reserving the power to enforce the transfer in case any difficulty should arise hereafter. Of course, it will take several months to make the division, as the Signor Marchese will only receive the direct inheritance of his great-grandfather, while the Saracinesca retain all that has come to them by their marriages during the last four generations."

"Of course. Who will be employed to make the division?"

"Half Rome, I fancy. It will be an endless business."

"But San Giacinto is prince. He will do homage for his titles next Epiphany."

"Yes. He must present his ten pounds of wax and a silver bowl—cheap!" observed Meschini with a grin.

It may be explained here that the families of the Roman nobility were all subject to a yearly tribute of merely nominal value, which they presented to the Pope at the Feast of the Epiphany. The custom was feudal, the Pope having been the feudal lord of all the nobles until 1870. The tribute generally consisted of a certain weight of pure wax, or of a piece of silver of a specified value, or sometimes of both. As an instance of the survival of such customs in other countries, I may mention the case of one great Irish family which to this day receives from another a yearly tribute, paid alternately in the shape of a golden rose and a golden spur.

"So we have won everything!" exclaimed Montevarchi after a pause, looking hard at the librarian, as though trying to read his thoughts. "We have won everything, and the thanks are due to you, my good friend, to you, the faithful and devoted companion who has helped me to accomplish this act of true justice. Ah, how can I ever express to you my gratitude!"

"The means of expression were mentioned in our agreement," answered Meschini with a servile inclination. "I agreed to do the work for your Excellency at a certain fixed price, as your Excellency may remember. Beyond that I ask nothing. I am too humble an individual to enjoy the honour of Prince Montevarchi's personal gratitude."

"Yes, of course, but that is mere money!" said the old gentleman somewhat hastily, but contemptuously withal. "Gratitude proceeds from the heart, not from the purse. When I think of all the work you have done, of the unselfish way in which you have devoted yourself to this object, I feel that money can never repay you. Money is sordid trash, Meschini, sordid trash! Let us not talk about it. Are we not friends? The most delicate sensibilities of my soul rejoice when I consider what we have accomplished together. There is not another man in Rome whom I would trust as I trust you, most faithful of men!"

"The Signor Principe is too kind," replied Meschini. "Nevertheless, I repeat that I am quite unworthy of such gratitude for having merely performed my part in a business transaction, especially in one wherein my own interests were so deeply concerned."

"My only regret is that my son-in-law can never know the share you have had in his success. But that, alas, is quite impossible. How, indeed, would it be practicable to inform him! And my daughter, too! She would remember you in all her innocent prayers, even as I shall do henceforth! No, Meschini, it is ordained that I, and I alone, should be the means of expressing to you the heartfelt thanks of those whom you have so highly benefited, but who unfortunately can never know the name of their benefactor. Tell me now, did the men of the law look long at the documents? Did they show any hesitation? Have you any reason to believe that their attention was roused, arrested by—by the writing?"

"No, indeed! I should be a poor workman if a parcel of lawyers could detect my handwriting!"

"It is a miracle!" exclaimed Montevarchi, devoutly. "I consider that heaven has interposed directly to accomplish the ends of justice. An angel guided your hand, my dear friend, to make you the instrument of good!"

"I am quite ready to believe it. The transaction has been as providential for me as for the Signor Marchese."

"Yes," answered the prince rather drily. "And now, my dear Meschini, will you leave me for a time? I have appointed this hour to see my last remaining daughter concerning her marriage. She is the last of those fair flowers! Ah, me! How sad a thing it is to part with those we love so well! But we have the consolation of knowing that it is for their good, that consolation, that satisfaction which only come to us when we have faithfully done our duty. Return to your library, therefore, Meschini, for the present. The consciousness of good well done is yours also today, and will soothe the hours of solitude and make your new labours sweet. The reward of righteousness is in itself and of itself. Good-bye, my friend, good-bye! Thank you, thank you—"

"Would it be agreeable to your Excellency to let me have the money now?" asked the librarian. There was a firmness in the tone that startled Montevarchi.

"What money?" he inquired with a well-feigned surprise. "I do not understand."

"Twenty thousand scudi, the price of the work," replied Meschini with alarming bluntness.

"Twenty thousand scudi!" cried the prince. "I remember that there was some mention of a sum—two thousand, I think I said. Even that is enormous, but I was carried away in the excitement of the moment. We are all liable to such weakness—"

"You agreed to pay me twenty thousand scudi in cash on the day that the verdict was given in favour of your son-in-law."

"I never agreed to anything of the kind. My dear friend, success has quite turned your head! I have not so much money at my disposal in the whole world."

"You cannot afford to make a fool of me," cried Meschini, making a step forward. His face was red with anger, and his long arms made odd gestures. "Will you pay me the money or not?"

"If you take this tone with me I will pay you nothing whatever. I shall even cease to feel any sense of gratitude—"

"To hell with your gratitude!" exclaimed the other fiercely. "Either you pay me the money now, or I go at once to the authorities and denounce the whole treachery."

"You will only go to the galleys if you do."

"You will go with me."

"Not at all. Have you any proof that I have had anything to do with the matter? I tell you that you are quite mad. If you wanted to play this trick on me you should have made me sign an agreement. Even then I would have argued that since you had forged the documents you had, of course, forged the agreement also. But you have nothing, not so much as a scrap of paper to show against me. Be reasonable and I will be magnanimous. I will give you the two thousand I spoke of in the heat of anticipation—"

"You will give me the twenty thousand you solemnly promised me," said Meschini, with concentrated anger.

Montevarchi rose slowly from his chair and rang the bell. He knew that Meschini would not be so foolish as to expose himself, and would continue to hope that he might ultimately get what he asked.

"I cannot argue with a madman," he said calmly.

He was not in the least afraid of the librarian. The idea never entered his mind that the middle-aged, round-shouldered scholar could be dangerous. A single word from Gouache, a glance of the artist's eye had cowed him less than an hour ago; but Meschini's fury left him indifferent. The latter saw that for the present there was nothing to be done. To continue such a scene before a servant would be the worst kind of folly.

"We will talk the matter over at another time," he said sullenly, as he left the study by a small door which opened upon a corridor in communication with the library.

Montevarchi sent the servant who answered the bell with a message begging Donna Faustina to come to the study at once. Since it was to be a day of interviews he determined to state the case plainly to his daughter, and bid her make ready to comply with his will in case the match with Frangipani turned out to be possible. He seemed no more disturbed by Meschini's anger than if the affair had not concerned him in the least. He had, indeed, long foreseen what would occur, and even at the moment when he had promised the bribe he was fully determined never to pay it. The librarian had taken the bait greedily, and it was his own fault if the result did not suit him. He had no redress, as Montevarchi had told him; there was not so much as a note to serve as a record of the bargain. Meschini had executed the forgery, and he would have to ruin himself in order to bring any pressure to bear upon his employer. This the latter felt sure that he would not do, even if driven to extremities. Meschini's nature was avaricious and there was no reason to suppose that he was tired of life, or ready to go to the galleys for a bit of personal vengeance, when, by exercising a little patience, he might ultimately hope to get some advantage out of the crime he had committed. Montevarchi meant to pay him what he considered a fair price for the work, and he did not see that Meschini had any means of compelling him to pay more. Now that the thing was done, he began to regret that he himself had not made some agreement with San Giacinto, but a moment's reflection sufficed to banish the thought as unworthy of his superior astuteness. His avarice was on a large scale and was merging into ambition. It might have been foreseen that, after having married one of his two remaining daughters to a man who had turned out to be Prince Saracinesca, his determination to match Faustina with Frangipani would be even stronger than it had been before. Hence his sudden wish to see Faustina and to prepare her mind for what was about to take place. All at once it seemed as though he could not act quickly enough to satisfy his desire of accomplishment. He felt as an old man may feel who, at the end of a busy life, sees countless things before him which he would still do, and hates the thought of dying before all are done. A feverish haste to complete this last step in the aggrandisement of his family, overcame the old prince. He could not understand why he had submitted to wasting his time with Gouache and Meschini instead of busying himself actively in the accomplishment of his purpose. There was no reason for waiting any longer. Frangipani's father had already half-agreed to the match, and what remained to be done involved only a question of financial details.

As he sat waiting for Faustina a great horror of death rose suddenly and clearly before him. He was not a very old man and he would have found it hard to account for the sensation. It is a notable fact, too, that he feared death rather because it might prevent him from carrying out his intentions, than because his conscience was burdened with the recollection of many misdeeds. His whole existence had been passed in such an intricate labyrinth of duplicity towards others and towards himself that he no longer distinguished between the true and the untrue. Even in this last great fraud he had so consistently deceived his own sense of veracity that he almost felt himself to be the instrument of justice he assumed to be. The case was a delicate one, too, for the most unprejudiced person could hardly have escaped feeling sympathy for San Giacinto, the victim of his ancestor's imprudence. Montevarchi found it very easy to believe that it was permissible to employ any means in order to gain such an end, and although he might have regarded the actual work of the forgery in the light of a crime, venial indeed, though contrary to the law, his own share in the transaction, as instigator of the deed itself, appeared to be defensible by a whole multitude of reasons. San Giacinto, by all the traditions of primogeniture dear to the heart of the Roman noble, was the head of the family of Saracinesca. But for a piece of folly, hardly to be equalled in Montevarchi's experience, San Giacinto would have been in possession of the estates and titles without opposition or contradiction since the day of his father's death. The mere fact that the Saracinesca had not defended the case proved that they admitted the justice of their cousin's claims. Had old Leone foreseen the contingency of a marriage in his old age, he would either never have signed the deed at all, or else he would have introduced just such a conditional clause as had been forged by Meschini. When a great injustice has been committed, through folly or carelessness, when those who have been most benefited by it admit that injustice, when to redress it is merely to act in accordance with the spirit of the laws, is it a crime then to bring about so much good by merely sacrificing a scruple of conscience, by employing some one to restore an inheritance to its rightful possessor with a few clever strokes of the pen? The answer seemed so clear to Montevarchi that he did not even ask himself the question. Indeed it would have been superfluous to do so, for he had so often satisfied all objections to doubtful courses by a similar sophistry that he knew beforehand what reply would present itself to his self-inquiry. He did not even experience a sense of relief as he turned from the contemplation of what he had just done to the question of Faustina's marriage, in which there was nothing that could torment his conscience. He was not even aware that he ought to recognise a difference between the two affairs. He was in great haste to settle the preliminaries, and that was all. If he should die, he thought, the princess would have her own way in everything, and would doubtless let Faustina throw herself away upon some such man as Gouache. The thought roused him from his reverie, and at the same time brought a sour smile to his face. Gouache, of all people! He looked up and saw that Faustina had entered and was standing before him, as though expecting him to speak. Her delicate, angelic features were pale, and she held her small hands folded before her. She had discovered by some means that Gouache had been with her father and she feared that something unpleasant had happened and that she was about to be called to account. The vision of Frangipani, too, was present in her mind, and she anticipated a stormy interview. But her mind was made up; she would have Anastase or she would have nobody. The two exchanged a preliminary glance before either spoke.

CHAPTER XX

MONTEVARCHI made his daughter sit beside him and took her hand affectionately in his, assuming at the same time the expression of sanctimonious superiority he always wore when he mentioned the cares of his household or was engaged in regulating any matter of importance in his family. Flavia used to imitate the look admirably, to the delight of her brothers and sisters. He smiled meaningly, pressed the girl's fingers, and smiled again, attempting in vain to elicit some response. But Faustina remained cold and indifferent, for she was used to her father's ways and did not like them.

"You know what I am going to say, I am sure," he began. "It concerns what must be very near your heart, my dear child."

"I do not know what it can be," answered Faustina, gravely. She was too well brought up to show any of the dislike she felt for her father's way of doing things, but she was willing to make it as hard as possible for him to express himself.

"Cannot you guess what it is?" asked the old man, with a ludicrous attempt at banter. "What is it that is nearest to every girl's heart? Is not that little heart of yours already a resort of the juvenile deity?"

"I do not understand you, papa."

"Well, well, my dear—I see that your education has not included a course of mythology. It is quite as well, perhaps, as those heathens are poor company for the young. I refer to marriage, Faustina, to that all-important step which you are soon to take."

"Have you quite decided to marry me to Frangipani?" asked the young girl with a calmness that somewhat disconcerted her father.

"How boldly you speak of it!" he exclaimed with a sigh of disapproval. "I will not, however, conceal from you that I hope—"

"Pray talk plainly with me, papa!" cried Faustina suddenly looking up. "I cannot bear this suspense."

"Ah! Is it so, little one?" Montevarchi shook his finger playfully at her. "I thought I should find you ready! So you are anxious to become a princess at once? Well, well, all women are alike!"

Faustina drew herself up a little and fixed her deep brown eyes upon her father's face, very quietly and solemnly.

"You misunderstand me," she said. "I only wish to know your decision in order that I may give you my answer."

"And what can that answer be? Have I not chosen, wisely, a husband fit for you in every way?"

"From your point of view, I have no doubt of it."

"I trust you are not about to commit the unpardonable folly of differing from me, my daughter," answered Montevarchi, with a sudden change of tone indicative of rising displeasure. "It is for me to decide, for you to accept my decision."

"Upon other points, yes. In the question of marriage I think I have something to say."

"Is it possible that you can have any objections to the match I have found for you? Is it possible that you are so foolish as to fancy that at your age you can understand these things better than I? Faustina, I would not have believed it!"

"How can you understand what I feel?"

"It is not a question of feeling, it is a question of wisdom, of foresight, of prudence, of twenty qualities which you are far too young to possess. If marriage were a matter of feeling, of vulgar sentiment, I ask you, what would become of the world? Of what use is it to have all the sentiment in life, if you have not that which makes life itself possible? Can you eat sentiment? Can you harness sentiment in a carriage and make it execute a trottata in the Villa Borghese? Can you change an ounce of sentiment into good silver scudi and make it pay for a journey in the hot weather? No, no, my child. Heaven knows that I am not avaricious. Few men, I think, know better than I that wealth is perishable stuff—but so is this mortal body, and the perishable must be nourished with the perishable, lest dust return to dust sooner than it would in the ordinary course of nature. Money alone will not give happiness, but it is, nevertheless, most important to possess a certain amount of it."

"I would rather do without it than be miserable all my life for having got it."

"Miserable all your life? Why should you be miserable? No woman should be unhappy who is married to a good man. My dear, this matter admits of no discussion. Frangipani is young, handsome, of irreproachable moral character, heir to a great fortune and to a great name. You desire to be in love. Good. Love will come, the reward of having chosen wisely. It will be time enough then to think of your sentiments. Dear me! If we all began life by thinking of sentiment, where would our existence end?"

"Will you please tell me whether you have quite decided that I am to marry Frangipani?" Faustina found her father's discourses intolerable, and, moreover, she had something to say which would be hard to express and still harder to sustain by her actions.

"If you insist upon my giving you an answer, which you must have already foreseen, I am willing to tell you that I have quite decided upon the match."

"I cannot marry him!" exclaimed Faustina, clasping her hands together and looking into her father's face.

"My dear," answered Montevarchi with a smile, "it is absolutely decided. We cannot draw back. You must marry him."

"Must, papa? Oh, think what you are saying! I am not disobedient, indeed I am not. I have always submitted to you in everything. But this—no, not this. Bid me do anything else—anything—"

"But, my child, nothing else would produce the same result. Be reasonable. You tell me to impose some other duty upon you. That is not what I want. I must see you married before I die, and I am an old man. Each year, each day, may be my last. Of what use would it be that you should make another sacrifice to please me, when the one thing I desire is to see you well settled with a good husband? I have done what I could. I have procured you the best match in all Rome, and now you implore me to spare you, to reverse my decision, to tell my old friend Frangipani that you will not have his son, and to go out into the market to find you another help-meet. It is not reasonable. I had expected more dutiful conduct from you."

"Is it undutiful not to be able to love a man one hardly knows, when one is ordered to do so?"

"You will make me lose my patience, Faustina!" exclaimed Montevarchi, in angry tones. "Have I not explained to you the nature of love? Have I not told you that you can love your husband as much as you please? Is it not a father's duty to direct the affections of his child as I wish to do, and is it not the child's first obligation to submit to its father's will and guidance? What more would you have? In truth, you are very exacting!"

"I am very unhappy!" The young girl turned away and rested her elbow on the table, supporting her chin in her hand. She stared absently at the old bookcases as though she were trying to read the titles upon the dingy bindings. Montevarchi understood her words to convey a submission and changed his tone once more.

"Well, well, my dear, you will never regret your obedience," he said. "Of course, my beloved child, it is never easy to see things as it is best that we should see them. I see that you have yielded at last—"

"I have not yielded in the least!" cried Faustina, suddenly facing him, with an expression he had never seen before.

"What do you mean?" asked Montevarchi in considerable astonishment.

"What I say. I will not marry Frangipani—I will not! Do you understand?"

"No. I do not understand such language from my daughter; and as for your determination, I tell you that you will most certainly end by acting as I wish you to act."

"You cannot force me to marry. What can you do? You can put me into a convent. Do you think that would make me change my mind? I would thank God for any asylum in which I might find refuge from such tyranny."

"My daughter," replied the prince in bland tones, "I am fully resolved not to be angry with you. Your undutiful conduct proceeds from ignorance, which is never an offence, though it is always a misfortune. If you will have a little patience—"

"I have none!" exclaimed Faustina, exasperated by her father's manner. "My undutiful conduct does not proceed from ignorance—it proceeds from love, from love for another man, whom I will marry if I marry any one."

"Faustina!" cried Montevarchi, holding up his hands in horror and amazement. "Do you dare to use *such* language to your father!"

"I dare do anything, everything—I dare even tell you the name of the man I love—Anastase Gouache!"

"My child! My child! This is too horrible! I must really send for your mother."

"Do what you will."

Faustina had risen to her feet and was standing before one of the old book-cases, her hands folded before her, her eyes on fire, her delicate mouth scornfully bent. Montevarchi, who was really startled almost out of his senses, moved cautiously towards the bell, looking steadily at his daughter all the while as though he dreaded some fresh outbreak. There was something ludicrous in his behaviour which, at another time, would not have escaped the young girl. Now, however, she was too much in earnest to perceive anything except the danger of her position and the necessity for remaining firm at any cost. She did not understand why her mother was to be called, but she felt that she could face all her family if necessary. She kept her eyes upon her father and was hardly conscious that a servant entered the room. Montevarchi sent a message requesting the princess to come at once. Then he turned again towards Faustina.

"You can hardly suppose," he observed, "that I take seriously what you have just said; but you are evidently very much excited, and your mother's presence will, I trust, have a soothing effect. You must be aware that it is very wrong to utter such monstrous untruths—even in jest—"

"I am in earnest. I will marry Monsieur Gouache or I will marry no one."

Montevarchi really believed that his daughter's mind was deranged. His interview with Gouache had convinced him that Faustina meant what she said, though he affected to laugh at it, but he was wholly unable to account for her conduct on any theory but that of insanity. Being at his wits' end he had sent for his wife, and while waiting for her he did not quite know what to do.

"My dear child, what is Monsieur Gouache? A very estimable young man, without doubt, but not such a one as we could choose for your husband."

"I have chosen him," answered Faustina. "That is enough."

"How you talk, my dear! How rashly you talk! As though choosing a husband were like buying a new hat! And you, too, whom I always believed to be the most dutiful, the most obedient of my children! But your mother and I will reason with you, we will endeavour to put better thoughts into your heart."

Faustina glanced scornfully at her father and turned away, walking slowly in the direction of the window.

"It is of no use to waste your breath on me," she said presently. "I will marry Gouache or nobody."

"You—marry Gouache?" cried the princess, who entered at that moment, and heard the last words. Her voice expressed an amazement and horror fully equal to her husband's.

"Have you come to join the fray, mamma?" inquired Faustina, in English.

"Pray speak in a language I can understand," said Montevarchi who, in a whole lifetime, had never mastered a word of his wife's native tongue.

"Oh, Lotario!" exclaimed the princess. "What has the child been telling you?"

"Things that would make you tremble, my dear! She refuses to marry Frangipani—"

"Refuses! But, Faustina, you do not know what you are doing! You are out of your mind!"

"And she talks wildly of marrying a certain Frenchman, a Monsieur Gouache, I believe—is there such a man, my dear?"

"Of course, Lotario! The little man you ran over. How forgetful you are!"

"Yes, yes, of course. I know. But you must reason with her, Guendalina—"

"It seems to me. Lotario, that you should do that—"

"My dear, I think the child is insane upon the subject. Where could she have picked up such an idea? Is it a mere caprice, a mere piece of impertinence, invented to disconcert the sober senses of a careful father?"

"Nonsense, Lotario! She is not capable of that. After all, she is not Flavia, who always had something dreadful quite ready, just when you least expected it."

"I almost wish she were Flavia!" exclaimed Montevarchi, ruefully. "Flavia has done very well." During all this time Faustina was standing with her back towards the window and her hands folded before her, looking from the one to the other of the speakers with an air of bitter contempt which was fast changing to uncontrollable anger. Some last remaining instinct of prudence kept her from interrupting the conversation by a fresh assertion of her will, and she waited until one of them chose to speak to her. She had lost her head, for she would otherwise never have gone so far as to mention Gouache's name, but, as with all very spontaneous natures, with her to break the first barrier was to go to the extreme, whatever it might be. Her clear brown eyes were very bright, and there was something luminous about her angelic face which showed that her whole being was under the influence of an extraordinary emotion, almost amounting to exaltation. It was impossible to foresee what she would say or do.

"Your father almost wishes you were Flavia!" groaned the princess, shaking her head and looking very grave. Then Faustina laughed scornfully and her wrath bubbled over.

"I am not Flavia!" she cried, coming forward and facing her father and mother. "I daresay you do wish I were. Flavia has done so very well. Yes, she is Princess Saracinesca this evening, I suppose. Indeed she has done well, for she has married the man she loves, as much as she is capable of loving anything. And that is all the more reason why I should do the same. Besides, am I as old as Flavia that you should be in such a hurry to marry me? Do you think I will yield? Do you think that while I love one man, I will be so base as to marry another?"

"I have explained to you that love—"

"Your explanations will drive me mad! You may explain anything in that way—and prove that Love itself does not exist. Do you think your saying so makes it true? There is more truth in a little of my love than in all your whole life!"

"Faustina!"

"What? May I not answer you? Must I believe you infallible when you use arguments that would not satisfy a child? Is my whole nature a shadow because yours cannot understand my reality?"

"If you are going to make this a question of metaphysics—"

"I am not, I do not know what metaphysic means. But I will repeat before my mother what I said to you alone. I will not marry Frangipani, and you cannot force me to marry him. If I marry any one I will have the man I love."

"But, my dearest Faustina," cried the princess in genuine distress, "this is a mere idea—a sort of madness that has seized upon you. Consider your position, consider what you owe to us, consider—"

"Consider, consider, consider! Do you suppose that any amount of consideration would change me?"

"Do you think your childish anger will change us?" inquired Montevarchi, blandly. He did not care to lose his temper, for he was quite indifferent to Faustina's real inclinations, if she would only consent to marry Frangipani.

"Childish!" cried Faustina, her eyes blazing with anger. "Was I childish when I followed him out into the midst of the revolution last October, when I was nearly killed at the Serristori, when I thought he was dead and knelt there among the ruins until he found me and brought me home? Was that a child's love?"

The princess turned pale and grasped her husband's arm, staring at Faustina in horror. The old man trembled and for a few moments could not find strength to speak. Nothing that Faustina could have invented could have produced such a sudden and tremendous effect as this revelation of what had happened on the night of the insurrection, coming from the girl's own lips with the unmistakable accent of truth. The mother's instinct was the first to assert itself. With a quick movement she threw her arms round the young girl, as though to protect her from harm.

"It is not true, it is not true," she cried in an agonised tone. "Faustina, my child—it is not true!"

"It is quite true, mamma," answered Faustina, who enjoyed an odd satisfaction in seeing the effect of her words, which can only be explained by her perfect innocence. "Why are you so much astonished? I loved him—I thought he was going out to be killed—I would not let him go alone—"

"Oh, Faustina! How could you do it!" moaned the princess. "It is too horrible—it is not to be believed—"

"I loved him, I love him still."

Princess Montevarchi fell into a chair and burst into tears, burying her face in her hands and sobbing aloud.

"If you are going to cry, Guendalina, you had better go away," said her husband, who was now as angry as his mean nature would permit him to be. She was so much accustomed to obey that she left the room, crying as she went, and casting back a most sorrowful look at Faustina.

Montevarchi shut the door and, coming back, seized his daughter's arm and shook it violently.

"Fool!" he cried angrily, unable to find any other word to express his rage.

Faustina said nothing but tried to push him away, her bright eyes gleaming with contempt. Her silence exasperated the old man still further. Like most very cowardly men he could be brutal to women when he was angry. It seemed to him that the girl, by her folly, had dashed from him the last great satisfaction of his life at the very moment when it was within reach. He could have forgiven her for ruining herself, had she done so; he could not forgive her for disappointing his ambition; he knew that one word of the story she had told would make the great marriage impossible, and he knew that she had the power to speak that word when she pleased as well as the courage to do so.

"Fool!" he repeated, and before she could draw back, he struck her across the mouth with the back of his hand.

A few drops of bright red blood trickled from her delicate lips. With an instinctive movement she pressed her handkerchief to the wound. Montevarchi snatched it roughly from her hand and threw it across the room. From his eyes she guessed that he would strike her again if she remained. With a look of intense hatred she made a supreme effort, and concentrating the whole strength of her slender frame wrenched herself free.

"Coward!" she cried, as he reeled backwards; then, before he could recover himself, she was gone and he was left alone.

He was terribly angry, and at the same time his ideas were confused, so that he hardly understood anything but the main point of her story, that she had been with Gouache on that night when Corona had brought her home. He began to reason again. Corona knew the truth, of course, and her husband knew it too. Montevarchi realised that he had already taken his revenge for their complicity, before knowing that they had injured him. His overwrought brain was scarcely capable of receiving another impression. He laughed aloud in a way that was almost hysterical.

"All!" he cried in sudden exultation. "All—even to their name—but the other—" His face changed quickly and he sank into his chair and buried his face in his hands, as he thought of all he had lost through Faustina's folly. And yet, the harm might be repaired—no one knew except—

He looked up and saw that Meschini had returned and was standing before him, as though waiting to be addressed. The suddenness of the librarian's appearance made the prince utter an exclamation of surprise.

"Yes, I have come back," said Meschini. "The matter we were discussing cannot be put off, and I have come back to ask you to be good enough to pay the money."

Montevarchi was nervous and had lost the calm tone of superiority he had maintained before his interview with Faustina. The idea of losing Frangipani, too, made his avarice assert itself very strongly.

"I told you," he replied, "that I refused altogether to talk with you, so long as you addressed me in that tone. I repeat it. Leave me, and when you have recovered your manners I will give you something for yourself. You will get nothing so long as you demand it as though it were a right."

"I will not leave this room without the money," answered Meschini, resolutely. The bell was close to the door. The librarian placed himself between the prince and both.

"Leave the room!" cried Montevarchi, trembling with anger. He had so long despised Meschini, that the exhibition of obstinacy on the part of the latter did not frighten him.

The librarian stood before the bell and the latch of the door, his long arms hanging down by his sides, his face yellow, his eyes red. Any one might have seen that he was growing dangerous. Instead of repeating his refusal to go, he looked steadily at his employer and a disagreeable smile played upon his ugly features. Montevarchi saw it and his fury boiled over. He laid his hands on the arms of his chair as though he would rise, and in that moment he would have been capable of striking Meschini as he had struck Faustina. Meschini shuffled forwards and held up his hand.

"Do not be violent," he said, in a low voice. "I am not your daughter, you know."

Montevarchi's jaw dropped, and he fell back into his chair again.

"You listened—you saw—" he gasped.

"Yes, of course. Will you pay me? I am desperate, and I will have it. You and your miserable secrets are mine, and I will have my price. I only want the sum you promised. I shall be rich in a few days, for I have entered into an affair in which I shall get millions, as many as you have perhaps. But the money must be paid tomorrow morning or I am ruined, and you must give it to me. Do you hear? Do you understand that I will have what is mine?"

At this incoherent speech, Montevarchi recovered something of his former nerve. There was something in Meschini's language that sounded like argument, and to argue was to temporise. The prince changed his tone.

"But, my dear Meschini, how could you be so rash as to go into a speculation when you knew that the case might not be decided for another week? You are really the most rash man I ever knew. I cannot undertake to guarantee your speculations. I will be just. I have told you that I would give you two thousand—"

"Twenty thousand!" Meschini came a little nearer.

"Not a single baiocco if you are exorbitant."

"Twenty thousand hard, good scudi in cash, I tell you. No more, but no less either." The librarian's hands were clenched, and he breathed hard, while his red eyes stared in a way that began to frighten Montevarchi.

"No, no, be reasonable! My dear Meschini, pray do not behave in this manner. You almost make me believe that you are threatening me. I assure you that I desire to do what is just—"

"Give me the money at once—"

"But I have not so much—murder! Ah-gh-gh—"

Arnodo Meschini's long arms had shot out and his hands had seized the prince's throat in a grip from which there was no escape. There lurked a surprising strength in the librarian's round shoulders, and his energy was doubled by a fit of anger that amounted to insanity. The old man rocked and swayed in his chair, and grasped at the green table-cover, but Meschini had got behind him and pressed his fingers tighter and tighter. His eye rested upon Faustina's handkerchief that lay on the floor at his feet. His victim was almost at the last gasp, but the handkerchief would do the job better. Meschini kept his grip with one hand and with the other snatched up the bit of linen. He drew it tight round the neck and wrenched at the knot with his yellow teeth. There was a convulsive struggle, followed by a long interval of quiet. Then another movement, less violent this time, another and another, and then Meschini felt the body collapse in his grasp. It was over. Montevarchi was dead. Meschini drew back against the bookcases, trembling in every joint. He scarcely saw the objects in the room, for his head swam and his senses failed him, from horror and from the tremendous physical effort he had made. Then in an instant he realised what he had done, and the consequences of the deed suggested themselves.

He had not meant to kill the prince. So long as he had kept some control of his actions he had not even meant to lay violent hands upon him. But he had the nature of a criminal, by turns profoundly cunning and foolishly rash. A fatal influence had pushed him onward so soon as he had raised his arm, and before he was thoroughly conscious of his actions the deed was done. Then came the fear of consequences, then again the diabolical reasoning which intuitively foresees the immediate results of murder, and provides against them at once.

"Nobody knows that I have been here. Nothing is missing. No one knows about the forgery. No one will suspect me. There is no one in the library nor in the corridor. The handkerchief is not mine. If it was not his own it was Donna Faustina's. No one will suspect her. It will remain a mystery."

Meschini went towards the door through which he had entered and opened it. He looked back and held his breath. The prince's head had fallen forward upon his hands as they lay on the table, and the attitude was that of a man overcome by despair, but not that of a dead body. The librarian glanced round the room. There was no trace of a struggle. The position of the furniture had not been changed, nor had anything fallen on the floor. Meschini went out and softly closed the door behind him, leaving the dead man alone.

The quiet afternoon sun fell upon the houses on the opposite side of the street, and cast a melancholy reflection into the dismal chamber where Prince Montevarchi had passed so many hours of his life, and in which that life had been cut short so suddenly. On the table before his dead hands lay the copy of the verdict, the testimony of his last misdeed, of the crime for which he had paid the forfeit upon the very day it was due. It lay there like the superscription upon a malefactor's gallows in ancient times, the advertisement of the reason of his death to all who chose to inquire. Not a sound was heard save the noise that rose faintly and at intervals from the narrow street below, the cry of a hawker, the song of a street-boy, the bark of a dog. Tomorrow the poor body would be mounted upon a magnificent catafalque, surrounded by the pomp of a princely mourning, illuminated by hundreds of funeral torches, an object of aversion, of curiosity, even of jest, perhaps, among those who bore the prince a grudge. Many of those who had known him would come and look on his dead face, and some would say that he was changed and others that he was not. His wife and his children would, in a few hours, be all dressed in black, moving silently and mournfully and occasionally showing a little feeling, though not more than would be decent. There would be masses sung, and prayers said, and his native city would hear the tolling of the heavy bells for one of her greatest personages. All this would be done, and more also, until the dead prince should be laid to rest beneath the marble floor of the chapel where his ancestors lay side by side.

But today he sat in state in his shabby chair, his head lying upon that table over which he had plotted and schemed for so many years, his white fingers almost touching the bit of paper whereon was written the ruin of the Saracinesca.

And upstairs the man who had killed him shuffled about the library, an anxious expression on his yellow face, glancing from time to time at his hands as he took down one heavy volume after another, practising in solitude the habit of seeming occupied, in order that he might not be taken unawares when an under-servant should be sent to tell the insignificant librarian of what had happened that day in Casa Montevarchi.

CHAPTER XXI

GIOVANNI came home late in the afternoon and found Corona sitting by the fire in her boudoir. She had known that he would return before long, but had not anticipated his coming with any pleasure. When he entered the room she looked up quietly, without a smile, to assure herself that it was he and no one else. She said nothing, and he sat down upon the other side of the fireplace. There was an air of embarrassment about their meetings, until one or the other had made some remark which led to a commonplace conversation. On the present occasion neither seemed inclined to be the first speaker and for some minutes they sat opposite to each other in silence. Giovanni glanced at his wife from time to time, and once she turned her head and met his eyes. Her expression was cold and grave as though she wished him to understand that she had nothing to say. He thought she had never been so beautiful before. The firelight, striking her face at an upward angle, brought out clearly the noble symmetry of her features, the level brow, the wide, delicate nostrils, the even curve of her lips, the splendid breadth of her smooth forehead, shaded by her heavy black hair. She seemed to feel cold, for she sat near the flames, resting one foot upon the fender, in an attitude that threw into relief the perfect curves of her figure, as she bent slightly forward, spreading her hands occasionally to the blaze.

"Corona—" Giovanni stopped suddenly after pronouncing her name, as though he had changed his mind while in the act of speaking.

"What is it?" she asked indifferently enough.

"Would you like to go away? I have been wondering whether it would not be better than staying here."

She looked up in some surprise. She had thought of travelling more than once of late, but it seemed to her that to make a journey together would be only to increase the difficulties of the situation. There would be of necessity more intimacy, more daily converse than the life in Rome forced upon her. She shrank from the idea for the very reason which made it attractive to her husband.

"No," she answered. "Why should we travel? Besides, with a child so young—"

"We might leave Orsino at home," suggested Giovanni. He was not prepared for the look she gave him as she replied.

"I will certainly not consent to that."

"Would you be willing to take him with you, and leave me here? You could easily find a friend to go with you—even my father. He would enjoy it immensely."

There was the shortest possible pause before she answered him this time. It did not escape him, for he expected it.

"No. I will not do that, either. I do not care to go away. Why should I, and at such a time?"

"I think I will go alone, in that case," said Giovanni quietly, but watching her face. She made no reply, but looked at him curiously as though she suspected him of laying a trap for her.

"You say nothing. Is silence consent?"

"I think it would be very unwise."

"You do not answer me. Be frank, Corona. Would you not be glad to be left alone for a time?"

"Why do you insist?" she asked with a little impatience. "Are you trying to make me say something that I shall regret?"

"Would you regret it, if it were said? Why not be honest? It would be an immense relief to you if I went away. I could find an excellent excuse and nobody would guess that there was anything wrong."

"For that matter—there is nothing wrong. Of course no one would say anything."

"I know you will think that I have no tact," Giovanni observed with considerable justice.

Corona could not repress a smile at the remark, which expressed most exactly what she herself was thinking.

"Frankly—I think it would be better to leave things alone. Do you not think so, too?"

"How coolly you say that!" exclaimed Giovanni. "It is so easy for you—so hard for me. I would do anything you asked, and you will not ask anything, because you would make any sacrifice rather than accept one from me. Did you ever really love me, Corona? Is it possible that love can be killed in a day, by a word? I wonder whether there is any woman alive as cold as you are! Is it anything to you that I should suffer as I am suffering, every day?"

"You cannot understand—"

"No—that is true. I cannot understand. I was base, cowardly, cruel—I make no defence. But if I was all that, and more too, it was because I loved you, because the least suspicion drove me mad, because I could not reason, loving you as I did, any more than I can reason now. Oh, I love you too much, too wholly, too foolishly! I will try and change and be another man—so that I may at least look at you without going mad!"

He rose to his feet and went towards the door. But Corona called him back. The bitterness of his words and the tone in which they were spoken hurt her, and made her realise for a moment what he was suffering.

"Giovanni—dear—do not leave me so—I am unhappy, too."

"Are you?" He had come to her side and stood looking down into her eyes.

"Wretchedly unhappy." She turned her face away again. She could not help it.

"You are unhappy, and yet I can do nothing. Why do you call me back?"

"If I only could, if I only could!" she repeated in a low voice.

There was silence for a few seconds, during which Giovanni could hear his heart beat loudly and irregularly.

"If I could but move you a little!" he said at last, almost inaudibly. "If I could do anything, suffer anything for you—"

She shook her head sorrowfully and then, as though afraid that she had given him pain, she took his hand and pressed it affectionately—affectionately, not lovingly. It was as cold as ice. He sighed and once more turned away. Just then the door opened, and old Pasquale appeared, his face pale with fright.

"Eccellenza, a note, and the man says that Prince Montevarchi has just been murdered, and that the note is from Donna Faustina, and the police are in the Palazzo Montevarchi, and that the poor princess is dying, and—"

Corona had risen quickly with a cry of astonishment. Giovanni had taken the letter and stood staring at the servant as though he believed that the man was mad. Then he glanced at the address and saw that it was for his wife.

"Faustina is accused of the murder!" she exclaimed. "I must go to her at once. The carriage, Pasquale, instantly!"

"Faustina Montevarchi—killed her own father!" cried Giovanni in the utmost astonishment.

Corona thrust the note into his hands. It only contained a few words scrawled in an irregular hand as though written in great emotion.

"Of course it is some horrible mistake," said Corona, "but I must go at once."

"I will go with you. I may be able to give some help."

Five minutes later, they were descending the stairs. The carriage was not ready, and leaving orders for it to follow them they went out into the street and took a passing cab. Under the influence of the excitement they acted together instinctively. During the short drive they exchanged but few words, and those only expressive of amazement at the catastrophe. At the Palazzo Montevarchi everything was already in confusion, the doors wide open, the servants hurrying aimlessly hither and thither with frightened faces. They had just been released from the preliminary examination held by the prefect of police. A party of gendarmes stood together in the antechamber talking, while one of their number mounted guard at the door with a drawn sabre, allowing no one to leave the house. A terrified footman led Giovanni and Corona to the great drawing-room.

The vast chamber was lighted by a single lamp which stood upon a yellow marble pier-table, and cast dim shadows on the tapestry of the walls. The old-fashioned furniture was ranged stiffly around the room as usual; the air was damp and cold, not being warmed even by the traditional copper brazier. The voices of the group of persons collected within the circle of the light sounded hollow, and echoed strangely in the huge emptiness. Dominant above the rest were heard the hard tones of the prefect of police.

"I can assure you," he was saying, "that I feel the greatest regret in being obliged to assert my decision."

Giovanni and Corona came forward, and the rest made way for them. The prefect stood with his back to the light and to the table, like a man who is at bay. He was of middle height, very dark, and inclining to stoutness. His aquiline features and his eyes, round in shape, but half veiled by heavy lids, gave him something of the appearance of an owl. When he spoke, his voice was harsh and mechanical, and he always seemed to be looking just over the head of the person he addressed. He made no gestures and held himself very straight.

Opposite him stood Faustina Montevarchi, her face luminously pale, her eyes almost wild in their fixed expression. She held her hands clasped before her, and her fingers worked nervously. Around her stood her brothers and their wives, apparently speechless with horror, crowding together like frightened sheep before the officer of the law. Neither her mother, nor Flavia, nor San Giacinto accompanied the rest. It would be impossible to imagine a number of persons more dumb and helpless with fear.

"Oh Corona, save me!" cried Faustina, throwing herself into her friend's arms as soon as she saw her face.

"Will you be good enough to explain what has occurred?" said Giovanni, confronting the prefect sternly. "Do you mean to tell me that you have accused this innocent child of murdering her father? You are mad, sir!"

"Pardon me, Signor Principe, I am not mad, and no one can regret more than I what has occurred here," replied the other in loud, metallic tones. "I will give you the facts in two minutes. Prince Montevarchi was found dead an hour ago. He had been dead some time. He had been strangled by means of this pocket handkerchief—observe the stains of blood—which I hold as part of the evidence. The Signora Donna Faustina is admitted to be the last person who saw the prince alive. She admits, furthermore, that a violent scene occurred between her and her father this afternoon, in the course of which his Excellency struck his daughter, doubtless in the way of paternal correction—observe the bruise upon the young lady's mouth. There is also another upon her arm. It is clear that, being young and vigorous and remarkably well grown, she opposed violence to violence. She went behind him, for the prince was found dead in his chair, leaning forward upon the table, and she succeeded in knotting the handkerchief so firmly as to produce asphyxia superinduced by strangulation without suspension. All this is very clear. I have examined every member of the household, and have reluctantly arrived at the conclusion, most shocking no doubt to these pacifically disposed persons, that this young lady allowed herself to be so far carried away by her feelings as to take the life of her parent. Upon this charge I have no course but to arrest her person, the case being very clear, and to convey her to a safe place."

Giovanni could scarcely contain his wrath while the prefect made this long speech, but he was resolved to listen to the account given without interrupting it. When the man had finished, however, his anger burst out.

"And do you take nothing into consideration," he cried, "but the fact that the prince was strangled with that handkerchief, and that there had been some disagreement between him and his daughter in the course of the day? Do you mean to say, that you, who ought to be a man of sense, believe it possible that this delicate child could take a hale old gentleman by the throat and throttle him to death? It is madness, I say! It is absurd!"

"It is not absurd," answered the prefect, whose mechanical tone never changed throughout the conversation. "There is no other explanation for the facts, and the facts are undeniable. Would you like to see the body?"

"There are a thousand explanations each ten thousand times as reasonable as the one you offer. He was probably murdered by a servant out of spite, or for the sake of robbing him. You are so sure of your idea that I daresay you did not think of searching the room to see whether anything had been taken or not."

"You are under a delusion. Everything has been searched. Moreover, it is quite well known that his deceased Excellency never kept money in the house. There was consequently nothing to take."

"Then it was done out of spite, by a servant, unless some one got in through the window."

"No one could get in through the window. It was done out of anger by this young lady."

"I tell you it was not!" cried Giovanni, growing furious at the man's obstinacy.

"There is reason to believe that it was," returned the prefect, perfectly unmoved.

Giovanni stamped his foot upon the floor angrily and turned away. Faustina had drawn back a little and was leaning upon Corona's arm for support, while the latter spoke words of comfort in her ear, such words as she could find at such a time. A timid murmur of approval arose from the others every time Giovanni spoke, but none of them ventured to say anything distinctly. Giovanni was disgusted with them all and turned to the young girl herself.

"Donna Faustina, will you tell me what you know?"

She had seemed exhausted by the struggle she had already endured, but at Sant' Ilario's question, she straightened herself and came forward again one or two steps. Giovanni thought her eyes very strange, but she spoke collectedly and clearly.

"I can only say what I have said before," she answered. "My father sent for me this afternoon, I should think about three o'clock. He spoke of my marriage, which he has been contemplating some time. I answered that I would not marry Prince Frangipani's son, because—" she hesitated.

"Because?"

"Because I love another man," she continued almost defiantly. "A man who is not a prince but an artist."

A murmur of horror ran round the little group of the girl's relations. She glanced at them scornfully.

"I am not ashamed of it," she said. "But I would not tell you unless it were necessary—to make you understand how angry he was. I forgot—he had called my mother, and she was there. He sent her away. Then he came back and struck me! I put my handkerchief to my mouth because it bled. He snatched it away and threw it on the floor. He took me by the arm—he was standing—I wrenched myself out of his hands and ran away, because I was afraid of him. I did not see him again. Beyond this I know nothing."

Giovanni was struck by the concise way in which Faustina told her story. It was true that she had told it for the second time, but, while believing entirely in her innocence, he saw that her manner might easily have made a bad impression upon the prefect. When she had done, she stood still a moment. Then her hands dropped by her sides and she shrank back again to Corona who put her arm round the girl's waist and supported her.

"I must say that my sister's tale seems clearly true," said the feeble voice of Ascanio Bellegra. His thin, fair beard seemed to tremble as he moved his lips.

"Seems!" cried Corona indignantly. "It is true! How can any one be so mad as to doubt it?"

"I do not deny its truth," said the prefect, speaking in the air. "I only say that the appearances are such as to oblige me to take steps—"

"If you lay a hand on her—" began Giovanni.

"Do not threaten me," interrupted the other calmly. "My men are outside."

Giovanni had advanced towards him with a menacing gesture. Immediately Faustina's sisters-in-law began to whimper and cry with fright, while her brothers made undecided movements as though wishing to part the two angry men, but afraid to come within arm's length of either.

"Giovanni!" exclaimed Corona. "Do not be violent—it is of no use. Hear me," she added, turning towards the prefect, and at the same time making a gesture that seemed to shield Faustina.

"I am at your service, Signora Principessa, but my time is valuable."

"Hear me—I will not detain you long. You are doing a very rash and dangerous thing in trying to arrest Donna Faustina, a thing you may repent of. You are no doubt acting as you believe right, but your heart must tell you that you are wrong. Look at her face. She is a delicate child. Has she the features of a murderess? She is brave against you, because you represent a horrible idea against which her whole nature revolts, but can you believe that she has the courage to do such a deed, the bad heart to will it, or the power to carry it out? Think of what took place. Her father sent for her suddenly. He insisted roughly on a marriage she detests. What woman would not put out her whole strength to resist such tyranny? What woman would submit quietly to be matched with a man she loathes? She said, 'I will not.' She even told her father and mother, together, that she loved another man. Her mother left the room, her mother, the only one from whom she might have expected support. She was alone with her father, and he was angry. Was he an enfeebled invalid, confined to his chair, broken with years, incapable of an effort? Ask his children. We all knew him well. He was not very old, he was tall, erect, even strong for his years. He was angry, beside himself with disappointment. He rises from his chair, he seizes her by the arm, he strikes her in the face with his other hand. You say that he struck her when he was seated. It is impossible—could she not have drawn back, avoiding the blow? Would the blow itself have had such force? No. He was on his feet, a tall, angry man, holding her by one arm. Is it conceivable that she, a frail child, could have had the physical strength to force him back to his seat, to hold him there while she tied that handkerchief round his neck, to resist and suppress his struggles until he was dead? Do you think such a man would die easily? Do you think that to send him out of the world it would be enough to put your fingers to his throat—such little fingers as these?" she held up Faustina's passive hand in her own, before their eyes. "A man does not die in an instant by strangling. He struggles, he strikes desperate blows, he turns to the right and the left, twisting himself with all his might. Could this child have held him? I ask it of your common sense. I ask of your heart whether a creature that God has made so fair, so beautiful, so innocent, could do such terrible work. The woman who could do such things would bear the sign of her badness in her face, and the fear of what she had done in her soul. She would tremble, she would have tried to escape, she would hesitate in her story, she would contradict herself, break down, attempt to shed false tears, act as only a woman who has committed a first great crime could act. And this child stands here, submitted to this fearful ordeal, defended by none, but defending herself with the whole innocence of her nature, the glory of truth in her eyes, the self-conscious courage of a stainless life in her heart. Is this assumed? Is this put on? You have seen murderers—it is your office to see them—did you ever see one like her? Do you not know the outward tokens of guilt when they are before your eyes? You would do a thing that is monstrous in absurdity, monstrous in cruelty, revolting to reason, outrageous to every instinct of human nature. Search, inquire, ask questions, arrest whom you will, but leave this child in peace; this child, with her angel face, her fearless eyes, her guiltless heart!"

Encouraged by Corona's determined manner as well as by the good sense of her arguments, the timid flock of relations expressed their approval audibly. Giovanni looked at his wife in some surprise; for he had never heard her make so long a speech before, and had not suspected her of the ability she displayed. He was proud of her in that moment and moved nearer to her, as though ready to support every word she had uttered. The prefect alone stood unmoved by her eloquence. He was accustomed in his profession to hear far more passionate appeals to his sensibilities, and he was moreover a man who, being obliged generally to act quickly, had acquired the habit of acting upon the first impulse of his intelligence. For a moment his heavy lids were raised a little, either in astonishment or in admiration, but no other feature of his face betrayed that he was touched.

"Signora Principessa," he said in his usual tone, "those are arguments which may be used with propriety by the persons who will defend the accused before the tribunals—"

Giovanni laughed in his face.

"Do you suppose, seriously, that Donna Faustina will ever be brought to trial?" he asked scornfully. The prefect kept his temper wonderfully well.

"It is my business to suppose so," he answered. "I am not the law, nor his Eminence either, and it is not for me to weigh the defence or to listen to appeals for mercy. I act upon my own responsibility, and it is for me to judge whether the facts are likely to support me. My reputation depends upon my judgment and upon nothing else. The fate of the accused depends upon a number of considerations with which I have nothing to do. I must tell you plainly that this interview must come to an end, I am very patient. I wish to overlook nothing. Arguments are of no avail. If there is any better evidence to offer against any one else in this house, I am here to take note of it."

He looked coolly round the circle of listeners. Faustina's relations shrank back a little under his glance.

"Not being able to find any person here who appears more likely to be guilty, and having found enough to justify me in my course, I intend to remove this young lady at once to the Termini."

"You shall not!" said Giovanni, placing himself in front of him in a threatening attitude. "If you attempt anything of the sort, I will have you in prison yourself before morning."

"You do not know what you are saying, Signor Principe. You cannot oppose me. I have an armed force here to obey my orders, and if you attempt forcible opposition I shall be obliged to take you also, very much against my will. Donna Faustina Montevarchi, I have the honour to arrest you. I trust you will make no resistance."

The semi-comic phrase fell from his lips in the professional tone; in speaking of the arrest as an honour to himself, he was making an attempt to be civil according to his lights. He made a step forward in the direction of the young girl, but Giovanni seized him firmly by the wrist. He made no effort to release himself, however, but stood still.

"Signor Principe, be good enough to let go of my hand."

"You shall not touch her," answered Giovanni, not relinquishing his grasp. He was beginning to be dangerous.

"Signor Principe, release me at once!" said the prefect in a commanding tone. "Very well, I will call my men," he added, producing a small silver whistle with his free hand and putting it to his lips. "If I call them, I shall have to send you to prison for hindering me in the execution of my duty," he said, fixing his eyes on Giovanni and preparing to sound the call.

Giovanni's blood was up, and he would not have let the man go. At that moment, however, Faustina broke from Corona's arms and sprang forward. With one hand she pushed back Sant' Ilario; with the other she seized the whistle.

"I will go with you!" she cried, speaking to the prefect. "I will go with him!" she repeated, turning to Giovanni. "It is a horrible mistake, but it is useless to oppose him any longer. I will go, I say!" An hysterical chorus of cries from her relations greeted this announcement.

Giovanni made a last effort to prevent her from fulfilling her intention. He was too much excited to see how hopeless the situation really was, and his sense of justice was revolted at the thought of the indignity.

"Donna Faustina, I implore you!" he exclaimed. "I can still prevent this outrage—you must not go. I will find the cardinal and explain the mistake—he will send an order at once."

"You are mistaken," answered the prefect. "He will do nothing of the kind.

Besides, you cannot leave this house without my permission. The doors are all guarded."

"But you cannot refuse that request," objected Corona, who had not spoken during the altercation. "It will not take half an hour for my husband to see his Eminence and get the order—"

"Nevertheless I refuse," replied the official firmly. "Donna Faustina must go with me at once. You are interfering uselessly and making a useless scandal. My mind is made up."

"Then I will go with her," said Corona, pressing the girl to her side and bestowing a contemptuous glance on the cowering figures around her.

By this time her sisters-in-law had fallen into their respective husband's arms, and it was hard to say whether the men or the women were more hopelessly hysterical. Giovanni relinquished the contest reluctantly, seeing that he was altogether overmatched by the prefect's soldiers.

"I will go too," he said. "You cannot object to our taking Donna Faustina in our carriage."

"I do not object to that. But male visitors are not allowed inside the Termini prison after dark. The Signora Principessa may spend the night there if it is her pleasure. I will put a gendarme in your carriage to avoid informality."

"I presume you will accept my promise to conduct Donna Faustina to the place," observed Giovanni. The prefect hesitated.

"It is informal," he said at last, "but to oblige you I will do it. You give your word?"

"Yes—since you are able to use force. We act under protest. You will remember that."

Faustina's courage did not forsake her at the last moment. She kissed each of her brothers and each of her sisters-in-law as affectionately as though they had offered to bear her company. There were many loud cries and sobs and protestations of devotion, but not one proposed to go with her. The only one who would have been bold enough was Flavia, and even if she had been present she would not have had the heart to perform such an act of unselfishness. Faustina and Corona, Giovanni and the prefect, left the room together.

"I will have you in prison before morning," said Sant'Ilario fiercely, in the ear of the official, as they reached the outer hall.

The prefect made no reply, but raised his shoulders almost imperceptibly and smiled for the first time, as he pointed silently to the gendarmes. The latter formed into an even rank and tramped down the stairs after the four persons whom they accompanied. In a few minutes the whole party were on their way to the Termini, Faustina with her friends in Sant' Ilario's carriage, the prefect in his little brougham, the soldiers on their horses, trotting steadily along in a close squad.

Faustina sat leaning her head upon Corona's shoulder, while Giovanni looked out of the window into the dark streets, his rage boiling within him, and all the hotter because he was powerless to change the course of events. From time to time he uttered savage ejaculations which promised ill for the prefect's future peace, either in this world or in the next, but the sound of the wheels rolling upon the uneven paving-stones prevented his voice from reaching the two women.

"Dear child," said Corona, "do not be frightened. You shall be free tonight or in the morning—I will not leave you."

Faustina was silent, but pressed her friend's hand again and again, as though she understood. She herself was overcome by a strange wonderment which made her almost incapable of appreciating what happened to her. She felt very much as she had felt once before, on the night of the insurrection, when she had found herself lying upon the pavement before the half-ruined barracks, stunned by the explosion, unable for a time to collect her senses, supported only by her physical elasticity, which was yet too young to be destroyed by any moral shock.

CHAPTER XXII

ON the following morning all Rome rang with the news that the Saracinesca had lost their title, and that Faustina Montevarchi had murdered her father. No one connected the two events, but the shock to the public mind was so tremendous that almost any incredible tale would have been believed. The story, as it was generally told, set forth that Faustina had gone mad and had strangled her father in his sleep. Every one agreed in affirming that he had been found dead with her handkerchief tied round his neck. It was further stated that the young girl was no longer in the Palazzo Montevarchi, but had been transferred to the women's prison at the Termini, pending further examination into the details of the case. The Palazzo Montevarchi was draped in black, and before night funeral hatchments were placed upon the front of the parish church bearing the Montevarchi arms. No one was admitted to the palace upon any pretext whatever, though it was said that San Giacinto and Flavia had spent the night there. No member of the family had been seen by any one, and nobody seemed to know exactly whence the various items of information had been derived.

Strange to say, every word of what was repeated so freely was true, excepting that part of the tale which accused Faustina of having done the deed. What had taken place up to the time when Corona and Giovanni had come may be thus briefly told.

Prince Montevarchi had been found dead by the servant who came to bring a lamp to the study, towards evening, when it grew dark. As soon as the alarm was given a scene of indescribable confusion followed, which lasted until the prefect of police arrived, accompanied by a party of police officials. The handkerchief was examined and identified. Thereupon, in accordance with the Roman practice of that day, the prefect had announced his determination of taking Faustina into custody. The law took it for granted that the first piece of circumstantial evidence which presented itself must be acted upon with the utmost promptitude. A few questions had shown immediately that Faustina was the last person who had seen Montevarchi alive. The young girl exhibited a calmness which surprised every one. She admitted that her father had been angry with her and had struck her, but she denied all knowledge of his death. It is sufficient to say that she fearlessly told the truth, so fearlessly as to prejudice even her own family with regard to her. Even the blood on the handkerchief was against her, though she explained that it was her own, and although the bruise on her lip bore out the statement. The prefect was inexorable. He explained that Faustina could be taken privately to the Termini, and that the family might use its influence on the next day to procure her immediate release, but that his duty compelled him for the present to secure her person, that he was responsible, that he was only doing his duty, and so forth and so on.

The consternation of the family may be imagined. The princess broke down completely under what seemed very like a stroke of paralysis. San Giacinto and Flavia were not to be found at their house, and as the carriage had not returned, nobody knew where they were. The wives of Faustina's brothers shut themselves up in their rooms and gave way to hysterical tears, while the brothers themselves seemed helpless to do anything for their sister.

Seeing herself abandoned by every one Faustina had sent for Corona Saracinesca. It was the wisest thing she could have done. In a quarter of an hour Corona and her husband entered the room together. The violent scene which followed has been already described, in which Giovanni promised the prefect of police that if he persisted in his intention of arresting Faustina he should himself be lodged in the Carceri Nuove in twelve hours. But the prefect had got the better of the situation, being accompanied by an armed force which Giovanni was powerless to oppose. All that could be obtained had been that Giovanni and Corona should take Faustina to the Termini in their carriage, and that Corona should stay with the unfortunate young girl all night if she wished to do so. Giovanni could not be admitted.

The prison of the Termini was under the administration of an order of nuns devoted especially to the care of prisoners. The prefect arrived in his own carriage simultaneously with the one which conveyed his prisoner and her friends. As the gate was opened and one of the sisters appeared, he whispered a few words into her ear. She looked grave at first, and then, when she saw Faustina's angel face, she shook her head incredulously. The prefect had accomplished his duty, however. The prison-gates closed after the two ladies, and the sentinel outside resumed his walk, while the carriages drove away, the one containing the officer of the law and the other Giovanni, who had himself driven at once to the Vatican, in spite of the late hour. The great cardinal received him but, to his amazement, refused an order of release.

The sister who admitted Corona and Faustina took the latter's hand kindly and looked into her face by the light of the small lantern she carried.

"It is some dreadful mistake, my child," she said. "But I have no course but to obey. You are Donna Faustina Montevarchi?"

"Yes—this is the Princess Sant' Ilario."

"Will you come with me? I will give you the best room we have—it is not very like a prison."

"This is," said Faustina, shuddering at the sight of the massive stone walls, quite as much as from the dampness of the night air.

"Courage, dear!" whispered Corona, drawing the girl's slight figure close to her and arranging the mantle upon her shoulders. But Corona herself was uneasy as to the result of the ghastly adventure, and she looked anxiously forward into the darkness beyond the nun's lantern.

At last they found themselves in a small whitewashed chamber, so small that it was brightly lighted by the two wicks of a brass oil-lamp on the table. The nun left them alone, at Corona's request, promising to return in the course of an hour. Faustina sat down upon the edge of the little bed, and Corona upon a chair beside her. Until now, the unexpected excitement of what had passed during the last three or four hours had sustained the young girl. Everything that had happened had seemed to be a part of a dream until she found herself at last in the cell of the Termini prison, abandoned by every one save Corona. Her courage broke down. She threw herself back upon the pillow and burst into tears. Corona did not know what to do, but tried to comfort her as well as she could, wondering inwardly what would have happened had the poor child been brought to such a place alone.

"What have I done, that such things should happen to me?" cried Faustina at last, sitting up and staring wildly at her friend. Her small white hands lay helplessly in her lap and her rich brown hair was beginning to be loosened and to fall upon her shoulders.

The tears stood in Corona's eyes. It seemed to her infinitely pathetic that this innocent creature should have been chosen as the victim to expiate so monstrous a crime.

"It will be all cleared up in the morning," she answered, trying to speak cheerfully or at least hopefully. "It is an abominable mistake of the prefect's. I will not leave you, dear—take heart, we will talk—the nun will bring you something to eat—the night will soon pass."

"In prison!" exclaimed Faustina, in a tone of horror and despair, not heeding what Corona said.

"Try and fancy it is not—"

"And my father dead!" She seemed suddenly to realise that he was gone for ever. "Poor papa! Poor papa!" she moaned. "Oh, I did not mean to be undutiful—indeed I did not—and I can never tell you so now—"

"You must not reproach yourself, darling," said Corona, trying to soothe her and to draw the pitiful pale face to her shoulder, while she wound her arm tenderly about the young girl's waist. "Pray for him, Faustina, but do not reproach yourself too much. After all, dear, he was unkind to you—"

"Oh, do not say that—he is dead!" She lowered her voice almost to a whisper as she spoke, and an expression of awe came over her features. "He is dead, Corona. I shall never see him again—oh, why did I not love him more? I am frightened when I think that he is dead—who did it?"

The question came suddenly, and Faustina started and shuddered. Corona pressed her to her side and smoothed her hair gently. She felt that she must say something, but she hardly expected that Faustina would understand reason. She gathered her energy, however, to make the best effort in her power.

"Listen to me, Faustina," she said, in a tone of quiet authority, "and try and see all this as I see it. It is not right that you should reproach yourself, for you have had no share in your father's death, and if you parted in anger it was his fault, not yours. He is dead, and there is nothing for you to do but to pray that he may rest in peace. You have been accused unjustly of a deed which any one might see you were physically incapable of doing. You will be released from this place tomorrow morning, if not during the night. One thing is absolutely necessary—you must be calm and quiet, or you will have brain fever in a few hours. Do not think I am heartless, dear. A worse thing might have happened to you. You have been suspected by an ignorant man who will pay dearly for his mistake; you might have been suspected by those you love."

Corona sighed, and her voice trembled with the last words. To her, Faustina was suffering far more from the shock to her sensibilities than from any real grief. She knew that she had not loved her father, but the horror of his murder and the fright at being held accountable for it were almost enough to drive her mad. And yet she could not be suffering what Corona had suffered in being suspected by Giovanni, she had not that to lose which Corona had lost, the dominating passion of her life had not been suddenly burnt out in the agony of an hour, she was only the victim of a mistake which could have no consequences, which would leave no trace behind. But Faustina shivered and turned paler still at Corona's words.

"By those I love? Ah, no! Not by him—by them!" The blood rushed to her white face, and her hand fell on her friend's shoulder.

Corona heard and knew that the girl was thinking of Anastase. She wondered vaguely whether the hot-headed soldier artist had learned the news and what he would do when he found that Faustina was lodged in a prison.

"And yet—perhaps—oh no! It is impossible!" Her sweet, low voice broke again, and was lost in passionate sobbing.

For a long time Corona could do nothing to calm her. The tears might be a relief to the girl's overwrought faculties, but they were most distressing to hear and see.

"Do you love him very much, dear?" asked Corona, when the paroxysm began to subside.

"I would die for him, and he would die for me," answered Faustina simply, but a happy smile shone through her grief that told plainly how much dearer to her was he who was left than he who was dead.

"Tell me about him," said Corona softly. "He is a friend of mine—"

"Indeed he is! You do not know how he worships you. I think that next to me in the world—but then, of course, he could not love you—besides, you are married."

Corona could not help smiling, and yet there was a sting in the words, of which Faustina could not dream. Why could not Giovanni have taken this child's straight-forward, simple view, which declared such a thing impossible—because Corona was married. What a wealth of innocent belief in goodness was contained in that idea! The princess began to discover a strange fascination in finding out what Faustina felt for this man, whom she, Corona, had been suspected of loving. What could it be like to love such a man? He was good-looking, clever, brave, even interesting, perhaps; but to love him—Corona suddenly felt that interest in the analysis of his character which is roused in us when we are all at once brought into the confidence of some one who can tell by experience what we should have felt with regard to a third person, who has come very near to our lives, if he or she had really become a part of our existence. Faustina's present pain and sense of danger momentarily disappeared as she was drawn into talking of what absorbed her whole nature, and Corona saw that by leading the conversation in that direction she might hope to occupy the girl's thoughts.

Faustina seemed to forget her misfortunes in speaking of Gouache, and Corona listened, and encouraged her to go on. The strong woman who had suffered so much saw gradually unfolded before her a series of pictures, constituting a whole that was new to her. She comprehended for the first time in her life the nature of an innocent girl's love, and there was something in what she learned that softened her and brought the moisture into her dark eyes. She looked at the delicate young creature beside her, seated upon the rough bed, her angelic loveliness standing out against the cold background of the whitewashed wall.

The outline seemed almost vaporous, as though melting into the transparency of the quiet air; the gentle brown eyes were at once full of suffering and full of love; the soft, thick hair fell in disorder upon her shoulders, in that exquisite disorder that belongs to beautiful things in nature when they are set free and fall into the position which is essentially their own; her white fingers, refined and expressive, held Corona's slender olive hand, pressing it and moving as they touched it, with every word she spoke. Corona almost felt that some spiritual, half divine being had glided down from another world to tell her of an angel's love.

The elder woman thought of her own life and compared it with what she saw. Sold to a decrepit old husband who had worshipped her in strange, pathetic fashion of his own, she had spent five years in submitting to an affection she loathed, enduring it to the very end, and sacrificing every instinct of her nature in the performance of her duty. Liberated at last, she had given herself up to her love for Giovanni, in a passion of the strong kind that never comes in early youth. She asked herself what had become of that passion, and whether it could ever be revived. In any case it was something wholly different from the love of which Faustina was speaking. She had fought against it when it came, with all her might; being gone, it had left her cold and indifferent to all she could still command, incapable of even pretending to love. It had passed through her life as a whirlwind through a deep forest, and its track was like a scar. What Faustina knew, she could never have known, the sudden growth within her of something beautiful against which there was no need to struggle, the whole-hearted devotion from the first, the joy of a love that had risen suddenly like the dawn of a fair day, the unspeakable happiness of loving intensely in perfect innocence of the world, of giving her whole soul at once and for ever, unconscious that there could be anything else to give.

"I would die for him, and he would die for me," Faustina had said, knowing that her words were true. Corona would die for Giovanni now, no doubt, but not because she loved him any longer. She would sacrifice herself for what had been, for the memory of it, for the bitterness of having lost it and of feeling that it could not return. That was a state very different from Faustina's; it was pain, not happiness, despair, not joy, emptiness, not fulness. Her eyes grew sad, and she sighed bitterly as though oppressed by a burden from which she could not escape. Faustina's future seemed to her to be like a beautiful vision among the clouds of sunrise, her own like the reflection of a mournful scene in a dark pool of stagnant water. The sorrow of her life rose in her eyes, until the young girl saw it and suddenly ceased speaking. It was like a reproach to her, for her young nature had already begun to forget its trouble in the sweetness of its own dream. Corona understood the sudden silence, and her expression changed, for she felt that if she dwelt upon what was nearest to her heart she could give but poor consolation.

"You are sad," said Faustina. "It is not for me—what is it?"

"No. It is not for you, dear child."

Corona looked at the young girl for a moment and tried to smile. Then she rose from the chair and turned away, pretending to trim the brass oil-lamp with the little metal snuffers that hung from it by a chain. The tears blinded her. She rested her hands upon the table and bent her head. Faustina watched her in surprise, then slipped from her place on the bed and stood beside her, looking up tenderly into the sad dark eyes from which the crystal drops welled up and trickled down, falling upon the rough deal boards.

"What is it, dear?" asked the young girl. "Will you not tell me!"

Corona turned and threw her arms round her, pressing her to her breast, almost passionately. Faustina did not understand what was happening.

"I never saw you cry before!" she exclaimed in innocent astonishment, as she tried to brush away the tears from her friend's face.

"Ah, Faustina! There are worse things in the world than you are suffering, child!"

Then she made a great effort and overcame the emotion that had taken possession of her. She was ashamed to have played such a part when she had come to the place to give comfort to another.

"It is nothing," she said, after a moment's pause. "I think I am nervous—at least, I am very foolish to let myself cry when I ought to be taking care of you."

A long silence followed, which was broken at last by the nun, who entered the room, bringing such poor food as the place afforded. She repeated her assurance that Faustina's arrest was the result of a mistake, and that she would be certainly liberated in the morning. Then, seeing that the two friends appeared to be preoccupied, she bade them good night and went away.

It was the longest night Corona remembered to have ever passed. For a long time they talked a little, and at length Faustina fell asleep, exhausted by all she had suffered, while Corona sat beside her, watching her regular breathing and envying her ability to rest. She herself could not close her eyes, though she could not explain her wakefulness. At last she lay down upon the other bed and tried to forget herself. After many hours she lost consciousness for a time, and then awoke suddenly, half stifled by the sickening smell of the lamp which had gone out, filling the narrow room with the odour of burning oil. It was quite dark, and the profound silence was broken only by the sound of Faustina's evenly-drawn breath. The poor child was too weary to be roused by the fumes that had disturbed Corona's rest. But Corona rose and groped her way to the window, which she opened as noiselessly as she could. Heavy iron bars were built into the wall upon the outside, and she grasped the cold iron with a sense of relief as she looked out at the quiet stars, and tried to distinguish the trees which, as she knew, were planted on the other side of the desolate grass-grown square, along the old wall that stood there, at that time, like a fortification between the Termini and the distant city. Below the window the sentry tramped slowly up and down in his beat, his steps alone breaking the intense stillness of the winter night. Corona realised that she was in a prison. There was something in the discomfort which was not repugnant to her, as she held the grating in her fingers and let the cold air blow upon her face.

After all, she thought, her life would seem much the same in such a place, in a convent, perhaps, where she could be alone all day, all night, for ever. She could not be more unhappy behind those bars than she had often been in the magnificent palaces in which her existence had been chiefly passed. Nothing gave her pleasure, nothing interested her, nothing had the power to distract her mind from the aching misery that beset it. She said to herself a hundred times a day that such apathy was unworthy of her, and she blamed herself when she found that even the loss of the great Saracinesca suit left her indifferent. She did no good to herself and none to any one else, so far as she could see, unless it were good to allow Giovanni to love her, now that she no longer felt a thrill of pleasure at his coming nor at the sound of his voice. At least she had been honest. She could say that, for she had not deceived him. She had forgiven him, but was it her fault if he had destroyed that which he now most desired? Was it her fault that forgiveness did not mean love? Her suffering was not the selfish pain of wounded vanity, for Giovanni's despair would have healed such a wound by showing her the strength of his passion. There was no resentment in her heart, either, for she longed to love him. But even the habit of loving was gone, broken away and forgotten in the sharp agony of an hour. She had done her best to bring it back, she had tried to repeat phrases that had once come from her heart with the conviction of great joy, each time they had been spoken. But the words were dead and meant nothing, or if they had a meaning they told her of the change in herself. She was willing to argue against it, to say again and again that she had no right to be so changed, that there had been enough to make any man suspicious, that she would have despised him had he overlooked such convincing evidence. Could a man love truly and not have some jealousy in his nature? Could a man have such overwhelming proof given him of guilt in the woman he adored and yet show nothing, any more than if she had been a stranger? But the argument was not satisfactory, nor conclusive. If human ills could be healed by the use of logic, there would long since have been no unhappiness left in the world. Is there anything easier than to deceive one's self when one wishes to be deceived? Nothing, surely, provided that the inner reality of ourselves which we call our hearts consents to the deception. But if it will not consent, then there is no help in all the logic that has been lavished upon the philosophy of a dozen ages.

Her slender fingers tightened upon the freezing bars, and once more, in the silent night, her tears flowed down as she looked up at the stars through the prison window. The new condition of her life sought an expression she had hitherto considered as weak and despicable, and against which she struggled even now. There was no relief in weeping, it brought her no sense of rest, no respite from the dull consciousness of her situation; and yet she could not restrain the drops that fell so fast upon her hands. She suffered always, without any intermittence, as people do who have little imagination, with few but strong passions and a constant nature. There are men and women whose active fancy is able to lend a romantic beauty to misfortune, which gives some pleasure even to themselves, or who can obtain some satisfaction, if they are poets, by expressing their pain in grand or tender language. There are others to whom sorrow is but a reality, for which all expression seems inadequate.

Corona was such a woman, too strong to suffer little, too unimaginative to suffer poetically. There are those who might say that she exaggerated the gravity of the position, that, since Giovanni had always been faithful to her, had acknowledged his error and repented of it so sincerely, there was no reason why she should not love him as before. The answer is very simple. The highest kind of love not only implies the highest trust in the person loved, but demands it in return; the two conditions are as necessary to each other as body and soul, so that if one is removed from the other, the whole love dies. Our relations with our fellow-creatures are reciprocal in effect, whatever morality may require in theory, from the commonest intercourse between mere acquaintances to the bond between man and wife. An honest man will always hesitate to believe another unless he himself is believed. Humanity gives little, on the whole, unless it expects a return; still less will men continue to give when their gifts have been denounced to them as false, no matter what apology is offered after the mistake has been discovered. Corona was very human, and being outwardly cold, she was inwardly more sensitive to suspicion than very expansive women can ever be. With women who express very readily what they feel, the expression often assumes such importance as to deceive them into believing their passions to be stronger than they are. Corona had given all, love, devotion, faithfulness, and yet, because appearances had been against her, Giovanni had doubted her. He had cut the plant down at the very root, and she had nothing more to give.

Faustina moved in her sleep. Corona softly closed the window and once more lay down to rest. The hours seemed endless as she listened for the bells. At last the little room grew gray and she could distinguish the furniture in the gloom. Then all at once the door opened, and the nun entered, bearing her little lantern and peering over it to try and see whether the occupants of the chamber were awake. In the shadow behind her Corona could distinguish the figure of a man.

"The prince is here," said the sister in a low voice, as she saw that Corona's eyes were open. The latter glanced at Faustina, whose childlike sleep was not interrupted. She slipped from the bed and went out into the corridor.

The nun would have led the two down to the parlour, but Corona would not go so far from Faustina. At their request she opened an empty cell a few steps farther on, and left Giovanni and his wife alone in the gray dawn. Corona looked eagerly into his eyes for some news concerning the young girl. He took her hand and kissed it.

"My darling—that you should have spent the night in such a place as this!" he exclaimed.

"Never mind me. Is Faustina at liberty? Did you see the cardinal?"

"I saw him." Giovanni shook his head.

"And do you mean to say that he would not give the order at once?"

"Nothing would induce him to give it. The prefect got there before me, and I was kept waiting half an hour while they talked the matter over. The cardinal declared to me that he knew there had been an enmity between Faustina and her father concerning her love for Gouache—"

"Her love for Gouache!" repeated Corona slowly, looking into his eyes. She could not help it. Giovanni turned pale and looked away as he continued.

"Yes, and he said that the evidence was very strong, since no one had been known to enter the house, and the servants were clearly innocent—not one of them betrayed the slightest embarrassment."

"In other words, he believes that Faustina actually did it?"

"It looks like it," said Giovanni in a low voice.

"Giovanni!" she seized his arm. "Do you believe it, too?"

"I will believe whatever you tell me."

"She is as innocent as I!" cried Corona, her eyes blazing with indignation. Giovanni understood more from the words than she meant to convey.

"Will you never forgive?" he asked sadly.

"I did not mean that—I meant Faustina. Giovanni—you must get her away from here. You can, if you will."

"I will do much for you," he answered quietly.

"It is not for me. It is for an unfortunate child who is the victim of a horrible mistake. I have comforted her by promising that she should be free this morning. She will go mad if she is kept here."

"Whatever I do, I do for you, and I will do nothing for any one else. For you or for no one, but I must know that it is really for you."

Corona understood and turned away. It was broad daylight now, as she looked through the grating of the window, watching the people who passed, without seeing them.

"What is Faustina Montevarchi to me, compared with your love?" Giovanni asked.

Something in the tone of his voice made her look at him. She saw the intensity of his feeling in his eyes, and she wondered that he should try to tempt her to love him with, such an insignificant bribe—with the hope of liberating the young girl. She did not understand that he was growing desperate. Had she known what was in his mind she might have made a supreme effort to deceive herself into the belief that he was still to her what he had been so long. But she did not know.

"For the sake of her innocence, Giovanni!" she exclaimed. "Can you let a child like that suffer so? I am sure, if you really would you could manage it, with your influence. Do you not see that I am suffering too, for the girl's sake?"

"Will you say that it is for your sake?"

"For my sake—if you will," she cried almost impatiently.

"For your sake, then," he answered. "Remember that it is for you, Corona."

Before she could answer, he had left the room, without another word, without so much as touching her hand. Corona gazed sadly at the open door, and then returned to Faustina.

An hour later the nun entered the cell, with a bright smile on her face.

"Your carriage is waiting for you—for you both," she said, addressing the princess. "Donna Faustina is free to return to her mother."

CHAPTER XXIII

WHEN Giovanni Saracinesca had visited Cardinal Antonelli on the previous evening, he had been as firmly persuaded that Faustina was innocent, as Corona herself, and was at first very much astonished by the view the great man took of the matter. But as the latter developed the case, the girl's guilt no longer seemed impossible, or even improbable. The total absence of any ostensible incentive to the murder gave Faustina's quarrel with her father a very great importance, which was further heightened by the nature of the evidence. There had been high words, in the course of which the Princess Montevarchi had left the room, leaving her daughter alone with the old man. No one had seen him alive after that moment, and he had been found dead, evidently strangled with her handkerchief. The fact that Faustina had a bruise on her arm and a cut on her lip pointed to the conclusion that a desperate struggle had taken place. The cardinal argued that, although she might not have had the strength to do the deed if the contest had begun when both were on their feet, it was by no means impossible that so old a man might have been overcome by a young and vigorous girl, if she had attacked him when he was in his chair, and was prevented from rising by the table before him. As for the monstrosity of the act, the cardinal merely smiled when Giovanni alluded to it. Had not fathers been murdered by their children before, and in Rome? The argument had additional weight, when Giovanni remembered

Faustina's wild behaviour on the night of the insurrection. A girl who was capable of following a soldier into action, and who had spent hours in searching for him after such an appalling disaster as the explosion of the Serristori barracks, might well be subject to fits of desperate anger, and it was by no means far from likely, if her father had struck her in the face from his place at the table, that she should have laid violent hands upon him, seizing him by the throat and strangling him with her handkerchief. Her coolness afterwards might be only a part of her odd nature, for she was undoubtedly eccentric. She might be mad, said the cardinal, shaking his head, but there was every probability that she was guilty. In those days there was no appeal from the statesman's decisions in such matters. Faustina would remain a prisoner until she could be tried for the crime.

His Eminence was an early riser, and was not altogether surprised that Giovanni should come to him at such an hour, especially as he knew that the Princess Sant' Ilario had spent the night with Faustina in the Termini prison. He was altogether taken aback, however, by Giovanni's manner, and by the communication he made.

"I had the honour of telling your Eminence last night, that Donna Faustina Montevarchi was innocent," began Giovanni, who refused the offer of a seat. "I trusted that she might be liberated immediately, but you have determined otherwise. I am not willing that an innocent person should suffer unjustly. I have come, therefore, to surrender myself to justice in this case."

The cardinal stared, and an expression of unmitigated astonishment appeared upon his delicate olive features, while his nervous hands grasped the arms of his chair.

"You!" he cried.

"I, your Eminence. I will explain myself. Yesterday the courts delivered their verdict, declaring that my cousin San Giacinto is Prince Saracinesca, instead of my father, and transferring to him all our hereditary property. The man who found out that there was a case against us, and caused it to be brought to trial, was Prince Montevarchi. You may perhaps understand my resentment against him. If you recollect the evidence which was detailed to you last night you will see that it was quite possible for me to go to him without being observed. The door chanced to be open, and there was no one in the hall. I am perfectly acquainted with the house. Several hours elapsed between the time when Donna Faustina left her father and the moment when he was found dead in his chair.

You can understand how I could enter the room unseen, how angry words naturally must have arisen between us, and how, losing my self-control, I could have picked up Donna Faustina's handkerchief which, as she says, lay upon the floor, and knotted it effectually round the old man's neck. What could he do in my hands? The study is far from the other rooms the family inhabit, and is near the hall. To go quietly out would not have been a difficult matter for any one who knew the house. Your Eminence knows as well as I the shallowness of circumstantial evidence."

"And do you tell me, calmly, like this, that you murdered a helpless old man out of revenge?" asked the cardinal, half-indignantly, half-incredulously.

"Would I surrender myself as the murderer, for a caprice?" inquired Giovanni, who was very pale.

The cardinal looked at him and was silent for a few moments. He was puzzled by what he heard, and yet his common sense told him that he had no course but to liberate Faustina and send Giovanni to prison. He felt, too, that he ought to experience an instinctive repulsion for the man before him, who, by his own showing, had been guilty of such a horrible crime; but he was conscious of no such sensation. He was a man of exceedingly quick and true intuitions, who judged the persons with whom he had business very accurately. There was a lack of correspondence between his intelligence and his feelings which roused his curiosity.

"You have told me a very strange story," he said.

"Less strange than the one your Eminence has believed since last night," returned Giovanni calmly.

"I do not know. It is more easy for me to believe that the girl was momentarily out of her mind than that you, whom I have known all my life, should have done such a thing. Besides, in telling me your story, you have never once positively asserted that you did it. You have only explained that it would have been possible for a man so disposed to accomplish the murder unsuspected."

"Is a man obliged to incriminate himself directly? It seems to me that in giving myself up I have done all that a man's conscience can possibly require— outside of the confessional. I shall be tried, and my lawyer will do what he can to obtain my acquittal."

"That is poor logic. Whether you confess or not, you have accused yourself in a way that must tell against you very strongly. You really leave me no choice."

"Your Eminence has only to do what I request, to liberate Donna Faustina and to send me to prison."

"You are a very strange man," said the cardinal in a musing tone, as he leaned back in his chair and scrutinised Giovanni's pale, impenetrable face.

"I am a desperate man, that is all."

"Will you give me your word of honour that Faustina Montevarchi is innocent?"

"Yes," answered Giovanni without the slightest hesitation, and meeting the gaze of the cardinal's bright eyes unflinchingly.

The latter paused a moment, and then turned in his chair, and taking a piece of paper wrote a few words upon it. Then he rang a little hand-bell that stood beside him. His servant entered, as he was folding and sealing the note.

"To the Termini prison," he said.

"The messenger had better take my carriage," observed Giovanni. "I shall not need it again."

"Take Prince Sant' Ilario's carriage," added the cardinal, and the man left the room. "And now," he continued, "will you be good enough to tell me what I am to do with you?"

"Send me to the Carceri Nuove, or to any convenient place."

"I will do nothing that can be an injury to you hereafter," answered the statesman. "Something tells me that you have had nothing to do with this dreadful murder. But you must know that though you may deceive me—I am not omniscient—I will not tolerate any contempt of the ways of justice. You have surrendered yourself as the criminal, and I intend to take you at your word."

"I ask for nothing else. Put me where you please, do what you please with me. It matters very little."

"You act like a man who has had an unfortunate love affair," remarked the cardinal. "It is true that you have just lost your fortune, and that may account for it. But I repeat that, whatever your motives may be, you shall not trifle with the law. You wish to be a prisoner. The law will oblige you so far as to comply with your request. I warn you that, after this, you can only obtain your freedom through a proper trial."

"Pray let it be so. My motives can be of no importance. The law shall judge the facts and give its verdict."

"The law will certainly do so. In the meantime, you will spend the day in a room of my apartments, and this evening, when it is dark, you will be quietly transferred to a place of safety—and secrecy. If the real murderer is ever found, I do not wish your life to have been ruined by such a piece of folly as I believe you are committing. You say you are a desperate man, and you are acting, I think, as though you were. Your family affairs may have led to this state, but they do not concern me. You will, however, be good enough to swear, here, solemnly, laying your hand upon this book, that you will not attempt to destroy yourself."

"I swear," said Giovanni, touching the volume which the cardinal presented to him.

"Very good. Now follow me, if you please, to the room where you must spend the day."

Giovanni found himself in a small chamber which contained only a large writing-table and a couple of chairs, and which seemed to have been destined for some sort of office. The cardinal closed the door, and Giovanni heard him turn the key and remove it from the lock. Then, for the first time, he reflected upon what he had done. He had spoken the truth when he had said that he was desperate. No other word could describe his state. A sort of madness had taken possession of him while he was talking with Corona, and he was still under its influence. There had been something in her manner which had seemed to imply that he was not doing his best to liberate Faustina, and indeed, when he remembered that the girl's innocence was by no means clear to him, he ought not to have been surprised at Corona's imputation. And yet, he had now pledged his word to the cardinal that Faustina had not done the deed. Corona's unwillingness to admit that it was for her own sake she asked his help had driven him nearly out of his mind, and when she had at last said it, even reluctantly, he had immediately resolved to show her what he was willing to do for one word of hers when she chose to speak it. He had from that moment but one thought, to free Faustina at any cost, and no plan suggested itself to him but to surrender himself in the girl's place. As a matter of fact, he could not have accomplished his purpose so quickly or surely in any other way, and perhaps he could not have otherwise accomplished it at all. It had been quite clear to him from the first that the cardinal was prejudiced against Faustina, owing, no doubt, to the representations of the prefect of police. Giovanni had carried the evidence against her clearly in his mind, and as soon as he thought of the expedient he saw how it would have been quite possible for himself, or for any other man who knew the house, to commit the murder. As for the detail concerning the doors being open, there was nothing improbable in it, seeing that there were many servants in the establishment, and that each one would suspect and accuse one of his companions of the carelessness. Nothing was easier than to construct the story, and he had supposed that nothing would be simpler than to make the cardinal believe it. He had been surprised to find himself mistaken upon this point, but he felt a thrill of triumph that more than repaid him for what he had done, when he saw the messenger leave the room with the order to liberate Faustina. Corona had spoken, had asked him to do a hard thing for her sake, and her caprice was satisfied, it mattered little at what cost. She had given him an opportunity of showing what he would do for her, and that opportunity had not been thrown away.

But as he sat alone in the little room the cardinal had assigned to him, he began to realise the magnitude of what he had been doing, and to see how his actions would be judged by others. He had surrendered himself as a murderer, and was to be treated as one. When the time came for the trial, might it not happen with him as with many another innocent man who has put himself into a false position? Might he not be condemned? Nothing that he could say hereafter could remove the impression created by his giving himself up to justice. Any denial hereafter would be supposed to proceed from fear and not from innocence. And if he were condemned, what would become of Corona, of his father, of little Orsino? He shuddered at the thought.

What, he asked himself, would be the defence? Yesterday afternoon he had been out of the house during several hours, and had walked alone, he hardly remembered where. Since the crisis in his life which had separated him from Corona in fact, if not in appearance, he often walked alone, wandering aimlessly through the streets. Would any of his acquaintance come forward and swear to having seen him at the time Montevarchi was murdered? Probably not. And if not, how could it be proved, in the face of his own statement to the cardinal, that he might not have gone to the palace, seeking an opportunity of expending his wrath on the old prince, that he might not have lost his self-control in a fit of anger and strangled the old man as he sat in his chair? As he himself had said, there was far more reason to believe that the Saracinesca had killed Montevarchi out of revenge, than that a girl like Faustina should have strangled her own father because he had interfered in her love affairs. If the judges took this view of the case, it was clear that Giovanni would have little chance of an acquittal. The thing looked so possible that even Corona might believe it—even Corona, for whose sake he had rushed madly into such desperate danger.

And today she would not see him; very possibly she would not know where he was. And tomorrow? And the next day? And all the days after that? He supposed that he would be allowed to write to her, perhaps to see her, but it would be hard to explain his position. She did not love him any longer, and she would not understand. He wondered how much she would care, if she really cared at all, beyond a discreet anxiety for his safety. She would certainly not comprehend a love like his, which had chosen such a sacrifice, rather than allow her wish to remain ungratified. How could she, since she did not love him? And yet, it was imperatively necessary that she should be informed of what had happened. She might otherwise suppose, naturally enough, that some accident had befallen him, and she would in that case apply to the police, perhaps to the cardinal himself, to find out where he was. Such a contingency must be prevented, by some means, before night. Until then, she would not be frightened by his absence. There would be time, perhaps, when he was removed to the prison—to the place of safety and secrecy, of which the cardinal had spoken, and which in all probability was the Holy Office. No questions were asked there.

There were writing materials on the broad table, and Giovanni began a letter to his wife. After a few minutes, however, he stopped, for he saw from what he had written that he was in no condition to attempt such a task. The words came quickly and fluently, but they expressed what he had no intention of telling Corona again. His love for her was still uppermost in his mind, and instead of trying to explain what had occurred, he found himself setting down phrases that told of nothing but a mad passion. The thought of her cold face when she should read the lines arrested his hand, and he threw down the pen impatiently, and returned to his meditations for a while. What he wanted to do was to tell her in the fewest possible words that he was alive and well. What else should he tell her? The statement would allay any anxiety she might feel, and his absence would doubtless be a relief to her. The thought was bitter, but he knew that nothing exasperates a woman like the constant presence of a man she has loved, who loves her more than ever, and for whom she no longer feels anything. At last he took another sheet of paper and tried again.

Dear Corona—when you get this, Faustina will be at liberty, according to your wish. Do not be anxious if you do not see me for a few days, as I am called away on urgent business. Tell my father, and any of our friends who ask about me, that I am at Saracinesca, superintending the removal of such effects as are not to go to San Giacinto. I will let you know when I am coming back—Your affectionate GIOVANNI

He read the note over twice, and then folded it, addressing it to his wife. His face expressed the most profound dejection when he had finished his task, and for a long time he leaned back in his chair, gazing at the morning sunlight that slowly crept across the floor, while his hands lay folded passively upon the table. The end of his love seemed very bitter as he thought of the words he had written. A few weeks ago to leave Corona thus unexpectedly would have caused her the greatest pain. Now, he felt that he need say nothing, that it would be useless to say anything, more than he had said. It was nothing to her, whether he stayed in Rome or went to the ends of the earth; indeed, he suspected that she would be glad to be left alone—unless she should discover why he had gone, and whither. This last consideration recalled to him his situation, and for a moment he was horrified at his own rashness. But the thought did not hold him long, and presently he asked himself apathetically what it could matter in the end. The hours passed slowly, and still he sat motionless by the table, the folded letter lying before him.

The cardinal had scarcely returned to his study when a second card was brought to him. The gentleman, said the servant, had assured him that his Eminence would receive him, as he had important information to give concerning the murder of Prince Montevarchi. The cardinal could not repress a smile as he read the name of Anastase Gouache.

The young man entered the room, and advanced in obedience to the cardinal's friendly gesture. He was as pale as death, and his soft dark eyes had an expression of despair in them such as the great man had rarely seen. For the rest, he wore his uniform, and was as carefully dressed as usual.

"Your Eminence has doubtless heard of this dreadful murder?" began Gouache, forgetting all formality in the extremity of his excitement.

"Yes," said the cardinal, sitting down. "You have something to communicate concerning it, I understand."

"Donna Faustina Montevarchi has been charged with the crime, and is in the prison of the Termini," answered the Zouave, speaking hurriedly. "I am here to ask your Eminence to order her release without delay—"

"On what grounds?" inquired the statesman, raising his eyebrows a little as though surprised by the way in which the request was made.

"Because she is innocent, because her arrest was due to the mistake of the prefect of police—the evidence was against her, but it was absurd to suppose that she could have done it—"

"The prefect of police received my approval. Have you any means of showing that she is innocent?"

"Showing it?" repeated Gouache, who looked dazed for a moment, but recovered himself immediately, turning white to the lips. "What could be easier?" he exclaimed. "The murderer is before you—I saw the prince, I asked him for his daughter's hand in marriage, he insulted me. I left the room, but I returned soon afterwards. I found him alone, and I killed him—I do not know how I did it—"

"With Donna Faustina's handkerchief," suggested the cardinal. "Perhaps you do not remember that it was lying on the floor and that you picked it up and knotted it—"

"Yes, yes! Round his neck," cried Gouache nervously. "I remember. But I saw red, everything swam, the details are gone. Here I am—your Eminence's prisoner—I implore you to send the order at once!"

The cardinal had hitherto maintained a grave expression. His features suddenly relaxed and he put out his hand.

"My dear Monsieur Gouache, I like you exceedingly," he said. "You are a man of heart."

"I do not understand—" Anastase was very much bewildered, but he saw that his plan for freeing Faustina was on the point of failure.

"I appreciate your motives," continued the statesman. "You love the young lady to distraction, she is arrested on a capital charge, you conceive the idea of presenting yourself as the murderer in her place—"

"But I assure your Eminence, I swear—"

"No," interrupted the other, raising his hand. "Do not swear. You are incapable of such a crime. Besides, Donna Faustina is already at liberty, and the author of the deed has already confessed his guilt."

Anastase staggered against the projecting shelf of the bookcase. The blood rushed to his face and for a moment he was almost unconscious of where he was. The cardinal's voice recalled him to himself.

"If you doubt what I tell you, you need only go to the Palazzo Montevarchi and inquire. Donna Faustina will return with the Princess Sant' Ilario. I am sorry that circumstances prevent me from showing you the man who has confessed the crime. He is in my apartments at the present moment, separated from us only by two or three rooms."

"His name, Eminence?" asked Gouache, whose whole nature seemed to have changed in a moment.

"Ah, his name must for the present remain a secret in my keeping, unless, indeed, you have reason to believe that some one else did the murder. Have you no suspicions? You know the family intimately, it seems. You would probably have heard the matter mentioned, if the deceased prince had been concerned in any quarrel—in any transaction which might have made him an object of hatred to any one we know. Do you recall anything of the kind? Sit down, Monsieur Gouache. You are acquitted, you see. Instead of being a murderer you are the good friend who once painted my portrait in this very room. Do you remember our charming conversations about Christianity and the universal republic?"

"I shall always remember your Eminence's kindness," answered Gouache, seating himself and trying to speak as quietly as possible. His nervous nature was very much unsettled by what had occurred. He had come determined that Faustina should be liberated at any cost, overcome by the horror of her situation, ready to lay down his life for her in the sincerity of his devotion. His conduct had been much more rational than Giovanni's. He had nothing to lose but himself, no relations to be disgraced by his condemnation, none to suffer by his loss. He had only to sacrifice himself to set free for ever the woman he loved, and he had not hesitated a moment in the accomplishment of his purpose. But the revulsion of feeling, when he discovered that Faustina was already known to be innocent, and that there was no need for his intervention, was almost more than he could bear. The tears of joy stood in his eyes while he tried to be calm.

"Have you any suspicions?" asked the cardinal again, in his gentle voice.

"None, Eminence. The only thing approaching to a quarrel, of which I have heard, is the suit about the title of the Saracinesca. But of course that can have nothing to do with the matter. It was decided yesterday without opposition."

"It could have nothing to do with the murder, you think?" inquired the statesman with an air of interest.

"No. How could it?" Gouache laughed at the idea. "The Saracinesca could not murder their enemies as they used to do five hundred years ago. Besides, your Eminence has got the murderer and must be able to guess better than I what were the incentives to the crime."

"That does not follow, my friend. A man who confesses a misdeed is not bound to incriminate any one else, and a man whose conscience is sensitive enough to make him surrender himself naturally assumes the blame. He suffers remorse, and does not attempt any defence, excepting such as you yourself just now gave me, when you said that the prince had insulted you. Enough to give a semblance of truth to the story. By the bye, is that true?"

"It is and it is not," answered Gouache, blushing a little. "The poor man, when I began to explain my position, thought—how shall I say? He thought I wanted to sell him a picture. It was not his fault."

"Poor man!" sighed the cardinal. "He had not much tact. And so, Monsieur Gouache, you think that the great Saracinesca suit has had nothing to do with the murder?"

"It seems to me impossible. It looks rather as though he had been murdered by a servant, out of spite. It is hard to believe that any one not belonging to the house could have done it."

"I think the public will agree with you. I will occupy myself with the matter. Perhaps I have got the man safe in that room, but who knows? If you had come first, you might have gone to the Carceri Nuove instead of him. After all, he may be in love too."

The cardinal smiled, but Gouache started at the suggestion, as though it hurt him.

"I doubt that," he said quickly.

"So do I. It would be a strange coincidence, if two innocent men had accused themselves of the same crime, out of love, within twenty-four hours of its being committed. But now that you are calm—yes, you were beside yourself with excitement—I must tell you that you have done a very rash thing indeed. If I had not chanced to be a friend of yours, what would have become of you? I cannot help liking your courage and devotion—you have shown it in sterner matters, and in the face of the enemy—but you might have destroyed yourself. That would have been a great sin."

"Is there no case in which a man may destroy himself deliberately?"

"You speak of suicide? It was almost that you contemplated. No. The church teaches that a man who takes his own life goes straight to hell. So does Moham-med, for that matter."

"In any case?"

"In any case. It is a mortal sin."

"But," objected Gouache, "let us suppose me a very bad man, exercising a destroying influence on many other people. Suppose, in short, for the sake of argument, that my life caused others to lose their own souls, and that by killing myself I knew that they would all become good again. Suppose then, that I sud-denly repented and that there was no way of saving these people but by my own suicide. Would it not be more honourable in me to say, 'Very well, I will submit to damnation rather than send all those others to eternal flames?' Should I not be justified in blowing out my brains?"

The cardinal did not know whether to smile or to look grave. He was neither a priest nor a theologian, but a statesman.

"My dear friend," he answered at last. "The ingenuity of your suppositions passes belief. I can only say that, when you find yourself in such a bad case as you describe, I will submit the matter for you to the Holy Father himself. But I would strongly advise you to avoid the situation if you possibly can."

Gouache took his leave with a light heart, little guessing as he descended the great marble staircase that Giovanni Saracinesca was the prisoner of whom the cardinal had spoken so mysteriously, still less that he, too, had falsely accused himself of having killed poor old Montevarchi. He wondered, as he walked rapidly along the streets in the bright morning sunshine, who the man was, and why he had done such a thing, but his thoughts were really with Faustina, and he longed to see her and to hear from her own lips the true version of what had happened.

CHAPTER XXIV

ARNOLDO Meschini was fully conscious of what he had done when he softly closed the door of the study behind him and returned to the library; but although he knew and realised that he had murdered his employer, he could not explain the act to himself. His temples throbbed painfully and there was a bright red spot in each of his sallow cheeks. He shuffled about from one bookcase to another, and his hands trembled violently as he touched the big volumes. Now and then he glanced towards one or the other of the doors expecting at every moment that some one would enter to tell him the news, if indeed any one at such a time should chance to remember the existence of the humble librarian. His brain was on fire and seemed to burn the sockets of his eyes. And yet the time passed, and no one came. The suspense grew to be unbearable, and he felt that he would do anything to escape from it. He went to the door and laid his hand upon the latch.

For an instant the flush disappeared from his cheeks, as a great fear took possession of him. He was not able to face the sight of Montevarchi's body lying across that table in the silent study. His hand fell to his side and he almost ran to the other side of the library; then, as though ashamed of his weakness he came back slowly and listened at the door. It was scarcely possible that any distant echo could reach his ears, if the household had been already roused, for the passage was long and tortuous, interrupted by other doors and by a winding staircase. But in his present state he fancied that his senses must be preternaturally sharpened and he listened eagerly. All was still. He went back to the books.

There was nothing to be done but to make a desperate effort to occupy himself and to steady his nerves. If any one came now, he thought, his face would betray him. There must be a light in his eyes, an uncertainty in his manner which would speak plainly enough to his guilt. He tried to imagine what would take place when the body was found. Some one would enter the room and would see the body. He, or she, would perhaps think that the prince was in a fit, or asleep—who could tell? But he would not answer the voice that called him. Then the person would come forward and touch him—Meschini forced himself to think of it—would touch the dead hand and would feel that it was cold. With a cry of horror the person would hasten from the room. He might hear that cry, if he left the door open. Again he laid his hand upon the latch. His fingers seemed paralysed and the cold sweat stood on his face, but he succeeded in mastering himself enough to turn the handle and look out. The cry came, but it was from his own lips. He reeled back from the entrance in horror, his eyes starting from his head. There stood the dead man, in the dusky passage, shaking at him the handkerchief.

It was only his fancy. He passed his hand across his forehead and a sickly look of relief crept over his face. He had been frightened by his own coat, that hung on a peg outside, long and thin and limp, a white handkerchief depending from the wide pocket. There was not much light in the corridor. He crept cautiously out and took the garment from its place with a nervous, frightened gesture. Dragging it after him, he hastily re-entered the library and rolled up the coat into a shape that could not possibly resemble anything which might frighten him. He laid it upon the table in the brightest place, where the afternoon sun fell upon it. There was a sort of relief in making sure that the thing could not again look like the dead man. He looked up and saw with renewed terror that he had left the door open. There was nothing but air between him and the place where that awful shadow had been conjured up by his imagination. The door must be shut. If it remained open he should go mad. He tried to think calmly, but it was beyond his power. He attempted to say that there was nothing there and that the door might as well remain open as be shut. But even while making the effort to reason with himself, he was creeping cautiously along the wall, in the direction of the entrance. By keeping his eyes close to the wooden panelling he could advance without seeing into the corridor. He was within a foot of the opening. Convulsed with fear, he put out his hand quickly and tried to pull the heavy oak on its hinges by the projecting bevel, but it was too heavy—he must look out in order to grasp the handle. The cold drops trickled down from his brow and he breathed hard, but he could not go back and leave the door unclosed. With a suppressed sob of agony he thrust out his head and arm. In a moment it was over, but the moral effort had been terrible, and his strength failed him, so that he staggered against the wainscot and would have fallen but for its support.

Some moments elapsed before he could get to a chair, and when he at last sat down in a ray of sunshine to rest, his eyes remained fixed upon the sculptured brass handle of the latch. He almost expected that it would turn mysteriously of itself and that the dead prince would enter the room. He realised that in his present condition he could not possibly face the person who before long would certainly bring him the news. He must have something to stimulate him and deaden his nerves. He had no idea how long a time had elapsed since he had done the deed, but it seemed that three or four hours must certainly have passed. In reality it was scarcely five and twenty minutes since he had left the study. He remembered suddenly that he had some spirits in his room at the top of the palace. Slowly and painfully he rose to his feet and went towards the other exit from the library, which, as in many ancient houses, opened upon the grand staircase, so as to give free access to visitors from without. He had to cross the broad marble landing, whence a masked door led to the narrow winding steps by which he ascended to the upper story. He listened to hear whether any one was passing, and then went out. Once on his way he moved more quickly than seemed possible for a man so bent and mis-shapen.

The bright afternoon sun streamed in through the window of his little chamber, a relief from the sombre gloominess of the lofty library, where the straggling rays seemed to make the great hall more shadowy by contrast. But Meschini did not stop to look about him. In a closet in the wall he kept his stores, his chemicals, his carefully-composed inks, his bits of prepared parchment, and, together with many other articles belonging to his illicit business, he had a bottle of old brandy, which the butler had once given him out of the prince's cellar, in return for a bit of legal advice which had saved the servant a lawyer's fee. Arnoldo Meschini had always been a sober man, like most Italians, and the bottle had stood for years unopened in the cupboard. He had never thought of it, but, having been once placed there, it had been safe. The moment had come when the stimulant was precious. His fingers shook as he put the bottle to his lips; when he set it down they were steady. The liquor acted like an enchantment, and the sallow-faced man smiled as he sat alone by his little table and looked at the thing that had restored him. The bottle had been full when he began to drink; the level of the liquid was now a good hand's breadth below the neck. The quantity he had swallowed would have made a temperate man, in his normal state, almost half drunk.

He sat still for a long time, waiting to see whether the draught would produce any other effect. He felt a pleasant warmth in his face and hands, the perspiration had disappeared from his brow, and he was conscious that he could now look out of the open door of the library without fear, even if his coat were hanging on the peg. It was incredible to him that he should have been so really terrified by a mere shadow. He had killed Prince Montevarchi, and the body was lying in the study. Yes, he could think of it without shuddering, almost without an unpleasant sensation. In the dead man's own words, it had been an act of divine justice and retribution, and since nobody could possibly discover the murderer, there was matter for satisfaction in the idea that the wicked old man no longer cumbered the earth with his presence. Strange, that he should have suffered such an agony of fear half an hour earlier. Was it half an hour? How pleasantly the sun shone in to the little room where he had laboured during so many years, and so profitably! Now that the prince was dead it would be amusing to look at those original documents for which he had made such skilfully-constructed substitutes. He would like to assure himself, however, that the deed had been well done. There was magic in that old liquor. Another little draught and he would go down to the study as though nothing had happened. If he should meet anybody his easy manner would disarm suspicion. Besides, he could take the bottle with him in the pocket of his long coat—the bottle of courage, he said to himself with a smile, as he set it to his lips. This time he drank but little, and very slowly. He was too cautious a man to throw away his ammunition uselessly.

With a light heart he descended the winding stair and crossed the landing. One of Ascanio Bellegra's servants passed at that moment. Meschini looked at the fellow quietly, and even gave him a friendly smile, to test his own coolness, a civility which was acknowledged by a familiar nod. The librarian's spirits rose. He did not resent the familiarity of the footman, for, with all his learning, he was little more than a servant himself, and the accident had come conveniently as a trial of his strength. The man evidently saw nothing unusual in his appearance. Moreover, as he walked, the brandy bottle in his coat tail pocket beat reassuringly against the calves of his legs. He opened the door of the library and found himself in the scene of his terror.

There lay the old coat, wrapped together on the table, as he had left it. The sun had moved a little farther during his absence, and the heap of cloth looked innocent enough. Meschini could not understand how it had frightened him so terribly. He still felt that pleasant warmth about his face and hands. That was the door before which he had been such a coward. What was beyond it? The empty passage. He would go and hang the coat where it had hung always, where he always left it when he came in the morning, unless he needed it to keep himself warm. What could be simpler, or easier? He took the thing in one hand, turned the handle and looked out. He was not afraid. The long, silent corridor stretched away into the distance, lighted at intervals by narrow windows that opened upon an inner court of the palace. Meschini suspended the coat upon the peg and stood looking before him, a contemptuous smile upon his face, as though he despised himself for his former fears. Then he resolutely walked towards the study, along the familiar way, down a flight of steps, then to the right—he stood before the door and the dead man was on the other side of it. He paused and listened. All was silent.

It was clear to him, as he stood before the table and looked at the body, that no one had been there. Indeed, Meschini now remembered that it was a rule in the house never to disturb the prince unless a visitor came. He had always liked to spend the afternoon in solitude over his accounts and his plans. The librarian, paused opposite his victim and gazed at the fallen head and the twisted, whitened fingers. He put out his hand timidly and touched them, and was surprised to find that they were not quite cold. The touch, however, sent a very unpleasant thrill through his own frame, and he drew back quickly with a slight shiver. But he was not terrified as he had been before. The touch, only, was disagreeable to him. He took a book that lay at hand and pushed it against the dead man's arm. There was no sign, no movement. He would have liked to go behind the chair and untie the handkerchief, but his courage was not quite equal to that. Besides, the handker-chief was Faustina's. He had seen her father snatch it from her and throw it upon the floor, as he watched the pair through the keyhole. A strange fascination kept him in the study, and he would have yielded to it had he not been fortified against any such morbid folly by the brandy he had swallowed. He thought, as he turned to go, that it was a pity the prince never kept money in the house, for, in that case, he might have helped himself before leaving. To steal a small value was not worth while, considering the danger of discovery.

He moved on tiptoe, as though afraid of disturbing the rest of his old employer, and once or twice he looked back. Then at last he closed the door and retraced his steps through the corridor till he gained the library. He was surprised at his own boldness as he went, and at the indifference with which he passed by the coat that hung, limp as ever, upon its peg. He was satisfied, too, with the result of his investigations. The prince was certainly dead. As a direct consequence of his death, the secret of the Saracinesca suit was now his own, no one had a share in it, and it was worth money. He pulled out a number of volumes from the shelves and began to make a pretence of working upon the catalogue. But though he surrounded himself with the implements and necessaries for his task, his mind was busy with the new scheme that unfolded itself to his imagination.

He and he alone, knew that San Giacinto's possession of the Saracinesca inheritance rested upon a forgery. The fact that this forgery must be revealed, in order to reinstate the lawful possessors in their right, did not detract in the least from the value of the secret. Two courses were open to him. He might go to old Leone Saracinesca and offer the original documents for sale, on receiving a guarantee for his own safety. Or he might offer them to San Giacinto, who was the person endangered by their existence. Montevarchi had promised him twenty thousand scudi for the job, and had never paid the money. He had cancelled his debt with his life, however, and had left the secret behind him. Either Saracinesca or San Giacinto would give five times twenty thousand, ten times as much, perhaps, for the original documents, the one in order to recover what was his own, the other to keep what did not belong to him. The great question to be considered was the way of making the offer. Meschini sat staring at the opposite row of books, engaged in solving the problem. Just then, one of the open volumes before him slipped a little upon another and the page turned slowly over. The librarian started slightly and glanced at the old-fashioned type. The work was a rare one, which he had often examined, and he knew it to be of great value. A new thought struck him. Why should he not sell this and many other volumes out of the collection, as well as realise money by disposing of his secret? He might as well be rich as possess a mere competence.

He looked about him. With a little care and ingenuity, by working at night and by visiting the sellers of old books during the day he might soon put together four or five hundred works which would fetch a high price, and replace them by so many feet of old trash which would look as well. With his enormous industry it would be a simple matter to tamper with the catalogue and to insert new pages which should correspond with the changes he contemplated. The old prince was dead, and little as he had really known about the library, his sons knew even less. Meschini could remove the stolen volumes to a safe place, and when he had realised the value of his secret, he would go to Paris, to Berlin, even to London, and dispose of his treasures one by one. He was amazed at the delights the future unfolded to him, everything seemed gilded, everything seemed ready to turn into gold. His brain dwelt with an enthusiasm wholly new to him upon the dreams it conjured up. He felt twenty years younger. His fears had gone, and with them his humility. He saw himself no longer the poor librarian in his slippers and shabby clothes, cringing to his employer, spending his days in studying the forgeries he afterwards executed during the night, hoarding his ill-gotten gains with jealous secrecy, afraid to show to his few associates that he had accumulated a little wealth, timid by force of long habit and by the remembrance of the shame in his early life. All that had disappeared under the potent spell of his new-found courage. He fancied himself living in some distant capital, rich and respected, married, perhaps, having servants of his own, astonishing the learned men of some great centre by the extent of his knowledge and erudition. All the vanity of his nature was roused from its long sleep by a new set of emotions, till he could scarcely contain his inexplicable happiness. And how had all this come to him so suddenly in the midst of his obscure life? Simply by squeezing the breath out of an old man's throat. How easy it had been.

The unaccustomed energy which had been awakened in him by the spirits brought with it a pleasant restlessness. He felt that he must go again to his little room upstairs, and take out the deeds and read them over. The sight of them would give an increased reality and vividness to his anticipations. Besides, too, it was just barely possible that there might be some word, some expression which he could change, and which should increase their value. To sit still, poring over the catalogue in the library was impossible. Once more he climbed to his attic, but he could not comprehend why he felt a nervous desire to look behind him, as though he were followed by some person whose tread was noiseless. It was not possible, he thought, that the effects of his draught were already passing off. Such courage as he felt in him could not leave him suddenly. He reached his room and took the deeds from the secret place in which he had hidden them, spreading them out lovingly before him. As he sat down the bottle in his long coat touched the floor behind him with a short, dull thud. It was as though a footstep had sounded in the silent room, and he sprang to his feet before he realised whence the noise came, looking behind him with startled eyes. In a moment he understood, and withdrawing the bottle from his pocket he set it beside him on the table. He looked at it for a few seconds as though in hesitation, but he determined not to have recourse to its contents so soon. He had undoubtedly been frightened again, but the sound that had scared him had been real and not imaginary. Besides, he had but this one bottle and he knew that good brandy was dear. He pushed it away, his avarice helping him to resist the temptation.

The old documents were agreeably familiar to his eye, and he read and re-read them with increasing satisfaction, comparing them carefully, and chuckling to himself each time that he reached the bottom of the sheet upon the copy, where there had been no room to introduce that famous clause. But for that accident, he reflected, he would have undoubtedly made the insertion upon the originals, and the latter would be now no longer in his possession. He did not quite under-stand why he derived such pleasure from reading the writing so often, nor why, when the surrounding objects in the room were clear and distinct to his eyes, the crabbed characters should every now and then seem to move of themselves and to run into each other from right to left. Possibly the emotions of the day had strained his vision. He looked up and saw the bottle. An irresistible desire seized him to taste the liquor again, even if he drank but a drop. The spirits wet his lips while he was still inwardly debating whether it were wise to drink or not. As he returned the cork to its place he felt a sudden revival within him of all he had experienced before. His face was warm, his fingers tingled. He took up one of the deeds with a firm hand and settled himself comfortably in his chair. But he could not read it through again. He laughed quietly at his folly. Did he not know every word by heart? He must occupy himself with planning, with arranging the details of his future. When that was done he could revel in the thought of wealth and rest and satisfied vanity.

To his surprise, his thoughts did not flow as connectedly as he had expected. He could not help thinking of the dead man downstairs, not indeed with any terror, not fearing discovery for himself, but with a vague wonderment that made his mind feel empty. Turn over the matter as he would, he could not foresee connectedly what was likely to happen when the murder was known. There was no sequence in his imaginings, and he longed nervously for the moment when everything should be settled. The restlessness that had brought him up to his room demanded some sort of action to quiet it. He would willingly have gone out to see his friend, the little apothecary who lived near the Ponte Quattro Capi. It would be a relief to talk to some one, to hear the sound of a human voice. But a remnant of prudence restrained him. It was not very likely that he should be suspected; indeed, if he behaved prudently nothing was more improbable. To leave the house at such a time, however, would be the height of folly, unless it could be proved that he had gone out some time before the deed could have been done. The porter was vigilant, and Meschini almost always exchanged a few words with him as he passed through the gates. He would certainly note the time of the librarian's exit more or less accurately. Moreover, the body might have been found already, and even now the gendarmes might be downstairs. The latter consideration determined him to descend once more to the library. A slight chill passed over him as he closed the door of his room behind him.

The great hall now seemed very gloomy and cold, and the solitude was oppressive. He felt the necessity for movement, and began to walk quickly up and down the length of the library between the broad tables, from one door to the other. At first, as he reached the one that separated him from the passage he experienced no disagreeable sensation, but turned his back upon it at the end of his walk and retraced his steps. Very gradually, however, he began to feel uncomfortable as he reached that extremity of the room, and the vision of the dead prince rose before his eyes. The coat was there again, on the other side of the door. No doubt it would take the same shape again if he looked at it. His varying courage was just at the point when he was able to look out in order to assure himself that the limp garment had not assumed the appearance of a ghost. He felt a painful thrill in his back as he turned the handle, and the cold air that rushed in as he opened the door seemed to come from a tomb. Although his eyes were satisfied when he had seen the coat in the corner, he drew back quickly, and the thrill was repeated with greater distinctness as he heard the bolt of the latch slip into its socket. He walked away again, but the next time he came back he turned at some distance from the threshold, and, as he turned, he felt the thrill a third time, almost like an electric shock. He could not bear it and sat down before the catalogue. His eyes refused to read, and after a lengthened struggle between his fears, his prudence and his economy, he once more drew the bottle from his pocket and fortified himself with a draught. This time he drank more, and the effect was different. For some seconds he felt no change in his condition. Presently, however, his nervousness disappeared, giving place now to a sort of stupid indifference. The light was fading from the clerestory windows of the library, and, within, the corners and recesses were already dark. But Meschini was past imagining ghosts or apparitions. He sat quite still, his chin leaning on his hand and his elbow on the table, wondering vaguely how long it would be before they came to tell him that the prince was dead. He did not sleep, but he fell into a state of torpor which was restful to his nerves. Sleep would certainly come in half an hour if he were left to himself as long as that. His breathing was heavy, and the silence around him was intense. At last the much-dreaded moment came, and found him dull and apathetic.

The door opened and a ray of light from a candle entered the room, which was now almost dark. A footman and a housemaid thrust in their heads cautiously and peered into the broad gloom, holding the candle high before them. Either would have been afraid to come alone.

"Sor Arnoldo, Sor Arnoldo!" the man called out timidly, as though frightened by the sound of his own voice.

"Here I am," answered Meschini, affecting a cheerful tone as well as he could. Once more and very quickly he took a mouthful from the bottle, behind the table where they could not see him. "What is the matter?" he asked.

"The prince is murdered!" cried the two servants in a breath. They were very pale as they came towards him.

If the cry he uttered was forced they were too much terrified to notice it. As they told their tale with every species of exaggeration, interspersed with expressions of horror and amazement, he struck his hands to his head, moaned, cried aloud, and, being half hysterical with drink, shed real tears in their presence. Then they led him away, saying that the prefect of police was in the study and that all the household had been summoned to be examined by him. He was now launched in his part, and could play it to the end without breaking down. He had afterwards very little recollection of what had occurred. He remembered that the stillness of the study and the white faces of those present had impressed him by contrast with the noisy grief of the servants who had summoned him. He remembered that he had sworn, and others had corroborated his oath, to the effect that he had spent the afternoon between the library and his room. Ascanio Bellegra's footman remembered meeting him on the landing, and said that he had smiled pleasantly in an unconcerned way, as usual, and had passed on. For the rest, no one seemed even to imagine that he could have done the deed, for no one had ever heard anything but friendly words between him and the prince. He remembered, too, having seen the dead body extended upon the great table of the study, and he recalled Donna Faustina's tone of voice indistinctly as in a dream. Then, before the prefect announced his decision, he was dismissed with the other servants.

After that moment all was a blank in his mind. In reality he returned to his room and sat down by his table with a candle before him. He never knew that after the examination he had begged another bottle of liquor of the butler on the ground that his nerves were upset by the terrible event. About midnight the candle burned down into the socket. Profiting by the last ray of light he drank a final draught and reeled to his bed, dressed as he was. One bottle was empty, and a third of the second was gone. Arnoldo Meschini was dead drunk.

CHAPTER XXV

CORONA was not much surprised when the messenger brought her carriage and presented the order for Faustina's liberation. When Giovanni had left her she had felt that he would find means to procure the young girl's liberty, and the only thing which seemed strange to her was the fact that Giovanni did not return himself. The messenger said he had seen him with the cardinal and that Sant' Ilario had given the order to use the carriage. Beyond that, he knew nothing. Corona at once took Faustina to the Palazzo Montevarchi, and then, with a promise to come back in the course of the day, she went home to rest.

She needed repose even more than Faustina, who, after all, had slept soundly on her prison bed, trusting with childlike faith in her friend's promise that she should be free in the morning. Corona, on the contrary, had passed a wakeful night, and was almost worn out with fatigue. She remained in her room until twelve o'clock, the hour when the members of the family met at the midday breakfast. She found her father-in-law waiting for her, and at a glance she saw that he was in a savage humour. His bronzed face was paler than usual and his movements more sudden and nervous, while his dark eyes gleamed angrily beneath his bent and shaggy brows. Corona, on her part, was silent and preoccupied. In spite of the tragic events of the night, which, after all, only affected her indirectly at present, and in spite of the constant moral suffering which now played so important a part in her life, she could not but be disturbed by the tremendous loss sustained by her husband and by his father. It fell most heavily upon the latter, who was an old man, and whose mind was not engaged by any other absorbing consideration, but the blow was a terrible one to the other also.

"Where is Giovanni?" asked Saracinesca brusquely, as they sat down to the table.

"I do not know," answered Corona. "The last I heard of him was that he was with Cardinal Antonelli. I suppose that after getting the order to release Faustina he stayed there."

"So his Eminence suffered himself to be persuaded that a little girl did not strangle that old tanner," remarked the prince.

"Apparently."

"If they had taken Flavia it would have been more natural. She would have inaugurated her reign as Princess Saracinesca by a night in the Termini. Delightful contrast! I suppose you know who did it?"

"No. Probably a servant, though they say that nothing was stolen."

"San Giacinto did it. I have thought the whole matter out, and I am convinced of it. Look at his hands. He could strangle an elephant. Not that he could have had any particular reason for liquidating his father-in-law. He is rich enough without Flavia's share, but I always thought he would kill somebody one of these days, ever since I met him at Aquila."

"Without any reason, why should he have done it?"

"My dear child, when one has no reason to give, it is very hard to say why a thing occurs. He looks like the man."

"Is it conceivable that after getting all he could desire he should endanger his happiness in such a way?"

"Perhaps not. I believe he did it. What an abominable omelet—a glass of water, Pasquale. Abominable, is it not, Corona? Perfectly uneatable. I suppose the cook has heard of our misfortunes and wants to leave."

"I fancy we are not very hungry," remarked Corona, in order to say something.

"I would like to know whether the murderer is eating his breakfast at this moment, and whether he has any appetite. It would be interesting from a psychological point of view. By the bye, all this is very like a jettatura."

"What?"

"Montevarchi coming to his end on the very day he had won the suit. In good old times it would have been Giovanni who would have cut his throat, after which we should have all retired to Saracinesca and prepared for a siege. Less civilised but twice as human. No doubt they will say now—even now—that we paid a man to do the work."

"But it was San Giacinto who brought the suit—"

"It was Montevarchi. I have seen my lawyer this morning. He says that Montevarchi sent the people out to Frascati to see San Giacinto and explained the whole matter to them beforehand. He discovered the clause in the deeds first. San Giacinto never even saw them until everything was ready. And on the evening of the very day when it was settled, Montevarchi is murdered. I wonder that it has not struck any one to say we did it."

"You did not oppose the suit. If you had, it would have been different."

"How could I oppose the action? It was clear from the beginning that we had no chance of winning it. The fact remains that we are turned out of our home. The sooner we leave this the better. It will only be harder to go if we stay here."

"Yes," answered Corona sadly. "It will be harder."

"I believe it is a judgment of heaven on Giovanni for his outrageous conduct," growled the prince, suddenly running away with a new idea.

"On Giovanni?" Corona was roused immediately by the mention of her husband in such a connection.

"Yes, for his behaviour to you, the young scoundrel! I ought to have disinherited him at once."

"Please do not talk in that way. I cannot let you say—"

"He is my own son, and I will say what I please," interrupted Saracinesca fiercely. "He treated you outrageously, I say. It is just like a woman to deny it and defend her husband."

"Since there is no one else to defend him, I must. He was misled, and naturally enough, considering the appearances. I did not know that you knew about it all."

"I do not know all, nor half. But I know enough. A man who suspects such a woman as you deserves to be hanged. Besides," he added irrelevantly, but with an intuitive keenness that startled Corona, "besides, you have not forgiven him."

"Indeed I have—"

"In a Christian spirit, no doubt. I know you are good. But you do not love him as you did. It is useless to deny it. Why should you? I do not blame you, I am sure."

The prince fixed his bright eyes on her face and waited for her answer. She turned a little paler and said nothing for several moments. Then as he watched her he saw the colour mount slowly to her olive cheeks. She herself could hardly have accounted for the unwonted blush, and a man capable of more complicated reasoning than her father-in-law would have misinterpreted it. Corona had at first been angry at the thought that he could speak as he did of Giovanni, saying things she would not say to herself concerning him. Then she felt a curious sensation of shame at being discovered. It was true that she did not love her husband, or at least that she believed herself unable to love him; but she was ashamed that any one else should know it.

"Why will you persist in talking about the matter?" she asked at length. "It is between us two."

"It seems to me that it concerns me," returned Saracinesca, who was naturally pertinacious. "I am not inquisitive. I ask no questions. Giovanni has said very little about it to me. But I am not blind. He came to me one evening and said he was going to take you away to the mountains. He seemed very much disturbed, and I saw that there had been trouble between you, and that he suspected you of something. He did not say so, but I knew what he meant. If it had turned out true I think I would have—well, I would not have answered for my conduct. Of course I took his part, but you fell ill, and did not know that. When he came and told me that he had been mistaken I abused him like a thief. I have abused him ever since whenever I have had a chance. It was a vile, dastardly, foolish, ridiculous—"

"For heaven's sake!" cried Corona, interrupting him. "Pray, pray leave the question in peace! I am so unhappy!"

"So am I," answered Saracinesca bluntly. "It does not add to my happiness to know that my son has made an ass of himself. Worse than that. You do not seem to realise that I am very fond of you. If I had not been such an old man I should have fallen in love with you as well as Giovanni. Do you remember when I rode over to Astrardente, and asked you to marry him? I would have given all I am—all I was worth, I mean, to be in Giovanni's shoes when I brought back your answer. Bah! I am an old fellow and no Apollo either! But you have been a good daughter to me, Corona, and I will not let any one behave badly to you."

"And you have been good to me—so good! But you must not be angry with Giovanni. He was misled. He loved me even then."

"I wish I were as charitable as you."

"Do not call me charitable. I am anything but that. If I were I would—" She stopped short.

"Yes, I know, you would love him as you did before. Then you would not be Corona, but some one else. I know that sort of argument. But you cannot be two persons at one time. The other woman, whom you have got in your mind, and who would love Giovanni, is a weak-minded kind of creature who bears anything and everything, who will accept any sort of excuse for an insult, and will take credit to herself for being long-suffering because she has not the spirit to be justly angry. Thank heaven you are not like that. If you were, Giovanni would not have had you for a wife nor I for a daughter."

"I think it is my fault. I would do anything in the world to make it otherwise."

"You admit the fact then? Of course. It is a misfortune, and not your fault.

It is one more misfortune among so many. You may forgive him, if you please. I will not. By the bye, I wonder why he does not come back. I would like to hear the news."

"The cardinal may have kept him to breakfast."

"Since seven o'clock this morning? That is impossible. Unless his Eminence has arrested him on charge of the murder." The old gentleman laughed gruffly, little guessing how near his jest lay to the truth. But Corona looked up quickly. The mere idea of such a horrible contingency was painful to her, absurd and wildly improbable as it appeared.

"I was going to ask him to go up to Saracinesca tomorrow and see to the changes," continued the prince.

"Must it be so soon?" asked Corona regretfully. "Is it absolutely decided? Have you not yielded too easily?"

"I cannot go over all the arguments again," returned her father-in-law with some impatience. "There is no doubt about it. I expended all my coolness and civility on San Giacinto when he came to see me about it. It is of no use to complain, and we cannot draw back. I suppose I might go down on my knees to the Pope and ask his Holiness for another title—for the privilege of being called something, Principe di Cavolfiore, if you like. But I will not do it. I will die as Leone Saracinesca. You can give Giovanni your old title, if you please—it is yours to give."

"He shall have it if he wants it. What does it matter? I can be Donna Corona."

"Ay, what does it matter, provided we have peace? What does anything matter in this unutterably ridiculous world—except your happiness, poor child! Yes. Everything must be got ready. I will not stay in this house another week."

"But in a week it will be impossible to do all there is to be done!" exclaimed Corona, whose feminine mind foresaw infinite difficulties in moving.

"Possible, or impossible, it must be accomplished. I have appointed this day week for handing over the property. The lawyers said, as you say, that it would need more time. I told them that there was no time, and that if they could not do it, I would employ some one else. They talked of sitting up all night—as if I cared whether they lost their beauty sleep or not! A week from today everything must be settled, so that I have not in my possession a penny that does not belong to me."

"And then—what will you do?" asked Corona, who saw in spite of his vehemence how much he was affected by the prospect.

"And then? What then? Live somewhere else, I suppose, and pray for an easy death."

No one had ever heard Leone Saracinesca say before now that he desired to die, and the wish seemed so contrary to the nature of his character that Corona looked earnestly at him. His face was discomposed, and his voice had trembled. He was a brave man, and a very honourable one, but he was very far from being a philosopher. As he had said, he had expended all his calmness in that one meeting with San Giacinto when he had been persuaded of the justice of the latter's claims. Since then he had felt nothing but bitterness, and the outward expression of it was either an unreasonable irritation concerning small matters, or some passionate outburst like the present against life, against the world in which he lived, against everything. It is scarcely to be wondered at that he should have felt the loss so deeply, more deeply even than Giovanni. He had been for many years the sole head and master of his house, and had borne all the hereditary dignities that belonged to his station, some of which were of a kind that pleased his love of feudal traditions. For the money he cared little. The loss that hurt him most touched his pride, and that generous vanity which was a part of his nature, which delighted in the honour accorded to his name, to his son, to his son's wife, in the perpetuation of his race and in a certain dominating independence, that injured no one and gave himself immense satisfaction. At his age he was not to be blamed for such feelings. They proceeded in reality far more from habit than from a vain disposition, and it seemed to him that if he bore the calamity bravely he had a right to abuse his fate in his own language. But he could not always keep himself from betraying more emotion than he cared to show.

"Do not talk of death," said Corona. "Giovanni and I will make your life happy and worth living." She sighed as she spoke, in spite of herself.

"Giovanni and you!" repeated the prince gloomily. "But for his folly—what is the use of talking? I have much to do. If he comes to you this afternoon please tell him that I want him."

Corona was glad when the meal was ended, and she went back to her own room. She had promised to go and see Faustina again, but otherwise she did not know how to occupy herself. A vague uneasiness beset her as the time passed and her husband did not come home. It was unlike him to stay away all day without warning her, though she was obliged to confess to herself that she had of late shown very little interest in his doings, and that it would not be very surprising if he began to do as he pleased without informing her of his intentions. Neverthe- less she wished he would show himself before evening. The force of habit was still strong, and she missed him without quite knowing it. At last she made an effort against her apathy, and went out to pay the promised visit.

The Montevarchi household was subdued under all the outward pomp of a ponderous mourning. The gates and staircases were hung with black. In the vast antechamher the canopy was completely hidden by an enormous hatchment before which the dead prince had lain in state during the previous night and a part of the day. According to the Roman custom the body had been already removed, the regulations of the city requiring that this should be done within twenty-four hours. The great black pedestals on which the lights had been placed were still standing, and lent a ghastly and sepulchral appearance to the whole. Numbers of servants in mourning liveries stood around an immense copper bra- zier in a corner, talking together in low tones, their voices dying away altogether as the Princess Sant' Ilario entered the open door of the hall. The man who came forward appeared to be the person in charge of the funeral, for Corona had not seen him in the house before.

"Donna Faustina expects me," she said, continuing to walk towards the entrance to the apartments.

"Your Excellency's name?" inquired the man. Corona was surprised that he should ask, and wondered whether even the people of his class already knew the result of the suit.

"Donna Corona Saracinesca," she answered in distinct tones. The appellation sounded strange and unfamiliar.

"Donna Corona Saracinesca," the man repeated in a loud voice a second later. He had almost run into San Giacinto, who was coming out at that moment. Corona found herself face to face with her cousin.

"You—princess!" he exclaimed, putting out his hand. In spite of the rela- tionship he was not privileged to call her by her name. "You—why does the man announce you in that way?"

Corona took his hand and looked quietly into his face. They had not met since the decision.

"I told him to do so. I shall be known by that name in future. I have come to see Faustina." She would have passed on.

"Allow me to say," said San Giacinto, in his deep, calm voice, "that as far as

I am concerned you are, and always shall be, Princess Sant' Ilario. No one can regret more than I the position in which I am placed towards you and yours, and I shall certainly do all in my power to prevent any such unnecessary changes."

"We cannot discuss that matter here," answered Corona, speaking more coldly than she meant to do.

"I trust there need be no discussion. I even hope that you will bear me no ill will."

"I bear you none. You have acted honestly and openly. You had right on your side. But neither my husband nor I will live under a borrowed name."

San Giacinto seemed hurt by her answer. He stood aside to allow her to pass, and there was something dignified in his demeanour that pleased Corona.

"The settlement is not made yet," he said gravely. "Until then the name is yours."

When she was gone he looked after her with an expression of annoyance upon his face. He understood well enough what she felt, but he was very far from wishing to let any unpleasantness arise between him and her family. Even in the position to which he had now attained he felt that there was an element of uncertainty, and he did not feel able to dispense with the good-will of his relations, merely because he was Prince Saracinesca and master of a great fortune. His early life had made him a cautious man, and he did not underestimate the value of personal influence. Moreover, he had not a bad heart, and preferred if possible to be on good terms with everybody. According to his own view he had done nothing more than claim what was legitimately his, but he did not want the enmity of those who had resigned all into his hands.

Corona went on her way and found Faustina and Flavia together. Their mother was not able to see any one. The rest of the family had gone to the country as soon as the body had been taken away, yielding without any great resistance to the entreaties of their best friends who, according to Roman custom, thought it necessary to "divert" the mourners. That is the consecrated phrase, and people of other countries may open their eyes in astonishment at the state of domestic relations as revealed by this practice. It is not an uncommon thing for the majority of the family to go away even before death has actually taken place. Speaking of a person who is dying, it is not unusual to say, "You may imagine how ill he is, for the family has left him!" The servants attend the Requiem Mass, the empty carriages follow the hearse to the gates of the city, but the family is already in the country, trying to "divert" itself.

Flavia and Faustina, however, had stayed at home, partly because the old princess was really too deeply moved and profoundly shocked to go away, and partly because San Giacinto refused to leave Rome. Faustina, too, was eccentric enough to think such haste after "diversion" altogether indecent, and she herself had been through such a series of emotions during the twenty-four hours that she found rest needful. As for Flavia, she took matters very calmly, but would have preferred very much to be with her brothers and their wives. The calamity had for the time subdued her vivacity, though it was easy to see that it had made no deep impression upon her nature. If the truth were told, she was more unpleasantly affected by thus suddenly meeting Corona than by her father's tragic death. She thought it necessary to be more than usually affectionate, not out of calculation, but rather to get rid of a disagreeable impression. She sprang forward and kissed Corona on both cheeks.

"I was longing to see you!" she said enthusiastically. "You have been so kind to Faustina. I am sure we can never thank you enough. Imagine, if she had been obliged to spend the night alone in prison! Such an abominable mistake, too. I hope that dreadful man will be sent to the galleys. Poor little Faustina! How could any one think she could do such a thing!"

Corona was not prepared for Flavia's manner, and it grated disagreeably on her sensibilities. But she said nothing, only returning her salutation with becoming cordiality before sitting down between the two sisters. Faustina looked on coldly, disgusted with such indifference. It struck her that if Corona had not accompanied her to the Termini, it would have been very hard to induce any of her own family to do so.

"And poor papa!" continued Flavia volubly. "Is it not too dreadful, too horrible? To think of any one daring! I shall never get over the impression it made on me—never. Without a priest, without any one—poor dear!"

"Heaven is very merciful," said Corona, thinking it necessary to make some such remark.

"Oh, I know," answered Flavia, with sudden seriousness. "I know. But poor papa—you see—I am afraid—"

She stopped significantly and shook her head, evidently implying that Prince Montevarchi's chances of blessedness were but slender.

"Flavia!" cried Faustina indignantly, "how can you say such things!"

"Oh, I say nothing, and besides, I daresay—you see he was sometimes very kind. It was only yesterday, for instance, that he actually promised me those ear-rings—you know, Faustina, the pearl drops at Civilotti's—it is true, they were not so very big after all. He really said he would give them to me as a souvenir if—oh! I forgot."

She stopped with some embarrassment, for she had been on the point of saying that the earrings were to be a remembrance if the suit were won, when she recollected that she was speaking to Corona.

"Well—it would have been very kind of him if he had," she added. "Perhaps that is something. Poor papa! One would feel more sure about it, if he had got some kind of absolution."

"I do not believe you cared for him at all!" exclaimed Faustina. Corona evi-dently shared this belief, for she looked very grave and was silent.

"Oh, Faustina, how unkind you are!" cried Flavia in great astonishment and some anger. "I am sure I loved poor papa as much as any of you, and perhaps a great deal better. We were always such good friends!"

Faustina raised her eyebrows a little and looked at Corona as though to say that her sister was hopeless, and for some minutes no one spoke.

"You are quite rested now?" asked Corona at last, turning to the young girl. "Poor child! What you must have suffered!"

"It is strange, but I am not tired. I slept, you know, for I was worn out."

"Faustina's grief did not keep her awake," observed Flavia, willing to say something disagreeable.

"I only came to see how you were," said Corona, who did not care to prolong the interview. "I hope to hear that your mother is better tomorrow. I met Saraci-nesca as I came in, but I did not ask him."

"Your father-in-law?" asked Faustina innocently. "I did not know he had been here."

"No; your husband, my dear," answered Corona, looking at Flavia as she spoke. She was curious to see what effect the change had produced upon her. Flavia's cheeks flushed quickly, evidently with pleasure, if also with some embar-rassment. But Corona was calm and unmoved as usual.

"I did not know you already called him so," said Flavia. "How strange it will be!"

"We shall soon get used to it," replied Corona, with a smile, as she rose to go. "I wish you many years of happiness with your new name. Good-bye." Faustina went with her into one of the outer rooms.

"Tell me," she said, when they were alone, "how did your husband manage it so quickly? They told me today that the cardinal had at first refused. I cannot understand it. I could not ask you before Flavia—she is so inquisitive!"

"I do not know—I have not seen Giovanni yet. He stayed with the cardinal when the carriage came for us. It was managed in some way, and quickly. I shall hear all about it this evening. What is it, dear?"

There were tears in Faustina's soft eyes, followed quickly by a little sob.

"I miss him dreadfully!" she exclaimed, laying her head on her friend's shoulder. "And I am so unhappy! We parted angrily, and I can never tell him how sorry I am. You do not think it could have had anything to do with it, do you?"

"Your little quarrel? No, child. What could it have changed? We do not know what happened."

"I shall never forget his face. I was dreadfully undutiful—oh! I could almost marry that man if it would do any good!"

Corona smiled sadly. The young girl's sorrow was genuine, in strange contrast to Flavia's voluble flippancy. She laid her hand affectionately on the thick chestnut hair.

"Perhaps he sees now that you should not marry against your heart."

"Oh, do you think so? I wish it were possible. I should not feel as though I were so bad if I thought he understood now. I could bear it better. I should not feel as though it were almost a duty to marry Frangipani."

Corona turned quickly with an expression that was almost fierce in its intensity. She took Faustina's hands in hers.

"Never do that, Faustina. Whatever comes to you, do not do that! You do not know what it is to live with a man you do not love, even if you do not hate him. It is worse than death."

Corona kissed her and left her standing by the door. Was it possible, Faustina asked, that Corona did not love her husband? Or was she speaking of her former life with old Astrardente? Of course, it must be that. Giovanni and Corona were a proverbially happy couple.

When Corona again entered her own room, there was a note lying upon the table, the one her husband had written that morning from his place of confinement. She tore the envelope open with an anxiety of which she had not believed herself capable. She had asked for him when she returned and he had not been heard of yet. The vague uneasiness she had felt at his absence suddenly increased, until she felt that unless she saw him at once she must go in search of him. She read the note through again and again, without clearly understanding the contents.

It was evident that he had left Rome suddenly and had not cared to tell her whither he was going, since the instructions as to what she was to say were put in such a manner as to make it evident that they were only to serve as an excuse for his absence to others, and not as an explanation to herself. The note was enigmatical and might mean almost anything. At last Corona tossed the bit of paper into the fire, and tapped the thick carpet impatiently with her foot.

"How coldly he writes!" she exclaimed aloud.

The door opened and her maid appeared.

"Will your Excellency receive Monsieur Gouache?" asked the woman from the threshold.

"No! Certainly not!" answered Corona, in a voice that frightened the servant. "I am not at home."

"Yes, your Excellency."

CHAPTER XXVI

THE amount of work which Arnoldo Meschini did in the twenty-four hours of the day depended almost entirely upon his inclinations. The library had always been open to the public once a week, on Mondays, and on those occasions the librarian was obliged to be present. The rest of his time was supposed to be devoted to the incessant labour connected with so important a collection of books, and, on the whole, he had done far more than was expected of him. Prince Montevarchi had never proposed to give him an assistant, and he would have rejected any such offer, since the presence of another person would have made it almost impossible for him to carry on his business of forging ancient manuscripts. The manual labour of his illicit craft was of course performed in his own room, but a second librarian could not have failed to discover that there was something wrong. Night after night he carried the precious manuscripts to his chamber, bringing them back and restoring them to their places every morning. During the day he studied attentively what he afterwards executed in the quiet hours when he could be alone. Of the household none but the prince himself ever came to the library, no other member of the family cared for the books or knew anything about them. His employer being dead, Meschini was practically master of all the shelves contained. No one disturbed him, no one asked what he was doing. His salary would be paid regularly by the steward, and he would in all probability be left to vegetate unheeded for the rest of his natural lifetime. When he died some one else would be engaged in his place. In the ordinary course of events no other future would have been open to him.

He awoke very late in the morning on the day after the murder, and lay for some time wondering why he was so very uncomfortable, why his head hurt him, why his vision was indistinct, why he could remember nothing he had done before going to bed. The enormous quantity of liquor he had drunk had temporarily destroyed his faculties, which were not hardened by the habitual use of alcohol. He turned his head uneasily upon the pillow and saw the bottles on the table, the candle burnt down in the brass candlestick and the general disorder in the room. He glanced at his own body and saw that he was lying dressed upon his bed. Then the whole truth flashed upon his mind with appalling vividness. A shock went through his system as though some one had struck him violently on the back of the head, while the light in the room was momentarily broken into flashes that pained his eyes. He got upon his feet with difficulty, and steadied himself by the bed-post, hardly able to stand alone.

He had murdered his master. The first moment in which he realised the fact was the most horrible he remembered to have passed. He had killed the prince and could recall nothing, or next to nothing, that had occurred since the deed. Almost before he knew what he was doing he had locked his door with a double turn of the key and was pushing the furniture against it, the table, the chairs, everything that he could move. It seemed to him that he could already hear upon the winding stair the clank of the gendarmes' sabres as they came to get him. He looked wildly round the room to see whether there was anything that could lead to discovery. The unwonted exertion, however, had restored the circulation of his blood, and with it arose an indistinct memory of the sense of triumph he had felt when he had last entered the chamber. He asked himself how he could have rejoiced over the deed, unless he had unconsciously taken steps for his own safety.

The body must have been found long ago.

Very gradually there rose before him the vision of the scene in the study, when he had been summoned thither by the two servants, the dead prince stretched on the table, the pale faces, the prefect, Donna Faustina's voice, a series of questions asked in a metallic, pitiless tone. He had not been drunk, therefore, when they had sent for him. And yet, he knew that he had not been sober. In what state, then, had he found himself? With a shudder, he remembered his terror in the library, his fright at the ghost which had turned out to be only his own coat, his visit to his room, and the first draught he had swallowed. From that point onwards his memory grew less and less clear. He found that he could not remember at all how he had come upstairs the last time.

One thing was evident, however. He had not been arrested, since he found himself in his chamber unmolested. Who, then, had been taken in his place? He was amazed to find that he did not know. Surely, at the first inquest, something must have been said which would have led to the arrest of some one. The law never went away empty-handed. He racked his aching brain to bring back the incident, but it would not be recalled—for the excellent reason that he really knew nothing about the matter. It was a relief at all events to find that he had actually been examined with the rest and had not been suspected. Neverthe-less, he had undoubtedly done the deed, of which the mere thought made him tremble in every joint. Or was it all a part of his drunken dreams? No, that, at least, could not be explained away. For a long time he moved uneasily from his barricade at the door to the window, from which he tried to see the street below. But his room was in the attic, and the broad stone cornice of the palace cut off the view effectually. At last he began to pull the furniture away from the entrance, slowly at first, as he merely thought of its uselessness, then with feverish haste, as he realised that the fact of his trying to entrench himself in his quarters would seem suspicious. In a few seconds he had restored everything to its place. The brandy bottles disappeared into the cupboard in the wall; a bit of candle filled the empty candlestick. He tore off his clothes and jumped into bed, tossing himself about to give it the appearance of having been slept in. Then he got up again and proceeded to make his toilet. All his clothes were black, and he had but a slender choice. He understood vaguely, however, that there would be a funeral or some sort of ceremony in which all the members of the household would be expected to join, and he arrayed himself in the best he had—a decent suit of broadcloth, a clean shirt, a black tie. He looked at himself in the cracked mirror. His face was ghastly yellow, the whites of his eyes injected with blood, the veins at the temples swollen and congested. He was afraid that his appearance might excite remark, though it was in reality not very much changed.

Then, as he thought of this, he realised that he was to meet a score of persons, some of whom would very probably look at him curiously. His nerves were in a shattered condition, he almost broke down at the mere idea of what he must face. What would become of him in the presence of the reality? And yet he had met the whole household bravely enough on the very spot where he had done the murder on the previous evening. He sat down, overpowered by the revival of his fear and horror. The room swam around him and he grasped the edge of the table for support. But he could not stay there all day. Any reluctance to make his appearance at such a time might be fatal. There was only one way to get the necessary courage, and that was to drink again. He shrank from the thought. He had not acquired the habitual drunkard's certainty of finding nerve and boldness and steadiness of hand in the morning draught, and the idea of tasting the liquor was loathsome to him in his disordered state. He rose to his feet and tried to act as though he were in the midst of a crowd of persons. Ape-like, he grinned at the furniture, walked about the room, spoke aloud, pretending that he was meeting real people, tried to frame sentences expressive of profound grief. He opened the door and made a pretence of greeting an imaginary individual. It was as though a stream of cold water had fallen upon his neck. His knees knocked together, and he felt sick with fear. There was evidently no use in attempting to go down without some stimulant. Almost sorrowfully he shut the door again, and took the bottle from its place. He took several small doses, patiently testing the effect until his hand was steady and warm.

Ten minutes later he was kneeling with many others before the catafalque, beneath the great canopy of black. He was dazed by the light of the great branches of candles, and confused by the subdued sound of whispering and of softly treading feet; but he knew that his outward demeanour was calm and collected, and that he exhibited no signs of nervousness. San Giacinto was standing near one of the doors, having taken his turn with the sons of the dead man to remain in the room. He watched the librarian and a rough sort of pity made itself felt in his heart.

"Poor Meschini!" he thought. "He has lost a friend. I daresay he is more genuinely sorry than all the family put together, poor fellow!"

Arnoldo Meschini, kneeling before the body of the man he had murdered, with a brandy bottle in the pocket of his long coat, would have come to an evil end if the giant had guessed the truth. But he looked what he was supposed to be, the humble, ill-paid, half-starved librarian, mourning the master he had faithfully served for thirty years. He knelt a long time, his lips moving mechanically with the words of an oft-repeated prayer. In reality he was afraid to rise from his knees alone, and was waiting until some of the others made the first move. But the rows of lacqueys, doubtless believing that the amount of their future wages would largely depend upon the vigour of their present mourning, did not seem inclined to desist from their orisons. To Meschini the time was interminable, and his courage was beginning to ooze away from him, as the sense of his position acquired a tormenting force. He could have borne it well enough in a church, in the midst of a vast congregation, he could have fought off his horror even here for a few minutes, but to sustain such a part for a quarter of an hour seemed almost impossible. He would have given his soul, which indeed was just then of but small value, to take a sip of courage from the bottle, and his clasped fingers twitched nervously, longing to find the way to his pocket. He glanced along the line, measuring his position, to see whether there was a possibility of drinking without being observed, but he saw that it would be madness to think of it, and began repeating his prayer with redoubled energy, in the hope of distracting his mind. Then a horrible delusion began to take possession of him; he fancied that the dead man was beginning to turn his head slowly, almost imperceptibly, towards him. Those closed eyes would open and look him in the face, a supernatural voice would speak his name. As on the previous afternoon the cold perspiration began to trickle from his brow. He was on the point of crying aloud with terror, when the man next to him rose. In an instant he was on his feet. Both bent again, crossed themselves, and retired. Meschini stumbled and caught at his companion's arm, but succeeded in gaining the door. As he passed out, his face was so discomposed that San Giacinto looked down upon him with increased compassion, then followed him a few steps and laid his hand on his shoulder. The librarian started violently and stood still.

"He was a good friend to you, Signor Meschini," said the big man kindly. "But take heart, you shall not be forgotten."

The dreaded moment had come, and it had been very terrible, but San Giacinto's tone was reassuring. He could not have suspected anything, though the servants said that he was an inscrutable man, profound in his thoughts and fearful in his anger. He was the one of all the family whom Meschini most feared.

"God have mercy on him!" whined the librarian, trembling to his feet. "He was the best of men, and is no doubt in glory!"

"No doubt," replied San Giacinto drily. He entertained opinions of his own upon the subject, and he did not like the man's tone. "No doubt," he repeated. "We will try and fulfil his wishes with regard to you."

"Grazie, Eccelenza!" said Meschini with great humility, making horns with his fingers behind his back to ward off the evil eye, and edging away in the direction of the grand staircase.

San Giacinto returned to the door and paid no more attention to him. Then Meschini almost ran down the stairs and did not slacken his speed until he found himself in the street. The cold air of the winter's day revived him, and he found himself walking rapidly in the direction of the Ponte Quattro Capi. He generally took that direction when he went out without any especial object, for his friend Tiberio Colaisso, the poor apothecary, had his shop upon the little island of Saint Bartholomew, which is connected with the shores of the river by a double bridge, whence the name, "the bridge of four heads."

Meschini paused and looked over the parapet at the yellow swirling water. The eddies seemed to take queer shapes and he watched them for a long time. He had a splitting headache, of the kind which is made more painful by looking at quickly moving objects, which, at the same time, exercise an irresistible fascination over the eye. Almost unconsciously he compared his own life to the river—turbid, winding, destroying. The simile was incoherent, like most of his fancies on that day, but it served to express a thought, and he began to feel an odd sympathy for the muddy stream, such as perhaps no one had ever felt before him. But as he looked he grew dizzy, and drew back from the parapet. There must have been something strange in his face, for a man who was passing looked at him curiously and asked whether he were ill. He shook his head with a sickly smile and passed on.

The apothecary was standing idly at his door, waiting for a custom that rarely came his way. He was a cadaverous man, about fifty years of age, with eyes of an uncertain colour set deep in his head. An ill-kept, grizzled beard descended upon his chest, and gave a certain wildness to his appearance. A very shabby green smoking cap, trimmed with tarnished silver lace, was set far back upon his head, displaying a wrinkled forehead, much heightened by baldness, but of proportions that denoted a large and active brain. That he took snuff in great quantities was apparent. Otherwise he was neither very dirty nor very clean, but his thumbs had that peculiar shape which seems to be the result of constantly rolling pills. Meschini stopped before him.

"Sor Arnoldo, good day," said the chemist, scrutinising his friend's face curiously.

"Good day, Sor Tiberio," replied the librarian. "Will you let me come in for a little moment?" There seemed to be an attempt at a jest in the question, for the apothecary almost smiled.

"Padrone," he said, retiring backwards through the narrow door. "A game of scopa today?"

"Have you the time to spare?" inquired the other, in a serious tone. They always maintained the myth that Tiberio Colaisso was a very busy man.

"Today," answered the latter, without a smile, and emphasising the word as though it defined an exception, "today, I have nothing to do. Besides, it is early."

"We can play a hand and then we can dine at Cicco's."

"Being Friday in Advent, I had intended to fast," replied the apothecary, who had not a penny in his pocket "But since you are so good as to invite me, I do not say no."

Meschini said nothing, for he understood the situation, which was by no means a novel one. His friend produced a pack of Italian cards, almost black with age. He gave Meschini the only chair, and seated himself upon a three-legged stool.

It was a dismal scene. The shop was like many of its kind in the poorer quarters of old Rome. There was room for the counter and for three people to stand before it when the door was shut. The floor was covered with a broken pavement of dingy bricks. As the two men began to play a fine, drizzling rain wet the silent street outside, and the bricks within at once exhibited an unctuous moisture. The sky had become cloudy after the fine morning, and there was little light in the shop. Three of the walls were hidden by cases with glass doors, containing an assortment of majolica jars which would delight a modern amateur, but which looked dingy and mean in the poor shop. Here and there, between them, stood bottles large and small, some broken and dusty, others filled with liquids and bearing paper labels, brown with age, the ink inscriptions fading into the dirty surface that surrounded them. The only things in the place which looked tolerably clean were the little brass scales and the white marble tablet for compounding solid medicines.

The two men looked as though they belonged to the little room. Meschini's yellow complexion was as much in keeping with the surroundings as the chemist's gray, colourless face. His bloodshot eyes wandered from the half-defaced cards to the objects in the shop, and he was uncertain in his play. His companion looked at him as though he were trying to solve some intricate problem that gave him trouble. He himself was a man who, like the librarian, had begun life under favourable circumstances, had studied medicine and had practised it. But he had been unfortunate, and, though talented, did not possess the qualifications most necessary for his profession. He had busied himself with chemistry and had invented a universal panacea which had failed, and in which he had sunk most of his small capital. Disgusted with his reverses he had gravitated slowly to his present position. Finding him careless and indifferent to their wants, his customers had dropped away, one by one, until he earned barely enough to keep body and soul together. Only the poorest class of people, emboldened by the mean aspect of his shop, came in to get a plaster, an ointment or a black draught, at the lowest possible prices. And yet, in certain branches, Tiberio Colaisso was a learned man. At all events he had proved himself able to do all that Meschini asked of him. He was keen, too, in an indolent way, and a single glance had satisfied him that something very unusual had happened to the librarian. He watched him patiently, hoping to find out the truth without questions. At the same time, the hope of winning a few coppers made him keep an eye on the game. To his surprise he won easily, and he was further astonished when he saw that the miserly Meschini was not inclined to complain of his losses nor to accuse him of cheating.

"You are not lucky today," he remarked at last, when his winnings amounted to a couple of pauls—a modern franc in all.

Meschini looked at him uneasily and wiped his brow, leaning back in the rickety chair. His hands were trembling.

"No," he answered. "I am not quite myself today. The fact is that a most dreadful tragedy occurred in our house last night, the mere thought of which gives me the fever. I am even obliged to take a little stimulant from time to time."

So saying, he drew the bottle from his pocket and applied it to his lips. He had hoped that it would not be necessary, but he was unable to do without it very long, his nerves being broken down by the quantity he had taken on the previous night. Colaisso looked on in silence, more puzzled than ever. The librarian seemed to be revived by the dose, and spoke more cheerfully after it.

"A most terrible tragedy," he said. "The prince was murdered yesterday afternoon. I could not speak of it to you at once."

"Murdered?" exclaimed the apothecary in amazement. "And by whom?"

"That is the mystery. He was found dead in his study. I will tell you all I know."

Meschini communicated the story to his friend in a disjointed fashion, interspersing his narrative with many comments intended to give himself courage to proceed. He told the tale with evident reluctance, but he could not avoid the necessity. If Tiberio Colaisso read the account in the paper that evening, as he undoubtedly would, he would wonder why his companion had not been the first to relate the catastrophe; and this wonder might turn into a suspicion. It would have been better not to come to the apothecary's, but since he found himself there he could not escape from informing him of what had happened.

"It is very strange," said the chemist, when he had heard all. Meschini thought he detected a disagreeable look in his eyes.

"It is, indeed," he answered. "I am made ill by it. See how my hand trembles. I am cold and hot."

"You have been drinking too much," said Colaisso suddenly, and with a certain brutality that startled his friend. "You are not sober. You must have taken a great deal last night. A libation to the dead, I suppose, in the manner of the ancients."

Meschini winced visibly and began to shuffle the cards, while he attempted to smile to hide his embarrassment.

"I was not well yesterday—at least—I do not know what was the matter—a headache, I think, nothing more. And then, this awful catastrophe—horrible! My nerves are unstrung. I can scarcely speak."

"You need sleep first, and then a tonic," said the apothecary in a business-like tone.

"I slept until late this morning. It did me no good. I am half dead myself. Yes, if I could sleep again it might do me good."

"Go home and go to bed. If I were in your place I would not drink any more of that liquor. It will only make you worse."

"Give me something to make me sleep. I will take it."

The apothecary looked long at him and seemed to be weighing something in his judgment. An evil thought crossed his mind. He was very poor. He knew well enough, in spite of Meschini's protestations, that he was not so poor as he pretended to be. If he were he could not have paid so regularly for the chemicals and for the experiments necessary to the preparation of his inks. More than once the operations had proved to be expensive, but the librarian had never complained, though he haggled for a baiocco over his dinner at Cicco's wine shop, and was generally angry when he lost a paul at cards. He had money somewhere. It was evident that he was in a highly nervous state. If he could be induced to take opium once or twice it might become a habit. To sell opium was very profitable, and Colaisso knew well enough the power of the vice and the proportions it would soon assume, especially if Meschini thought the medicine contained only some harmless drug.

"Very well," said the apothecary. "I will make you a draught. But you must be sure that you are ready to sleep when you take it. It acts very quickly."

The draught which Meschini carried home with him was nothing but weak laudanum and water. It looked innocent enough, in the little glass bottle labelled "Sleeping potion." But the effect of it, as Colaisso had told him, was very rapid. Exhausted by all he had suffered, the librarian closed the windows of his room and lay down to rest. In a quarter of an hour he was in a heavy sleep. In his dreams he was happier than he had ever been before. The whole world seemed to be his, to use as he pleased. He was transformed into a magnificent being such as he had never imagined in his waking hours. He passed from one scene of splendour to another, from glory to glory, surrounded by forms of beauty, by showers of golden light in a beatitude beyond all description. It was as though he had suddenly become emperor of the whole universe. He floated through wondrous regions of soft colour, and strains of divine music sounded in his ears. Gentle hands carried him with an easy swaying motion to transcendent heights, where every breath he drew was like a draught of sparkling life. His whole being was filled with something which he knew was happiness, until he felt as though he could not contain the overflowing joy. At one moment he glided beyond the clouds through a gorgeous sunset; at another he was lying on a soft invisible couch, looking out to the bright distance—distance that never ended, never could end, but the contemplation of which was rapture, the greater for being inexplicable. An exquisite new sense was in him, corresponding to no bodily instinct, but rejoicing wildly in something that could not be defined, nor understood, nor measured, but only felt.

At last he began to descend, slowly at first and then with increasing speed, till he grew giddy and unconscious in the fall. He awoke and uttered a cry of terror. It was night, and he was alone in the dark. He was chilled to the bone, too, and his head was heavy, but the darkness was unbearable, and though he would gladly have slept again he dared not remain an instant without a light. He groped about for his matches, found them, and lit a candle. A neighbouring clock tolled out the hour of midnight, and the sound of the bells terrified him beyond measure. Cold, miserable, in an agony of fear, his nervousness doubled by the opium and by a need of food of which he was not aware, there was but one remedy within his reach. The sleeping potion had been calculated for one occasion only, and it was all gone. He tried to drain a few drops from the phial, and a drowsy, half-sickening odour rose from it to his nostrils. But there was nothing left, nothing but the brandy, and little more than half a bottle of that. It was enough for his present need, however, and more than enough. He drank greedily, for he was parched with thirst, though hardly conscious of the fact. Then he slept till morning. But when he opened his eyes he was conscious that he was in a worse state than on the previous day. He was not only nervous but exhausted, and it was with feeble steps that he made his way to his friend's shop, in order to procure a double dose of the sleeping mixture. If he could sleep through the twenty-four hours, he thought, so as not to wake up in the dead of night, he should be better. When he made his appearance Tiberio Colaisso knew what he wanted, and although he had half repented of what he had done, the renewed possibility of selling the precious drug was a temptation he could not withstand.

One day succeeded another, and each morning saw Arnoldo Meschini crossing the Ponte Quattro Capi on his way to the apothecary's. In the ordinary course of human nature a man does not become an opium-eater in a day, nor even, perhaps, in a week, but to the librarian the narcotic became a necessity almost from the first. Its action, combined with incessant doses of alcohol, was destructive, but the man's constitution was stronger than would have been believed. He possessed, moreover, a great power of controlling his features when he was not assailed by supernatural fears, and so it came about that, living almost in solitude, no one in the Palazzo Montevarchi was aware of his state. It was bad enough, indeed, for when he was not under the influence of brandy he was sleeping from the effects of opium. In three days he was willing to pay anything the apothecary asked, and seemed scarcely conscious of the payments he made. He kept up a show of playing the accustomed game of cards, but he was absent-minded, and was not even angry at his daily losses. The apothecary had more money in his pocket than he had possessed for many a day. As Arnoldo Meschini sank deeper and deeper, the chemist's spirits rose, and he began to assume an air of unwonted prosperity. One of the earliest results of the librarian's degraded condition was that Tiberio Colaisso procured himself a new green smoking cap ornamented profusely with fresh silver lace.

CHAPTER XXVII

SANT' Ilario had guessed rightly that the place of safety and secrecy to which he was to be conveyed was no other than the Holy Office, or prison of the Inquisition. He was familiar with the interior of the building, and knew that it contained none of the horrors generally attributed to it, so that, on the whole, he was well satisfied with the cardinal's choice. The cell to which he was conveyed after dark was a large room on the second story, comfortably furnished and bearing no sign of its use but the ornamented iron grating that filled the window. The walls were not thicker than those of most Roman palaces, and the chamber was dry and airy, and sufficiently warmed by a huge brazier of coals. It was clear from the way in which he was treated that the cardinal relied upon his honour more than upon any use of force in order to keep him in custody. A silent individual in a black coat had brought him in a carriage to the great entrance, whence a man of similar discretion and of like appearance had conducted him to his cell. This person returned soon afterwards, bringing a sufficient meal of fish and vegetables—it was Friday—decently cooked and almost luxuriously served. An hour later the man came back to carry away what was left. He asked whether the prisoner needed anything else for the night.

"I would like to know," said Giovanni, "whether any of my friends will be allowed to see me, if I ask it."

"I am directed to say that any request or complaint you have to make will be transmitted to his Eminence by a special messenger," answered the man. "Anything," he added in explanation, "beyond what concerns your personal comfort. In this respect I am at liberty to give you whatever you desire, within reason."

"Thank you. I will endeavour to be reasonable," replied Giovanni. "I am much obliged to you."

The man left the room and closed the door softly, so softly that the prisoner wondered whether he had turned the key. On examining the panels he saw, however, that they were smooth and not broken by any latch or keyhole. The spring was on the outside, and there was no means whatever of opening the door from within.

Giovanni wondered why a special messenger was to be employed to carry any request he made directly to the cardinal. The direction could not have been given idly, nor was it without some especial reason that he was at once told of it. Assuredly his Eminence was not expecting the prince to repent of his bargain and to send word that he wished to be released. The idea was absurd. The great man might suppose, however, that Giovanni would desire to send some communication to his wife, who would naturally be anxious about his absence. Against this contingency, however, Sant' Ilario had provided by means of the note he had despatched to her. Several days would elapse before she began to expect him, so that he had plenty of time to reflect upon his future course. Meanwhile he resolved to ask for nothing. Indeed, he had no requirements. He had money in his pockets and could send the attendant to buy any linen he needed without getting it from his home.

He was in a state of mind in which nothing could have pleased him better than solitary imprisonment. He felt at once a sense of rest and a freedom from all responsibility that soothed his nerves and calmed his thoughts. For many days he had lived in a condition bordering on madness. Every interview with Corona was a disappointment, and brought with it a new suffering. Much as he would have dreaded the idea of being separated from her for any length of time, the temporary impossibility of seeing her was now a relief, of which he realised the importance more and more as the hours succeeded each other. There are times when nothing but a forcible break in the current of our lives can restore the mind to its normal balance. Such a break, painful as it may be at first, brings with it the long lost power of rest. Instead of feeling the despair we expect, we are amazed at our own indifference, which again is succeeded by a renewed capacity for judging facts as they are, and by a new energy to mould our lives upon a better plan.

Giovanni neither reflected upon his position nor brooded over the probable result of his actions. On the contrary, he went to bed and slept soundly, like a strong man tired out with bodily exertion. He slept so long that his attendant at last woke him, entering and opening the window. The morning was fine, and the sun streamed in through the iron grating. Giovanni looked about him, and realised where he was. He felt calm and strong, and was inclined to laugh at the idea that his rashness would have any dangerous consequences. Corona doubtless was already awake too, and supposed that he was in the country shooting wild boar, or otherwise amusing himself. Instead of that he was in prison. There was no denying the fact, after all, but it was strange that he should not care to be at liberty. He had heard of the moral sufferings of men who are kept in confinement. No matter how well they are treated they grow nervous and careworn and haggard, wearing themselves out in a perpetual longing for freedom. Giovanni, on the contrary, as he looked round the bright, airy room, felt that he might inhabit it for a year without once caring to go out into the world. A few books to read, the means of writing if he pleased—he needed nothing else. To be alone was happiness enough.

He ate his breakfast slowly, and sat down in an old-fashioned chair to smoke a cigarette and bask in the sunshine while it lasted. It was not much like prison, and he did not feel like a man arrested for murder. He was conscious for a long time of nothing but a vague, peaceful contentment. He had given a list of things to be bought, including a couple of novels, to the man who waited upon him, and after a few hours everything was brought. The day passed tranquilly, and when he went to bed he smiled as he blew out the candle, partly at himself and partly at his situation.

"My friends will not say that I am absolutely lacking in originality," he reflected as he went to sleep.

On the morrow he read less and thought more. In the first place he wondered how long he should be left without any communication from the outside world. He wondered whether any steps had been taken towards bringing him to a trial, or whether the cardinal really knew that he was innocent, and was merely making him act out the comedy he had himself invented and begun. He was not impatient, but he was curious to know the truth. It was now the third day since he had seen Corona, and he had not prepared her for a long absence. If he heard nothing during the next twenty-four hours it would be better to take some measures for relieving her anxiety, if she felt any. The latter reflection, which presented itself suddenly, startled him a little. Was it possible that she would allow a week to slip by without expecting to hear from him or asking herself where he was? That was out of the question. He admitted the impossibility of such indifference, almost in spite of himself. He was willing, perhaps, to think her utterly heartless rather than accept the belief in an affection which went no farther than to hope that he might be safe; but his vanity or his intuition, it matters little which of the two, told him that Corona felt more than that. And yet she did not love him. He sat for many hours, motionless in his chair, trying to construct the future out of the past, an effort of imagination in which he failed signally. The peace of his solitude was less satisfactory to him than at first, and he began to suspect that before very long he might even wish to return to the world. Possibly Corona might come to see him. The cardinal would perhaps think it best to tell her what had happened. How would he tell it? Would he let her know all? The light faded from the room, and the attendant brought his evening meal and set two candles upon the table.

Hitherto it could not be said that he had suffered. On the contrary, his character had regained its tone after weeks of depression. Another day was ended, and he went to rest, but he slept less soundly than before, and on the following morning he awoke early. The monotony of the existence struck him all at once in its reality. The fourth day would be like the third, and, for all he knew, hundreds to come would be like the fourth if it pleased his Eminence to keep him a prisoner. Corona would certainly never suspect that he was shut up in the Holy Office, and if she did, she might not be able to come to him. Even if she came, what could he say to her? That he had committed a piece of outrageous folly because he was annoyed at her disbelief in him or at her coldness. He had probably made himself ridiculous for the first time in his life. The thought was the reverse of consoling. Nor did it contribute to his peace of mind to know that if he had made himself a laughing-stock, the cardinal, who dreaded ridicule, would certainly refuse to play a part in his comedy, and would act with all the rigour suitable to so grave a situation. He might even bring his prisoner to trial. Giovanni would submit to that, rather than be laughed at, but the alternative now seemed an appalling one. In his disgust of life on that memorable morning he had cared nothing what became of him, and had been in a state which precluded all just appreciation of the future. His enforced solitude had restored his faculties. He desired nothing less than to be tried for murder, because he had taken a short cut to satisfy his wife's caprice. But that caprice had for its object the liberty of poor Faustina Montevarchi. At all events, if he had made himself ridiculous, the ultimate purpose of his folly had been good, and had been accomplished.

All through the afternoon he paced his room, alternately in a state of profound dissatisfaction with himself, and in a condition of anxious curiosity about coming events. He scarcely touched his food or noticed the attendant who entered half a dozen times to perform his various offices. Again the night closed in, and once more he lay down to sleep, dreading the morning, and hoping to lose himself in dreams. The fourth day was like the third, indeed, as far as his surroundings were concerned, but he had not foreseen that he would be a prey to such gnawing anxiety as he suffered, still less, perhaps, that he should grow almost desperate for a sight of Corona. He was not a man who made any exhibition of his feelings even when he was alone. But the man who served him noticed that when he entered Giovanni was never reading, as he had always been doing at first. He was either walking rapidly up and down or sitting idly in the big chair by the window. His face was quiet and pale, even solemn at times. The attendant was doubtless accustomed to sudden changes of mood in his prisoners, for he appeared to take no notice of the alteration in Giovanni's manner.

It seemed as though the day would never end. To a man of his active strength to walk about a room is not exercise; it hardly seems like motion at all, and yet Giovanni found it harder and harder to sit still as the hours wore on. After an interval of comparative peace, his love for Corona had overwhelmed him again, and with tenfold force. To be shut up in a cell without the possibility of seeing her was torture such as he had never dreamt of in his whole life. By a strange revulsion of feeling it appeared to him that by taking her so suddenly at her word he had again done her an injustice. The process of reasoning by which he arrived at this conclusion was not clear to himself, and probably could not be made intelligible to any one else. He had assuredly sacrificed himself unhesitatingly, and at first the action had given him pleasure. But this was destroyed by the thought of the possible consequences. He asked whether he had the right to satisfy her imperative demand for Faustina's freedom by doing that which might possibly cause her annoyance, even though it should bring no serious injury to any one. The time passed very slowly, and towards evening he began to feel as he had felt before he had taken the fatal step which had placed him beyond Corona's reach, restless, miserable, desperate. At last it was night, and he was sitting before his solitary meal, eating hardly anything, staring half unconsciously at the closed window opposite.

The door opened softly, but he did not look round, supposing the person entering to be the attendant. Suddenly, there was the rustle of a woman's dress in the room, and at the same moment the door was shut. He sprang to his feet, stood still a moment, and then uttered a cry of surprise. Corona stood beside him, very pale, looking into his eyes. She had worn a thick veil, and on coming in had thrown it back upon her head—the veils of those days were long and heavy, and fell about the head and neck like a drapery.

"Corona!" Giovanni cried, stretching out his hands towards her. Something in her face prevented him from throwing his arms round her, something not like her usual coldness and reproachful look that kept him back.

"Giovanni—was it kind to leave me so?" she asked, without moving from her place.

The question corresponded so closely with his own feelings that he had anticipated it, though he had no answer ready. She knew all, and was hurt by what he had done. What could he say? The reasons that had sent him so boldly into danger no longer seemed even sufficient for an excuse. The happiness he had anticipated in seeing her had vanished almost before it had made itself felt. His first emotion was bitter anger against the cardinal. No one else could have told her, for no one else knew what he had done nor where he was. Giovanni thought, and with reason, that the great man might have spared his wife such a blow.

"I believed I was doing what was best when I did it," he answered, scarcely knowing what to say.

"Was it best to leave me without a word, except a message of excuse for others?"

"For you—was it not better? For me—what does it matter? Should I be happier anywhere else?"

"Have I driven you from your home, Giovanni?" asked Corona, with a strange look in her dark eyes. Her voice trembled.

"No, not you," he answered, turning away and beginning to walk up and down by the force of the habit he had acquired during the last two or three days. "Not you," he repeated more than once in a bitter tone.

Corona sank down upon the chair he had left, and buried her face in her hands, as though overcome by a great and sudden grief. Giovanni stopped before her and looked at her, not clearly understanding what was passing in her mind.

"Why are you so sorry?" he asked. "Has a separation of a few days changed you? Are you sorry for me?"

"Why did you come here?" she exclaimed, instead of answering his question. "Why here, of all places?"

"I had no choice. The cardinal decided the matter for me."

"The cardinal? Why do you confide in him? You never did before. I may be wrong, but I do not trust him, kind as he has always been. If you wanted advice, you might have gone to Padre Filippo—"

"Advice? I do not understand you, Corona."

"Did you not go to the cardinal and tell him that you were very unhappy and wanted to make a retreat in some quiet place where nobody could find you? And did he not advise you to come here, promising to keep your secret, and authorising you to stay as long as you pleased? That is what he told me."

"He told you that?" cried Giovanni in great astonishment.

"Yes—that and nothing more. He came to see me late this afternoon. He said that he feared lest I should be anxious about your long absence, and that he thought himself justified in telling me where you were and in giving me a pass, in case I wanted to see you. Besides, if it is not all as he says, how did you come here?"

"You do not know the truth? You do not know what I did? You do not guess why I am in the Holy Office?"

"I know only what he told me," answered Corona, surprised by Giovanni's questions.

But Giovanni gave no immediate explanation. He paced the floor in a state of excitement in which she had never seen him, clasping and unclasping his fingers nervously, and uttering short, incoherent exclamations. As she watched him a sensation of fear crept over her, but she did not ask him any question. He stopped suddenly again.

"You do not know that I am in prison?"

"In prison!" She rose with a sharp cry and seized his hands in hers.

"Do not be frightened, dear," he said in an altered tone. "I am perfectly innocent. After all, you know it is a prison."

"Ah, Giovanni!" she exclaimed reproachfully, "how could you say such a dreadful thing, even in jest?" She had dropped his hands again, and drew back a step as she spoke.

"It is not a jest. It is earnest. Do not start. I will tell you just what happened. It is best, after all. When I left you at the Termini, I saw that you had set your heart on liberating poor Faustina. I could not find any way of accomplishing what you desired, and I saw that you thought I was not doing my best for her freedom. I went directly to the cardinal and gave myself up in her place."

"As a hostage—a surety?" asked Corona, breathlessly.

"No. He would not have accepted that, for he was prejudiced against her. I gave myself up as the murderer."

He spoke quite calmly, as though he had been narrating a commonplace occurrence. For an instant she stood before him, dumb and horror-struck. Then with a great heart-broken cry she threw her arms round him and clasped him passionately to her breast.

"My beloved! My beloved!"

For some moments she held him so closely that he could neither move nor see her face, but the beating of his heart told him that a great change had in that instant come over his life. The cry had come from her soul, irresistibly, spontaneously. There was an accent in the two words she repeated which he had never hoped to hear again. He had expected that she would reproach him for his madness. Instead of that, his folly had awakened the love that was not dead, though it had been so desperately wounded.

Presently she drew back a little and looked into his eyes, a fierce deep light burning in her own.

"I love you," she said, almost under her breath.

A wonderful smile passed over his face, illuminating the dark, stern lines of it like a ray of heavenly light. Then the dusky eyelids slowly closed, as though by their own weight, his head fell back, and his lips turned white. She felt the burden of his body in her arms, and but for her strength he would have fallen to the floor. She reeled on her feet, holding him still, and sank down until she knelt and his head rested on her knee. Her heart stood still as she listened for the sound of his faint breathing. Had his unconsciousness lasted longer she would have fainted herself. But in a moment his eyes opened again with an expression such as she had seen in them once or twice before, but in a less degree.

"Corona—it is too much!" he said softly, almost dreamily. Then his strength returned in an instant, like a strong steel bow that has been bent almost to breaking. He scarcely knew how it was that the position was changed so that he was standing on his feet and clasping her as she had clasped him. Her tears were flowing fast, but there was more joy in them than pain.

"How could you do it?" she asked at length, looking up. "And oh, Giovanni! What will be the end of it? Will not something dreadful happen?"

"What does anything matter now, darling?"

At last they sat down together, hand in hand, as of old. It was as though the last two months had been suddenly blotted out. As Giovanni said, nothing could matter now. And yet the situation was far from clear. Giovanni understood well enough that the cardinal had wished to leave him the option of telling his wife what had occurred, and, if he chose to do so, of telling her in his own language. He was grateful for the tact the statesman had displayed, a tact which seemed also to show Giovanni the cardinal's views of the case. He had declared that he was desperate. The cardinal had concluded that he was unhappy. He had said that he did not care what became of him. The cardinal had supposed that he would be glad to be alone, or at all events that it would be good for him to have a certain amount of solitude. If his position were in any way dangerous, the great man would surely not have thought of sending Corona to his prisoner as he had done. He would have prepared her himself against any shock. And yet he was undeniably in prison, with no immediate prospect of liberty.

"You cannot stay here any longer," said Corona when they were at last able to talk of the immediate future.

"I do not see how I am to get out," Giovanni answered, with a smile.

"I will go to the cardinal—"

"It is of no use. He probably guesses the truth, but he is not willing to be made ridiculous by me or by any one. He will keep me here until there can be a trial, or until he finds the real culprit. He is obstinate. I know him."

"It is impossible that he should think of such a thing!" exclaimed Corona indignantly.

"I am afraid it is very possible. But, of course, it is only a matter of time—a few days at the utmost. If worst comes to worst I can demand an inquiry, I suppose, though I do not see how I can proclaim my own innocence without hurting Faustina. She was liberated because I put myself in her place—it is rather complicated."

"Tell me, Giovanni," said Corona, "what did you say to the cardinal? You did not really say that you murdered Montevarchi?"

"No. I said I gave myself up as the murderer, and I explained how I might have done the deed. I did more, I pledged my honour that Faustina was innocent."

"But you were not sure of it yourself—"

"Since you had told me it was true, I believed it," he answered simply.

"Thank you, dear—"

"No. Do not thank me for it. I could not help myself. I knew that you were sure—are you sure of something else, Corona? Are you as certain as you were of that?"

"How can you ask? But you are right—you have the right to doubt me. You will not, though, will you? Hear me, dear, while I tell you the whole story."

She slipped from her chair and knelt before him, as though she were to make a confession. Then she took his hands and looked up lovingly into his face. The truth rose in her eyes.

"Forgive me, Giovanni. Yes, you have much to forgive. I did not know myself. When you doubted me, I felt as though I had nothing left in life, as though you would never again believe in me. I thought I did not love you. I was wrong. It was only my miserable vanity that was wounded, and that hurt me so. I felt that my love was dead, that you yourself were dead and that another man had taken your place. Ah, I could have helped it! Had I known you better, dear, had I been less mistaken in myself, all would have been different. But I was foolish—no, I was unhappy. Everything was dark and dreadful. Oh, my darling, I thought I could tell what I felt—I cannot! Forgive me, only forgive me, and love me as you did long ago. I will never leave you, not if you stay here for ever, only let me love you as I will!"

"It is not for me to forgive, sweetheart," said Giovanni, bending down and kissing her sweet dark hair. "It is for you—"

"But I would so much rather think it my fault, dear," she answered, drawing his face down to hers. It was a very womanly impulse that made her take the blame upon herself.

"You must not think anything so unreasonable, Corona. I brought all the harm that came, from the first moment."

He would have gone on to accuse himself, obstinate and manlike, recapitulating the whole series of events. But she would not let him. Once more she sat beside him and held his hand in hers. They talked incoherently and it is not to be wondered at if they arrived at no very definite conclusion after a very long conversation. They were still sitting together when the attendant entered and presented Giovanni with a large sealed letter, bearing the Apostolic arms, and addressed merely to the number of Giovanni's cell.

"There is an answer," said the man, and then left the room.

"It is probably the notice of the trial, or something of the kind," observed Giovanni, suddenly growing very grave as he broke the seal. He wished it might have come at any other time than the present. Corona held her breath and watched his face while he read the lines written upon one of the two papers he took from the envelope. Suddenly the colour came to his cheeks and his eyes brightened with a look of happiness and surprise.

"I am free!" he cried, as he finished. "Free if I will sign this paper! Of course I will! I will sign anything he likes."

The envelope contained a note from the cardinal, in his own hand, to the effect that suspicion had fallen upon another person and that Giovanni was at liberty to return to his home if he would sign the accompanying document. The latter was very short, and set forth that Giovanni Saracinesca bound himself upon his word to appear in the trial of the murderer of Prince Montevarchi, if called upon to do so, and not to leave Rome until the matter was finally concluded and set at rest.

He took the pen that lay on the table and signed his name in a broad firm hand, a fact the more notable because Corona was leaning over his shoulder, watching the characters as he traced them. He folded the paper and placed it in the open envelope which accompanied it. The cardinal was a man of details. He thought it possible that the document might be returned open for lack of the means to seal it. He did not choose that his secrets should become the property of the people about the Holy Office. It was a specimen of his forethought in small things which might have an influence upon great ones.

When Giovanni had finished, he rose and stood beside Corona. Each looked into the other's eyes and for a moment neither saw very clearly. They said little more, however, until the attendant entered again.

"You are at liberty," he said briefly, and without a word began to put together the few small things that belonged to his late prisoner.

Half an hour later Giovanni was seated at dinner at his father's table. The old gentleman greeted him with a half-savage growl of satisfaction.

"The prodigal has returned to get a meal while there is one to be had," he remarked. "I thought you had gone to Paris to leave the agreeable settlement of our affairs to Corona and me. Where the devil have you been?"

"I have been indulging in the luxury of a retreat in a religious house," answered Giovanni with perfect truth.

Corona glanced at him and both laughed happily, as they had not laughed for many days and weeks. Saracinesca looked incredulously across the table at his son.

"You chose a singular moment for your devotional exercises," he said. "Where will piety hide herself next, I wonder? As long as Corona is satisfied, I am. It is her business."

"I am perfectly satisfied, I assure you," said Corona, whose black eyes were full of light. Giovanni raised his glass, looked at her and smiled lovingly. Then he emptied it to the last drop and set it down without a word.

"Some secret, I suppose," said the old gentleman gruffly.

CHAPTER XXVIII

Arnoldo Meschini was not, perhaps, insane in the ordinary sense of the word; that is to say, he would probably have recovered the normal balance of his faculties if he could have been kept from narcotics and stimulants, and if he could have been relieved from the distracting fear of discovery which tormented him when he was not under the influence of one or the other. But the latter condition was impossible, and it was the extremity of his terror which almost forced him to keep his brain in a clouded state. People have been driven mad by sudden fright, and have gradually lost their intellect through the constant presence of a fear from which there is no escape. A man who is perpetually producing an unnatural state of his mind by swallowing doses of brandy and opium may not be insane in theory; in actual fact, he may be a dangerous madman. As one day followed another Meschini found it more and more impossible to exist without his two comforters. The least approach to lucidity made him almost frantic. He fancied every man a spy, every indifferent glance a look full of meaning. Before long the belief took possession of him that he was to be made the victim of some horrible private vengeance. San Giacinto was not the man, he thought, to be contented with sending him to the galleys for life. Few murderers were executed in those days, and it would be a small satisfaction to the Montevarchi to know that Arnoldo had merely been transferred from his study of the library catalogue to the breaking of stones with a chain gang at Civitavecchia. It was more likely that they would revenge themselves more effectually. His disordered imagination saw horrible visions. San Giacinto might lay a trap for him, might simply come at dead of night and take him from his room to some deep vault beneath the palace. What could he do against such a giant? He fancied himself before a secret tribunal in the midst of which towered San Giacinto's colossal figure. He could hear the deep voice he dreaded pronouncing his doom. He was to be torn to shreds piecemeal, burnt by a slow fire, flayed alive by those enormous hands. There was no conceivable horror of torture that did not suggest itself to him at such times. It is true that when he went to bed at night he was generally either so stupefied by opium or so intoxicated with strong drink that he forgot even to lock his door. But during the day he was seldom so far under the power of either as not to suffer from his own hideous imaginings. One day, as he dragged his slow pace along a narrow street near the fountain of Trevi, his eyes were arrested by an armourer's window. It suddenly struck him that he had no weapon of defence in case San Giacinto or his agents came upon him unawares. And yet a bullet well placed would make an end even of such a Hercules as the man he feared. He paused and looked anxiously up and down the street. It was a dark day and a fine rain was falling. There was nobody about who could recognise him, and he might not have another such opportunity of providing himself unobserved with what he wanted. He entered the shop and bought himself a revolver. The man showed him how to load it and sold him a box of cartridges. He dropped the firearm into one of the pockets of his coat, and smiled as he felt how comfortably it balanced the bottle he carried in the other. Then he slunk out of the shop and pursued his walk.

The idea of making capital out of the original deeds concerning the Saracinesca, which had presented itself to him soon after the murder, recurred frequently to his mind; but he felt that he was in no condition to elaborate it, and promised himself to attend to the matter when he was better. For he fancied that he was ill and that his state would soon begin to improve. To go to San Giacinto now was out of the question. It would have been easier for him to climb the cross on the summit of St. Peter's, with his shaken nerves and trembling limbs, than to face the man who inspired in him such untold dread. He could, of course, take the alternative which was open to him, and go to old Saracinesca. Indeed, there were moments when he could almost have screwed his courage to the point of making such an attempt, but his natural prudence made him draw back from an interview in which he must incur a desperate risk unless he had a perfect command of his faculties. To write what he had to say would be merely to give a weapon against himself, since he could not treat the matter by letter without acknowledging his share in the forgeries. The only way to accomplish his purpose would be to extract a solemn promise of secrecy from Saracinesca, together with a guarantee for his own safety, and to obtain these conditions would need all the diplomacy he possessed. Bad as he was, he had no experience of practical blackmailing, and he would be obliged to compose his speeches beforehand with scrupulous care, and with the wisest forethought. For the present, such work was beyond his power, but when he was half drunk he loved to look at the ancient parchments and build golden palaces in the future. When he was strong again, and calm, he would realise all his dreams, and that time, he felt sure, could not be far removed.

Nevertheless the days succeeded each other with appalling swiftness, and nothing was done. By imperceptible degrees his horror of San Giacinto began to invade his mind even when it was most deadened by drink. So long as an idea is new and has not really become a habit of the brain, brandy will drive it away, but the moment must inevitably come when the stimulant loses its power to obscure the memory of the thing dreaded. Opium will do it more effectually, but even that does not continue to act for ever. The time comes when the predominant thought of the waking hours reproduces itself during the artificial sleep with fearful force, so that the mind at last obtains no rest at all. That is the dangerous period, preceding the decay and total collapse of the intellect under what is commonly called the fixed idea. In certain conditions of mind, and notably with criminals who fear discovery, the effects of opium change very quickly; the downward steps through which it would take months for an ordinary individual to pass are descended with alarming rapidity, and the end is a thousand times more horrible. Meschini could not have taken the doses which a confirmed opium-eater swallows with indifference, but the result produced was far greater in proportion to the amount of the narcotic he consumed. Before the week which followed the deed was ended, he began to see visions when he was apparently awake.

Shapeless, slimy things crawled about the floor of his room, upon his table, even upon the sheets of his bed. Dark shadows confronted him, and changed their outlines unexpectedly. Forms rose out of the earth at his feet and towered all at once to the top of the room, taking the appearance of San Giacinto and vanishing suddenly into the air. The things he saw came like instantaneous flashes from another and even more terrible world, disappearing at first so quickly as to make him believe them only the effects of the light and darkness, like the ghost he had seen in his coat. In the beginning there was scarcely anything alarming in them, but as he started whenever they came, he generally took them as a warning that he needed more brandy to keep him up. In the course of a day or two, however, these visions assumed more awful proportions, and he found it impossible to escape from them except in absolute stupor. It would have been clear to any one that this state of things could not last long. There was scarcely an hour in which he knew exactly what he was doing, and if his strange behaviour escaped observation this was due to his solitary way of living. He did not keep away from the palace during the whole day, from a vague idea that his absence might be thought suspicious. He spent a certain number of hours in the library, doing nothing, although he carefully spread out a number of books before him and dipped his pen into the ink from time to time, stupidly, mechanically, as though his fingers could not forget the habit so long familiar to them. His eyes, which had formerly been unusually bright, had grown dull and almost bleared, though they glanced at times very quickly from one part of the room to another. That was when he saw strange things moving in the vast hall, between him and the bookcases. When they had disappeared, his glassy look returned, so that his eyeballs seemed merely to reflect the light, as inanimate objects do, without absorbing it, and conveying it to the seat of vision. His face grew daily more thin and ghastly. It was by force of custom that he stayed so long in the place where he had spent so much of his life. The intervals of semi-lucidity seemed terribly long, though they were in reality short enough, and the effort to engage his attention in work helped him to live through them. He had never gone down to the apartments where the family lived, since he had knelt before the catafalque on the day after the murder. Indeed, there was no reason why he should go there, and no one noticed his absence. He was a very insignificant person in the palace. As for any one coming to find him among the books, nothing seemed more improbable. The library was swept out in the early morning and no one entered it again during the twenty-four hours.

He never went out into the corridor now, but left his coat upon a chair near him, when he remembered to bring it. As a sort of precautionary measure against fear, he locked the door which opened upon the passage when he came in the morning, unlocking it again when he went away in order that the servant who did the sweeping might be able to get in.

The Princess Montevarchi was still dangerously ill, and Faustina had not been willing to leave her. San Giacinto and Flavia were not living in the house, but they spent a good deal of time there, because San Giacinto had ideas of his own about duty, to which his wife was obliged to submit even if she did not like them. Faustina was neither nervous nor afraid of solitude, and was by no means in need of her sister's company, so that when the two were together their conversation was not always of the most affectionate kind. The consequence was that the young girl tried to be alone as much as possible when she was not at her mother's bedside. One day, having absolutely nothing to do, she grew desperate. It was very hard not to think of Anastase, when she was in the solitude of her own room, with no occupation to direct her mind. A week earlier she had been only too glad to have the opportunity of dreaming away the short afternoon undisturbed, letting her girlish thoughts wander among the rose gardens of the future with the image of the man she loved so dearly, and who was yet so far removed from her. Now she could not think of him without reflecting that her father's death had removed one very great obstacle to her marriage. She was by no means of a very devout or saintly character, but, on the other hand, she had a great deal of what is called heart, and to be heartless seemed to her almost worse than to be bad. In excuse of such very untheological doctrines it must be allowed that her ideas concerning wickedness in general were very limited indeed, if not altogether childish in their extreme simplicity. It is certain, however, that she would have thought it far less wrong to run away with Gouache in spite of her family than to entertain any thought which could place her father's tragic death in the light of a personal advantage. If she had nothing to do she could not help thinking of Anastase, and if she thought of him, she could not escape the conclusion that it would be far easier for her to marry him, now that the old prince was out of the way. It was therefore absolutely necessary to find some occupation.

At first she wandered aimlessly about the house until she was struck, almost for the first time, by the antiquated stiffness of the arrangement, and began to ask herself whether it would be respectful to the memory of her father, and to her mother, to try and make a few changes. Corona's home was very different. She would like to take that for a model. But one or two attempts showed her the magnitude of the task she had undertaken. She was ashamed to call the servants to help her—it would look as though there were to be a reception in the house. Her ideas of what could take place in the Palazzo Montevarchi did not go beyond that staid form of diversion. She was ashamed, however, and reflected, besides, that she was only the youngest of the family and had no right to take the initiative in the matter of improvements. The time hung very heavily upon her hands. She tried to teach herself something about painting by looking at the pictures on the walls, spending a quarter of an hour before each with conscientious assiduity. But this did not succeed either. The men in the pictures all took the shape of Monsieur Gouache in his smartest uniform and the women all looked disagreeably like Flavia. Then she thought of the library, which was the only place of importance in the house which she had not lately visited. She hesitated a moment only, considering how she could best reach it without passing through the study, and without going up the grand staircase to the outer door. A very little reflection showed her that she could get into the corridor from a passage near her own room. In a few minutes she was at the entrance to the great hall, trying to turn the heavy carved brass handle of the latch. To her surprise she could not open the door, which was evidently fastened from within. Then as she shook it in the hope that some one would hear her, a strange cry reached her ears, like that of a startled animal, accompanied by the shuffling of feet. She remembered Meschini's walk, and understood that it was he.

"Please let me in!" she called out in her clear young voice, that echoed back to her from the vaulted chamber.

Again she heard the shuffling footsteps, which this time came towards her, and a moment afterwards the door opened and the librarian's ghastly face was close before her. She drew back a little. She had forgotten that he was so ugly, she thought, or perhaps she would not have cared to see him. It would have been foolish, moreover, to go away after coming thus far.

"I want to see the library," she said quietly, after she had made up her mind. "Will you show it to me?"

"Favorisca, Excellency," replied Meschini in a broken voice. He had been frightened by the noise at the door, and the contortion of his face as he tried to smile was hideous to see. He bowed low, however, and closed the door after she had entered. Scarcely knowing what he did, he shuffled along by her side while she looked about the library, gazing at the long rows of books, bound all alike, that stretched from end to end of many of the shelves. The place was new to her, for she had not been in it more than two or three times in her life, and she felt a sort of unexplained awe in the presence of so many thousands of volumes, of so much written and printed wisdom which she could never hope to understand. She had come with a vague idea that she should find something to read that should be different from the novels she was not allowed to touch. She realised all at once that she knew nothing of what had been written in all the centuries whose literature was represented in the vast collection. She hardly knew the names of twenty books out of the hundreds of millions that the world contained. But she could ask Meschini. She looked at him again, and his face repelled her. Nevertheless, she was too kindhearted not to enter into conversation with the lonely man whom she had so rarely seen, but who was one of the oldest members of her father's household.

"You have spent your life here, have you not?" she asked, for the sake of saying something.

"Nearly thirty years of it," answered Meschini in a muffled voice. Her presence tortured him beyond expression. "That is a long time, and I am not an old man."

"And are you always alone here? Do you never go out? What do you do all day?"

"I work among the books, Excellency. There are twenty thousand volumes here, enough to occupy a man's time."

"Yes—but how? Do you have to read them all?" asked Faustina innocently. "Is that your work?"

"I have read many more than would be believed, for my own pleasure. But my work is to keep them in order, to see that there is no variation from the catalogue, so that when learned men come to make inquiries they may find what they want. I have also to take care of all the books, to see that they do not suffer in any way. They are very valuable. There is a fortune here."

Somehow he felt less nervous when he began to speak of the library and its contents and the words came more easily to him. With a little encouragement he might even become loquacious. In spite of his face, Faustina began to feel an interest in him.

"It must be very hard work," she remarked. "Do you like it? Did you never want to do anything else? I should think you would grow tired of being always alone."

"I am very patient," answered Meschini humbly. "And I am used to it. I grew accustomed to the life when I was young."

"You say the collection is valuable. Are there any very beautiful books? I would like to see some of them."

The fair young creature sat down upon one of the high carved chairs at the end of a table. Meschini went to the other side of the hall and unlocked one of the drawers which lined the lower part of the bookcases to the height of three or four feet. Each was heavily carved with the Montevarchi arms in high relief. It was in these receptacles that the precious manuscripts were kept in their cases. He returned bringing a small square volume of bound manuscript, and laid it before Faustina.

"This is worth an enormous sum," he said. "It is the only complete one in the world. There is an imperfect copy in the library of the Vatican."

"What is it?"

"It is the Montevarchi Dante, the oldest in existence."

Faustina turned over the leaves curiously, and admired the even writing though she could not read many of the words, for the ancient characters were strange to her. It was a wonderful picture that the couple made in the great hall. On every side the huge carved bookcases of walnut, black with age, rose from the floor to the spring of the vault, their dark faces reflected in the highly-polished floor of coloured marble. Across the ancient tables a ray of sunlight fell from the high clerestory window. In the centre, the two figures with the old manuscript between them; Faustina's angel head in a high light against the dusky background, as she bent forward a little, turning the yellow pages with her slender, transparent fingers, the black folds of her full gown making heavy lines of drapery, graceful by her grace, and rendered less severe by a sort of youthfulness that seemed to pervade them, and that emanated from herself. Beside her, the bent frame of the broken down librarian, in a humble and respectful attitude, his long arms hanging down by his sides, his shabby black coat almost dragging to his heels, his head bent forward as he looked at the pages. All his features seemed to have grown more sharp and yellow and pointed, and there was now a deep red flush in the upper part of his cheeks. A momentary light shone in his gray eyes, from beneath the bushy brows, a light of intelligence such as had formerly characterised them especially, brought back now perhaps by the effort to fix his attention upon the precious book. His large, coarse ears appeared to point themselves forward like those of an animal, following the direction of his sight. In outward appearance he presented a strange mixture of dilapidation, keenness, and brutality. A week had changed him very much. A few days ago most people would have looked at him with a sort of careless compassion. Now, there was about him something distinctly repulsive. Beside Faustina's youth and delicacy and freshness, he hardly seemed like a human being.

"I suppose it is a very wonderful thing," said the young girl at last, "but I do not know enough to understand its value. Do my brothers ever come to the library?" She leaned back from the volume and glanced at Meschini's face, wondering how heaven could have made anything so ugly.

"No. They never come," replied the librarian, drawing the book towards him instinctively, as he would have done if his visitor had been a stranger, who might try to steal a page or two unless he were watched.

"But my poor father was very fond of the books, was he not? Did he not often come to see you here?"

She was thinking so little of Meschini that she did not see that he turned suddenly white and shook like a man in an ague. It was what he had feared all along, ever since she had entered the room. She suspected him and had come, or had perhaps been sent by San Giacinto to draw him into conversation and to catch him in something which could be interpreted to be a confession of his crime. Had that been her intention, his behaviour would have left little doubt in her mind as to the truth of the accusation. His face betrayed him, his uncontrollable fear, his frightened eyes and trembling limbs. But she had only glanced at him, and her sight wandered to the bookcases for a moment. When she looked again he was moving away from her, along the table. She was surprised to see that his step was uncertain, and that he reeled against the heavy piece of furniture and grasped it for support. She started a little but did not rise.

"Are you ill?" she asked. "Shall I call some one?"

He made no answer, but seemed to recover himself at the sound of her voice, for he shuffled away and disappeared behind the high carved desk on which lay the open catalogue. She thought she saw a flash of light reflected from some smooth surface, and immediately afterwards she heard a gurgling sound, which she did not understand. Meschini was fortifying himself with a draught. Then he reappeared, walking more steadily. He had received a severe shock, but, as usual, he had not the courage to run away, conceiving that flight would inevitably be regarded as a proof of guilt.

"I am not well," he said in explanation as he returned. "I am obliged to take medicine continually. I beg your Excellency to forgive me."

"I am sorry to hear that," answered Faustina kindly. "Can we do nothing for you? Have you all you need?"

"Everything, thank you. I shall soon be well."

"I hope so, I am sure. What was I saying? Oh—I was asking whether my poor father came often to the library. Was he fond of the books?"

"His Excellency—Heaven give him glory!—he was a learned man. Yes, he came now and then." Meschini took possession of the manuscript and carried it off rather suddenly to its place in the drawer. He was a long time in locking it up. Faustina watched him with some curiosity.

"You were here that day, were you not?" she asked, as he turned towards her once more. The question was a natural one, considering the circumstances.

"I think your Excellency was present when I was examined by the prefect," answered Meschini in a curiously disagreeable tone.

"True," said Faustina. "You said you had been here all day as usual. I had forgotten. How horrible it was. And you saw nobody, you heard nothing? But I suppose it is too far from the study."

The librarian did not answer, but it was evident from his manner that he was very much disturbed. Indeed, he fancied that his worst fears were realised, and that Faustina was really trying to extract information from him for his own conviction. Her thoughts were actually very far from any such idea. She would have considered it quite as absurd to accuse the poor wretch before her as she had thought it outrageous that she herself should be suspected. Her father had always seemed to her a very imposing personage, and she could not conceive that he should have met his death at the hands of such a miserable creature as Arnoldo Meschini, who certainly had not the outward signs of physical strength or boldness. He, however, understood her words very differently and stood still, half way between her and the bookcases, asking himself whether it would not be better to take immediate steps for his safety. His hand was behind him, feeling for the revolver in the pocket of his long coat. Faustina was singularly fearless, by nature, but if she had guessed the danger of her position she would probably have effected her escape very quickly, instead of continuing the conversation.

"It is a very dreadful mystery," she said, rising from her chair and walking slowly across the polished marble floor until she stood before a row of great volumes of which the colour had attracted her eye. "It is the duty of us all to try and explain it. Of course we shall know all about it some day, but it is very hard to be patient. Do you know?" she turned suddenly and faced Meschini, speaking with a vehemence not usual for her. "They suspected me, as if I could have done it, I, a weak girl! And yet—if I had the man before me—the man who murdered him—I believe I would kill him with my hands!"

She moved forward a little, as she spoke, and tapped her small foot upon the pavement, as though to emphasise her words. Her soft brown eyes flashed with righteous anger, and her cheek grew pale at the thought of avenging her father. There must have been something very fierce in her young face, for Meschini's heart failed him, and his nerves seemed to collapse all at once. He tried to draw back from her, slipped and fell upon his knees with a sharp cry of fear. Even then, Faustina did not suspect the cause of his weakness, but attributed it to the illness of which he had spoken. She sprang forward and attempted to help the poor creature to his feet, but instead of making an effort to rise, he seemed to be grovelling before her, uttering incoherent exclamations of terror.

"Lean on me!" said Faustina, putting out her hand. "What is the matter? Oh! Are you going to die!"

"Oh! Do not hurt me—pray—in God's name!" cried Meschini, raising his eyes timidly.

"Hurt you? No! Why should I hurt you? You are ill—we will have the doctor. Try and get up—try and get to a chair."

Her tone reassured him a little, and her touch also, as she did her best to raise him to his feet. He struggled a little and at last stood up, leaning upon the bookcase, and panting with fright.

"It is nothing," he tried to say, catching his breath at every syllable. "I am better—my nerves—your Excellency—ugh! What a coward I am!"

The last exclamation, uttered in profound disgust of his own weakness, struck Faustina as very strange.

"Did I frighten you?" she asked in surprise. "I am very sorry. Now sit down and I will call some one to come to you."

"No, no! Please—I would rather be alone! I can walk quite well now. If—if your Excellency will excuse me, I will go to my room. I have more medicine—I will take it and I shall be better."

"Can you go alone? Are you sure?" asked Faustina anxiously. But even while she spoke he was moving towards the door, slowly and painfully at first, as it seemed, though possibly a lingering thought of propriety kept him from appearing to run away. The young girl walked a few steps after him, half fearing that he might fall again. But he kept his feet and reached the threshold. Then he made a queer attempt at a bow, and mumbled some words that Faustina could not hear. In another moment he had disappeared, and she was alone.

For some minutes she looked at the closed door through which he had gone out. Then she shook her head a little sadly, and slowly went back to her room by the way she had come. It was all very strange, she thought, but his illness might account for it. She would have liked to consult San Giacinto, but though she was outwardly on good terms with him, and could not help feeling a sort of respect for his manly character, the part he had played in attempting to separate her from Gouache had prevented the two from becoming intimate. She said nothing to any one about her interview with Meschini in the library, and no one even guessed that she had been there.

CHAPTER XXIX

IN spite of his haste to settle all that remained to be settled with regard to the restitution of the property to San Giacinto, Saracinesca found it impossible to wind up the affair in a week as he had intended. It was a very complicated matter to separate from his present fortune that part of it which his cousin would have inherited from his great-grandfather. A great deal of wealth had come into the family since that time by successive marriages, and the management of the original estate had not been kept separate from the administration of the dowries which had from time to time been absorbed into it. The Saracinesca, however, were orderly people, and the books had been kept for generations with that astonishing precision of detail which is found in the great Roman houses, and which surpasses, perhaps, anything analogous which is to be found in modern business. By dint of perseverance and by employing a great number of persons in making the calculations, the notaries had succeeded in preparing a tolerably satisfactory schedule in the course of a fortnight, which both the principal parties agreed to accept as final. The day fixed for the meeting and liquidation of the accounts was a Saturday, a fortnight and two days after the murder of Prince Montevarchi. A question arose concerning the place of meeting.

Saracinesca proposed that San Giacinto and the notaries should come to the Palazzo Saracinesca. He was ready to brave out the situation to the end, to face his fate until it held nothing more in store for him, even to handing over the inventory of all that was no longer his in the house where he had been born. His boundless courage and almost brutal frankness would doubtless have supported him to the last, even through such a trial to his feelings, but San Giacinto refused to agree to the proposal. He repeatedly stated that he wished the old prince to inhabit the palace through his lifetime, and that he should even make every effort to induce him to retain the title. Both of these offers were rejected courteously, but firmly. In the matter of holding the decisive meeting in the palace, however, San Giacinto made a determined stand. He would not on any account appear in the light of the conqueror coming to take possession of the spoil. His wife had no share in this generous sentiment. She would have liked to enjoy her triumph to the full, for she was exceedingly ambitious, and was, moreover, not very fond of the Saracinesca. As she expressed it, she felt when she was with any of them, from the old prince to Corona, that they must be thinking all the time that she was a very foolish young person. San Giacinto's action was therefore spontaneous, and if it needs explanation it may be ascribed to an inherited magnanimity, to a certain dignity which had distinguished him even as a young man from the low class in which he had grown up. He was, indeed, by no means a type of the perfect nobleman; his conduct in the affair between Faustina and Gouache had shown that. He acted according to his lights, and was not ashamed to do things which his cousin Giovanni would have called mean. But he was manly, for all that, and if he owed some of his dignity to great stature and to his indomitable will, it was also in a measure the outward sign of a good heart and of an innate sense of justice. There had as yet been nothing dishonest in his dealings since he had come to Rome. He had acquired a fortune which enabled him to take the position that was lawfully his. He liked Flavia, and had bargained for her with her father, afterwards scrupulously fulfilling the terms of the contract. He had not represented himself to be what he was not, and he had taken no unfair advantage of any one for his own advancement. In the matter of the suit he was the dupe of old Montevarchi, so far as the deeds were concerned, but he was perfectly aware that he actually represented the elder branch of his family. It is hard to imagine how any man in his position could have done less than he did, and now that it had come to a final settlement he was really anxious to cause his vanquished relations as little humiliation as possible. To go to their house was like playing the part of a bailiff. To allow them to come to his dwelling suggested the journey to Canossa. The Palazzo Montevarchi was neutral ground, and he proposed that the formalities should be fulfilled there. Saracinesca consented readily enough and the day was fixed.

The notaries arrived at ten o'clock in the morning, accompanied by clerks who were laden with books, inventories and rolls of manuscript. The study had been selected for the meeting, both on account of its seclusion from the rest of the house and because it contained an immense table which would serve for the voluminous documents, all of which must be examined and verified. San Giacinto himself awaited the arrival of the Saracinesca in the great reception-room. He had sent his wife away, for he was in reality by no means so calm as he appeared to be, and her constant talk disturbed him. He paced the long room with regular steps, his head erect, his hands behind him, stopping from time to time to listen for the footsteps of those he expected. It was the great day of his life. Before night, he was to be Prince Saracinesca.

The moments that precede a great triumph are very painful, especially if a man has looked forward to the event for a long time. No matter how sure he is of the result, something tells him that it is uncertain. A question may arise, he cannot guess whence, by which all may be changed. He repeats to himself a hundred times that failure is impossible, but he is not at rest. The uncertainty of all things, even of his own life, appears very clearly before his eyes. His heart beats fast and slow from one minute to another. At the very instant when he is dreaming of the future, the possibility of disappointment breaks in upon his thoughts. He cannot explain it, but he longs to be beyond the decisive hour. In San Giacinto's existence, the steps from obscurity to importance and fortune had, of late, been so rapidly ascended that he was almost giddy with success. For the first time since he had left his old home in Aquila, he felt as though he had been changed from his own self to some other person.

At last the door opened, and Saracinesca, Giovanni, and Corona entered the room. San Giacinto was surprised to see Giovanni's wife on an occasion when the men alone of the family were concerned, but she explained that she had come to spend the morning with Faustina, and would wait till everything was finished. The meeting was not a cordial one, though both parties regarded it as inevitable. If Saracinesca felt any personal resentment against San Giacinto he knew that it was unreasonable and he had not the bad taste to show it. He was silent, but courteous in his manner. Giovanni, strange to say, seemed wholly indifferent to what was about to take place.

"I hope," said San Giacinto, when all four were seated, "that you will consent to consider this as a mere formality. I have said as much through my lawyers, but I wish to repeat it myself in better words than they used."

"Pardon me," answered Saracinesca, "if I suggest that we should not discuss that matter. We are sensible of your generosity in making such offers, but we do not consider it possible to accept them."

"I must ask your indulgence if I do not act upon your suggestion," returned San Giacinto. "Even if there is no discussion I cannot consent to proceed to business until I have explained what I mean. If the suit has been settled justly by the courts, it has not been decided with perfect justice as regards its consequences. I do not deny, and I understand that you do not expect me to act otherwise, that it has been my intention to secure for myself and for my children the property and the personal position abandoned by my ancestor. I have obtained what I wanted and what was my right, and I have to thank you for the magnanimity you have displayed in not attempting to contest a claim against which you might have brought many arguments, if not much evidence. The affair having been legally settled, it is for us to make whatever use of it seems better in our own eyes. To deprive you of your name and of the house in which you were born and bred, would be to offer you an indignity such as I never contemplated."

"You cannot be said to deprive us of what is not ours, by any interpretation of the word with which I am acquainted," said Saracinesca in a tone which showed that he was determined to receive nothing.

"I am a poor grammarian," answered San Giacinto gravely, and without the slightest affectation of humility. "I was brought up a farmer, and was only an innkeeper until lately. I cannot discuss with you the subtle meanings of words. To my mind it is I who am taking from you that which, if not really yours, you have hitherto had every right to own and to make use of. I do not attempt to explain my thought. I only say that I will neither take your name nor live in your house while you are alive. I propose a compromise which I hope you will be willing to accept."

"I fear that will be impossible. My mind is made up."

"I propose," continued San Giacinto, "that you remain Prince Saracinesca, that you keep Saracinesca itself, and the palace here in Rome during your lifetime, which I trust may be a long one. After your death everything returns to us. My cousin Giovanni and the Princess Sant' Ilario—"

"You may call me Corona, if you please," said the princess suddenly. Her eyes were fixed on his face, and she was smiling.

Both Saracinesca and Giovanni looked at her in surprise. It seemed strange to them that she should choose such a moment for admitting San Giacinto to a familiarity he had never before enjoyed. But for some time she had felt a growing respect for the ex-innkeeper, which was quickened by his present generosity. San Giacinto's swarthy face grew a shade darker as the blood mounted to his lean cheeks. Corona had given him one of the first sensations of genuine pleasure he had ever experienced in his rough life.

"Thank you," he said simply. "You two, I was going to say, have palaces of your own and cannot have such close associations with the old places as one who has owned them during so many years. You," he continued, turning to the old prince, "will, I hope, accept an arrangement which cannot affect your dignity and which will give me the greatest satisfaction."

"I am very much obliged to you," answered Saracinesca promptly. "You are very generous, but I cannot take what you offer."

"If you feel that you would be taking anything from me, look at it from a different point of view. You would be conferring a favour instead of accepting one. Consider my position, when I have taken your place. It will not be a pleasant one. The world will abuse me roundly, and will say I have behaved abominably towards you. Do you fancy that I shall be received as a substitute for the Prince Saracinesca your friends have known so long? Do you suppose that the vicissitudes of my life are unknown, and that no one will laugh behind my back and point at me as the new, upstart prince? Few people know me in Rome, and if I have any friends besides you, I have not been made aware of the fact. Pray consider that in doing what I ask, you would be saving me from very unpleasant social consequences."

"I should be doing so at the cost of my self-respect," replied the old man firmly. "Whatever the consequences are to you, the means of bearing them will be in your hands. You will have no lack of friends tomorrow, or at least of amiable persons anxious to call themselves by that name. They will multiply this very night, like mushrooms, and will come about you freshly shaved and smiling tomorrow morning."

"I am afraid you do not understand me," said San Giacinto. "I can leave you the title and yet take one which will serve as well. You would call yourself Prince Saracinesca and I should be Saracinesca di San Giacinto. As for the palace and the place in the mountains, they are so insignificant as compared with the rest that it could not hurt your self-respect to live in them. Can you not persuade your father?" He turned to Giovanni who had not spoken yet.

"You are very good to make the proposal," he answered. "I cannot say more than that. I agree with my father."

A silence followed which lasted several minutes. Corona looked from one to the other of the three men, wondering how the matter would end. She understood both parties better than they understood each other. She sympathised with the refusal of her husband and his father. To accept such an offer would put them in a position of obligation towards San Giacinto which she knew they could never endure, and which would be galling to herself. On the other hand she felt sorry for their cousin, who was evidently trying to do what he felt was right and generous, and was disappointed that his advances should be repelled. He was very much in earnest, or he would not have gone so far as to suggest that it would be a favour to him if they took what he offered. He was so simple, and yet so dignified withal, that she could not help liking him. It was not clear to her, however, that she could mend matters by interfering, nor by offering advice to the one or sympathy to the other.

Saracinesca himself was the first to break the silence. It seemed to him that everything had been said, and that nothing now remained but to fulfil the requisite formalities.

"Shall we proceed to business?" he inquired, as though ignoring all the previous conversation. "I believe we have a great deal to do, and the time is passing."

San Giacinto made no reply, but rose gravely and made a gesture signifying that he would show the way to the study. Saracinesca made a show of refusing to go out first, then yielded and went on. San Giacinto waited at the door for Corona and Giovanni. "I will join you in a moment—I know the way," said the latter, remaining behind with his wife.

When they were alone he led her towards one of the windows, as though to be doubly sure that no one could hear what he was about to say. Then he stood still and looked into her eyes.

"Would you like us to accept such a favour from him?" he asked. "Tell me the truth."

"No," answered Corona without the least hesitation. "But I am sorry for San Giacinto. I think he is really trying to do right, and to be generous. He was hurt by your father's answer."

"If I thought it would give you pleasure to feel that we could go to Saracinesca, I would try and make my father change his mind."

"Would you?" She knew very well what a sacrifice it would be to his pride.

"Yes, dear. I would do it for you."

"Giovanni—how good you are!"

"No—I am not good. I love you. That is all. Shall I try?"

"Never! I am sorry for San Giacinto—but I could no more live in the old house, or in Saracinesca, than you could. Do I not feel all that you feel, and more?"

"All?"

"All."

They stood hand in hand looking out of the window, and there were tears in the eyes of both. The grasp of their fingers tightened slowly as though they were drawn together by an irresistible force. Slowly they turned their faces towards each other, and presently their lips met in one of those kisses that are never forgotten. Then Giovanni left her where she was. All had been said; both knew that they desired nothing more in this world, and that henceforth they were all to each other. It was as though a good angel had set a heavenly seal upon the reunion of their hearts.

Corona did not leave the room immediately, but remained a few moments leaning against the heavy frame of the window. Her queenly figure drooped a little, and she pressed one hand to her side. Her dark face was bent down, and the tears that had of old come so rarely made silver lines upon her olive cheeks. There was not one drop of bitterness in that overflowing of her soul's transcendent joy, in that happiness which was so great and perfect that it seemed almost unbearable.

And she had reason to be glad. In the midst of a calamity which would have absorbed the whole nature of many men, Giovanni had not one thought that was not for her. Giovanni, who had once doubted her, who had said such things to her as she dared not remember—Giovanni, suffering under a blow to his pride, that was worse almost than total ruin, had but one wish, to make another sacrifice for her. That false past, of which she hated to think, was gone like an evil dream before the morning sun, that true past, which was her whole life, was made present again. The love that had been so bruised and crushed that she had thought it dead had sprung up again from its deep, strong roots, grander and nobler than before. The certainty that it was real was overwhelming, and drowned all her senses in a trance of light.

Faustina Montevarchi entered the drawing-room softly, then, seeing no one, she advanced till she came all at once upon Corona in the embrasure of the window. The princess started slightly when she saw that she was not alone.

"Corona!" exclaimed the young girl. "Are you crying? What is it?"

"Oh, Faustina! I am so happy!" It was a relief to be able to say it to some one.

"Happy?" repeated Faustina in surprise. "But there are tears in your eyes, on your cheeks—"

"You cannot understand—I do not wonder—how should you? And besides, I cannot tell you what it is."

"I wish I were you," answered her friend sadly. "I wish I were happy!"

"What is it, child?" asked Corona kindly. Then she led Faustina to a stiff old sofa at one end of the vast room and they sat down together. "What is it?" she repeated, drawing the girl affectionately to her side.

"You know what it is, dear. No one can help me. Oh, Corona! We love each other so very much!"

"I know—I know it is very real. But you must have a little patience, darling. Love will win in the end. Just now, too—" She did not finish the sentence, but she had touched a sensitive spot in Faustina's conscience.

"That is the worst of it," was the answer. "I am so miserable, because I know he never would have allowed it, and now—I am ashamed to tell you, it is so heartless!" She hid her face on her friend's shoulder.

"You will never be heartless, my dear Faustina," said Corona. "What you think, is not your fault, dear. Love is master of the world and of us all."

"But my love is not like yours, Corona. Perhaps yours was once like mine. But you are married—you are happy. You were saying so just now."

"Yes, dear. I am very, very happy, because I love very, very dearly. You will be as happy as I am some day."

"Ah, that may be—but—I am dreadfully wicked, Corona!"

"You, child? You do not know what it is to think anything bad!"

"But I do. I am so much ashamed of it that I can hardly tell you—only I tell you everything, because you are my friend. Corona—it is horrible—it seems easier, more possible—now that he is gone—oh! I am so glad I have told you!" Faustina began to sob passionately, as though she were repenting of some fearful crime.

"Is that all, darling?" asked Corona, smiling at the girl's innocence, and pressing her head tenderly to her own breast. "Is that what makes you so unhappy?"

"Yes—is it not—very, very dreadful?" A fresh shower of tears accompanied the question.

"Perhaps I am very bad, too," said Corona. "But I do not call that wickedness."

"Oh no! You are good. I wish I were like you!"

"No, do not wish that. But, I confess, it seems to me natural that you should think as you do, because it is really true. Your father, Faustina, may have been mistaken about your future. If—if he had lived, you might perhaps have made him change his mind. At all events, you can hope that he now sees more clearly, that he understands how terrible it is for a woman to be married to a man she does not love—when she is sure that she loves another."

"Yes—you told me. Do you remember? It was the other day, after Flavia had been saying such dreadful things. But I know it already. Every woman must know it."

There was a short pause, during which Corona wondered whether she were the same person she had been ten days earlier, when she had delivered that passionate warning. Faustina sat quite still, looking up into the princess's face. She was comforted and reassured and the tears had ceased to flow.

"There is something else," she said at last. "I want to tell you everything, for I can tell no one else. I cannot keep it to myself either. He has written to me, Corona. Was it very wrong to read his letter?" This time she smiled a little and blushed.

"I do not think it was very wrong," answered her friend with a soft laugh. She was so happy that she would have laughed at anything.

"Shall I show you his letter?" asked the young girl shyly. At the same time her hand disappeared into the pocket of her black gown, and immediately afterwards brought out a folded piece of paper which looked as though it had been read several times.

Corona did not think it necessary to express her assent in words. Faustina opened the note, which contained the following words, written in Gouache's delicate French handwriting:

MADEMOISELLE—when you have read these lines, you will understand my object in writing them, for you understand me, and you know that all I do has but one object. A few days ago it was still possible for us to meet frequently. The terrible affliction which has fallen upon you, and in which none can feel deeper or more sincere sympathy than I, has put it out of your power and out of mine to join hands and weep over the present, to look into each other's eyes and read there the golden legend of a future happiness. To meet as we have met, alone in the crowded church—no, we cannot do it! For you, at such a time, it would seem like a disrespect to your father's memory. For myself, I should deem it dishonourable, I should appear base in my own eyes. Did I not go to him and put to him the great question? Was I not repulsed—I do not say with insult, but with astonishment—at my presumption? Shall I then seem to take advantage of his death—of his sudden and horrible death—to press forward a suit which he is no longer able to oppose? I feel that it would be wrong. Though I cannot express myself as I would, I know that you understand me, for you think as I do. How could it be otherwise? Are we not one indivisible soul, we two? Yes, you will understand me. Yes, you will know that it is right. I go therefore, I leave Rome immediately. I cannot inhabit the same city and not see you. But I cannot quit the Zouaves in this time of danger. I am therefore going to Viterbo, whither I am sent through the friendly assistance of one of our officers. There I shall stay until time has soothed your grief and restored your mother to health. To her we will turn when the moment has arrived. She will not be insensible to our tears and entreaties. Until then good-bye—ah, the word is less terrible than it looks, for our souls will be always together! I leave you but for a short space—no! I leave your sweet eyes, your angel's face, your dear hands that I adore, but yourself I do not leave. I bear you with me in a heart that loves you—God knows how tenderly.

Corona read the letter carefully to the end. To her older appreciation of the world, such a letter appeared at first to be the forerunner of a definite break, but a little reflection made her change her mind. What he said was clearly true, and corresponded closely with Faustina's own view of the case. The most serious obstacle to the union of the lovers had been removed by Prince Montevarchi's death, and it was inconceivable that Gouache should have ceased to care for Faustina at the very moment when a chance of his marrying her had presented itself. Besides, Corona knew Gouache well, and was not mistaken in her estimate of his character. He was honourable to Quixotism, and perfectly capable of refusing to take what looked like an unfair advantage. Considering Faustina's strange nature, her amazing readiness to yield to first impulses, and her touching innocence of evil, it would have been an easy matter for the man she loved to draw her into a runaway match. She would have followed him as readily to the ends of the earth as she had followed him to the Serristori barracks. Gouache was not a boy, and probably understood her peculiarities as well as any one. In going away for the present he was undoubtedly acting with the greatest delicacy, for his departure showed at once all the respect he felt for Faustina, and all that devotion to an ideal honour which was the foundation of his being. Though his epistle was not a model of literary style it contained certain phrases that came from the heart. Corona understood why Faustina was pleased with it, and why instead of shedding useless tears over his absence, she had shown such willingness to let her friend read Gouache's own explanation of his departure. She folded the sheet of paper again and gave it back to the young girl.

"I am glad he wrote that letter," she said after a moment's pause. "I always believed in him, and now—well, I think, he is almost worthy of you, Faustina."

Faustina threw her arms around Corona's neck, and kissed her again and again.

"I am so glad you know how good he is!" she cried. "I could not be happy unless you liked him, and you do."

All through the morning the two friends sat together in the great drawing-room talking, as such women can talk to each other, with infinite grace about matters not worth recording, or if they spoke of things of greater importance, repeating the substance of what they had said before, finding at each repetition some new comment to make, some new point upon which to agree, after the manner of people who are very fond of each other. The hours slipped by, and they were unconscious of the lapse of time. The great clocks of the neighbouring church towers tolled eleven, twelve, and one o'clock, and yet they had more to say, and did not even notice the loud ringing of the hundred bells. The day was clear, and the bright sunlight streamed in through the high windows, telling the hour with a more fateful precision than the clocks outside. All was peace and happiness and sweet intercourse, as the two women sat there undisturbed through the long morning. They talked, and laughed, and held their hands clasped together, unconscious of the rest of the world. No sound penetrated from the rest of the house to the quiet, sunlit hall, which to Faustina's mind had never looked so cheerful before since she could remember it. And yet within the walls of the huge old palace strange things were passing, things which it was well that neither of them should see.

Before describing the events which close this part of my story, it is as well to say that Faustina has made her last appearance for the present. From the point of view which would have been taken by most of her acquaintances, her marriage with Gouache was a highly improbable event. If any one desires an apology for being left in uncertainty as to her fate, I can only answer that I am writing the history of the Saracinesca and not of any one else. There are certain stages in that history which are natural halting-places for the historian himself, and for his readers if he have any; and it is impossible to make the lives of a number of people coincide so far as to wind them up together, and yet be sure that they will run down at the same moment like the clocks of his Majesty Charles the Fifth. If it were, the world would be a very different place.

CHAPTER XXX

THE scene in the study, while the notary read through the voluminous documents, is worth describing. At one end of the large green table sat San Giacinto alone, his form, even as he sat, towering above the rest. The mourning he wore harmonised with his own dark and massive head. His expression was calm and thoughtful, betraying neither satisfaction nor triumph. From time to time his deep-set eyes turned towards Saracinesca with a look of inquiry, as though to assure himself that the prince agreed to the various points and was aware that he must now speak for the last time, if he spoke at all. At the other end of the board the two Saracinesca were seated side by side. The strong resemblance that existed between them was made very apparent by their position, but although, allowing for the difference of their ages, their features corresponded almost line for line, their expressions were totally different. The old man's gray hair and pointed beard seemed to bristle with suppressed excitement. His heavy brows were bent together, as though he were making a great effort to control his temper, and now and then there was an angry gleam in his eyes. He sat square and erect in his seat, as though he were facing an enemy, but he kept his hands below the table, for he did not choose that San Giacinto should see the nervous working of his fingers. Giovanni, on the other hand, looked upon the proceedings with an indifference that was perfectly apparent. He occasionally looked at his watch, suppressed a yawn, and examined his nails with great interest. It was clear that he was not in the least moved by what was going on. It was no light matter for the old nobleman to listen to the documents that deprived him one by one of his titles, his estates, and his other wealth, in favour of a man who was still young, and whom, in spite of the relationship, he could not help regarding as an inferior. He had always considered himself as the representative of an older generation, who, by right of position, was entitled to transmit to his son the whole mass of those proud traditions in which he had grown up as in his natural element. Giovanni, on the contrary, possessed a goodly share of that indifference that characterises the younger men of the nineteenth century. He was perfectly satisfied with his present situation, and had been so long accustomed to depend upon his personality and his private fortune, for all that he enjoyed or required in life, that he did not desire the responsibilities that weigh heavily upon the head of a great family. Moreover, recent events had turned the current of his thoughts into a different direction. He was in his way as happy as Corona, and he knew that real happiness proceeds from something more than a score of titles and a few millions of money, more or less. He regarded the long morning's work as an intolerable nuisance, which prevented him from spending his time with his wife.

In the middle of the table sat the two notaries, flanked by four clerks, all of them pale men in black, clean shaved, of various ages, but bearing on their faces the almost unmistakable stamp of their profession. The one who was reading the deeds wore spectacles. From time to time he pushed them back upon his bald forehead and glanced first at San Giacinto and then at Prince Saracinesca, after which he carefully resettled the glasses upon his long nose and proceeded with his task until he had reached the end of another set of clauses, when he repeated the former operation with mechanical regularity, never failing to give San Giacinto the precedence of the first look.

For a long time this went on, with a monotony which almost drove Giovanni from the room. Indeed nothing but absolute necessity could have kept him in his place. At last the final deed was reached. It was an act of restitution drawn up in a simple form so as to include, by a few words, all the preceding documents. It set forth that Leone Saracinesca being "free in body and mind," the son of Giovanni Saracinesca deceased, "whom may the Lord preserve in a state of glory," restored, gave back, yielded, and abandoned all those goods, titles, and benefices which he had inherited directly from Leone Saracinesca, the eleventh of that name, deceased, "whom may the Lord preserve in a state of glory," to Giovanni Saracinesca, Marchese di San Giacinto, who was "free in body and mind," son of Orsino Saracinesca, ninth of that name, deceased, "whom may the Lord, etc." Not one of the quaint stock phrases was omitted. The notary paused, looked round, adjusted his spectacles and continued. The deed further set forth that Giovanni Saracinesca, Marchese di San Giacinto aforesaid, acknowledged the receipt of the aforesaid goods, titles, and benefices, and stated that he received all as the complete inheritance, relinquishing all further claims against the aforesaid Leone and his heirs for ever. Once more the reader paused, and then read the last words in a clear voice: "Both the noble parties promising, finally, in regard to the present cession, to take account of it, to hold it as acceptable, valid, and perpetual, and, for the same, never to allow it to be spoken of otherwise."

A few words followed, setting forth the name of the notary and the statement that the act was executed in his presence, with the date. When he had finished reading all, he rose and turned the document upon the table so that the two parties could stand opposite to him and sign it. Without a word he made a slight inclination and offered the pen to Saracinesca. The old gentleman pushed back his chair and marched forward with erect head and a firm step to sign away what had been his birthright. From first to last he had acknowledged the justice of his cousin's claims, and he was not the man to waver at the supreme moment. His hair bristled more stiffly than ever, and his dark eyes shot fire, but he took the pen and wrote his great strong signature as clearly as he had written it at the foot of his marriage contract five and thirty years earlier. Giovanni looked at him with admiration.

Then San Giacinto, who had risen out of respect to the old man, came forward and took the pen in his turn. He wrote out his name in straight, firm characters as usual, but at the end the ink made a broad black mark that ended abruptly, as though the writer had put the last stroke to a great undertaking.

"There should be two witnesses," said the notary in the awkward silence that followed. "Don Giovanni can be one," he added, giving the latter the only name that was now his, with a lawyer's scrupulous exactness.

"One of your clerks can be the other," suggested Saracinesca, who was anxious to get away as soon as possible.

"It is not usual," replied the notary. "Is there no one in the palace? One of the young princes would do admirably."

"They are all away," said San Giacinto. "Let me see—there is the librarian. Will he answer the purpose? He must be in the library at this hour. A respectable man—he has been thirty years in the house. For that matter, the steward is probably in his office, too."

"The librarian is the best person," answered the notary.

"I will bring him at once—I know the way." San Giacinto left the study by the door that opened upon the passage. The others could hear his heavy steps as he went rapidly up the paved corridor. Old Saracinesca walked up and down the room unable to conceal his impatience. Giovanni resumed his seat and waited quietly, indifferent to the last.

Arnoldo Meschini was in the library, as San Giacinto had anticipated. He was seated at his usual place at the upper end of the hall, surrounded by books and writing materials which he handled nervously without making any serious attempt to use them. He had lost all power of concentrating his thoughts or of making any effort to work. Fortunately for him no one had paid any attention to him during the past ten days. His appearance was dishevelled and slovenly, and he was more bent than he had formerly been. His eyes were bleared and glassy as he stared at the table before him, assuming a wild and startled expression when, looking up, he fancied he saw some horrible object gliding quickly across the sunny floor, or creeping up to him over the polished table. All his former air of humility and shabby respectability was gone. His disordered dress, his straggling grayish hair that hung from beneath the dirty black skullcap around his misshapen ears, his face, yellow in parts and irregularly flushed in others, as though it were beginning to be scorched from within, his unwashed hands, every detail of his appearance, in short, proclaimed his total degradation. But hitherto no one had noticed him, for he had lived between his attic, the deserted library and the apothecary's shop on the island of Saint Bartholomew. His mind had almost ceased to act when he was awake, except in response to the fear which the smallest circumstances now caused him. If he had dreams by night, he saw visions also in the day, and his visions generally took the shape of San Giacinto. He had not really seen him since he had met him when the prince lay in state, but the fear of him was, if anything, greater than if he had met him daily. The idea that the giant was lying in wait for him had become fixed, and yet he was powerless to fly. His energy was all gone between his potations and the constant terror that paralysed him.

On that morning he had been as usual to the Ponte Quattro Capi and had returned with the means of sleep in his pocket. He had no instinct left but to deaden his sensations with drink during the hours of light, while waiting for the time when he could lie down and yield to the more potent influence of the opium. He had therefore come back as usual, and by force of habit had taken his place in the library, the fear of seeming to neglect his supposed duties forbidding him to spend all his time in his room. As usual, too, he had locked the door of the passage to separate himself from his dread of a supernatural visitation. He sat doubled together in his chair, his long arms lying out before him upon the books and papers.

All at once he started in his seat. One, two, one two—yes, there were footsteps in the corridor—they were coming nearer and nearer—heavy, like those of the dead prince—but quicker, like those of San Giacinto—closer, closer yet. A hand turned the latch once, twice, then shook the lock roughly. Meschini was helpless. He could neither get upon his feet and escape by the other exit, nor find the way to the pocket that held his weapon. Again the latch was turned and shaken, and then the deep voice he dreaded was heard calling to him.

"Signor Meschini!"

He shrieked aloud with fear, but he was paralysed in every limb. A moment later a terrible crash drowned his cries. San Giacinto, on hearing his agonised scream, had feared some accident. He drew back a step and then, with a spring, threw his colossal strength against the line where the leaves of the door joined.

The lock broke in its sockets, the panels cracked under the tremendous pressure, and the door flew wide open. In a moment San Giacinto was standing over the librarian, trying to drag him back from the table and out of his seat. He thought the man was in a fit. In reality he was insane with terror.

"An easy death, for the love of heaven!" moaned the wretch, twisting himself under the iron hands that held him by the shoulders. "For God's sake! I will tell you all—do not torture me—oh! oh!—only let it be easy—and quick—yes, I tell you—I killed the prince—oh, mercy, mercy, for Christ's sake!"

San Giacinto's grip tightened, and his face grew livid. He lifted Meschini bodily from the chair and set him against the table, holding him up at arm's length, his deep eyes blazing with a rage that would soon be uncontrollable. Meschini's naturally strong constitution did not afford him the relief of fainting.

"You killed him—why?" asked San Giacinto through his teeth, scarcely able to speak.

"For you, for you—oh, have mercy—do not—"

"Silence!" cried the giant in a voice that shook the vault of the hall. "Answer me or I will tear your head from your body with my hands! Why do you say you killed him for me?"

Meschini trembled all over, and then his contorted face grew almost calm. He had reached that stage which may be called the somnambulism of fear. The perspiration covered his skin in an instant, and his voice sank to a distinct whisper.

"He made me forge the deeds, and would not pay me for them. Then I killed him."

"What deeds?"

"The deeds that have made you Prince Saracinesca. If you do not believe me, go to my room, the originals are in the cupboard. The key is here, in my right-hand pocket."

He could not move to get it, for San Giacinto held him fast, and watched every attempt he made at a movement. His own face was deathly pale, and his white lips were compressed together.

"You forged them altogether, and the originals are untouched?" he asked, his grasp tightening unconsciously till Meschini yelled with pain.

"Yes!" he cried. "Oh, do not hurt me—an easy death—"

"Come with me," said San Giacinto, leaving his arms and taking him by the collar. Then he dragged and pushed him towards the splintered door of the passage. At the threshold, Meschini writhed and tried to draw back, but he could no more have escaped from those hands that held him than a lamb can loosen the talons of an eagle when they are buried deep in the flesh.

"Go on!" urged the strong man, in fierce tones. "You came by this passage to kill him—you know the way."

With a sudden movement of his right hand he launched the howling wretch forward into the corridor. All through the narrow way Meschini's cries for mercy resounded, loud and piercing, but no one heard him. The walls were thick and the distance from the inhabited rooms was great. But at last the shrieks reached the study.

Saracinesca stood still in his walk. Giovanni sprang to his feet. The notaries sat in their places and trembled. The noise came nearer and then the door flew open. San Giacinto dragged the shapeless mass of humanity in and flung it half way across the room, so that it sank in a heap at the old prince's feet.

"There is the witness to the deeds," he cried savagely. "He forged them, and he shall witness them in hell. He killed his master in this very room, and here he shall tell the truth before he dies. Confess, you dog! And be quick about it, or I will help you."

He stirred the grovelling creature with his foot. Meschini only rolled from side to side and hid his face against the floor. Then the gigantic hands seized him again and set him on his feet, and held him with his face to the eight men who had all risen and were standing together in wondering silence.

"Speak!" shouted San Giacinto in Meschini's ear. "You are not dead yet—you have much to live through, I hope."

Again that trembling passed over the unfortunate man's limbs, and he grew quiet and submissive. It was all as he had seen it in his wild dreams and visions, the secret chamber whence no sound could reach the outer world, the stern judges all in black, the cruel strength of San Giacinto ready to torture him. The shadow of death rose in his eyes.

"Let me sit down," he said in a broken voice.

San Giacinto led him to a chair in the midst of them all. Then he stood before one of the doors, and motioned to his cousin to guard the other. But Arnoldo Meschini had no hope of escape. His hour was at hand, and he knew it.

"You forged the deeds which were presented as originals in the court. Confess it to those gentlemen." It was San Giacinto who spoke.

"The prince made me do it," answered Meschini in low tones. "He promised me twenty thousand scudi for the work."

"To be paid—when? Tell all."

"To be paid in cash the day the verdict was given."

"You came to get your money here?"

"I came here. He denied having promised anything definite. I grew angry. I killed him." A violent shudder shook his frame from head to foot.

"You strangled him with a pocket handkerchief?"

"It was Donna Faustina's?"

"The prince threw it on the ground after he had struck her. I saw the quarrel. I was waiting for my money. I watched them through the door."

"You know that you are to die. Where are the deeds you stole when you forged the others?"

"I told you—in the cupboard in my room. Here is the key. Only—for God's sake—"

He was beginning to break down again. Perhaps, by the habit of the past days he felt the need for drink even in that supreme moment, for his hand sought his pocket as he sat. Instead of the bottle he felt the cold steel barrel of the revolver, which he had forgotten. San Giacinto looked towards the notary.

"Is this a full confession, sufficient to commit this man to trial?" he asked. But before the notary could answer, Meschini's voice sounded through the room, not weak and broken, but loud and clear.

"It is! It is!" he cried in sudden and wild excitement. "I have told all. The deeds will speak for themselves. Ah, you would have done better to leave me amongst my books!" He turned to San Giacinto. "You will never be Prince Saracinesca. But I shall escape you. You shall not give me a slow death—you shall not, I say—"

San Giacinto made a step towards him. The proximity of the man who had inspired him with such abject terror put an end to his hesitation.

"You shall not!" he almost screamed. "But my blood is on your head—Ah!"

Three deafening reports shook the air in rapid succession, and all that was left of Arnoldo Meschini lay in a shapeless heap upon the floor. While a man might have counted a score there was silence in the room. Then San Giacinto came forward and bent over the body, while the notaries and their clerks cowered in a corner. Saracinesca and Giovanni stood together, grave and silent, as brave men are when they have seen a horrible sight and can do nothing. Meschini was quite dead. When San Giacinto had assured himself of the fact, he looked up. All the fierce rage had vanished from his face.

"He is dead," he said quietly. "You all saw it. You will have to give your evidence in half an hour when the police come. Be good enough to open the door."

He took up the body in his arms carefully, but with an ease that amazed those who watched him. Giovanni held the door open, and San Giacinto deposited his burden gently upon the pavement of the corridor. Then he turned back and re-entered the room. The door of the study closed for ever on Arnoldo Meschini.

In the dead silence that followed, San Giacinto approached the table upon which the deed lay, still waiting to be witnessed. He took it in his hand and turned to Saracinesca. There was no need for him to exculpate himself from any charge of complicity in the abominable fraud which Montevarchi had prepared before he died. Not one of the men present even thought of suspecting him. Even if they had, it was clear that he would not have brought Meschini to confess before them a robbery in which he had taken part. But there was that in his brave eyes that told his innocence better than any evidence or argument could have proclaimed it. He held out the document to Saracinesca.

"Would you like to keep it as a memento?" he asked. "Or shall I destroy it before you?"

His voice never quavered, his face was not discomposed. Giovanni, the noble-hearted gentleman, wondered whether he himself could have borne such a blow so bravely as this innkeeper cousin of his. Hopes, such as few men can even aspire to entertain, had been suddenly extinguished. A future of power and wealth and honour, the highest almost that his country could give any man, had been in a moment dashed to pieces before his eyes. Dreams, in which the most indifferent would see the prospect of enormous satisfaction, had vanished into nothing during the last ten minutes, almost at the instant when they were to be realised. And yet the man who had hoped such hopes, who had looked forward to such a future, whose mind must have revelled many a time in the visions that were already becoming realities—that man stood before them all, outwardly unmoved, and proposing to his cousin that he should keep as a remembrance the words that told of his own terrible disappointment. He was indeed the calmest of those present.

"Shall I tear it to pieces?" he asked again, holding the document between his fingers. Then the old prince spoke.

"Do what you will with it," he answered. "But give me your hand. You are a braver man than I."

The two men looked into each other's eyes as their hands met.

"It shall not be the last deed between us," said Saracinesca. "There shall be another. Whatever may be the truth about that villain's work you shall have your share—"

"A few hours ago, you would not take yours," answered San Giacinto quietly. "Must I repeat your own words?"

"Well, well—we will talk of that. This has been a terrible morning's work, and we must do other things before we go to business again. That poor man's body is outside the door. We had better attend to that matter first, and send for the police. Giovanni, my boy, will you tell Corona? I believe she is still in the house."

Giovanni needed no urging to go upon his errand. He entered the drawing-room where Corona was still sitting beside Faustina upon the sofa. His face must have been pale, for Corona looked at him with a startled expression.

"Is anything the matter?" she asked.

"Something very unpleasant has occurred," he answered, looking at Faustina. "Meschini, the librarian, has just died very suddenly in the study where we were."

"Meschini?" cried Faustina in surprise and with some anxiety.

"Yes. Are you nervous, Donna Faustina? May I tell you something very startling?" It was a man's question.

"Yes—what is it?" she asked quickly.

"Meschini confessed before us all that it was he who was the cause—in fact that he had murdered your father. Before any one could stop him, he had shot himself. It is very dreadful."

With a low cry that was more expressive of amazement than of horror, Faustina sank into a chair. In his anxiety to tell his wife the whole truth Giovanni forgot her at once. As soon as he began to speak, however, Corona led him away to the window where they had stood together a few hours earlier.

"Corona—what I told her is not all. There is something else. Meschini had forged the papers which gave the property to San Giacinto. Montevarchi had promised him twenty thousand scudi for the job. It was because he would not pay the money that Meschini killed him. Do you understand?"

"You will have everything after all?"

"Everything—but we must give San Giacinto a share. He has behaved like a hero. He found it all out and made Meschini confess. When he knew the truth he did not move a muscle of his face, but offered my father the deed he had just signed as a memento of the occasion."

"Then he will not take anything, any more than you would, or your father. Is it quite sure, Giovanni? Is there no possible mistake?"

"No. It is absolutely certain. The original documents are in this house."

"I am glad then, for you, dear," answered Corona. "It would have been very hard for you to bear—"

"After this morning? After the other day in Holy Office?" asked Giovanni, looking deep into her splendid eyes. "Can anything be hard to bear if you love me, darling?"

"Oh my beloved! I wanted to hear you say it!" Her head sank upon his shoulder, as though she had found that perfect rest for which she had once so longed.

Here ends the second act in the history of the Saracinesca. To trace their story further would be to enter upon an entirely different series of events, less unusual perhaps in themselves, but possibly worthy of description as embracing that period during which Rome and the Romans began to be transformed and modernised. In the occurrences that followed, both political and social, the Saracinesca bore a part, in that blaze of gaiety which for many reasons developed during the winter of the Oecumenical Council, in the fall of the temporal power, in the social confusion that succeeded that long-expected catastrophe, and which led by rapid degrees to the present state of things. If there are any left who still feel an interest in Giovanni and Corona, the historian may once more resume his task and set forth in succession the circumstances through which they have passed since that memorable morning they spent at the Palazzo Montevarchi. They themselves are facts, and, as such, are a part of the century in which we live; whether they are interesting facts or not, is for others to judge, and if the verdict denounces them as flat, unprofitable and altogether dull, it is not their fault; the blame must be imputed to him who, knowing them well, has failed in an honest attempt to show them as they are.

THE END

Designed by Fiona Cecile Clarke, the CLUNY MEDIA *logo depicts a monk at work in the scriptorium, with a cat sitting at his feet.*

The monk represents our mission to emulate the invaluable contributions of the monks of Cluny in preserving the libraries of the West, our strivings to know and love the truth.

The cat at the monk's feet is Pangur Bán, from the eponymous Irish poem of the 9th century. The anonymous poet compares his scholarly pursuit of truth with the cat's happy hunting of mice. The depiction of Pangur Bán is an homage to the work of the monks of Irish monasteries and a sign of the joy we at Cluny take in our trade.

"Messe ocus Pangur Bán,
cechtar nathar fria saindan:
bíth a menmasam fri seilgg,
mu memna céin im saincheirdd."

Made in the USA
Middletown, DE
20 April 2023

29028355R00219